D0227367

4am in
LAS VEGAS

LIBRARIES NI
WITHDRAWN FROM STOCK

MICHELLE JACKSON

POOLBEG

This novel is entirely a work of fiction. The names, characters and incidents portrayed in it are the work of the author's imagination. Any resemblance to actual persons, living or dead, events or localities is entirely coincidental.

Published 2011
by Poolbeg Press Ltd
123 Grange Hill, Baldoyle
Dublin 13, Ireland
E-mail: poolbeg@poolbeg.com
www.poolbeg.com

© Michelle Jackson 2011

Copyright for typesetting, layout, design
© Poolbeg Press Ltd

The moral right of the author has been asserted.

1

A catalogue record for this book is available from the British Library.

ISBN 978-1-84223-424-2

All rights reserved. No part of this publication may be reproduced or transmitted in any form or by any means, electronic or mechanical, including photography, recording, or any information storage or retrieval system, without permission in writing from the publisher. The book is sold subject to the condition that it shall not, by way of trade or otherwise, be lent, resold or otherwise circulated without the publisher's prior consent in any form of binding or cover other than that in which it is published and without a similar condition, including this condition, being imposed on the subsequent purchaser.

Typeset by Patricia Hope in Sabon 11/15
Printed by CPI Group (UK), Croydon, CR0 4YY

LIBRARIES NI	
C700776115	
RONDO	04/10/2011
F	£ 12.99
RAN	

About the author

Michelle Jackson attended the National College of Art and Design and kicked off her early career as a sock designer. She has taught Art and Design to second and third-level students for more years than she would like to admit.

4am in Las Vegas is her fourth novel to be published by Poolbeg Press. Her other novels *One Kiss in Havana*, *Two Days in Biarritz* and *Three Nights in New York* will soon be translated into foreign languages including Dutch, German, Portuguese and Norwegian. In October 2010 her first non-fiction title *What Women Know*, which she co-wrote with Dr Juliet Bressan, was published.

Extracts of her work have been chosen for publication by the *Irish Daily Mail*, the *Irish Independent*, the *Sunday Tribune* and various Irish women's magazines.

She is a native of Howth, County Dublin, where she lives with her husband and two children.

To contact Michelle visit her website www.michellejackson.ie.

Also by Michelle Jackson

One Kiss in Havana
Two Days in Biarritz
Three Nights in New York

Acknowledgements

I am blessed to have so many people to thank on my path to this my fourth novel but I am determined not to make this thank-you too long, as I fear I have done in the past! So, I would like to begin by expressing my heartfelt thanks to everyone who has helped me on my way here.

My deepest thanks go to all the wonderful staff and support system at my publishers Poolbeg, especially those at the coalface: Paula Campbell, Kieran Devlin, Sarah Ormston and David Prendergast. Thanks to my FGE, the extremely talented and all-knowing editor Gaye Shortland – what a journey we have been on together – I truly am Lucky!

To Ros Edwards and Helenka Fuglewicz of Edwards Fuglewicz Literary Agency who have had such faith in my novels and have worked so hard to get my books published in other languages.

To my long-suffering friends who have had the arduous task of reading first and second drafts and spotting typos and errors – especially Clodagh Hoey, Suzanne Barry, Wendy Buckley, Tryphavana Cross, Maressa O'Brien Raleigh and Carla Cerasi.

This book would not have been written had it not been for the inspiration and drive of John Donohue at Aereps who sold the idea of Las Vegas to me with such gusto he has now left me longing to visit the city again! Together with Tryphavana Cross and his terrific team, he compiled a Vegas itinerary for me that I could never have dreamt of, so a massive thank-you to the generosity of the Las Vegas Convention and Visitors Authority and all of the businesses that sponsored me on my research trip to Las Vegas. Especially Joni Moss at LV Wedding Connections for giving me a day I will never forget – five weddings in two hours!

Special thanks to the generosity of those who shared their inside knowledge of Las Vegas, especially Stella Clery for the very interesting chat, and thanks to Jeanne and Nick Heather who informed me of the finer details of gambling.

Thanks to Angela Forte and Michelle Mulvany for introducing me to Shamanism and inspiring me during the writing of this book.

There are so many other people that I would like to thank but the list is endless and I am afraid of leaving anybody out – so, for the support and friendship of all the readers, writers and friends who have helped me online, over the phone and over cups of coffee, many thanks.

Finally but most importantly, I would like to thank my family – my parents Jim and Pauline who have supported and encouraged me in every single part of my life. Thanks to my husband Brian who was the best possible companion to take to Las Vegas and had the restraint to hold me back from losing our spending money at the roulette wheel!!! And final thanks to my beautiful children Mark and Nicole who are so understanding about having a mother who writes – you have taught me more than you will ever know.

This book is for my dearly departed maternal grandmother, Peggy Cashell, and anyone who knew her will know why!

Many thanks to the organisations who sponsored my
visit to Las Vegas:

Las Vegas Convention and Visitors Authority
Aereps
British Airways
MGM Resorts International
Cirque du Soleil Productions
Scenic Airlines

And the wedding chapels:

Joni Moss at Las Vegas Wedding Connections
Viva Las Vegas Wedding Chapel
The Graceland Wedding Chapel
The Chapel of the Flowers

Dedicated to the memory of my grandmother Peggy Cashell – a remarkable woman who was ahead of her time and who would have loved Las Vegas!

The Great Spirit is in all things: he is in the air we breathe.
The Great Spirit is our father, but the earth is our mother.
She nourishes us; that which we put into the ground
she returns to us.

~ Big Thunder (Bedagi), WABANAKI ALGONQUIN *~*

Prologue

Viva Las Vegas Wedding Chapel

OCTOBER 31ST

Vicky jumped out of the Cadillac and slammed the door shut. She gasped for air, trembling as the adrenalin rushed through her.

"Wait for me," John called as he catapulted out of the car and followed her through the doorway of the wedding chapel.

Vicky pushed past the man standing inside the door – knocking over his television camera. Dry ice rose from the floor, tinted lilac by the flashing spotlights. Candlelight illuminated the dark walls and the strains of a church organ playing a macabre melody filled the air. Large cobwebs draped down from the rafters and hung over the aisles – Vicky pushed them out of her way to get to the bizarre altar. Standing in the middle was a gentleman wearing a black suit and top hat, his fangs exposed as his mouth opened in shock at the intruders. On his left was a young man with a pallid face and blood dripping down his chin. To his right stood the bride, wearing a long green satin dress and black shawl.

Vicky tripped over a tombstone in her anxiety to reach her daughter. Hysterically she waved her arms in the air and screamed.

"Tina, what do you think you're doing?"

The organ started up with the Dead March as two trapeze vampires glided through the air over their heads.

"I'm getting married," Tina replied. Her voice trembled – this wasn't the way she had planned it.

1

Vicky shook her head in disbelief. "Tell me this is some kind of joke – you can't honestly be getting married!"

Tina moved in by her groom's side and he put his arm protectively around her.

"This is my wife," the boy said brazenly. "And we *are* married!"

"Tina Hughes, come with me now!" Vicky roared.

"Her name is Tina Haycock now," the young man said coolly. "And she's going with me!"

They had started to walk away when Dracula called them back.

"Hey, kids – you gotta sign the register."

"We'll do that outside," the groom said and continued to walk, with his arm wrapped around his wife's shoulders.

John put his arm around Vicky who was shaking so hard she wasn't conscious of the tears dripping down her cheeks.

"It's okay – calm down. At least we know she's safe and nothing has happened to her," he said gently.

Dracula approached Vicky respectfully.

"I'm sorry, ma'am, but you'll have to leave – there's another wedding in two minutes."

As the strains of Aerosmith's rock classic "Love Bites" filled the chapel, Vicky and John walked back down the aisle.

"We're all done here!" the cameraman said to his assistant and they gathered up their equipment and left through the side door.

"What's going on?" Vicky said in dismay. "Why the TV crew?"

The camera crew had come to film the spectacle, *Fox News* emblazoned across their equipment. Vicky would only have to look at the TV later to see the evidence that the wedding had taken place.

"Let's go back to the hotel," John said gently. "Connie will help sort this mess out."

Vicky could hardly speak with shock. "Tina's eighteen – there's nothing I can do about this."

"She probably got carried away. Don't worry!"

But John knew that she was right – an eighteen-year-old was perfectly within her rights to get married, but now he was going to have to cope with this mess on top of everything else that had happened over the last few days in Las Vegas.

Chapter 1

*You can't wake a person who is
pretending to be asleep.*

~ Navajo proverb ~

Connie Haycock flicked open her diary – it was that crazy time of year again. Halloween in Las Vegas meant even more weddings than usual. So many people chose to blend their big day with a stay in the city of excess and fun that she loved so much.

She was a Californian girl who had run away at a time when she felt there was no hope. Fourteen years ago, with a Chrysler Estate and two snotty-nosed little boys in the back, she had checked into a motel room off The Strip and spent her first night in the city that she now called home – relieved to be away from the sham of a marriage she had endured for six years, but frightened about how she would survive in this new city of neon.

She had come a long way from those early days of working on the blackjack tables in the Golden Nugget to the point where she was one of the most successful wedding planners in Las Vegas. She lived in a smart bungalow in the suburb of Summerlin and last year had a pool installed in her garden. Her life had blossomed in a way she could never have dreamed before leaving California. Her eldest son, Troy, was now at the Arizona State University on a football scholarship and doing exceptionally well. Unfortunately, she still worried abut her moody and mixed-up son Kyle – he had always been a sensitive child. So different from his brother who seemed to love life with the same passion as his mother.

Yes, Connie had a lot to be thankful for. She loved her role as wedding planner – such a pity that she never seemed to meet anyone to marry herself.

She looked through the diary. Yes, she had everything covered up to Sunday 31st – which was Halloween of course – and knew that all arrangements made would go ahead and work like clockwork as usual. Connie's organisational skills were honed to perfection at this point in her career and all her support systems had been tried and tested over the years.

She checked to see what she had in store for the following week. First up was that Irish couple.

Tuesday November 2nd
at 2.30pm

Marriage of Vicky Hughes and Frank Proctor
Witnesses and guests: Tina Hughes and John Proctor

Reception at the Bellagio Hotel

Wedding chapel to be arranged on arrival in Vegas.

At Heathrow Airport Vicky and Tina Hughes were running frantically to the boarding gate. It was a long way from Terminal 1, where they had arrived from Dublin. They had ten more minutes to get to Terminal 5 where a shiny British Airways 777 was waiting to take them to McCarran International Airport, Las Vegas.

Finally reaching Gate 35, the two sat down in relief and waited to be called to board.

Vicky was fearful, and disappointed that her fiancé wasn't with them – she wasn't a good traveller and she'd have liked the security of his presence.

"I really hope Frank gets away tomorrow," she said, her emerald eyes peeking out widely through the attractive new fringe she'd had cut into the soft brunette curls that fell to her shoulders. "I didn't want to do all of the planning on my own!"

"You're not on your own," Tina assured her. "I'm here."

Vicky reached out and gave her daughter's hand a squeeze. Her words of comfort were sweet but unrealistic. Tina was more likely to be a liability than an asset. And Vicky knew that the minute her fiancé landed in Las Vegas, Tina's hackles would rise and it would be eggshells all the way after that. Vicky wished she could soothe her daughter's worries and concerns. She wished she was a bigger part of her life.

Tina turned on her iPod and Vicky looked at her in dismay. So much for company and support! Tina seldom communicated with her any more – she was always tweeting or Facebooking or listening to her iPod. Any technical device was more appealing than having an actual conversation with her mother. Vicky felt as though she had failed her, spending too many hours working since her husband, David, had left and earning as much as she could so that her daughter could have everything that her friends had. Maybe, if she had spent more time with her, she wouldn't be the way she was now. Always sombre and solemn in black – with tattoos and piercings which made her appear fierce and unlike the lovely little girl she used to be when her daddy was around.

Vicky went out of her mind when Tina got her first tattoo. It was a source of constant anxiety for her. She had to tell someone because her ex-husband wasn't interested in hearing about his daughter and it was during a conversation about Tina with her boss, Frank, that a relationship between them had started to develop. Frank was so sympathetic and understanding – their initial little chats after work turned into drinks in the Residency Club and quickly became dinner at least twice a week. It was such a delight to be with a man who could support her emotionally. So unlike her ex-husband.

Vicky had met David in her first year of commercial college. He was a student in the neighbouring Dublin Institute of Technology – studying architecture. They had been inseparable all the way through their college years, then she got a job as a secretary and married at twenty-one. Vicky never dreamed that there would ever be another man for her but, after twelve years of what she thought was a very happy and successful marriage, David announced one day out of the blue that he was leaving her. She was stunned beyond belief and fell into a deep depression that lasted for three years. Meanwhile, he was riding high on the Celtic Tiger property boom and quickly filled her shoes with a younger blonde woman who since had produced twin boys.

Vicky felt terribly for Tina who was marginalised by her father in favour of his new family. She blamed the birth of the twins for Tina's transformation into a Goth. It happened within days of their birth and Tina was still rebelling.

Frank Proctor shook hands with the bank manager and pulled his navy-blue linen jacket on over his pinstriped shirt. It had been a tense meeting, and warm and sticky in the office of the Bank of Ireland. Frank had a lot of pressures weighing down on him today – he was wondering if he was doing the right thing at all. Business wasn't good and hadn't been for some time and this wedding was enough to bring his blood pressure to boiling point.

He walked out onto Baggot Street and hurried down to the premises of his most popular restaurant. He had been in the business so long he couldn't remember a time when he wasn't involved in catering. As a teenager he used to wait on tables and dream of owning his own place. He was fortunate to get the position of commis chef in the King Sitric restaurant in Howth and that set him up with the know-how to move in the right circles when the time came to open his own place. The boom had given him the opportunity to expand and develop at a rate he had never dreamed he could. He had mixed with property developers and bankers who were only too keen to steer him into all sorts of schemes and investments that were now coming back to haunt him. If only he had concentrated on the restaurant business and kept away from property speculation! But everyone was doing it during the noughties and you didn't have anything to talk about if you weren't involved in it too. Now, pushing forty-two, he was in a mess and not just financially!

He came to the door of his restaurant and went inside, only to be greeted by the sight of his brother on the way out.

"Hey, John. What's up?"

"You said to be here an hour ago – I got tired of waiting. You asked me to get the rings – remember?"

Frank ran his fingers through his black mane which curled slightly at the ends where it reached the collar of his shirt. "Sorry, John – I forgot!" He didn't want to trouble John with his worries.

John Proctor shrugged and shook his dark-brown hair that also was longer than the norm for men. He was a ruggedly handsome man who fitted his 6 foot 3 inch frame squarely – the type who commanded a natural respect from other men. He was used to his brother's unreliable ways and this latest offence was merely one in a long list over the years.

"I've got to go home and pack – unless you've also forgotten that you're going to Las Vegas tomorrow?"

Frank shook his head. "No, of course not – I'll see you at the airport at eleven – okay?"

"I'll be there," John said.

John brushed past his brother, walked out onto Baggot Street and headed in the direction of Stephen's Green and his apartment. John had bought it the previous year on the advice of his older brother. Frank had been desperate to offload properties to increase his cash flow and John had a stash of cash in the bank from the previous two years' heavy gigging around the globe. Frank assured him that he was getting a bargain. Now he was really pleased that he had a place of his own and the views down the quays and over the River Liffey were spectacular.

John was happy with his decision to settle back in Ireland. He had lived a Bohemian life in his twenties, playing in all sorts of bands and shows. There was nothing to hold him in Ireland: his father was dead and he had an awkward relationship with his mother. Frank was always the golden boy in his mother's eyes and John felt that it gave him free rein to go off and pursue the life of a musician, whereas if he had been his mother's pet she would have wanted him to go into a solid reliable profession. Sometimes he felt that Frank had got the short straw, for all that favouritism came with a price. John couldn't remember his father. Frank had been six when he died and could still recall snippets of him but John was only three and couldn't honestly say that he remembered anything about him. Kieran Proctor was a merchant seaman who drank his way through his days on shore and offered little support or comfort to his poor wife. Bernadette Proctor scrubbed floors and took any job that she could get to put her boys through school and give them a good start. When Frank was set up as a chef she was happy enough to let John leave school early to pursue whatever career took his fancy, and if that was the life of a wandering musician she didn't care. As long as she had Frank to fuss over and make Sunday lunch for, then her life was fulfilled.

Now John was enjoying a less nomadic lifestyle, largely based in Dublin, but he still wasn't interested in putting down roots. He was a free spirit and wasn't in any rush to get married – if he ever would. He had moved in with a Japanese girl in Amsterdam when he was twenty-five and that had lasted three years. So far that was the longest he had spent in any relationship with the opposite sex. He usually spent months contentedly without any steady female company, usually while on tour, and then would fall into meeting someone when the mood took him. No, he wasn't in any rush to settle into a life of responsibility. He went with the flow and did whatever felt right at that time and this was how he intended to continue for the foreseeable future.

The British Airways aircraft rumbled down the runway and rose up and into the air.

Vicky leaned over and whispered in her daughter's ear, "Isn't it lovely, Tina?"

The teenager shrugged. They were sitting in spacious reclining seats – an upgrade from economy that Frank had insisted upon, which was going to make their ten-hour-plus journey really comfortable.

Vicky savoured the little luxuries she had come to experience since Frank and she became a couple. Her daughter didn't seem to have the same appreciation of her future stepfather. Even the World Traveller Class seats and extra pampering couldn't raise a smile on her daughter's face.

Tina had cried for hours and insisted on spending the weekend with her father in Limerick when she heard the news of her mother's forthcoming nuptials – but her father's new partner Maria was even less appealing than Frank. At least Frank flashed his cash regularly and she took it from him without batting an eye.

Vicky couldn't understand why Tina wasn't thrilled at the prospect of having a man about the house again. Vicky had her own demons from her childhood which brought her pain. Her own father had died when she was only seven years of age. It was no wonder that her relationship with her own mother was so intense and in its final years so strained. She wished that her mother had told her more about her father, but she had felt that it was okay to brush aside an entire part of the family's history, leaving Vicky always longing to find out what her life would have been like if he had lived longer. Maybe then she would have had brothers and sisters and Tina would have more cousins and extended family. It was one of the reasons why she was so keen to begin again with Frank.

Frank went over to the till and had a look to see the takings. He was lucky that the turnover hadn't dropped too badly – he would be in the soup without the cash flow from the business. Twenty apartments and houses around the city had his name on them and half were without tenants – the other half brought in well below what was needed to pay the mortgages. He had kept this mounting debt secret from his fiancée. He didn't think that Vicky would be able to cope with the weight of his worries. He would be on the plane with her now only for the meeting demanded by his bank manager – the same man who had encouraged him to borrow cash so liberally a few years back.

He hadn't wanted to travel to Las Vegas to get married – it had been Vicky's idea, but when he realised that by doing so he would be able to save on the expense of the occasion, he changed his mind. Two weeks was too long to be spending away from the business at this crucial point but she had managed to convince him to stay long enough to have their honeymoon as well when it occurred to him that, if he was lucky, the trip to Vegas could solve all his problems in one swoop.

Then there was the matter of his mother's absence from the occasion – at first Frank thought she would be so dreadfully hurt that he would have to insist on getting married in Ireland, but he was surprised when she took the practical stand and encouraged him to save his money. He wondered if she had an idea that something was amiss with her once-affluent son's finances. She was no fool when it came to money. Besides, it was on her insistence that Frank had hotly pursued a wife and Vicky was there in his restaurant working as the temporary maitre d' at the right time. Frank realised that part of the reason his mother wanted him to get married so badly was her desire for grandchildren. And Vicky was so feminine and gentle with her pretty little-girl-lost appeal that he had no need to look any further.

The pressures were mounting so heavily on Frank that his temples were aching. He went over to the bar and poured himself a quick brandy. There was so much to do before the next day.

Chapter 2

Humankind has not woven the web of life
We are but one thread within it.
Whatever we do to the web, we do to ourselves.
All things are bound together.
All things connect.

~ *Chief Seattle, 1854* ~

Suzanne flicked through her emails and then clicked on the Facebook icon. It was all very new to her. Her friend Eddie had shown her how to navigate the pages but she was finding it difficult.

Suddenly her mother called out, "Lily, are you there?"

Suzanne's mother often called her Lily. Lily was Mary Quinn's older sister who she had loved dearly but lost to TB in her twenties.

Suzanne ran up the stairs and into the bedroom to see her once-beautiful mother fiddling around the drawer of her dressing table.

"Have you taken my pearls? I can't find them and I'm going to the dance now."

She looked up from the drawer at Suzanne. "Who are you?"

It was a question she asked her several times a day.

"Come on now, Mary," Suzanne said softly. "Time you had some lunch."

Suzanne worked part-time in Temple Street Children's Hospital. She had studied physiotherapy and once thought she'd have a good solid career and the opportunity to meet varied and interesting people. How different her life had actually turned out! She'd had few boyfriends of any significance since her schooldays – and had only one steady in college who ended up marrying the girl that she loathed most in her class. For the last four years she'd been caring for her mother on a full-time basis outside work hours, so her social life had taken a serious dive in the wrong direction.

Eddie tried to convince her to put her mother into a home – but that was something that she would not do. Eddie was a very different person to her. He had no family ties. He only briefly visited his family in County Mayo once a year at Christmas and lived his life completely independently for the rest of the time. He had moved five years ago to a cottage in Clontarf which was around the corner from Kincora Road where Suzanne lived with her mother – he was nice company for them both.

Using Facebook had given Suzanne a chance to communicate with the outside world while still in her home and she was very grateful to Eddie for showing her how. So far she'd found several school-friends that she'd lost touch with over the years and she was enjoying the frequent updates on their lives. Most were married – some lived abroad – but others were only a few miles away and it was amazing that she hadn't seen them for so long. She envied those that had photos of beautiful little children in their profile picture. They were displayed like badges of success and she wished that she had a file of photos of her children, but so far that had not been the path for her.

She decided to change her profile picture and uploaded a photo that her brother Leo had taken of her with her six-year-old niece Wendy when they were home from Devon last Christmas. She immediately felt better and didn't care what sort of a signal that sent out to the rest of the Facebook users.

Suzanne clicked on chat and Eddie was on-line as he often was at lunch-time when at work.

She tapped into the box: Hi Eddie

He replied immediately: Good to see you on line. What are you up to?

She typed: Just browsing – am envious of all the people who are planning on heading away for the weekend or going to some exciting party. She waited, fingers crossed that he would be able to call around some evening over the coming weekend.

A pause and the response came: Well, I'm in for a quiet one so you're not alone – for starters, I'll call around with a bottle of wine tomorrow night and we can watch Dancing on Ice – have got some on DVD!

She smiled. Sounds divine – are you not meeting your boyfriend?

The answer was swift. Change subject – not good at the mo – see you when you get in here xx

Suzanne clicked off and went to see how her mother was doing. At least Eddie had a boyfriend to have an argument with. It had been four years since she had last dated – he was one of the doctors in Temple Street and he was such an egotist that he almost put her off dating for good.

Mary was smearing make-up all over her face, like a little girl attempting to use her mother's foundation for the first time.

Suzanne felt a pang inside as she remembered how beautifully her mother always used to present herself in public. It was so unfair that she was rambling around the house each and every day like a lost child. It was so degrading and sad to see someone without their mind at the end of their life. She wasn't old either – only seventy, which meant that she should be able to have a good life. Suzanne went over to her and took the foundation gently from her mother's hand.

"I'm not finished!" Mary declared.

"You need to brush your hair first – I'll finish off your make-up for you."

"Thanks, Lily – you're so much better at that sort of thing anyway."

Suzanne found her easy to distract – like a small child in many ways. She was looking forward to going to work. The doorbell rang, signalling the arrival of Kate, the home help. She always let herself in but carried out the courtesy of ringing the doorbell to announce her arrival. Suzanne ran down the stairs to where Kate stood in the hallway.

"Hi, Suzanne," she smiled cheerily.

"How are you, Kate? You're going to have fun today – Mum wants to do dressing- up!"

13

"I'm ready for anything!" Kate said as she rolled up her sleeves and climbed the stairs. She was a small stocky woman in her fifties, down-to-earth and unflappable, and well able to handle Mary.

Suzanne grabbed her coat and bag and went out to catch the Number 130 bus.

Ronan sat at the desk of his office checking through his messages. He had started to use Facebook for work a couple of years back when advised by one of the other directors but found that he actually enjoyed the chat with old friends that he had left in Ireland and found in the recent months. He swung around on his leather chair and viewed the towering skyline of Boston. The Charles River sparkled in the distance. He loved the onset of the fall. It was late coming this year and not all of the leaves had turned which was particularly unseasonal. The cold snap hadn't come until two weeks ago and the skies were still a wonderful cerulean blue when he woke up every morning. Things had been bleak for the last three months – since the break-up of his marriage to Laura. He often wondered whether, had they been lucky enough to have children, it would have come to this. He had moved all of his things out of their house on Arlington Street and moved into an apartment in Fulton Street after the news of her relationship with a colleague in work. He was still hurting inside but wouldn't admit it to another soul.

He had a good network of friends and a nice life in Boston but it didn't stop him hankering for Dublin. Whenever he reminisced he always travelled back to the same time and place in his memory. It was always the summer of 1989 and he was coming home from school. She would be waiting for him at the entrance to St Anne's Park and they would walk home through the rose gardens together. He closed his eyes as he pictured her blonde hair – she was an Irish Lady Diana and the most exotic schoolgirl in Dublin. Well, in his eyes. He often wondered what had happened to her and what she was doing now. Over the years he had tried to Google her several times but only found images of brunette and red-haired Suzannes. He had searched for her on Facebook a couple of times before, but not recently.

He swivelled around in his chair, tapped her name into the vacant slot on Facebook and pressed search. Yet again he was surprised to see so many Suzanne Quinns show up in the results. He flicked down along the side of the screen and after two searches there she was. He took a sharp breath and had to look twice. It definitely was his Suzanne. She hadn't changed at all – still so fair and classically beautiful. He hadn't expected to find her so easily. He paused for a moment to take stock. Of course it might not be her but another Suzanne who looked like her. But in his heart he knew that it was his Suzanne looking out through those beautiful blue eyes from the screen. He had to think hard – what was he going to say to her? Because he was certainly going to contact her.

His hand started trembling as he clicked to send a message.

He tapped into the subject box Hello stranger.

He couldn't think of anything clever or witty to say. His brain turned to mush as he continued to type.

I hope you're keeping well – your little girl is lovely. You have obviously been busy over the years – if you fancy dropping me a line I can update you on life in Boston. Ronan

He pressed send and leaned back on his seat. He was wobbly inside. What a blast from the past! Suzanne Quinn – the one woman he thought about whenever he dwelt on happy days long ago when he still had his youth and his dreams.

In Temple Street Children's hospital Suzanne was tending to a young boy who was recovering from a dislocated thumb.

"How did you injure this?" she asked him gently.

"I was throwing a ball to my sister," the young boy replied, all innocence and wide eyes.

Suzanne looked through the patient's notes on the table beside her.

"And how did you manage to hit your hand off the concrete wall?"

"Oh, she jumped out of the way . . ."

Suzanne took his hand and rubbed the thumb – taking care not to press too hard on the limp muscles. The bone had set back in place very well but the lack of exercise while the hand had been in plaster meant that she would prefer to see this little boy one more time.

"Try bending it this way," she demonstrated.

Kids were such fun to work with. At thirty-six her biological clock had gone past the stage of panic and was now ticking slowly and steadily with the concern that it might never come to any use. Her married colleagues assured her that lots of women didn't start their families until they were well into their forties but she found their comfort patronising and sometimes insulting – even though they never meant it to be.

How could they possibly understand what it was like to be her? To live with your mother who was controlled by her crippling Alzheimer's disease! It was a situation that was impossible to understand unless you were in it yourself. Even Eddie, who was the most empathetic man she had ever met and was regularly in her home, often made statements that showed he had no idea of the commitment that she was obliged to honour. It was like living with a very large four-year-old who could do an enormous amount of damage to herself and her home if she wasn't monitored twenty-four hours a day.

"Hey, Sue – you due for a break?"

Suzanne looked up from the little boy she was treating and smiled. "Hi, Eddie – yeah, I can meet you in the staff room in ten if you like."

"I'll make you an Eddie Special," he said as he retreated.

"What's an Eddie Special?" the little boy asked.

"A creamy cappuccino with extra sprinkles," Suzanne informed him. "Keep doing those exercises that I showed you and you'll be back playing football in four weeks."

The little boy's face dropped. "Four weeks! But I have a match on Saturday!"

"Four weeks – if you push me it will be five!"

The little boy grimaced and skulked over to where his mother sat on the other side of the treatment area.

Suzanne had a quick word with the boy's mother, then washed her hands and made her way briskly to the staff canteen. Eddie had installed a coffee machine during the summer and it was proving to be a big hit with all the physios. Most were women and Eddie was more comfortable with his female colleagues than other men on the staff.

Suzanne went over to the Formica table and sat down beside her friend who was busily tapping away on the keys of his laptop.

"Just sending an email, pet. Finished in a minute."

"Who is it to or can I ask?"

Eddie looked up. "My boyfriend, who is melting my head at the minute."

"And what's up between you?"

"He's been taking me totally for granted," Eddie sighed and took a sip of his cappuccino. "It's a really long story – maybe save it for our bottle of wine tomorrow?"

Suzanne nodded. "Hey, I'm having fun on Facebook – can you check out my messages when you've finished? And I need to add information to my profile."

"Sure!" he said, tapping away frantically. "Done! What's your password?"

"It's '*Eddie*' – you came up with it so that I would remember!"

"Of course," he said as he continued to fiddle with the keys. "Someone called Linda wrote on your wall and you've got a new message."

Eddie swung the laptop around so that she could take a look.

Suzanne opened the document and the colour drained from her face as she read the words.

"Suzanne – are you okay?"

Suzanne nodded but her startled expression showed that she wasn't.

"What is it?" Eddie asked.

"It's from Ronan Power. He's an old boyfriend – I haven't seen him for years – not since I was in college. He emigrated with his family just after he did his first year in college. I can't believe it!"

Eddie moved in to get a closer look at the screen.

"Wooo – well, he looks very fit for his late thirties!"

"He does look good, doesn't he? And he thinks my niece is my little girl."

"Have you selected your marriage status on your profile?"

"No."

Eddie smiled cheekily. "Well, don't tell him yet – keep him guessing. Let's take a look at his profile."

Together they flicked through his page and scanned for snippets of information.

"A director of a software company – must have a bob or two!" Eddie said with a big grin.

"He's married, it says here, and living in Boston!"

"That's only a short six-hour flight! You could have an affair!"

Suzanne gave him a look that said she didn't approve and he reciprocated with a cheesy grin.

"My boyfriend's in a relationship – it's the way of the world."

"I'm not able for that sort of heartache, Eddie – you know me!"

"I can't understand why you haven't been snapped up years ago, Sue. You're the best girl I know!"

Suzanne smiled at the compliment but inside her gut a discomfort was rearing. "Well, maybe if Ronan hadn't gone off to Boston when we were young we would have got together."

"Was he *the one*?"

"I don't know if there's such a thing."

She stood up and walked over to the sink to rinse her cup. Her head flooded with memories and in the background she could hear her mother's voice dictating how and why she needed to end it with Ronan. How strange it seemed now to remember those days and the pain and the tears.

Eddie was oblivious to Suzanne's emotions. "Are you going to answer him?"

Suzanne turned around and nodded. "I just don't know what to say!"

"I'll call around later after work and help you reply – my boyfriend can wait for me – he's a jerk!"

Ronan was preparing for the convention in Vegas and sorting out the last few pieces of paperwork that needed to be sent away. He found himself casting his eyes every few minutes over the emails and messages in his iPhone. There were several coming in every hour but none from the person he was watching out for. Since sending the Facebook message, he couldn't get Suzanne Quinn out of his mind.

His secretary knocked on the office door and entered with a pile of files in her arms.

"Thanks, Carla – just leave them on my desk." He knew what they were.

"I'm just finalising details of your Las Vegas trip – will you be staying in your usual suite?"

Ronan nodded. "Yes, thank you, Carla – and be sure to book a table at Mix for two of the nights."

"No problem," the pretty girl smiled as she left the room.

Ronan liked the peace and tranquillity of the Signature Hotel at the MGM Grand. It didn't have slots in the foyer and the entrance was in a side street away from the crowds and The Strip. He had spent a weekend there with Laura only last year at the very same convention. He should have known then by her constant texting and phone-calls that there was someone else.

He went on to the net to read his daily fix of the *Irish Times*. It was a little ritual that kept him in touch with the country that he still thought of as his home – even though he had lived as long on the other side of the Atlantic as he had in Ireland.

Suzanne opened the door. "Hi, Eddie – I've just got Mum to bed – perfect timing!"

Eddie gave Suzanne a peck on the cheek and followed her into the kitchen.

"So, honey, have you decided what you're going to say to this old lover of yours?"

Suzanne gave a timid laugh as she went over to the fridge. "He was more than just a lover," she said sadly. "Wine?"

"Only if you have a bottle open," he replied.

"I always have a bottle open, Eddie!" she said, taking out a nice

Mâcon-Lugny from the fridge. "Am I keeping you from your boyfriend?"

"I told you I want him to pay – he's such a pain at the moment. I'm really much more interested in your saga – tell me the nitty-gritty – you have me intrigued. And it's been ages since you've had a little romance, Sue!"

"I would hardly call one email a romance," she smiled.

Eddie opened his laptop and hit the keys.

"Let's see what information we can get from his Facebook page. Sue, you're hopeless! You haven't even accepted his 'friend' request!" He tapped more frantically at the keys. "Right, that's done. Now we can get properly started."

Suzanne poured generous measures into wineglasses and put them on the table before sitting down.

"He says that his favourite book is *One Hundred Years of Solitude* by Gabriel García Márques – very macho and deep!" said Eddie. "And *The Departed* is his favourite movie – I bet that's because it's set in Boston – although Leonardo is *sooo* gorgeous in it!"

Suzanne giggled anxiously as Eddie continued with his voyeuristic analysis of her old boyfriend's tastes. Ronan was part of her past and they had separated on difficult terms. She didn't want to divulge the circumstances of their relationship to Eddie because she could barely admit them to herself. Her relationship with Ronan Power was tucked away in the deepest recesses of her memory and had been for many years. It would be too painful to dredge those feelings back up . . . yet she was desperate to know how he was and what he was doing now.

Suddenly she wished she hadn't involved Eddie – she didn't want her contact with Ronan to be treated as a giggle. "Oh, let me just send a brief reply and be done with it!" she said. "I'll do it later."

Eddie wasn't listening. "Hmm . . . a very typical A-type male . . . maybe we should keep him hanging on a while . . ."

Suzanne was losing patience with Eddie. She needed to get him away from the computer but he knew her too well not to start quizzing if she gave any information away.

"Come on, Eddie – it's not a romance! He's married – and he thinks I am too!"

"But everyone likes a little cyber-flirting now and again – he could be your cyber boyfriend!"

"I *would* like to reply. But I won't do it now – leave it and I'll get back to it later!"

Eddie shook his head vehemently. "No, no, no – have you learnt nothing from me? Strike while the iron is hot!"

She laughed nervously. "A moment ago you were telling me to keep him hanging! Make up your mind!"

"Never!" Eddie declared, unabashed.

Suzanne really didn't know if she could handle full communication with Ronan just yet. The shock of contact was enough to digest for the moment.

"Well, if I do answer I think it should be just friendly. And honest!"

"Please let him think Wendy is your daughter! That's the least you can do for me!"

"You mean, then he mightn't think I'm such a loser in the relationship stakes?" She felt a bit offended.

Eddie raised his hands in a 'don't shoot me' gesture. "I only meant it would add a bit of intrigue – get him wondering!"

Suzanne shook her head. She could feel her jaw tighten. She was like a clam in a shell and bursting to get out. "I'm not very good at lying. It just gets people in a mess."

"For heaven's sake, Sue, he's in Boston! Let me write it," he said, starting to type, reading aloud as he did. "*Dear Ronan, it's so lovely to hear from you after all these years! I'm still living in Clontarf – I didn't move far. I'm so glad that you like the photo of Wendy and me – she's such a sweetheart. I'm working in Temple Street Hospital and living life to the full. Please tell me all your news and we can reminisce about the 'old days'! Suzanne.*" Eddie stopped, a big grin across his face. "What do you think?"

"'*Living life to the full*'! How corny is that? And not putting him right about Wendy is the same as lying about her!"

Eddie dramatically lifted his index finger and pressed it down onto the send key.

"Well, it's sent now!"

"Eddie!"

Suzanne looked at the screen in dismay. Too late to do anything now. Her heart sank. It was a wasted opportunity because she had really wanted to send Ronan a serious message, an honest one. She didn't want to get cross with Eddie because he would smell a rat and be able to draw the truth from her with ease. It was something that he had quite a knack of doing.

"That's very naughty of you, Eddie – you should have let me do it."

"You probably wouldn't have replied at all if I had left it up to you – at least this way you didn't have time to think about it!"

Suzanne knew that he was right – Eddie knew her better than she knew herself. He had been such a supportive and encouraging part of her life since her mother had taken ill. As time passed, her confidence had waned to a point where she was afraid to go on dates any more. She wished she could tell Eddie the truth – the fact that re-acquaintance with Ronan Power would ultimately re-awaken memories of the most difficult and painful period in her life. But this was something that she wanted to keep from Eddie.

Ronan was on his way home from work before he realised he had received a message from Suzanne. While stopped at the lights by Boston Common he had flicked on his iPhone. He couldn't take the smile off his face and pulled the car in to the side of the road to read and re-read her words. His heart was thumping and he wanted to respond immediately but decided to wait until later when he was in the comfort of his apartment with a nice glass of beer at his side.

A letter had arrived to his work from Laura's solicitor and now he was relieved to have something to focus on apart from the divorce. Yet he couldn't prevent his thoughts from sliding back to his failed marriage. He couldn't understand how the woman who had been so loving and adoring for years could change and pour so much hatred on him in such a short time. Laura and he were extremely happy until she decided that she wanted to start a family. The urgency she suddenly felt to get pregnant was as great as the repulsion she had held towards pregnancy at the start of their marriage. She was a highly successful businesswoman and saw the challenge of having a baby as an immediate target to be met – much in the same way as the products that she marketed.

But in this instance she wasn't meant to have it all instantly. Ronan had handed himself to her after a work party on Cape Cod eight years before. They married soon after and settled into a comfortable and desirable apartment on Arlington Street. He could recall with clarity the day that Laura decided they should start a family. It was a shock at first and she didn't want to discuss the details – all she wanted was Ronan to take her to the bedroom immediately and impregnate her. She couldn't understand after the first month why she wasn't pregnant but as she was in her thirties she decided to give it another month before seeking help and advice. By the third month of trying she was losing patience with her husband and had booked an appointment at a private maternity clinic. Ronan felt that her actions were premature but she insisted she had to know how and why she was not pregnant. When she was told that there was no apparent reason why she wasn't, she demanded that Ronan be examined.

He was told that his sperm count was low and this could be a reason why they were not conceiving a child. As the doctor read the report on his findings Laura let her hand slip symbolically from her husband's grasp and covered her mouth. It was a simple gesture but enough to show Ronan that his relationship with his wife had changed beyond repair. They continued having something of a sexual relationship for another six months and then their lovemaking stopped. Laura had found a colleague in her office who was five years her junior and hungry with desire for her. It was almost in the same breath as she asked for the divorce that she announced she was pregnant.

Ronan pulled up to the underground car park beside his apartment and opened the gates with the zapper, reeling with the reawakened pain of rejection and underlying feelings of failure. It was dark. He parked quickly and made his way into the lift and up to his apartment on the second floor.

He didn't relish the prospect of a TV dinner. That was why he had forced himself to eat a good lunch in the middle of the day – since living on his own his appetite had vanished. He went over to the fridge, pulled out a Miller and put on the lights and music in his living room. Settling down on the armchair, he took out his laptop and turned it on.

Chapter 3

Certain things catch your eye,
But pursue only those that capture your heart.

~ NATIVE AMERICAN PROVERB ~

Vicky and Tina sat silently beside each other in the cab.

"Where to?" the taxi-driver asked in his husky Mexican accent.

"The Mirage, please."

He suddenly became very animated and waved an arm around. "You gotta see the dolphins in the gardens – and the volcano – you're gonna have a real good stay!"

Vicky leaned over to whisper in her daughter's ear but Tina was listening to her iPod.

"Did you hear that, love? There are dolphins in the grounds of the hotel – that's why Frank chose it – he knows they're your favourite animal."

Tina threw her mother a look of contempt. "They should be left in the wild. I don't think they should be kept in the middle of a desert."

It was exactly the sort of repartee that Vicky had become used to between herself and her daughter. It was difficult to win. Sometimes it was better just to keep her mouth shut.

"You got the Beatles musical in the Mirage," the driver continued. "I saw that – it's real good. You like the Beatles?"

Vicky felt a tightening in her stomach – this wasn't how she wanted to start off her new life. She had hoped that Frank would be with her when they arrived in Vegas. She opened her bag and took out the card that he had given her. It read *Connie Haycock, Wedding Planner*. She would ring her the next morning.

The bright lights of The Strip were coming into view and the spectacle of Vegas at night was so exhilarating and stimulating to the senses that even Tina was enthralled. She stared out the window in disbelief at the brightly lit Statue of Liberty and the Brooklyn Bridge.

"We got the Eiffel Tower here," the driver continued with his brief tour info.

On both sides the skyscraper hotels reached up and into the night like beacons of man's conquest of the desert.

"What do you think?" Vicky asked her daughter enthusiastically.

Tina nodded. It was a spectacular sight to behold. To their left a long line of fountains rained down in front of a huge majestic hotel that she had recognised from the pictures that Connie had sent.

"That's the Bellagio, and look – there's Caesar's Palace!" Vicky clapped her hands with delight as the buildings whizzed by. They were much more impressive in reality than they had looked in the travel brochure.

They drove off The Strip and up to a tall geometric building.

"Here it is," the driver said as he hopped out of the car and went to the trunk to get their bags.

The street was alive with people hustling and bustling in all directions. It looked like it was almost as busy inside the hotel.

Vicky tipped the driver and made her way with her daughter into the lobby. The reception area was in front of an enormous aquarium filled with tropical fish. Vicky and Tina dragged their bags over to the receptionist's desk where they were taken from them by the bellboy to be delivered up to their room. Vicky signed the register and took the keys, giving her daughter one. Tina had a room of her own but the two rooms were adjoining so that Vicky wouldn't worry about her.

"Can we book dinner?" Vicky asked the receptionist.

"Might I suggest Stack for your dinner tonight – it's in our hotel and one of the best steak houses on The Strip."

"That would be lovely, thank you," Vicky said, smiling widely to make up for her daughter's apparent lack of interest and enthusiasm. "Come on, love."

The two walked over to the elevators for the rooms, passing a waterfall surrounded by tropical vegetation and exotic displays of fresh fruit and flowers. They might as well have arrived in Hawaii, were it not for the slot machines that blinked in the distance.

It was Vicky's first exposure to the business that was the original purpose of Vegas. Vicky wasn't a gambler so it didn't attract her but she knew that Frank was fond of the casinos in Dublin and it would be interesting and fun to watch him play in the gambling capital of the world.

They arrived at their rooms at last. Vicky went over to the window – glad to be on her own for a few moments after the tension of the long flight spent in almost total silence with her daughter. She didn't feel the excitement that she thought she would as a bride-to-be. Her stomach was flitting alright but it was more with concern that she was doing the right thing. She didn't doubt for a moment that Frank was the man for her and that she should marry him but how her new husband would affect her relationship with her daughter was causing her concern.

Suddenly the sound of drums reverberated through the thick double-glazed windows. It was followed by the strains of Polynesian music and singing. Vicky rushed over to take a look outside and to her amazement lights were flashing and a substance resembling lava was erupting from the sculpted mound in the gardens below.

Tina ran into the room through the adjoining doors.

"What's going on?" she asked shakily. "Is it an earthquake?"

The vibrations were coming faster and longer now.

"I don't think so, love – take a look outside." Vicky pointed down to the mock volcano in the Polynesian garden with lava spurting out from the top. "I think it's just Vegas at night! Something tells me we're going to see lots of wonderful things on this trip!"

The two stood staring out the window at the vast spectacle below. Every now and then it was accompanied by cries from the crowd down on the street. It was a surreal moment where the eyes of both mother and daughter were fixed on the sight below but their minds were in completely different sets.

Tina sighed. "I still can't believe that you're actually going to marry him, Mum."

"Don't, Tina – please. It's our first night – let's just enjoy the experience."

Tina shook her head and walked back into her room.

Vicky could feel a choking sensation in her throat. She hadn't been able to talk properly to her daughter since her marriage had broken up – it wasn't her fault but she secretly felt that Tina blamed her for driving her husband into the arms of another woman. The closeness that had always been between them was gone and at times Vicky felt like she was living with a stranger. When Frank said that he had to come out to Vegas a day later than originally planned she secretly thought that it would be an opportunity for herself and her daughter to foster their relationship but she realised now that she had been too optimistic. And as for Frank, she was carrying concern in her gut every time she thought about the way he had been behaving for the last three weeks – something was up but she hadn't the courage to ask him or the confidence to be told the truth if there was something seriously wrong. No, this was not how she wanted her new life with Frank to start out.

Vicky and Tina walked out onto The Strip. The place was alive and throbbing with energy. Even Tina couldn't hide the amazement in her wide eyes.

"Where do you want to go? Venice?"

Tina shrugged and they walked across the road, dodging the beeping cars and heaving crowds. The Venetian Hotel had been Vicky's preferred choice for their stay but she had asked Frank to change it after she thought there might be objections from Tina that it was too romantic.

Now that they were entering the vast canalled shopping mall that led into the heart of the hotel Vicky felt sad and wished that Frank was with her. It was, after all, meant to be the lead-up to the happiest day of her life. But with the sour looks from Tina it wasn't going to go exactly the way that she had planned. The ceiling of the main entrance was adorned with copies of Tintoretto and the great artists of the Venetian Renaissance. Cherubs and gilt gave the décor that distinctly Italian flavour.

"Let's do some shopping?" Vicky suggested.

Tina's eyes moved swiftly from store to store. Exotic masks and vintage costumes filled the shop window to her right and she was enthralled by the magical water wonderland they passed as they walked through the mall. Above, the painted sky was a perfect powder blue adorned with little fluffy clouds.

"I'm going to buy you anything that you want in here – call it an early bridesmaid's present from me!" Vicky said affectionately.

Tina wandered over to the mask shop and ran her fingers over the beautiful vintage brooches and earrings that hung in the display case. On the bottom row were rings sculpted in silver with fine filigree. One of them caught Tina's eye particularly – it had a large sapphire garnet in the middle and was cut like a teardrop.

"Do you like it?" Vicky whispered over her shoulder.

"It's the most beautiful ring I have ever seen."

"Well, then, it's yours," Vicky said hurriedly – delighted to see something appeal to her daughter and take the scowl from her brow – if only for a moment.

They ventured back into the mall and stood and watched the gondoliers singing as they came to a dead end and turned their crafts around. It wasn't anything like the Venice that Vicky remembered. She had spent a weekend there with Frank when he whisked her away to get engaged earlier in the year but this place was a cleaner and simpler version – there was something wholesome about it and she liked it.

"Mum, do you love Frank?" Tina asked as she left the shop with one eye on her new ring which she had put on the ring-finger of her right hand.

"Of course I do, darling. You don't really need to ask that – I wouldn't be marrying him if I didn't."

"You might be marrying him because he's rich."

"I wouldn't marry for any other reason than love."

Tina shook her head. "I just don't get it – I don't think he's right for you, Mum."

Vicky looked at the long black-dyed locks of her daughter's hair and the piercings through her eyebrow, nose and lip and thought for a moment how ironic the comment was. Tina hadn't fitted in at school. She had rebelled so much in her last two years in the Loretto Convent School that Vicky was pleased that she managed to finish at all, as the principal was always on about her hair and piercings – it was just as well she didn't know about Tina's tattoos. Then Vicky had found a place in the Institute for her after she had done really badly in her Leaving Certificate the first time.

"Tina, we don't always like the person that someone in our family falls in love with and we have to try hard to overcome it."

Tina shook her head. "But it's much harder when I'm getting a new dad!"

"He's not your dad – David's your father and always will be – okay?"

Tina's eyes started to well up. "Dad doesn't want me!"

Vicky could feel her pain like a weight in her heart. "Oh, love – I'm sorry that your dad has been preoccupied with the twins but he does love you."

"Not as much as his sons!" The tears were streaming down her cheeks now and dragging lines of black liner and mascara along with them.

Vicky put her arm consolingly around her daughter. "Come on, let's go back to the hotel!"

The young girl sniffled into the sleeve of her black top and allowed her mother to lead her across the road and back to the hotel.

"Come on into the bathroom and we'll fix your make-up and then paint the town red – it's our first night in Vegas!"

After Tina had allowed her mother to pamper her and fuss over her, they went into the sumptuous surroundings of the Japonais

Lounge that overlooked the roulette wheels and crap tables of the Mirage Hotel.

They settled down on the leather couches and Vicky ordered a Margarita for herself and a Coke for Tina. The waitress was swift and, although she gave Tina a funny look, presumably for being in a bar and looking under twenty-one years of age, she returned with their drinks.

Tina had turned eighteen two weeks earlier and Vicky hoped that with her coming of age that she might revise her dark moody look and revert to the pretty fair-haired girl that she used to be. She watched her daughter lift her drink and take a sip.

"Have you decided what you're going to put down on your CAO form?"

Tina put her Coke down on the table with a bang. "I thought you were going to back off, Mum? I thought we were trying to enjoy ourselves?"

"It's just chit-chat, love." Vicky said defensively. "It's normal to talk about work and college."

Tina threw her eyes heavenward. "I thought we were just having some quality time together! You can't help yourself, can you?" She stood up. "I'm going to my room."

Vicky got up. "Wait, Tina – do you know where you're going?"

But Tina had moved so swiftly down the steps she no longer heard her.

Vicky called over the waiter and fixed up the tab before rushing off to follow her daughter.

The elevators were numerous and Tina was apparently already in one of them and on her way to the room.

Vicky kicked herself for saying the wrong thing. But that was the problem with their relationship as mother and daughter – everything she said lately was the 'wrong thing'!

Tina shut the bedroom door and went over to turn the lock on the adjoining suite. She didn't want to see her mother for the rest of the evening. Outside the volcano was erupting again to cheers from the crowd on the street below. She lay down on the bed and put a pillow over her head. It almost drowned out the knocking on the door.

"Tina – are you in there, love?"

Tina didn't want to answer – her mother was overprotective – where did she expect her to be?

"Yes. I'm here and I'm going to bed."

"Are you okay? Do you want to talk?"

Of course I don't want to talk – that's when the bloody problems always start!

"No. I want to go to sleep now."

"Alright, love. See you in the morning."

Tina's head spun. She wanted a drink so badly. In Ireland she was old enough to be served in loads of places. She sat up and tiptoed over to the mini-bar. Without making a sound she took out a bottle of baby vodka and unscrewed the cap. She couldn't be bothered with adding orange or cola. If she knocked it back really quickly it would have greater effect. The spirit was sharp and tart on her tongue and she reached for her bottle of water to dilute the aftertaste. That was better – she was more comfortable now. Maybe just one more, she thought. It reminded her of the times that she used to sneak into the living room, when she was sure that her mother was asleep, and take a shot from the cocktail cabinet. She had been doing it since she was fourteen.

Her mother never noticed because she often needed a nightcap before she could get a night's sleep after her father left home. In fact she only stopped drinking vodka when she started dating Frank. Now her mother only brought expensive bottles of wine into the house and Tina abhorred the way Frank studied every label carefully before removing the cork. There were so many things about Frank that annoyed her that she didn't know where to start.

She didn't trust his motives with her mother either. Sure her mother was an attractive woman and she held herself really well for almost forty but why would Frank be so keen to marry her when he had the choice of so many younger women? There was so much about Frank that didn't make any sense at all.

Tina slugged back the last drop from the second bottle of vodka and went over to the bed. She was numb now and ready for sleep. Sleep was the best part of her day.

Chapter 4

When a man moves away from nature
his heart becomes hard.

~ LAKOTA PROVERB ~

John rose into the Dog Pose and took a deep breath. His yoga routine in the mornings was a ritual that he relished. The best part of his day, he had said to his last girlfriend. When she'd been scornful, he'd known it was the beginning of the end with her. He was in tune with his body and his environment and, if somebody couldn't respect that, then John didn't want to be with that person.

He had plenty of time to make breakfast and pack the few things that he was taking to Vegas before taking the airlink bus to the airport. It wasn't that he couldn't afford a taxi but he liked to travel on public transport. It came with living in the city and a respect and regard for the social system that he grew up in. When they were kids, Frank and he always took the bus to school or to football matches from their little house in Cabra as they didn't have a car. His working-class roots didn't do him any harm and John felt as happy sitting chatting on a bus as he did when being driven around the capitals of the world in limousines belonging to the bands that he played with. As he had said to Frank, "They all do the same thing and get you from A to B."

Frank's view on transport, as with many other things, was very

34

different from his brother's. He liked the comfortable life that he had earned for himself with hard work. He had also dropped his accent even before he left school. Bernadette had nurtured its improvement with relish and care. John had a fairly neutral accent that was strong and soft at the same time. He didn't feel the need to hide his roots like his brother by cultivating his accent and anyway his mother didn't seem to care how her younger son spoke.

It was almost time to catch the bus. As he took a last sip from his cup of green tea, a few drops dribbled from the base of the mug and on to his white T-shirt. He smiled to himself as he brushed the stains away. It was a John Proctor trait and one that used to torment his mother whenever he spilt his breakfast on his shirt before going out the door to school. It didn't warrant changing – he wasn't dressing to impress anyone. He picked up his bag and, without rushing, left the house and walked down the quays to the Busárus.

He liked Vegas and had been there many times in his capacity as a musician but the thing he liked best about Vegas was the desert and visiting what he called his spiritual home – the Grand Canyon. He had spent some time camping out in the desert with an American rock group several years before. They had eaten scorpions and washed in the tiny lakes formed along the Colorado River. At night the stars illuminated the desert sky like flash-lamps. It was a special time and he hoped to escape the wedding party for a few days after the ceremony and spend some time near the Indian reservations and out in the wide-open spaces.

Frank was restlessly tossing and turning at the back of the aircraft while John was sound asleep in the comfortable first-class beds at the front of the plane. His brother was a complete enigma – he was happy to pay thousands to travel in luxury on a plane but wouldn't pay for a taxi. He wished that he was up at the front enjoying a good sleep but instead he had saved enough by travelling economy to go some way towards paying for the wedding and his accommodation for the two-week stay in Vegas. He had to be more organised – his bank manager had shown him how truly desperate his financial situation was and he didn't know for how much longer he could keep the truth from Vicky. Poor Vicky deserved so much more. She was getting a booby prize for a new husband.

Frank closed his eyes and tried to think of the night before. It was the most amazing lovemaking that he had experienced in years. Maybe the fact that he was about to commit to Vicky made it more exciting. So what was it, he asked himself – was it the last fling he had promised himself . . . or the first in a series of infidelities? Would he really be able to turn over a new leaf? Leave the past behind?

His eyes sprang open as he suffered a crisis of confidence. What he had done was wrong but now he was worried that marrying Vicky was even more wrong. He wanted to give her a good life. She deserved to live in comfort after the difficult situation she had experienced with her ex for the last few years. And she was keen and anxious to have another baby before she got any older which ticked another box for him. He smiled as he imagined himself as a father. His mother would be ecstatic.

He had put everything into his courtship of Vicky, his efforts culminating in taking her off to Venice a few months earlier. He knew that no woman could resist the romance of the beautiful watery Renaissance city. But the passion of the city and romance of getting engaged couldn't stop him thinking of the lover he had left behind in Dublin.

He took out his laptop and tried to distract his thoughts with business. He had streamlined his menus and staff. He couldn't be more efficient. If only he hadn't got involved in property! Now he ran the risk of losing everything he had set up and worked so hard to build.

Money was a great motivator for Frank. As a child coming from a working-class background, he wanted to have enough to live in relative comfort and not scrimp and save the way he watched his poor mother do to bring himself and his brother up on her own – washing floors and cleaning people's houses.

That was why it grieved Frank so much to still have an attachment to someone else when he was about to marry the most wonderful woman that he had ever had a relationship with. And there had been many. When the celebrity chefs came into vogue, Frank was already a successful restaurateur. He used to go to the top spots at least five nights a week and have one beautiful model after another fawn over him.

He was in a Catch 22 situation and he was careering along at over five hundred miles an hour into a marriage that could leave him in the biggest mess of his life.

Chapter 5

*Give thanks for unknown blessings
already on their way.*

~ NATIVE AMERICAN PROVERB ~

Vicky opened her eyes. For a moment she thought she was at home in Howth but the ray of bright sunshine beaming in through the crack in the curtains told her she was not. She pulled on her dressing gown and went over to the window to see the blue sky and early morning buzz on The Strip below. She hoped that Tina had slept well and knocked on the door that separated her suite from her daughter's adjoining room. There was no reply. She went out to the hall and knocked on the door there but there was still no reply. She had to see that Tina was okay and took out the second key that the receptionist had given her.

Tina was sprawled out on the bed – face down. All of her clothes were still on. She was only a child in many ways and Vicky rushed over to sit down on the side of the bed and stroke her daughter's tear-stained face. Smudged mascara and black eyeliner covered her eyelids.

Tina moved her head slightly and Vicky brushed her hair off her face. She always seemed so much younger when she was asleep. It reminded Vicky of when she was a little girl and how much she loved her to stroke her hair as she fell asleep. Tina was her little shadow when she was a child. Vicky never went out without her. When Vicky played a tennis match her daughter would sit at the sideline and keep the score. David used to complain that they needed more time together as a couple but Vicky loved having her little girl involved in every aspect of her life. Maybe it was because she was an only child, but Tina was such a good little girl it was so easy to take her around with her. Things had certainly changed and Vicky felt a pang of regret for the loss of her little girl and the challenges of placating her teenager.

She whispered into the air. "Good morning, darling – I'm sorry I upset you last night."

Tina rose slowly like a small animal and yawned. "What time is it?"

"It's ten o'clock – do you want to go and get some breakfast – then we can meet the wedding planner if you don't mind?"

Tina shrugged. "Okay."

They showered and dressed, then had a light breakfast in the Paradise Café downstairs and went out to get a taxi from reception.

"Where to?" the taxi driver asked.

"The Graceland Chapel, please," Vicky instructed.

"How do you like Vegas?"

He spoke like a cartoon character and Tina and Vicky had to swallow their laughter so as not to be rude.

"It's lovely, thanks – we only arrived last night," Vicky replied.

"Last night? You gotta go to Fremont Street – that's the real Vegas!"

"Is it far from the Graceland Chapel?"

"It's just around the corner, ma'am. Why don't I drive by and show you?"

"Why not!" Vicky agreed.

Vicky watched the Vegas skyline pass by as they drove up the Las Vegas Freeway. They turned off at West Charleston Boulevard and the driver pointed out the different chapels as they passed along the way.

Most of the shops were pawnbroker stores and jewellers – no surprise considering the end of town that they were in.

"That one over there is the chapel you want but I'm gonna drop you at Fremont Street – you can't go home without seeing it."

Vicky looked at Tina who seemed interested in going anywhere rather than a wedding chapel.

"Okay," Vicky agreed. They were early for their appointment with Connie the wedding planner. Frank would be arriving soon and then there would be little time for sightseeing with her daughter on her own.

The taxi brought them to the entrance of Fremont Street. A futuristic canopy one hundred feet high covered the shoppers and gamblers below from the heat of the midday sun. Banners draped the pillars and billboards advertising the Oktober Frightfest. German beer-cellar music bellowed from the loudspeakers and followed them as they walked past the famous icon of Vegas Vic – the neon cowboy. The street was lined on both sides with casinos, jewellers and cheap souvenir stores but there was something incredibly clean and shiny about the place. The tiled street was immaculate and there wasn't a shred of litter or vandalism. Signs in neon flashed to show that they had arrived at the Four Queens, the Golden Nugget and Binions. These names were part of the fabric and history of the city and Vicky thrilled just being there.

She looked around but couldn't see Tina anywhere – only tourists, a couple of Native Americans and some vintage-car salesmen huddled around their convertibles. No matter how hard she tried she couldn't see her daughter and she started to panic until she recognised the silhouette of a young girl reading a sign on a small caravan that wasn't unlike an old Irish traveller's. It was painted a dark brown with red trims on the edging and wheels. Handwritten over the doorway were the words *Past, Present and Future*. The door was left open, revealing an old lady inside who was sitting at a cloth-covered table.

Vicky rushed over to Tina. "I didn't know where you had gone!"

"Let's go in," Tina said, stepping up and into the van. "It's only ten dollars to get your palm read."

Vicky looked at her watch. They did have plenty of time and even though she had no inclination to dabble in the supernatural or superstitious nonsense, she was willing to do anything to make her daughter's time in Vegas more enjoyable.

Madame Lauren, as the sign on the door informed, was wearing a red scarf and black cardigan. Her skin was tanned dark from the sun and she spoke with a Hispanic accent.

"Come inside," she smiled, revealing her chipped front tooth.

Tina went straight over to the chair at the table and sat down. She boldly placed her open palm on the table unprompted.

Vicky took the big step up into the caravan and sat at a chair beside Tina.

"Would you like me to read yours too?" Madame Lauren asked.

Vicky shook her head. She gave the old woman a ten-dollar bill then sat back to listen.

The soothsayer set to work.

"I see a long and eventful life for you. Many jobs in different things but you will always be close to the television. You will have good health if you learn to relax and I see a man with the initial K in his name." Her smile widened. "And you will be married soon."

Vicky let out a giggle – she had no time for pranksters or phonies and this woman was obviously not a real clairvoyant. Her daughter's ideas on marriage were made perfectly clear to her after the break-up of her parents' marriage. She let the old woman continue but stood up abruptly as soon as the session was coming to an end.

Madame Lauren looked up. "Are you sure you don't want me to read your palm?"

"No, thanks – I think I've heard enough. Especially as I'm the one that's getting married and that's what lots of people come to Vegas to do."

The old woman laughed out loud. "You may have been married once but you're not getting married again!" she said, shaking her head vehemently.

"Come on, Tina – we've heard enough," Vicky said uncomfortably. The certainty in the woman's voice disturbed her.

Tina jumped up and followed her mother out of the tiny enclosed space. It was not the news she had wanted to hear. The old woman was crazy to think that she would ever want to get married

41

but, on the positive side, if there was a grain of truth in her predictions maybe her mother wouldn't be getting married after all.

Kyle called out to his mother but there was no reply. He looked at his watch – it was way later than he had figured. His mom would be out working with some couple who had come to Vegas to get hitched. She worked too hard. He pushed back the duvet and swung his long skinny legs out of the bed and on to the wooden floor. He loved this time of year – not too hot. Now that he had finished school, he loved life. The last three years had been so dumb in Las Vegas High. He should have left when he was sixteen but had stayed on to keep his mom happy. He stood up, scratched his head and pushed his long black fringe away from his eyes. Eleven thirty and he was no way near ready to meet the day. He picked up a black T-shirt off the floor and pulled it down over his head – then stepped into a pair of black jeans. He put on his freedom feather necklace and walked into the bathroom. College wasn't for him – he wasn't like his brother. It would be another day of doing nothing and nothing to do. But Kyle didn't mind that – he would strum a few chords later and watch the heat of the day evaporate from the porch.

He looked into the bathroom mirror at another spot that had erupted overnight on his chin. It hurt so bad when he tried to shave. He pushed his fringe back and examined the rest of his face. He wasn't bad-looking – he realised that. And he was a darn sight better-looking than the dorks on *American Idol*. But he had never been in love. He couldn't understand why some guys had no trouble picking up girls – but his problem had always been finding a girl interesting enough to fall in love with. Most high-school girls were so dumb and only cared about how they looked and how much money a guy had. The clever girls were boring and opinionated. The one girl he had kind of liked and dated on and off for the last year was now living with a Hell's Angel old enough to be her dad. Even his friends had changed – Greg who swore he would hang out with him or go and travel the country had enrolled for a geeky computer course in the University of Las Vegas. His other friend Len, a Native American, had got a job on the Hualapai Ranch and was returning to his roots – opting out of the world they had shared. He looked down at his freedom feather, carved beautifully in silver, that Len had given him on his last day in school. Now four months later it was even more symbolic and poignant. The freedom to be who he wanted to be was up to him – but who was that?

He went to the kitchen and poured himself a bowl of cereal. A scribbled note lay beside the phone.

I'm working at the Graceland Chapel with a couple who have come from Ireland. Like to meet for lunch? I'll be there until 1 o'clock.

Love Mom xx

Kyle scrunched up the piece of paper and threw it into the garbage bin. He definitely didn't want to meet some Irish couple – why did all these people come to Vegas to get married? The world had gone crazy. Marriage was out of date. He took some milk from the fridge and poured it over his cereal, then brought it out to the porch where he sat and ate it in the sunshine. It was a good day to go for a ride – out to the desert – maybe bring his guitar and strum to the sound of the crickets and lizards.

Suddenly he remembered he had no money. He looked out the window at his SUV, which was a gift from his mom for finishing high school. He barely had enough gas to get home from Greg's the night before. Damn, he thought. He looked at his watch. If his mom was on Las Vegas Boulevard maybe he could call in and get some cash – he just about had enough to get there. She could be going anywhere after her meeting. He took out his phone and texted her. Meet you at 1 – I need gas! K

Standing at the door of the Graceland Chapel was a woman wearing a tiger-print shawl draped over her shoulders and white palazzo trousers. Her manicured toenails peeped out through exceptionally high silver sandals. Sunglasses rested on the top of her head and pulled back her long brunette hair.

Vicky knew this had to be Connie – she was even more vivacious in the flesh than she had been on the telephone during their brief conversations.

Connie put out her hand and wagged it in anticipation of meeting her client and her daughter.

"Vicky – that has to be you – my gosh, you're even prettier than your photos – you're going to make a beautiful bride!" Connie threw her arms around Vicky once they were close enough and embraced her as if she had known her all of her life. Her phone beeped and she reached into her pocket to quickly read the message. When she had finished she stood back and looked Tina up and down. "And you must be Tina – my, what a lovely young woman – and such lovely skin – you should ease up on that black stuff – you really don't need it!"

Before a disgusted Tina could respond, Connie was guiding her mother in through the doors of the wedding chapel.

"Jon Bon Jovi walked these steps before you twenty years ago – you're in very good company coming here."

Tina walked behind with absolute disdain for the whole sordid event that was being planned.

Suddenly the strains of "It's Now or Never" struck up on an acoustic guitar and from behind a doorway stepped the spectre of Elvis in his heyday.

Vicky was agog at the likeness.

"This is Brendan," Connie introduced. "But naturally he prefers to be called 'The King'!"

"I'm very pleased to meet you," Vicky replied as Elvis leaned forward and planted a warm kiss on her right cheek. He was so handsome she started to giggle and silently berated herself for it.

It was more than Tina could stand and she excused herself and went outside. She couldn't do it, not even for her mother. The whole process was just awful. The sun was beating down and she searched for a spot to sit. She didn't normally like getting the sun on her skin but she rolled up her sleeves and stretched out her legs. She closed her eyes and held her face up to the sun.

Suddenly the roar of a jeep interrupted her thoughts. She looked around as the machine pulled up a few metres from where she sat.

Tina tried not to stare as the driver's door opened and a tall, lean guy stepped down – about her age, she guessed. He was wearing a black T-shirt and jeans. He walked by her as if she was invisible and she felt her insides flutter. His arrival was the most interesting thing to happen since she arrived in Vegas.

Connie was showing Vicky the flower brochure when her son came into the reception of the chapel.

"Kyle, honey, I'm still working – can you wait for a bit?" Connie looked at Vicky. "This is my son Kyle."

Vicky smiled and nodded at the young man. He had a small tattoo on his neck and stud in his eyebrow and ear and she shuddered at what poor Connie must be going through with her rebellious teenager. *Could he be any worse than Tina?*

"I need some gas, Mom – can't stay for lunch – did you get my text?"

Connie couldn't hide the disappointment she felt. She reached into her purse and pulled out two fifty-dollar bills.

"There you go, son," she said, handing over the cash. "What are your plans?"

"I might go for a ride before I go to meet Troy at the bus station – that's if he comes home for Halloween."

Connie gave a sad smile and nodded. Troy had become very unpredictable since he started college. "See you later, son."

Kyle nodded and walked out of building.

"How old is your son?" Vicky asked.

Connie shook her head. "Eighteen – sometimes I feel he's going on forty and then others he acts just like a little kid."

"I know how you feel – it's the same with my daughter!"

Connie slapped her hand down on big book of floral bouquets. "My, why don't I get him to talk to your girl?"

Quick as a flash Connie was scurrying out of the door and running to where Kyle was starting up his vehicle. She waved her arms and called.

Kyle stalled and leaned out the window.

"Kyle, honey – would you show my client's daughter some of the sights of Las Vegas? Like Circus Circus?" Connie pointed over at the small figure in black who sat on the stone wall, now clutching her knees.

"Mom!" Kyle exclaimed. He hated awkward scenes like this – why did his mom think it okay to thrust people together just because they were the same age?

"I did give you one hundred – and it would give me more time with her mother?"

Kyle knew that it was only a couple of hours out of his day while his mother could get a lot of business if he helped her out.

"Okay," he sighed.

Connie was delighted – this could work out very well.

Kyle cut the engine and walked over to where Tina was sitting. By now Vicky had come out to see what was going on.

"Vicky – my son would like to show Tina some of the sights – the fairground in the Circus Circus Hotel is unmissable – and it will give us more time to discuss plans."

Vicky thought hard. Tina didn't seem to mind too much, to judge by the expression on her face and at least it would give her some time to put all the final arrangements in place. Frank had given her *carte blanche*. Vicky looked at Kyle. The youth seemed less than impressed by the prospect.

"An hour or so might be good," Kyle shrugged and nodded at Tina. "Okay with you?"

She stood up with the start of a pink blush on her cheeks that could have been caused by the sun, but Vicky knew that she was embarrassed and attracted to the young man.

Connie was flapping about with excitement. "That's so great – now come on, Vicky, and we can check out some more chapels just to be sure that you're happy."

Vicky would have been happier if her daughter was staying with her but she didn't want to upset Connie and the plan.

Kyle turned to Tina. "Ready?" he said curtly.

Vicky bit her lip. She didn't like the idea of her daughter going out in a car driven by a kid in her own country, let alone in a strange country with a young guy she had only just met – even if she did know his mother professionally.

Tina was revelling in the discomfort she could see etched all over her mother's face. She couldn't have made the scenario up if she'd tried and, even if the guy turned out to be a complete idiot, at least she got to be with someone her own age and away from the wedding-from-hell plans.

Vicky decided to bite her tongue because, for the first time since leaving Dublin airport, Tina was smiling.

"We'll meet back at the hotel then – is that okay?" she asked her daughter.

"Sure – I'll be by the pool if I'm not in my room."

"Have you got any money?" Vicky asked.

Tina nodded then ran around to the passenger side of the car and jumped in.

"Later," Kyle nodded to his mother then revved up and was off.

"Are they going to be okay?" Vicky asked, realising that it was too late now.

"My Kyle has been driving for two years and he is very sensible even if I say so myself. Anyway the Circus Circus is only a couple of blocks down the boulevard. Come now, honey, this is going to be the happiest day of your life – okay?"

Vicky wished she had Connie's confidence as she let her lead her back into the chapel and the host of catalogues on offer.

Kyle pulled in to the gas station which was only a couple of hundred metres from the chapel they had left.

"Stay here," he said coolly.

He got out and filled up, then went into the shop to pay.

Tina sat and watched. She hoped she hadn't made a mistake by letting this strange guy take her off. But it had to be better than staying with her mum.

Kyle jumped back into the car and put a can of Coke on the dash. He didn't look at her as he started the car again and drove off.

Tina liked the warm breeze that rushed through the window as they sped down the road. It was so different being with someone who knew the place – was part of the city – this was his home. He was also nice and tall and Tina really liked tall men – like her dad. She hated the fact that Frank was only slightly taller than her mother. She berated herself for thinking of him again. Soon he would be here and she would have to look at him – the least she should do now was forget about him until he landed.

They passed the tall tower of the Stratosphere Hotel and the iconic Sahara Hotel before the brightly coloured red-and-white big-top structure of the Circus Circus came into view and they were on the boulevard at last.

Kyle parked up. He brushed his fingers through his dark fringe and nodded at the entrance.

"Where you stayin'?" he asked. He stared right at her with penetrating brown eyes.

It was the first time he had addressed her and Tina was tongue-tied. She didn't want to come across as a silly naïve kid. She also didn't want Kyle to realise how much she was in awe of him.

"In the Mirage."

Kyle nodded but gave nothing away by his expression.

They went into the tunnel that led to the Adventuredome and the noise level went up by several decibels. It was remarkable that all these fairground rides were happening in a hotel. Sublime and unexpected.

Tina stayed close to Kyle for support – she didn't want to get lost.

"Want a Coke?"

He was spare with his words, Tina thought to herself – but this was part of the attraction of the strange guy. She imagined what music he might like – what his favourite movie might be. All the time he was looking ahead and leading her into the unknown.

When they reached the entrance to the massive big top Kyle paid the woman in the ticket booth.

The Adventuredome was loud. A cacophony of screams and wheels on runners flooded Tina's ears.

Kyle seemed unimpressed. He walked over to the biggest rollercoaster in the middle of the arena – *Canyon Blaster* was emblazoned across it. He joined the queue without saying a word and she followed. His profile was fine and he gave her a half smile.

"Want to try this? It's really the best one."

Tina nodded vehemently. "Cool." She hated herself for the way she had wagged her head. Why couldn't she think of something funny to say? She was completely out of her depth.

Vicky looked at her watch. She had spent three hours going from wedding chapel to wedding chapel and Connie was keen to bring her to just one more.

But Connie sensed the concern and anticipation in Vicky's voice every time she mentioned her daughter.

"Don't worry about the kids – Kyle will be showing her all the hotels along the way back to the Mirage."

"I'm just not used to her being in a strange country on her own." Vicky was almost apologising.

"No need to worry – my Kyle is a tour-guide proper. It's one thing that seems to have rubbed off on him. So – have you decided where you want to have the ceremony?"

Vicky was even more confused than she had been before she came to Vegas. She'd thought that she wanted the Graceland Chapel to be her chosen venue until she went to the Chapel of the Flowers and Connie showed her the beautiful grotto and garden outside. Coming from Ireland Vicky had never considered getting married out of doors but, then again, with so many days' perfect sunshine a year, the Nevada desert was not somewhere that you would have to think of rain on the day.

"Maybe we should break for something to eat – what do you think?" she suggested as her stomach rumbled.

"Okay!" Connie said. "Let's go to Paris – or would you rather New York?"

It all sounded so very exotic. Vicky was curious. "I really don't mind – I'm sure I'll like it wherever – which is closer to the hotel? Do you think the kids will be back there yet?"

Connie laughed out loud. "Not a chance!" she said with a shake of her head. "They'll be hours yet. Troy ain't coming home after all – he's just sent me a message – so Kyle wouldn't be doing anything else anyway."

Vicky followed Connie out to her car and they sat in the Chrysler while Connie put down the hood. A rose protruded from the dashboard and they set off down the boulevard like Thelma and Louise.

"Are you going to the Grand Canyon while in Vegas?"

"Frank has something lined up but he didn't tell me the details – I hope it's not a helicopter," Vicky said nervously.

Connie slapped her palm on the driving wheel. "Oh my, you have to get a helicopter into the Canyon – it's the only way to see it! Unless you want the pain of trekking on a donkey for hours and hours."

The helicopter didn't appeal but the donkey appealed even less.

Tina held her arms in the air as the rollercoaster sped down to the ground and the cheers and cries from the rest of the crowd rang out all around. Even Kyle had a big grin on his face as the car rammed to a complete and abrupt stop.

She was a spunky girl and much cuter than he had first noticed. He liked the ring in her eyebrow and the way she painted her eyes.

"Do you want to go somewhere different?"

"I don't mind!" she said shakily. "I'm not really into rollercoasters that much!"

"Would you like to go for a drive somewhere different? It isn't far – about thirty minutes."

"Sounds good – I'd like to get away from all the noise and hotels."

Kyle smiled to himself. She was just like him. He would try playing his music in the car and see if she liked it. That was always a good test – Linkin Park and My Chemical Romance – something told him that she not only looked different to the girls that he knew at high school but she *was* different. He had never met an Irish girl before and this could turn into fun.

"Where are we going?" Tina asked as they got back to the car.

Kyle tilted his head and looked shyly out from under his fringe. He grinned before answering her.

"It's called Red Rock Canyon – one of my favourite places! Jump in."

Tina obediently did as she was told and jumped into the jeep. She was anxious and excited at the prospect of driving out into the Mojave Desert with this cute guy who had already shown her the only excitement she had seen in Vegas so far. They drove past the stream of cars backed up along the boulevard and quickly hit the freeway. As they passed the lush suburb of Summerlin, Kyle informed her that was where he lived. After about ten minutes they were in the midst of wide-open space and the towers of the Vegas hotels were behind them. The mountains of the Nevada desert reflected burnt orange light from the earth and sunlight.

Tina felt like she was riding across the moon and entering a whole new world a million miles from home. She wasn't herself and this guy was unlike anyone she had ever been with before. Somehow the guys in the Institute were too studious – all in the brain factory to get their 600 points. There was so much more to life than 600 points and Tina wished her mother would just accept that all she wanted to do was go to art college. But this was out of the question – her mother saw no future for her as an artist. She wanted to see her daughter with some dull degree that guaranteed her a good job – or rather her mother's view of what a good job was. Why couldn't she see that such things didn't really exist and were not part of the future? She was still thinking in the mindset of the last millennium. Vicky had believed all the deep dark oppressive media hype that had settled over Europe like an ash cloud. She really couldn't see the hope and opportunities for the future that Tina and her generation wanted to be a part of. Sometimes she wished that her grandmother was still alive. That woman had been so in touch with the world and lived her life to the full. She was nothing but an embarrassment to Vicky in her final days and this really upset Tina. It all happened around the time that her father left home. Her gran lived on the other side of the city in an incredible house that would

51

have been a perfect setting for a Dickensian novel. Vicky used to visit her mother on Sundays and check that she had everything that she needed. They would exchange few words because every sentence ended in an argument. Tina was the peacekeeper and going through her transition from shiny-faced schoolgirl to Goth. Her grandmother used to spur her on to get another piercing or tattoo and sometimes Tina figured that she was really only encouraging her in order to annoy her daughter. The visits always ended in the same way with Vicky marching down the steps of the house and not looking back while Tina and her grandmother embraced. It was with complete and utter shock that Vicky arrived one Sunday a little over a year ago to find that her mother had turned to stone and had possibly been in the same position for two days. It was little comfort for her to find out that her mother had died peacefully and without pain. She was only seventy-two and in perfect health and fitness right up until the end. She had always told Tina that that was the way she would go – out like a light one day. A psychic that she had met in the sixties at Woodstock had told her and she was at peace with that truth.

Her gran would be so happy and proud to see Tina now, driving off on an adventure with this elusive and enigmatic American guy.

A jagged mountain range cut like torn paper lay ahead of them – orange light reflecting off it in brilliant contrast to the uninterrupted blue sky. Their jeep slid along the snakelike road, twisting and creeping into the distance, and the wide-open space of the desert and all the freedom that came with it.

Kyle seemed to know exactly where he wanted to be – they passed a sign for Red Rock Canyon and continued until he pulled the jeep off the road and they were riding out into the wilderness over the sandy soil.

Suddenly he stopped the jeep and cut the engine. The sun was behind them now. He got out of the car and she did the same. They were in the middle of nowhere. Small tufts of coarse cactus plants and yuccas sprouted out from the earth. Aromatic purple sage and yellow flowering blackbrush threw colour and texture over the landscape that contrasted beautifully with the colourful mineral-rich hills of the Canyon.

The fauna of the desert were well hidden beneath the spiky plants and stones, sheltering from the baking sun, or so Tina surmised. Unusual rock formations stuck out on the mountainside like sticks of seaside rock split in places at right angles, exposing marbled deposits.

Kyle handed her a drink from the Coke that he had bought at the gas station earlier. She took a sip and thrilled from the knowledge that her lips were touching the rim that had touched his a few seconds earlier.

Kyle walked over to a small group of spliced rocks and sat on the largest one.

Tina felt awkward and suddenly very naïve as she looked around for a place to sit.

"What you think of this place?" he asked.

Tina nodded. "It's good," she said, sitting down.

"Sometimes if you're lucky you can see a desert tortoise or a mountain goat – plenty of lizards under those bushes too."

He pointed down at the rock – an imprint of a spiral motif was dug into it, resembling the symbols she had seen on a school trip to Newgrange, the amazing Stone Age Passage Tomb, with her art class.

"That's Paiute artwork – they own this land – we should never have taken it from them."

"What's Paiute?"

"They were the local Native Americans. You know, when they came here and found the ponderosa pines that had fossilised and become solid white stone – they believed them to be weapons of the wolf god Shinarav." He rolled up his sleeve and revealed a similar motif on his bicep.

"Wow, that looks good! I have a Celtic symbol on my back." She blushed as the words left her mouth and didn't offer to show it. She wasn't about to lift her top to reveal it – even though the thought of him running his fingers along the base of her spine excited her. "How do you know all that Indian stuff?"

"My friend Len in school is Hualapai Indian – but he has gone back to the reservation. He told me about this place. He says that here is good – but there are better places out by the Grand Canyon."

He tossed his head back and looked out over the plain to the hills in the distance. His profile was strong and his stare intense. He was exactly the type of guy that she'd dreamed of meeting but it had never happened – until now. Halfway across the world she had found him. She wanted to know more about him but she didn't know how to get the conversation going. She was happy when he asked her a question.

"How long are you staying?"

"Two weeks."

They were well away from the long snake-like line of concrete that had brought them here – where motor cars and trucks could still be seen in the distance. It was an oasis and Tina was comfortable in the quiet with this guy who didn't really have much to say but didn't really need to. His movements were enough.

Chapter 6

Like the grasses showing tender faces to each other,
thus should we do,
for this was the wish of the Grandfathers of the World.

~ Black Elk, OGLALA SIOUX *~*

"I think *Dancing on Ice* should be compulsory viewing for everyone in the country – nothing else puts me in such a good mood!" Eddie exclaimed as Suzanne handed him a very large and very full glass of white wine.

"Nachos?" she asked, producing a massive bag and throwing it down on the couch.

"Yummy! Isn't it such a shame that we can't get married – you're the partner of my dreams – apart from one little thing of course!"

Suzanne picked up a cushion and gave him a friendly thump on the shoulder with it.

"Move up the couch!" she said as she proceeded to open the nachos.

"Have you checked Facebook today?"

"Of course I have and no, Ronan hasn't replied yet – he probably won't after the signals you sent out!"

Eddie took a slug from his wineglass. "Oh, he'll be on to you alright. We just have to decide how to play it."

"You know, Eddie, much as I love you and your theories, sometimes I wonder how come they haven't worked for you!"

"That is a complete enigma – apart from the fact that I always fall for the wrong guys. They are either desperately polygamous or still in the closet or the worst of all – gay and don't know it. Actually change that to – gay and hiding it from their wives!"

"We're a couple of hopeless romantics, aren't we? So what is wrong with your current boyfriend?"

"Oh, he's a bit of all of the above!"

Suzanne spluttered into her chardonnay. "Eddie, I do love you! Maybe I'll marry you – your quirky sense of humour would make up for handicaps in other departments!"

"Hey! You haven't tried me out yet!"

Giggling, she pelted him with nachos as he made a mock lunge for her.

Suzanne was dying to see if there was a reply from Ronan yet but didn't want to let Eddie know. She waited until he had fallen asleep on the couch before sneaking into the kitchen to see if there were any messages on Facebook.

She did a quick check of her email first, to see if there was anything from her brother Leo. They had been discussing the possibility of his coming over for a week or so, as they needed to get together and go through the legalities of their mother's paperwork. Yes, there was an email. He was flying over the following day. Suzanne sighed. One more person to take care of!

Holding her breath, she turned to Facebook.

There was a reply. It was a letter this time.

Hi Suzanne

So good to be back in touch – there's so much I want to talk about. Who's the father of your little girl? Anyone I knew back then? Are you partners or legally married? She's gorgeous and the image of you.

I have thought about you plenty of times over the years. Especially in the spring – when we met. I have been back to Ireland a couple of times and have to admit that I dropped out to Clontarf and wandered the places where we used to go after school. The Rose Garden wasn't how

I remembered it – much smaller. I guess living in the States changes your perspective on places too. Ireland has changed so much since we were kids.

So you qualified as a physiotherapist. Good for you! My wife had a busy career – I should say my ex-wife because we are in the process of divorcing at the moment. We didn't have kids. It's such a shame. I really envy you. It has been a difficult few months and I have been thinking so much of Ireland and the happy times we shared in our teens. Why does life have to get so complicated just because you get older? I moved out of our apartment three months ago and am now living in a small but nice place in the north end – have you ever been to Boston? You must come sometime and bring your partner and family.

I'm director for a computer software company that has seen some hard times but is coming out of a dip finally this year. I'm off to Las Vegas soon to a convention which is usually a lot of hard work crammed into a couple of days. Not much time for enjoying myself, though I do intend to get there a couple of days in advance to chill a little beforehand.

I finished college in MIT and went on to do a postgrad. I loved America when I came here first but now seem to hanker more and more for Ireland. I guess it's because I realise my own mortality now and see so many years that have gone by that I have so little to show for. Laura and I travelled all around the States in our early years together but Laura is American and they aren't very adventurous about visiting destinations outside their own country. I was down in Argentina a couple of years back and had to go to Italy too but would really like to explore Europe at some stage. I guess I can do what I want now that I'm free and single?

My dad moved back to Ireland five years ago – crazy but my parents split up and my mother has a newer, younger husband – a fitter version of Dad! My sisters are settled and married. Rosaline has two boys and is living in Texas and Martina has a girl and lives with a yoga master in San Diego.

Write soon and tell me what happened over the missing years – I'm so glad to hear that you're having a wonderful life – no more than you deserve.

All the best
Ronan

Suzanne wanted to cry after reading this. Why had she let Eddie answer with a misleading response? She did want Ronan to know the truth but she didn't want him to know how difficult and sad her life was either. She would have to think carefully before responding to this mail. And she wouldn't need Eddie's help!

Suddenly she heard a rustling on the stairs.

"Lily – is that you? Are you back from the dance?"

Suzanne ran to the stairs where her mother stood in her dressing gown and slippers.

"Who are you?" Mary asked for the tenth time that day.

"It's me. Suzanne. You have to go back to bed, Mary."

"It's not fair – I wish I was allowed to go to the dance."

"You will be soon – back to bed now," Suzanne said as she ushered her mother into her bedroom and fixed her comfortably under the duvet.

"I want to know what happened – was Paddy Jones there?"

"Just rest now, Mary."

Suzanne kissed her mother on the forehead as if she were a small child and turned out the light as she left the room. These were the hard nights – when she should be tending to her own small ones or out enjoying herself like her other single friends. She went downstairs and took the throw off the armchair and put it over Eddie. He was in need of lots of loving tender care too. But who was going to give any loving care to her, she wondered?

Eddie was woken by a dribble of saliva running down his chin. He pulled himself up on the couch and looked around to realise that he was on his own. The TV was still on and he thought he could hear Suzanne moving around the kitchen. It always hit him hardest on first waking – the realisation that the man he loved was utterly unobtainable and would always be. How simple his life would be if he had given Kevin's Eurovision party a miss!

Kevin lived in a swanky apartment near Grand Canal Dock and threw the best parties. There was always an eclectic mix of talented artists, people in media and other creative professions attending. Eddie was on his way to the party that night with Suzanne but Kate had rung and asked her to return as her mother was not well. After driving her back to Clontarf, Eddie nearly drove home too. Instead he turned around and hit the party just before the points were being called out. Only half of the guests were listening – the other half were in the kitchen enjoying the line of tasty hors d'oeuvres spread along the counter and on the kitchen table. Eddie helped himself to a beer from the fridge and, when he turned around, there he was – standing beside the sink with a tiny vol-au-vent in his hand. He had a presence about him that was different to everyone else in the room – a confidence that said he was a man who was in control of his life and everything and everybody that was in it. Eddie didn't wait for him to make the first move. He went over and helped himself to the nibblets beside the handsome man wearing a polo shirt which revealed tanned, strong arms.

"Are you not watching the show?" Eddie said with a glint in his eyes.

"I'm not really into the Eurovision, to be honest!" the guy replied in a confident, well-spoken voice.

Eddie was swooning from there. He talked to the stranger for two hours in the kitchen while the others danced in the living room, but they never exchanged names or details. It was only when the dancers filtered into the kitchen that the two went into a bedroom where they could speak in peace. It was to be the first of many nights that they would spend together.

Eddie felt for his glass of wine and took a large gulp. He was an addict now and needed this man like no one he had ever wanted before. He looked at his watch. Damn, he couldn't ring him – he couldn't give in this soon. He had to think of something else to get him out of his mind.

He looked around for Suzanne but she was nowhere to be seen. He got up and went into the kitchen. Then he heard her footsteps lightly descending the stairs.

"You fell asleep," she said with a smile.

"Sorry, hon – everything okay?"

Suzanne nodded. But Eddie could tell that everything wasn't okay. He had watched his friend become more and more restricted by her mother's illness over the last few years. He went and put his arm around her.

"Come on, Sue – let's fill up our glasses. We always have each other."

Suzanne followed him into the living room and sat in front of the TV.

"I got an email from Ronan," she said.

Eddie perked up in his seat. "Please tell more – how fab!"

Suzanne smiled and took a sip of her wine. "He's lovely and was updating me about his family. It's very hard to fill in so many years in a short email. But he managed to tell me that his wife is with another man and that he is living alone now in Boston. I know all about his sisters and his job and that he is going to Las Vegas soon for a convention!"

"Las Vegas?"

"Yes," Suzanne nodded.

"I've always wanted to go there – how fantastic!"

Suzanne shrugged. "It's just work for him – I'm sure that he won't be out partying."

Eddie shook his head. "Las Vegas doesn't sleep – it's open 24/7."

"I'm sure it's great if you're into that sort of thing!"

Eddie's mind was working overtime. "You know, Sue, I think you could do with a holiday."

"Oh, now you're talking," she sighed. "Some chance! Apart from my mother, I just heard Leo is coming tomorrow for maybe a week – which is the longest he's spent in Dublin in twenty years!"

Eddie slapped his thigh. "Now *that* is a sign if ever I heard one!"

Suzanne laughed. "A sign that I'll have a houseguest to mind now also?"

Eddie turned around and looked his friend in the eyes. "No, I really mean it – I've known you how many years and you have never had a proper holiday!"

Suzanne brushed her hands through her hair. "Minding my

mother is not a job I can leave just like that!" she replied curtly, then regretted her tone. Eddie was only trying to be kind. "There's no one to look after her."

"But your brother will be here!"

Suzanne shook her head. "He couldn't cope with Mum."

"It's not fair that he leaves you to take all of the responsibility."

"Well, he does come over at least twice a year."

"Is he coming on his own?"

Suzanne nodded. "He wants us to go through the legalities of mum's paperwork – in case anything happens."

Eddie lifted his glass of wine. "Wants to get his share of the house," he muttered into it.

Suzanne clicked the roof of her mouth with her tongue. "Don't go presuming things like that – Leo is comfortable and has no intention of coming over and kicking me out of my home."

"So why is he coming for such a long time and without his family?"

Suzanne had asked herself the same question when she'd received the email from her brother. He never came without Grace and Wendy. He also never stayed more than two nights. It was something that she had managed to convince herself was not important, but in her gut she did feel that something was wrong.

"What time does he arrive tomorrow?" Eddie asked.

"Not exactly sure – but in the morning anyway."

Eddie smiled to himself. He had a plan – it would be perfect!

Chapter 7

Treat the earth well – it was not given to you by
your parents – it was loaned to you by your children.

~ NATIVE AMERICAN PROVERB ~

Frank and John showed their passports to the laughing customs officers and collected their bags, then made their way to get a cab.

"How far is the airport from the hotel?" Frank asked his brother.

"About ten minutes – depending on the traffic on The Strip of course."

"Have you ever been to the Mirage before?"

"No – there are lots of hotels in Vegas – you'd have to stay many times before you get to see every one and even then there's always a new place opening."

"It's really wild then?"

"Vegas is whatever you want it to be – if you want a crazy stag weekend you got it – if you want to go gamble and drink your head off – you got it. If you want to see some of the best shows on the planet – you got it! It's Disneyland for adults."

They fell silent for a while and then Frank said, "Thanks for being my best man, John."

John shrugged. "You're family – it's what we do." He grinned to avoid the risk of sounding too emotional. "Anyway I don't have any gigs lined up for eight months – your timing was good!"

Connie followed Vicky up to the hotel room. "I hope they've given you a suite," she said.

"Frank made the arrangements – the room is lovely and Tina is beside us with adjoining doors and that is more important than anything."

Connie wasn't so sure about that.

"I expect Tina should be back by now," Vicky said anxiously.

"Well, maybe." Connie hoped that Kyle had been a gentleman and was showing the young Irish girl a nice time.

The suite was empty and Connie took the chance to glance around the room and bathroom while Vicky went next door.

"Hey, you got a good view!" she called out.

It was one of the smaller suites but Connie was pleased – the view was spectacular. Caesar's Palace and the Eiffel Tower to the right and the Venezia Tower, a perfect replica of the Campanile of St Mark's and the Venetian Hotel just ahead.

"She's not here," Vicky said.

"Maybe she's down by the pool?" Connie suggested.

"Her swimsuit and shorts are on the chair in her room and her flip-flops on the floor. I'll just give her a ring."

Connie sat down on the chair beside the bed and took the opportunity to check her manicure.

Vicky listened to her daughter's phone ring out and waited to leave a message.

"Tina, it's Mum here – give me a call and let me know where you are, okay?"

Connie didn't seem the slightest bit perturbed. "I bet those kids are still in the Circus Circus having fun in the Adventuredome. Or maybe went on to the Stratosphere."

Vicky gulped. "You mean that tall tower we passed where you said they had the rollercoaster rides hanging from the top?"

Connie thought it best to change the subject. "I'm only kidding

– Kyle doesn't really like heights. Maybe they went for a coffee – they could be downstairs now in the Carnegie Deli – Kyle just loves the pancakes there. Why don't we go for a drink and then you can tell me what you have decided. Have you had a cocktail in the Rhumbar yet?"

Vicky shook her head. There seemed to be no end of bars, restaurants and clubs in this one hotel alone – how many must there be in all the hotels along The Strip? Vicky looked at her watch. It was gone half past five. She didn't want to be overly concerned but she would like to see Tina this side of six o'clock.

"What time is your fiancé flying in?"

"He should be here in the next hour if his flight is on time."

Connie lifted the phone beside the bed. "I'll leave them a message in reception that they can find us in the Rhumbar. Same if your daughter comes to the desk looking for anything."

Vicky was anxious but did as she was told. She texted Tina while Connie was on the phone.

Ring me now please – where are you? Mum x

Then the two women took the lift back down to the reception.

The waitress was dressed like she had stepped out of a New York downtown café.

"Pancakes with maple syrup and cherries!" she said, placing the two plates down on the table in front of Tina and Kyle.

"You're gonna love these," said Kyle. "If I were you I'd eat here for the next two weeks."

They looked delicious and were accompanied with clotted cream and all sorts of decoration.

"This is a crazy city – do you come down to The Strip much?"

Kyle laughed. He shook his head. "Only when my mom has a job for me – you try to stay away from the neon when you live here. The 'burbs are very different – like any others in the mid-west. Real estate was the buzz word for a few years – I hate all that – we don't own one grain of sand in this desert. It belongs to the Native Americans – we shouldn't have done this to their country."

Tina knew nothing about this part of the world and its history – she had seen a couple of western films but hadn't really digested what they were about – she wished now that she had taken more notice when her dad was watching Clint Eastwood movies when she was a little girl.

"So tell me about Ireland."

Tina could feel herself blush. "Well, we're famous for U2, Riverdance and Guinness."

"I love U2 – especially their album *The Joshua Tree* – just like the yuccas we saw today at Red Rock Canyon. You like music, Tina?"

Tina felt the blush spread across her cheeks and down her neck. It was the first time that Kyle had used her name and she hadn't even been sure before this that it had registered with him when his mother had introduced them.

"I live in a place called Howth where the drummer from U2 lives."

Suddenly she was pleased they had moved to the northside – she had something to say that was interesting and Kyle's eyebrows rose at the mention. She had hated the move to Howth so much at the time – she was far away from all her friends and her gran. But lately she had come to appreciate the natural beauty of the small seaside town.

"I like old music – I'm not into all this regenerated hype – the music industry is sick – it's like everything else – corrupt and falling apart."

Tina nodded as the waitress came back – this time bringing over two milkshakes and putting them down in front of them.

"This food is so good!" Tina munched and smiled widely.

Kyle looked at the girl with the big blue eyes – he wondered what her real hair colour was – for now it was jet black but that was out of a bottle. It suited her – she wasn't cheerleader-like as the girls in his school had been.

"So when is your mom getting hitched?"

"On Tuesday," Tina said with a roll of her eyes.

"What's your new stepdad like?"

Tina ran her fingers through her black fringe and shook her head. "He's awful. He's really into money and his businesses!"

Kyle laughed. He liked the words she used. She really was a cute girl. He'd never before had to entertain a girl like this for his mom and he was so glad that she had asked him. The way this girl seemed to understand what he loved about the desert and the music they had listened to in the car on the way – she knew American music and liked the things that he liked – even the pancakes.

"Would you like to go to Lake Mead tomorrow?"

Tina blushed. Of course she would happily go anywhere with Kyle tomorrow – that would mean that she wouldn't have to watch her mother and Frank being all foolish and romantic.

"Yeah, sure." She tried not to sound over-enthusiastic but couldn't hide it.

Vicky followed Connie through the loud clattering of coins falling into the slot-machine tills and the clicking of the chips on the roulette and poker tables.

It didn't seem to matter what time it was – day or night the casino was packed with punters gambling busily. It was dusk outside but inside the casino it could be 11 a.m. or 2 a.m. It didn't really make any difference. She was told before going that there were never any clocks inside the casinos so that the gamblers wouldn't be distracted by the time. She also heard that oxygen was pumped into the casinos to keep people awake but the night before she was so tired with jet lag she hadn't noticed.

The foyer was vast and Connie was racing ahead – she knew exactly where she was going.

"Connie!" Vicky called. "Do you mind if we take a look in that place where you said your son likes the pancakes?"

"Sure, honey," Connie said, turning abruptly and heading off in the opposite direction. Vicky anxiously followed her.

"It's right over here," Connie said, "and, hey, I can see our two beauties – they're having a good time."

Vicky let out a sigh of relief. Now that she had found her

daughter she could think straight again. She followed Connie over to the corner table where Kyle and Tina were deep in conversation and hadn't noticed their mothers' arrival until Connie was almost on top of them.

"How did you guys enjoy the day?" she beamed.

Tina looked up from under her fringe and nodded at her mother. This was not how she wanted her time with Kyle to end.

"We went out to Red Rock," Kyle said.

"You guys really did get around!" Connie was, still beaming. "We're going to Rhumbar – do you two want to stay here for a while?"

"I'd better go and see if Troy is home yet," Kyle said to his mother.

"Oh, he's decided to stay in school for the weekend. He sent me a message just after you left. Stay and have fun."

Kyle took his phone out of his pocket and saw that there was a message from his brother – he'd been having such a good time with Tina he hadn't noticed his phone bleep.

"Have you got enough money?" Vicky asked her daughter. "Frank and John will be here in a little while and then we can go out for dinner – okay?"

It wasn't okay for Tina – after the wonderful afternoon she had spent the thought of meeting Frank was enough to bring her mood down. Then she remembered Kyle's offer of a visit to Lake Mead.

"Eh, Mum, can I go to Lake Mead with Kyle tomorrow?"

Vicky was taken aback. "But we have to make the final arrangements for the wedding and then get our shoes and hair sorted."

"Please! I've always wanted to see Lake Mead."

Vicky was sure that Tina had never heard of Lake Mead until Kyle had suggested it but it was an indication of how much fun her daughter had had and how much she wanted to be with this boy. "Oh well – I guess if that's okay with Kyle?"

Kyle shrugged.

"That would be lovely," Connie barged in. "It's so great that you kids have hit it off! Now come on, Vicky, and let's have a cocktail to celebrate all our great work today!"

Vicky was stuck between two very strong emotions – she did want her daughter to be happy but things were not working out the way that she had planned. She wasn't as happy with the teenage match as Connie was – she hadn't had a chance to get to know Kyle. Still, it might be good to have time on her own with Frank before the wedding.

"Come out to us when you're finished here – or text me – is your phone working?"

"It needs to be charged," Tina said with a shrug.

It conveniently ran out of power whenever Tina didn't want to speak with her mother.

Connie linked arms with Vicky and coaxed her gently out of the deli.

John and Frank stood in front of the large aquarium set in the walls behind the reception. They were only one person away from the receptionist.

"Whaddya think?" John asked.

"It's good – mad but good." Frank was stiff and tired after the long journey but could feel his second wind coming on in the midst of this tropical paradise.

Suddenly he heard his name being called.

"Frank!" Vicky rushed over and flung her arms around his neck, in utter joy at his arrival.

Connie loved scenes like this – it was the romantic in her being fulfilled. And there was another romantic sight standing at Frank's side. He was tall with the most gorgeous early-morning shadow cast across his rugged chin. He seemed oblivious to the attention he was getting from the receptionist who was clearly ushering her client on so that she could help the new arrival at her desk.

Connie decided to move in first.

"Hi there, you must be the groom's brother – I'm Connie the wedding planner."

She held out her hand and he took it firmly and shook it.

"I'm John." He looked around. "Are we missing Tina?"

"Oh she's been taken care of," Connie chuckled. "She's hit it off with my son – they're having pancakes."

Frank pulled himself away from his fiancée and held his hand out to Connie, while Vicky and John hugged.

"Frank Proctor, pleased to meet you," he said with a suave smile.

Connie was more than surprised. This was not how she had imagined Vicky's groom would be. He was slightly flashy, wearing a navy pinstriped shirt and chinos. For some reason she had thought he would be more typically Irish. But of course, according to her files, he was a renowned chef so she should have expected him to be a bit flamboyant! On the other hand, Vicky was a sweet woman who was able to make smart and casual dress look sexy and she could see why a man like Frank would choose her for a partner.

"Do you want to go to your room?" Connie asked.

"I'd like to go to the bar," Frank said with a grin.

"That's just where we were going," Connie said. "Why don't you get the bellhop to take your stuff up to your room?"

John looked at Frank. "Sounds good to me!"

Connie knew that she really should be leaving these people but she was enthralled by John Proctor. She was going to give the best man the best time that he had ever had in his life!

Tina looked at her watch. Time had stood still since this morning when she had first driven off in Kyle's truck. She had been exposed to a whole new world that she had never dreamed of and something told her that the next day was going to be even better.

"I'm going to meet my friend now but I'll see you tomorrow – and bring your swimming costume."

Tina's imagination went into overdrive. She could picture herself almost naked, lying under the desert sun beside this gorgeous guy.

Kyle paid the check and the two set off through the casino and out under the night sky. It was only seven o'clock but the madness and mayhem of the night on The Strip was already in full swing. A symphony of neon flashed across the street from the façades of Bally's and Harrah's casino. Venezia Tower lit up like a candle on a birthday cake at one side and the Eiffel Tower on the other.

Along the side of the Mirage was the cascading waterfall which set the scene for the beautiful outdoor Rhumbar.

Tina spotted her mother sitting at the table next to John and Connie. Frank was nowhere in sight. She liked John – he was cool. She had only met him twice but on each of those occasions he was thoughtful and didn't speak patronisingly to her – unlike other adults and especially Frank.

Kyle stopped just outside the bar. "They won't let us in there – see you tomorrow then. I'll call for you from reception – about nine thirty okay?"

Tina nodded her head. "And thanks for today, Kyle – I had a really cool time!" Her eyes widened and he smiled into them. For a moment they froze but neither dared make the move for even a friendly peck on the cheek. They both knew that it wouldn't be right and neither wanted to create an awkward moment.

"Later," Kyle said with a nod.

As he walked away Tina watched him go, meanwhile keeping an eye on her mother and the other adults. Her holiday had begun and maybe her mother marrying Frank wasn't the worst thing that could happen in the world.

She went into the bar and was immediately approached by the waitress asking her to leave.

"I must just have a word with my mum."

"Okay, honey, but be quick!"

Vicky was on her second Piña Colada and was loving the world. She hadn't noticed that her fiancé had been missing for almost twenty minutes.

But Connie had – she was drinking a non-alcoholic cocktail because she was driving. Besides, she wanted to remember every word of her conversation with the dishy Irishman.

"Hi, Mum."

"Where have you been?" Vicky stood up, reeling with giddiness.

4am in LAS VEGAS

"Just left Kyle now – in fact I'm pretty tired so I was going up to the room."

"Oh, darling, you need to have some dinner – we're all going to the Bellagio for a lovely meal – Connie has organised it."

"I'd like to go up to my room, Mum – I've just had pancakes and I can get room service if that's okay with you?"

Vicky kissed her daughter on the head. "Okay, darling – we won't be long."

"Please take as long as you like," Tina assured her. A tipsy mother and Frank would be enough to give her nightmares.

"Hi, John – have a good flight?"

"Cool, Tina – thanks for asking! How do you like Vegas?"

He was sipping mineral water and sitting back on the chair with his right ankle resting on his left knee. He raised his glass and it slipped out of his hand momentarily, spilling on to his jeans. It didn't phase him at all as he wiped the liquid off, put the glass onto the table with a cheeky grin that said *'what the heck'*.

Tina giggled. "Good, thanks," she smiled and something told her that she was going to like it even more after tomorrow.

"Are you sure you'll be okay up there on your own?" Vicky was slurring her words now.

"I'm sure, Mum – see you in the morning in case I fall asleep – you go and enjoy yourself."

Vicky held on to her daughter tightly. "She's such a good girl," she said, squeezing her and looking down at Connie.

"Have a good time tomorrow, honey, and I'll make sure that Kyle looks after you," Connie smiled.

Tina was delighted to be away from the adults and she hadn't even had to see Frank. As she started her trek through the tropical foyer she spotted him deep in conversation on his mobile phone. He didn't see her at all and looked so intense that it made her feel curious. She stepped behind a nearby palm tree and listened.

"Look, I'm afraid she'll find out!" Frank said.

There was a long pause.

"Okay, okay!" he said then. "Yes, you're right, love – we do need to talk."

Tina couldn't believe her ears. Was this the same man who had sworn to her that he loved only her mother and that he was going to look after her for the rest of her days?

"I miss you already . . . terribly."

Tina was astounded. This was much more information than she ever needed to know.

What would she say to her mother – what could she say?

Frank hoped that no one would comment on his long absence.

"Here comes the groom – I've booked a table for us at Sensi in the Bellagio, Frank – I think you're going to love it!" Connie beamed and glanced over at John.

John didn't flinch. "Important call?" he asked Frank.

"Just work," Frank said nervously and sat down to drink the last drop of his Long Island Iced Tea.

"Oh, you've missed Tina, sweetheart – she's gone up to her room. Connie has organised dinner for us."

Frank knew by Vicky's tone and the way she had repeated what Connie had said that she was way over her limit. He would have to be sure that she didn't drink any more during dinner.

John stood up and rubbed the palms of his hands on his jeans. "Are we off then?"

The four stepped out along the path that wound its way out of the Mirage and on to The Strip. The cars were in gridlock which wasn't anything unusual apparently. Caesar's Palace was illuminated by beams of light that shone up from the perfectly manicured garden and flowerbeds in front of the Forum Shops. It was the only building between them and the towering splendour of the Bellagio Hotel.

Violet shades crept up from the base of the building, turning to pink and peach as the hues changed every few stories until reaching the turret and penthouse suites that were crowned majestically with golden light.

Suddenly the strains of Rachmaninov's Rhapsody sounded. It bellowed out from the speakers dotted around the lake and spread across the breadth of the hotel. Perfectly sculpted bushes created the borders and led the cobble-locked pathways up to the hotel foyer. The spectacle was too wonderful for Vicky. She squealed and ran over to the water's edge to get a better view of the dancing fountains and light show. Her mouth hung open as the torrents of water gushed up in perfectly arranged formations, co-ordinating with the classical music.

Frank went over and stood at his future bride's side – she was mesmerised by the display and innocent like a little girl. It was cruel what he was doing to her – she deserved so much better. But in his heart he felt that it would be crueller to finish with her. She loved living in the smart bungalow they co-owned in Howth – she had sold her modest three-bedroomed semi in Terenure before moving out to his side of the city. She was so trusting – he was lucky to have her. He really needed to sort his situation out – get rid of this entanglement he was enmeshed in.

"I never tire of seeing that show!" Connie said to John.

"It's good – I stayed here the last time I was in Vegas."

"You'll have to tell me all about your work as a musician, John – Vicky has been raving about your talents!"

John wondered how much of that was true. Vicky seemed to tut-tut his travels and Bohemian lifestyle – at least according to Frank she did – though he had always found Vicky to be sweet and gentle and in need of lots of TLC, and he wasn't so sure his brother was the best person to give her what she needed.

Jet lag was taking over Tina – it was the middle of the night back in Dublin but she couldn't sleep. Her head was full of Kyle and his beautiful brown eyes. She tried to think of the words that had passed between them during the day but she couldn't put structure on her thoughts at all. She was visually transfixed by his moody and handsome looks and the way he moved – whether he was driving his jeep or eating a pancake – he just seemed to do everything so well – compared to the geeks she had studied with back in Dublin.

She picked up a magazine that lay beside her bed with adverts for all that was going on in Vegas. Her eyes were drawn to the picture of Lake Mead and the Hoover Dam and she read the article to see where she would be visiting the next day.

The four walked past the uniformed bellhops and doormen and into the opulent world of the Bellagio hotel.

Vicky had never seen anything like it in her life.

"Oh wow!" she exclaimed, looking up at the glass floral sculptures hanging from the foyer ceiling.

There was much more in store for her senses as they passed the magnificent display of autumnal harvest and Halloween-themed sculptures. A miniature model of the hotel was in the corner of a massive display that included wood sprites and giant pumpkin creatures. It even had a perfectly replicated fountain in front of the entrance.

Connie was finding it difficult to catch John's attention – he seemed to be in his own world. Nothing she said seemed to interest him. He was polite and charming but totally nonchalant.

"Vicky told me that you were in a band – would I know them?"

John smiled. People always wanted to know who he had worked with. He didn't like to drop names but decided to indulge her.

"Well, I have played with Sting . . ."

"*The* Sting – the Police Sting?" Connie was agog.

"Sure," he said, then regretted having gone there with the conversation – he found it was usually better to play down his appearances.

Vicky was feeling her tiredness now, especially after so many drinks, and slipped her hand into the crook of Frank's arm.

"You okay?" he asked as he steadied her grip and her wobbly stance.

"Fine," she grinned. "So much better now you're here."

Frank said nothing and guided her in Connie's footsteps.

"How many restaurants are there in this place?" he asked Connie.

"About fourteen or fifteen, I guess," she replied.

74

Frank had counted that they had already passed six.

"Almost there," Connie said with a smile.

The entrance to Sensi was glass, and it was minimalist in colour and styling. It was, however, incredibly chic and Frank was instantly impressed by the sophisticated ambience. Striking waterfalls cascaded down the carved stone walls and mirrored chrome touched the edgings and features around the kitchen in the centre of the dining space. As a chef he never ceased to be amazed by what other chefs did with their restaurants. A place like this would have been at the cutting edge of Celtic Tiger Ireland – but now it would seem too decadent for a city in recession. He longed for the days when money used to roll so easily into the tills of his restaurants and the bank accounts from his properties. Everything was so uncertain now – he wasn't sure that he would still be in business in a couple of months. And after the phone call earlier even his stay in Vegas was cast into uncertainty. He needed a buzz – a fix. Drink and drugs didn't give it to him – he loved to gamble. It was just as well that he was in the best place in the world to indulge. He had brought along his last one hundred thousand euros and hoped to translate that into double the amount – that way he could cover himself for another while at least.

The maitre d' showed them to a table and fussed over Connie which made her feel special. She hoped that John would feel that she was special too by the end of the evening.

The waiter appeared and handed out menus. He then went around the table and gave the wine list to John.

"That's okay – I don't drink – give it to him," he said, pointing to Frank.

Frank ran his fingers through his hair as he scanned the menu. It was impressive to say the least. How did they manage to have such a huge variety of fare in the one space? The fish dishes sounded exquisite providing the product was fresh – but this was Vegas and since arriving from the airport he had seen that everything was done well. He would normally be ultra-critical and keen to observe how another chef organised his kitchen and menu but for now he had more pressing concerns. A fiancée, for one, who was naïve – and a lover who was insatiable and the cause of his mixed-up moods.

Connie started ordering and was deep in conversation with Vicky about the wedding venue as the wine appeared. The waiter poured and was followed closely by a man carrying two ice-sculptures shaped like giant teardrops. The insides of the drops had been carved out and a lobster amuse-bouche sat on a sprig of lettuce in the centre of each sculpture.

"I have never seen anything like that in my life!" Vicky exclaimed.

Frank hid how impressed he was by giving a blasé shrug of his shoulders. "A lot of work for such a tiny morsel." He wished that he had thought of it. Even when his business was at its height he was too distracted by all the money that he was making to invest in clever and different ideas like this one. He missed the buzz from his craft that he used to have when he started out first.

His whole world had turned upside down and all he could do was watch himself as an onlooker. The next forty-eight hours would tell a lot in the life of Frank Proctor.

Kyle didn't stay long at Greg's house. Greg didn't want to talk the way they used to when they were in high school. Greg just wanted to talk about money and getting a part-time job. He only got excited when he spoke about the geeky course that he was studying and it didn't seem to bother him that there weren't many girls in his part of the college either. It would be cold soon and the mountains at Lake Tahoe would have snow. When Kyle had asked him about snowboarding the night before Greg wasn't as interested as he used to be either. He had said that he would be busy with project work and have to concentrate on that for the rest of term.

Kyle drove up the road of the lush and beautiful suburb that was his home. Maybe he had it too good. He had no desire to rush off and find new things to consume his head. He just wanted to play his music and find where he wanted to go with his life before doing it. He pulled up in front of the garage – his mom's car wasn't there. He felt relief. He let himself in and went to the kitchen to get a glass of water before going to bed.

Tina popped into his head and he smiled. He liked her cute accent and intense blue eyes. It had turned into a really cool day – and when he hadn't planned it that way it made it even sweeter. He was intrigued by this Irish girl. He had made a good call fixing a date to see her the next day. He could have some fun over the next few days – Halloween was a crazy time in Vegas. They could go to a Native American party – she seemed like the type of girl who would be up for anything.

When dinner was finished the four made their way into the casino. The Bellagio was vast – they passed a theatre and shops en-route. The casino smacked of Italian opulence – the floor was covered in panels of shiny cream marble and embellished carpets with rich plum and golden paisley motifs. Canopies made from rich brocades in stripes and floral designs hung over the roulette and card tables.

"Have you seen the Cirque du Soleil show 'O'?" Connie asked John.

"I can't say that I have – it's meant to be good."

Connie had to contain the excitement from bursting out. "Well, that's just great because I have tickets for that show any time – it would be lovely to go along – what do you think?"

John shrugged. "If the others would like to go, I guess we could."

Connie had to think for a second – she hadn't planned on taking the others – but she could swing another two tickets no problem. "Fine. Tomorrow night okay?"

"See what Vicky and Frank think – I'm easy."

Connie wasn't going to waste any time – she went over to Vicky and slipped her hand into the crook of her arm.

"Vicky, honey – would you guys like to go and see the Cirque du Soleil show with John and me tomorrow night?"

"Sure!"

Frank let the women walk on a little and waited behind to talk to John.

"Looks like you have a fan there, John!" he said with a cheeky wink.

John grinned nonchalantly. "She's a nice lady."

"Not your type though!"

"Are you asking or telling me?"

Frank sensed the change in tone and wasn't sure if he was out of line. He, after all, had his own skeletons in his closet.

"I'm only messing with you!" Frank said. "Right – what are we going to take on first – blackjack, I think – how about you?"

"You know me, Frank – I don't play but I'll watch you."

Frank sidled up to the nearest table and put five hundred dollars down. The dealer handed him a pile of brown chips.

Connie and Vicky were giggling as they took the last two seats at the table.

"Are we playing, guys?" Connie asked.

Frank handed Vicky a one-hundred-dollar bill. "There you go, Vicky – play a hand or two." He offered the same to Connie but she declined.

Vicky trembled – this was part of her attraction to Frank in the first place – the way he took control of situations and his generosity.

The dealer put two cards each in front of Frank and Vicky and the four other people who were playing.

"What do I do now?" Vicky was shaking with excitement.

Frank lifted his cards to see a queen and a ten. He couldn't get much better – it was an easy decision to stick.

"What have you got, honey?" Connie asked Vicky.

Vicky lifted the cards and left them in full view of the entire table. An eight and a five.

Not great, Connie figured. She could bust easily on one more card. It was twenty more dollars just to stay at the table.

"What the heck – you go for it, girl!" she urged.

Vicky put her chips out and asked the dealer for another card. Frank was upping the stakes and grinning widely.

The dealer stuck too and all eyes were on Frank as he put four hundred dollars' worth of chips on to bet. The dealer didn't flinch and met his hand.

Eyes turned to Vicky as she took her third card. Connie looked at her and then at the card – a king – she had bust. But it was looking good for Frank. Again all eyes on the table were on Frank and the dealer.

Frank grinned as he took his hand of twenty and flipped the cards over. The dealer dealt himself one more card – he had a perfect twenty-one. Frank couldn't believe his eyes – he was wiped out in one hand. He shrugged.

"You win some, you lose some!" he said and tipped the dealer with the fifty-dollar chip that he had left.

Vicky was aghast. She still had seventy-five dollars' worth. She slipped it into her pocket – she was changing it at the cashier's before they left – this gambling was a mug's game and she was seriously concerned by the way her husband-to-be had thrown away five hundred dollars with just one hand.

"Hey, guys, let's have a nightcap!" Connie said and beckoned them over to the bar. It was in the middle of the casino and adorned with opulent couches and chandeliers with tiny golden lampshades hanging from the panelled ceiling.

Vicky had suddenly become very sober and was confused and edgy after the display of decadence on the blackjack table.

"I'll get these," John said. "What would you like?"

They took a pair of couches in the corner and a waitress came straight over.

"What can I get for you tonight?" she beamed with perfect shiny white teeth.

"A Jack Daniel's," Frank said.

"Can I have a white wine?" Connie said and Vicky nodded the same.

"Just a Perrier for me," John replied. He rarely drank alcohol and he had to be in control tonight because he had a feeling that he was possibly the only one who was.

"I can't believe you lost five hundred dollars in one bet!" Vicky exclaimed.

"Hey, baby – it's our first night in Vegas – it's okay to go a little crazy!" Frank said reassuringly as he put his hand on her thigh gently.

Vicky nodded. Maybe she did need to relax. It was a once-off – not like he did foolish things like that all of the time. And after all they were in Vegas to get married so it should be the happiest time of her life . . .

79

Chapter 8

Lose your temper and you lose a friend;
lie and you lose yourself.

~ HOPI PROVERB ~

Ronan was about to turn the light out beside his bed when the phone rang. He looked at the time on his clock. Who could be ringing him at 12.45 a.m.? He recognised the sobs instantly when he put the phone to his ear.

Laura sounded like a seal in pain when she cried and he had heard her outbursts plenty of times over the years.

"Laura – it's a quarter to one in the morning."

"Ronan – can I come over?"

She must be in a pretty bad state to be calling him like this after sending the papers for divorce, he thought.

"What's wrong? It's the middle of the night!"

"I need to see you – can I come over?"

Ronan let out a sigh. He still cared for Laura though their relationship had become toxic – he wasn't the one that had abandoned the marriage. The rejection that went with their separation had cut him and the fact that she was carrying another man's child had cut him even deeper.

"Okay, come over."

With a click from the other end of the line, Laura hung up the phone.

Ronan pulled himself up onto his elbows and rubbed his forehead. He truly wondered what Laura was going to spring on him. That was the thing about Laura – he just never really knew what she was up to. It had kept him intrigued for the duration of their eight years together. But this call worried him. He had been hurt so badly that the last three months were simply a period of survival but now he was starting to feel what it was like to be himself again and not Laura's keeper. Along with the pain of the loss of her came the relief from the responsibility of keeping her happy.

Suzanne was sitting at her kitchen table eating a late breakfast with the radio on. She didn't hear Eddie come in the back door and creep up on her until he said, "*Boo!*"

"Eddie!" she cried.

Eddie giggled as he took a seat opposite her at the table. He was giddy with the thrill of what he was about to reveal to his friend.

"What are you up to?" she asked with a lowered brow.

"Don't be cross – you have to promise?" he grinned.

"Eddie – I can't trust you – what's going on?"

Eddie reached into his back pocket and revealed a British Airways envelope. He put it on the table and looked up into Suzanne's eyes.

"Open it."

Suzanne gasped – she had a hunch that this was something that would be complicated and she didn't underestimate Eddie's enthusiasm.

"What is it?"

"It's meant to be – the signs are all in place and you can't say no to me!"

Suzanne opened the envelope and scanned the tickets. Her name was printed across the top of one book. They were for a five-day return flight to Las Vegas. She was exhilarated and thrilled at the prospect for about five seconds and then reality struck . . .

"But these are for today!"

"Yes! Meet me – Superman!" Eddie flexed his biceps.

"How did you . . .?"

"Contacts are everything – remember that friend I had that wee fling with recently? Who works in a travel agent's? I phoned him and he came up with these last-minute cancellations at a great price!"

"You're crazy! How could we go today?"

"Throw a few things in a bag, call a cab! We can shop when we get there!" Eddie was on a high.

"Oh Eddie, that would have been so lovely!"

"What do you mean '*would have*' – those tickets have our names on them and we are going to Las Vegas!"

Suzanne shook her head. "I told you Leo is coming – I need to be here."

"Nonsense – that's why you need to get out of here – it will do him no harm to see all the work and effort that you put into minding your mother – you need a break!"

"It's not that simple – oh dear sweet Eddie, I'm so sorry to burst your bubble but you don't understand! I can't just up and leave like that!"

But Eddie wasn't giving up that easily. "I spoke to Kate and she said that you deserved the break and she would be happy to spend more hours with your mum, showing your brother the ropes."

"No way," Suzanne shook her head. "I know you have the best intentions in the world but my mother is my responsibility."

Eddie took a strong hold of Suzanne's wrist and looked at her firmly. "You owe it to yourself to take a break – besides, these tickets are non-refundable."

"I'm sure your friend can do something about that!" Suzanne shook her arm loose and stood up. "Anyway, you should have spoken to me before making any bookings. I'm sorry, Eddie – you go but I can't. How could I suddenly announce that anyway? With Leo only just coming in the door!"

"I'm not going to Vegas alone! Don't let me down, Sue!"

"Please, Eddie, Have a bit of sense! It can't be done!"

Suzanne left the kitchen and went into the front room where she threw herself into an armchair and hid her face in her hands. She felt terrible inside. Quite apart from the madness of just rushing off to the airport at the drop of a hat, the prospect of leaving her mother for five days on her own was too much to cope with – even with her brother there in her place. She couldn't rely on Leo to do the things that she did. Her mother had special needs and she wouldn't let a man clean up after her when she had an accident in the bed at night. She was a proud woman and strong-willed – and, besides, she wouldn't understand who her son was. Eddie was out of order and showing a lack of empathy to her situation as far as she was concerned. He was coming from a different place to her and she needed him to leave as quickly as possible before she could feel the tears that represented a mixture of hurt and annoyance swell up and pour out.

Eddie was more cross with himself than Suzanne. She was always so straight with him and he had never done anything like this before. But he had never felt the urge or desire to do something so impulsive before.

He really thought that he knew his friend but he had misjudged her. Her attachment to her mother was natural but her complete sense of responsibility was unfathomable. No adult should be so tied to another that they cannot have any room to have their own needs met. He was angry at his own lack of sensitivity and madder at her doggedness. Anyway, he had to get her to go!

He followed her through to the front room where a cosy fire blazed.

"I know winter is here when you light your fire, Sue."

The air had turned sharper and cooler and all the trees on Castle Avenue and Kincora Road had turned to a delicious array of autumnal yellows, oranges and browns.

"Mum likes to sit looking at the fire during the day." Suzanne stood up, feeling that perhaps she had been a bit harsh on her friend. "Would you like a cup of coffee?" she asked.

"Coffee would be grand, thanks," he said as he took a seat on the couch.

In the kitchen Suzanne found that her mother had come downstairs and was now sitting in the corner knitting. A blue cardigan for her baby brother Matthew who had died ten years ago, aged fifty-four. Some days it was more difficult than others to live with her mother's eccentricities but Suzanne was touched by the knitting of the cardigan.

Mary didn't look up. Her tongue stuck out slightly between her barely parted lips and she took each stitch with great care.

Suzanne didn't say a word. She made two coffees and left as quietly as she had entered. Back in the front room she silently handed one to Eddie and he thanked her graciously.

Both were afraid of the conversation that was to follow but both knew that it was coming. They sat silently and drank their coffee.

"Anything new from Boston?" Eddie asked at last as an ice-breaker.

Suzanne shook her head. "I haven't answered him yet."

Eddie hated to see Suzanne so dejected. Her self-esteem had been this way since her mother had become ill.

"So there really is no point in going to Las Vegas!" she added.

Here comes the crunch, thought Eddie.

"This isn't just about meeting with your old flame, Suzanne – this is about a well-deserved break. Vegas is somewhere I've always wanted to visit – and I really would love to get away with you more than anyone!"

"And I think we'd have fun too but you know Mum – I can't really. And Leo will be here and I really need to be too – we need to go through those papers."

"You Skype him all the time, Sue – and you could sort those papers any old time!"

Suzanne shook her head. Then she paused for a moment – totally still. "What's that smell?"

Eddie shrugged. He didn't smell anything unusual.

"It's gas – there's a smell of gas!" she cried.

Suzanne jumped up and ran into the kitchen with Eddie following closely behind.

A pot of milk rested on the hob with the ring beside it spewing out gas – its burner unlit. In the corner Mary was still knitting, intent on her next stitch.

"Oh my God, I didn't even realise that she had put the cooker on!"

Suzanne turned off the gas and quickly opened the back door and windows. She turned around and looked at Eddie dolefully.

"See – looking after Mum is a full-time job – you have to understand!"

Eddie felt awful – every day there was something for Suzanne to consider – another catastrophe to divert. If only she could understand that this was the very reason that he wanted to see her get away for a break! Okay, so he was thinking of himself too, admittedly – he was desperate to go – but he sincerely wanted to rescue his friend from the soul-destroying life she was living.

After a downcast Eddie left, Suzanne went to her computer and started to write.

Hi Ronan

I don't know where to begin. First I have to apologise for the first message that I sent – in fact, I didn't actually write it! My friend and work colleague was messing with my Facebook and he is responsible for it.

It's great to hear from you and all your news. I have often dreamed of visiting America – would you believe I have never been! I'm not really sure what I have been doing with my time!

I'm a physiotherapist and living in Clontarf but I never got married. I don't know where the years have gone. It's so lovely to connect with you again. I have thought of you several times to be honest. I always wondered if you were still in the States and what your life was like. I'm glad you're well but sorry to hear of your marriage breakdown. It must be terribly hard for you at the moment. Feel free to email me – if you want to get anything off your chest – not that I'm the best person to ask about marriage!

My mum has been ill for years and I take care of her when I'm not working. She has Alzheimer's – it's so sad, Ronan – you remember how feisty she was and remarkably bright and clever. She just turned after I finished college. It was like all the lights went out. She never refers to

Dad now – it's like he was never part of her life. Most of the time she doesn't recognise me or she confuses me with her sister who died decades ago. It's the most debilitating and cruel disease and I feel so protective of her because really I'm the only one who can look after her. My brother Leo – I'm sure you remember him – lives in Devon now and the little girl in my profile picture is his daughter Wendy. I don't have any kids either – I guess it's not meant for everyone! I do work with kids though and love it!

I told Eddie about your email and said that you were going to Las Vegas – he is trying to organise a trip for me to go there but unfortunately it's impossible with Mum. People don't understand that it's a full-time commitment looking after a loved one with Alzheimer's. I hope you have a nice time though – maybe I'll get to America some day!

Keep in touch – it's great to be at the other end of the internet, isn't it?

Suzanne x

Suzanne had hesitated before putting the kiss after her name and then deleted it. Then she put it back in. What were the boundaries with a man who was separating from his wife? She didn't want to be too overt yet she wanted to be affectionate and show Ronan that he was someone who at one stage was very important in her life.

As she watched the icon swirl and read that it had been sent she felt her stomach churn. A whole well of emotions flooded out and trickled down her cheeks. She had carried their secret bravely and with as little emotion as she could stand for nearly twenty years. It was too hard to put a perspective on the whole relationship. To think of how it turned out and how it might have been. Never a day went by when she didn't ask herself the same question and she was bereft and couldn't share how she felt with a single soul in the entire world.

If only her mother hadn't left the gas on earlier! Who knows, maybe Eddie might have talked her into going to Vegas. But the incident highlighted how much her mother needed her. God, everything she did was determined by her mother and always had been.

She couldn't feel anger towards her mother any more – it was much worse than that. The person with whom she was maddest was herself.

Ronan looked at the woman in the bed beside him and sighed – saddened by his weakness of character. He swore when Laura walked out of his life that he would never have her back but the way that she had pleaded and begged and sobbed had thrown him into a spin. He was shocked that she no longer wanted to have anything to do with the father of her child. He wondered what had *really* happened and if he would ever be told the truth. He hadn't made love to her because that would have been one bridge too many to cross. The bump that the child made in her stomach had helped him make his decision. She had craved and cried that she wanted him to make love to her but now in the light of day he was glad that he hadn't . . . but he hadn't been able to resist her giving him oral sex. He was so confused and really didn't think that he knew women at all.

He got out of bed and went into the shower. And in that instant he thought of Suzanne and wondered how his life would have been if he had stayed in Ireland and married her. As the warm water hit his body he found himself wandering back to the beautifully scented rose garden in St Anne's Park. He closed his eyes and pictured her. She was only eighteen in his daydream but that seemed natural because in it he was eighteen too. His erection started to swell as he remembered her lips and beautiful soft skin – her golden hair caressing her shoulders – he could almost smell her.

His dream was shattered as Laura entered the bathroom. He jumped with a start.

Laura was wearing his dressing gown and she let it slip from her shoulder to reveal her nakedness.

"Mind if I join you?" she asked.

Ronan stepped out of the shower and covered himself with a towel.

"It's all yours," he said as he hurriedly left the bathroom.

He really wanted to give his head some space before dealing with Laura. She was toying with him as usual and he didn't know what her game was.

His head buzzed and he felt ill inside. He wished he had someone to talk to – it was too early to ring his sister Martina in California. It always helped to run his issues by her – she was in a different mental zone to anyone that he knew in Boston. Martina and her husband had opted out of the rat race and shared a holistic existence in the sunshine. He had visited immediately after Laura had left and found great help and healing from being with her. All that meditation and relaxation might as well have never happened now – he was in such a state that everything seemed shrouded in a yellow haze and he couldn't connect his thoughts clearly.

Thank God he had to leave for Las Vegas that day.

When he was ready, he decided to go out for a quick breakfast and a newspaper. He really didn't want to be in the apartment with Laura.

When he got back she was gone. He breathed a sigh of relief and then noticed the note on the kitchen counter. Laura had gone to *Bella Sante*, a luxurious day spa on Newbury Street, to recover from the upsetting events of the previous night and would be back at seven o'clock. She had booked a table at Marco's for eight and would meet him there. He heard a bleep on his phone and saw the same details in a text message. It was very presumptuous of her but she was always that way. It annoyed him and he wasn't going to jump to her tune any more. But he recognised that he did still care for her. It was all too much to digest. He needed his space from Laura right now.

He rubbed his chin and thought hard. How strange of Suzanne to say that she would like to go to Vegas – he wouldn't mind spending some time with her, catching up on the missing years. From the tone of her email it was unlikely that she would get to this side of the Atlantic any time soon. He had been fantasising about her since opening the email. He settled down at his Apple iPad to reply to her. He wasn't sure what he was going to say but right now he knew that he had to make a gesture to tell her that he still thought of her.

He went into Google Earth and typed in St Anne's Park. He clicked on the application that showed a photograph of the area and it was perfect. The roses were in full bloom and it must have been taken at the height of summer. He found the leafy corner near the entrance. That was the exact spot – where they had shared their first kiss. He stuck the link into an attachment and added simply – Remember this?

If she had the same memories of their time together she would get it – sometimes it was better to say less than more.

Suzanne was upstairs when something made her look at her phone – an email with an attachment that she couldn't open. She trembled like she was a teenager again, anxious and excited to see what Ronan had sent her. She ran down the stairs and into the kitchen to turn on the computer.

She could feel a tingling in her legs and arms. It was a long time since she had felt so excited by someone. She punched in the keys and code to get to her email and clicked on the link. Her internet connection flickered as it had a habit of doing sometimes and she lost the link. She hit it again and this time it worked. A small pinpoint highlighted St Anne's Park – she knew exactly why he had taken her there – she followed the links and clicked again and this time a photograph of the area popped up. She recognised the spot instantly – her heart pounded. Nothing else accompanied the message. It was subtle but thrilling and she wanted to speak with him right away. She needed to know what he was thinking. She needed to talk to him – to see him. She was so full of him she just kept staring at the image and shivering inside. She really needed to pull herself together – her mother had always warned her of falling too hard for a man. Mary always said that it wasn't right to make yourself too available. She had said a lot of things over the years that had shaped and formed Suzanne's thoughts and opinions but lately Mary hadn't been able to say anything much that made any sense and in a way that felt like an incredible relief now. Mary wouldn't be able to burst her bubble on this or tell her that Ronan was only toying with her. She could form her own opinion and conclusion on the email because Mary was no longer coherent. And for the first time since her mother was diagnosed with Alzheimer's she felt free and in a strange and thwarted way glad that she could enjoy her moment of romance with her thoughts and with Ronan.

Especially after the way their relationship had ended. Ronan might be vague about how it happened but it was with clarity she remembered the events in the run-up to the ending of their romance. She remembered the pain in her solar plexus as her mother sat her down in the kitchen all those years ago and sealed her future. Why had she let her mother have so much control? But it was okay now – now she could say and be who she wanted to be with Ronan.

How wonderful it would be to see him again!

Eddie did have a point about Leo – he really did always suit himself. It might be good for him to see the responsibility that she carried on her shoulders every day. Leo was seven years older than her but he might as well be from a different generation. She was always her mother's little shadow, while Leo was out with his friends, and from the time she could remember he was in college and had left home altogether. When her father died her mother was still a relatively young woman but instead of seeking a new relationship she chose to follow Suzanne's life carefully and mould and advise her at every stage of it. Sometimes it was suffocating for Suzanne but part of it was a reaction, Suzanne felt, by her mother to the loss of her husband and later to the loss of her son when he went to college. The two happened within a year of each other and Suzanne was only twelve and became the centre of her mother's world. She remained so until Mary started to lose her mind. Even when she was dating, Mary would find something wrong with the man the moment she brought him home. It was an unnatural bond that took so much energy from Suzanne that she found it difficult to see where she started and Mary ended, for their lives were so intertwined.

Maybe Eddie was right – she had forgotten who she was. She was so consumed with looking after her mother she couldn't make a decision for herself.

Maybe Eddie had more points in his favour than she thought. A break away would be wonderful – an adventure – it was just what she needed. She wasn't going to let him pay for the trip to Vegas but she might go with him.

Ronan packed his case and closed the zip on his suit bag. It had been strange sleeping with his wife again. She had given him the most amazing oral sex. It had felt wonderful while he was receiving it but the pleasure didn't last – instead he was sad and sick with himself afterwards.

He couldn't fathom if she was toying with him or using him as a stopgap or if she would return to her lover. He wasn't sure how he felt about her either. Part of him felt duty bound to her – technically she was still his wife. They had been through so much together – achieved so much as a couple. So much but yet not the most important thing in his perspective. They had not had a child. And even though he felt that he could love any child, he wasn't sure that he could accept the baby in Laura's womb.

He was so unsettled after getting the email from Suzanne and touched by her response to his Google Earth Map. He wasn't sure if it was the correct signal to send to a woman that he hadn't seen in over seventeen years but now he knew that he had done the right thing. She had sent him a link to Jim Fitzpatrick's website and an image of Palu the Cat Goddess. It was a strikingly beautiful woman that he had drawn for her and made into a card for her birthday. The instant he'd seen the image he had gasped.

His head was full of Suzanne after seeing the Celtic goddess image. He wanted to be whisked off to another world on the other side of the Atlantic – another time – another place. The trust was broken between him and Laura. He'd carried out the motions and allowed her to feel powerful and in control but the bond was lost and no matter how hard she tried it could not be repaired. As he'd let her bring him to orgasm the only image in his mind's eye was Suzanne's smiling face and the thought of her had helped him to feel real and escape the horrible toxic relationship that he was now sharing with the woman that he once had loved so much.

But this was another day and Ronan just wanted to be as far away from Laura as possible and this escape to Las Vegas was perfect.

Eddie couldn't believe it! He wondered what had made Suzanne change her mind so suddenly. In his mind he was already halfway across the Atlantic. He had been dreaming of Vegas for all of the previous night and that morning had his dreams dashed. But now she had agreed.

He was more excited than he had ever been in his life. He had assured Suzanne that he had organised the time off for both of them but that was only partially true – he had got his leave but he didn't know how his supervisor would react when he told her that Suzanne would be going as well at exactly the same time. He had checked to see that nobody else had put in for annual leave for those days over Halloween – they were lucky this year that mid-term break had fallen early and all the mothers on the roster hadn't put in for the same days. With a bit of luck there would be no objection to Suzanne taking leave. And he was feeling lucky.

Chapter 9

We will be known forever by the tracks we leave.

~ DAKOTA PROVERB ~

Tina was nearly ready to go by nine o'clock. Her stomach was fluttering with anticipation and excitement.

Vicky appeared in her daughter's room, holding the sides of her head, and Tina knew that could mean only one thing. That was another thing about Frank she hated – her mother always drank too much when she was around him and he never seemed to get drunk.

"Darling – I'm sorry that we took so long. You were asleep when we got in – do you want to go down and get some breakfast?"

"That's okay – Kyle is picking me up soon." She was wearing a long purple sundress and black sandals – the one dress that she had brought with her. She would be wearing a bikini when they got out to the lake.

"Oh – very good." Vicky was unsettled by the way her daughter had her own plans made and they didn't include her mother.

Tina was busily putting a towel and shorts into her beach bag and anything else that she thought she might need.

"Will you be gone all day?"

Tina didn't look up as she folded a T-shirt and sweatshirt and put them into the bag.

"I don't really know – my phone is charged – I'll call you."

Vicky's head was pounding even louder with the thought of her daughter out in the desert with a strange kid.

"Okay, honey – well, be careful."

Tina went over to her mother and brushed her lips off her cheek.

Vicky wanted to hold her tightly. She didn't know why she was suddenly feeling overly protective. "Frank hasn't seen you yet – why don't you say hi?"

"I'll see him later, Mum."

Tina slipped her bag on to her shoulder and walked out the door.

Vicky wrapped her arms around herself for comfort. She didn't often get feelings about things – usually she liked her life to be all neatly planned out and organised. She liked safety and sure things – she didn't like feeling out of control and that was exactly the way she was feeling right now.

Tina was not herself. It was a pleasure to see her animated about something and the fact that she had organised her trip with Kyle all by herself was out of character but in a positive way. Vicky usually had to do everything for her daughter – even though most girls her age would make their own breakfast and lunch and even prepare the dinner when they came home from school, Tina did none of these things. She didn't even do her own washing and ironing. Vicky didn't mind – she was dedicated to her daughter's happiness – she would do anything to bring a smile to her face. But she wasn't comfortable about her driving out into the desert with a boy – anything could happen to her.

Vicky's mind began to wander and imagine all sorts of scenarios. What if she became pregnant or if the boy was a psycho or just downright irresponsible and crashed his car? There was nothing she could do for now – she had a wedding to prepare and only four days to do it!

Tina waited at the east entrance of the Mirage Hotel where the buses collected people who were taking excursions. Kyle was right on time and drove up to her just as she looked at her watch. His arm rested on the window frame and he smiled as she opened the passenger door.

"Hi," she said with a tilt of her head. He was even more gorgeous than she had remembered.

The back of the car was filled with bags. She wondered what was in them.

They drove in the direction of the morning sun this time and followed signs for Boulder City and Hoover Dam. The hills were as impressive as they had been on the road to Red Rock Canyon but the road was a straight path of dark grey which went on for at least twenty miles before she saw anything that wasn't desert. She spotted a sign for Lake Mead after they were driving for twenty minutes. Kyle wasn't very chatty this early in the morning but he had thoughtfully put on some good music.

"Did you sleep well?" he asked.

"Yeah – the jet lag has been hitting me every now and again but I had no problem waking up this morning," she said with a shy smile. God, why did she sound so bashful? He had this incredible effect on her.

"I called around to Greg last night but didn't stay long. It's strange how quickly people change when they leave high school."

"I found that too – I used to have a really good friend called Jenny who became a total pain when she started college."

Kyle stretched his right arm forward and changed the CD.

"Have you ever heard of the Doors?" he asked. "They're a band who were around in the sixties – Jim Morrison was their lead singer."

"Oh, I've heard of him – he died in Paris – they have tours to see his headstone. Actually my friend Jenny went there with her family – her dad is a big Doors fan."

"Ah, only two steps of separation!"

"What do you mean?" Tina was puzzled.

"They say there are only six steps of separation – max – between anybody or thing or event in the world. It doesn't have to be that closely related but it's proof that everything and everybody is connected."

"I still don't get what you mean by 'steps of separation'?"

Kyle jerked his head back and rearranged his posture in the driving seat. "It's like this – we were talking about friends changing and you mention your friend Jenny – then I change the CD to the Doors and you tell me that Jenny is connected to the Doors – it's kind of like a series of links or chain of events that connects everybody." He gave a little laugh. "You're gonna think I'm crazy now – right?"

"No! No, not at all! I find that kind of thing really interesting – I mean, what happened there about Jenny and the Doors is a bit like synchronicity, too, isn't it? You know, when you feel something strongly in your gut and then you're proved right. Or you think of someone and then they phone you."

Kyle nodded his head vehemently. "Yeah!"

"There are patterns we don't always understand the meaning of – like how my mum marrying Frank was the worst thing that could happen – until now!"

"Is she not going to marry him?"

Tina chuckled. "Unfortunately she is still marrying him – but, you know, if she wasn't I'd never have come to Vegas and we'd never have met." There, she had said it – it was really bold and totally out of character for her but this guy was special. She could feel electric vibrations from him when they spoke. She was so connected to his every move that she didn't want to be with anyone else in the world since she had met him. The sweetest part was that he didn't realise she was under his spell. At least not until now!

Kyle smiled shyly and turned his head to the side to hide his reaction. He was right about this girl. The Doors track changed from "Love Her Madly" to "Light my Fire" – they didn't need to preach – his fire had been lit by this enigmatic Irish girl and he was going to enjoy every minute of this day.

John shivered as he entered the shower – that air-con needed adjusting. He cleared his mind as the drops of water cleansed his body. It was his first meditation of the day. It would be easy in the distraction and buzz of Vegas to lose himself but that never happened to him. He was more centred now than he had ever been at any stage in his life.

Vicky, however, was in trouble. He wasn't too worried about Frank – he would ferret his way around business and his life in a way that would bring him some sort of satisfaction.

But he didn't think Frank would ever be truly happy until he started to be honest with himself – and John doubted very much if that would ever happen.

But he did feel an obligation to Vicky. She was so naïve in the ways of the world and she had no idea what Frank was really like. He feared that she was still on some kind of rebound and wondered how content she truly was with the way things were.

He would spend some time by the pool today and take it easy while Frank and Vicky made their plans. He would put up with this charade for a few more days and then head out into the desert – that was where he really wanted to be and one of the reasons that he had agreed to come.

Vicky looked at Frank as he stepped out of the shower and wrapped a towel around his waist. He had been too tired to make love the night before and she was disappointed. Somehow she had thought that everything would be incredibly romantic and wonderful when they got to Vegas – but there was a sense of sameness about their relationship. They had been living together for six months so it wasn't as if they didn't know each other. But, still, she expected to feel different.

"Where do you want to go today?" he asked, taking his towel and giving his head a good drying.

"I want to show you the chapel that I chose for the wedding."

Frank stopped. "I told you, honey, that I would go along with whatever you chose. You said that you wanted to go shopping too!"

"I know," Vicky said. "I just wanted to show you."

Frank threw his towel down on the bed. "Okay then – let's go and I'll take you shopping later. Connie was telling me last night that there's this great mall just twenty minutes from here."

Vicky had thought they were going to be shopping in the Forum mall at Caesar's Palace. She noticed Frank was looking at his phone. Again. He'd been doing it a lot.

"Is everything okay at home?" she asked.

"Sure," he said, so quickly that he sounded doubly unconvincing. "My mum is feeling bad because she isn't coming to Vegas."

"I knew this would happen. I did warn you!"

"It's okay, honey." Frank put his arms around her waist and held her closely. "She'll get over it. Let's just have a good time. Hey, is there any movement from Tina this morning?"

"Oh, she's up already and gone off with Kyle for the day."

"Who's Kyle?"

"Connie's son. They did a little sightseeing yesterday and seemed to hit it off." Vicky somehow felt that, if she conveyed that she was happy to Frank, she might believe it herself. "Do you think she'll be okay?"

Frank nodded his head. "Of course!" That was one less distraction out of the way. "What time will she be back?"

"Eh, she didn't say. They're taking a trip out to a lake. She doesn't want to come to the theatre with us later either. I hope she'll be okay in the room on her own tonight."

"We won't be late. You can always come back after the show and stay here with her."

Vicky was aghast. "And what about you?"

"I was going to do a little high-rolling tonight – you don't mind, do you?"

Vicky pushed his arms away from her and took a step back. She did mind actually. She was feeling really disconnected from everyone around her.

"Where do you want to have breakfast?" Frank asked as he started to get dressed. "John said that the Paradise Café downstairs is good for breakfast."

Vicky was blown away by her fiancé's lack of sensitivity. He was like a different person since he had landed in Vegas.

"Why don't you give him a ring and see if he wants to come down with us?" he suggested as he pulled his trousers on.

Vicky obediently did as he proposed. She wondered how she would get through the day.

John was already sitting at a table when Frank and Vicky arrived in the tropical habitat of the Paradise Café. "Hi guys, over here!" he called.

He watched his brother and his fiancée walk over and he noticed, not for the first time, how odd they appeared together. Frank was wearing pressed grey trousers and a white polo shirt with a cotton jumper tied loosely around his neck. He smacked of Hugo Boss and other designer brands that to John were like relics of the last decade. Vicky on the other hand was wearing a simple purple figure-hugging T-shirt dress. Her brown soft curls fell gently to her shoulders. She certainly didn't look almost forty – he often thought that she looked like Tina's older sister and she could pass as Frank's daughter easier than his partner.

She sat down beside John and gave him a friendly kiss on the cheek.

"Did you have a good rest?" she asked.

"Yes, I did – slept well, thanks, and have been up for a while."

"I fell asleep the minute my head hit the pillow!" Frank declared as he picked up a menu and scanned it. "I can't get used to this time-zone thing."

"It's crazy, isn't it?" Vicky said. "Although you're probably used to it, John?"

"You never get used to jet lag. But it's a good idea not to drink too much when you're adjusting to a new time zone. Where's Tina?"

"She has gone out for the day with Connie's son – again!"

"It's nice for her to have someone her own age," John said with a nod.

Vicky couldn't hide her concern. "He's only eighteen and I'm not really mad about her going off in a car with a kid! But I dare not say it to her or she would freak out!"

"Kids all drive over here – they don't have an option. Don't worry – I'm sure she'll be fine."

Vicky shook her head. "I don't know what I've done wrong!"

John smiled at his future sister-in-law. "You've done nothing wrong – it's just a phase. She's a really good kid." He lifted his glass of orange juice and, as he took a sip, it dribbled down his chin and onto his clean T-shirt. "Whoops!"

Vicky tried not to laugh as he pulled a face and wiped his chest with a napkin. John had the cutest way of turning a mishap into a funny spectacle. He was always outwardly cool and collected and then turned out to be so normal and natural a few moments later.

"Have you ordered yet?" Frank asked, his eyes still glued to the menu card.

"I'm getting the eggs and bacon," John said. "I ordered a pot of coffee for us."

"Good, I'll have the same," Frank said, throwing the card down on the table. "So what are you doing today?"

John shrugged. "I was going to take a swim after breakfast."

"We're going shopping!" Frank said.

John looked at Vicky. He watched as her emerald eyes scanned the menu. He knew she was hiding her concerns about Tina behind the menu card. She really needed to be minded. The funny thing was that Frank did too – she wouldn't find her caretaker in him – but did she realise that yet?

Tina and Kyle came to a small town that was called Boulder Beach and passed signs for boat and wave-runner rental.

"What's a wave-runner?" Tina asked.

"It's a jet ski – you have them in Ireland, I'm sure?" Kyle pointed over to a row of them waiting to be hired. "See, there they are."

Tina grinned. "I love the way you say certain words and the way you use different words in America – like 'sidewalk' for 'pavement'!"

"Well, jet skis are cool whatever their name! Hey, would you like to go for a ride on one?" Kyle pulled the car over.

Tina could feel the adrenalin rush coming over her. Her

grandmother would be thrilled and would definitely tell her to go for it. It was just as well, however, that her mother had no idea what she was about to do – things like jet skis scared the life out of Vicky. Anything that smacked of adventure or danger and she would run a mile. That made Tina's mind up for her.

"I'd love to – are they very expensive?"

"Don't worry about that – my mom gave me another hundred today."

Tina smiled. "Your mum is cool!"

Kyle nodded. "I guess so. Sometimes I feel like she is a good friend and then when she hollers at me to do chores she goes back to being my mom again."

"She's kind of trendy – what music does she like?"

"She loves the Doors – we both do. You know, Jim Morrison always thought that he was possessed by the spirit of an American Indian."

"Wow, that sounds kind of strange."

Kyle nodded. "I guess to be a genius it helps to be strange."

"Some people think I'm strange – my mum for one!" Tina said with a laugh.

"I think you're beautiful." Kyle had said it before he realised that he had let the words slip from his lips. He had only meant to think them – his mouth was out of control and he suddenly became really embarrassed and jumped out of the car. "I'll go see about hiring those jet skis!"

Tina sat in the car and internalised his words. She had been told she was beautiful before – by her mother and her father – and she had been told by some girls in school. But she had never been told by a guy – what's more, a guy that she really liked. There were boys who had been sweet and given her compliments but they had never said straight out that she was beautiful. The compliment sent her spirit levitating into the air.

Kyle came back all matter of fact and hopped into the car. "He says we can collect them down at the marina." He handed her a life-vest and threw his into the back. "They sit two – is that okay with you?"

Tina nodded. "Fine by me." Way better in fact. She could sit on the back and wrap her arms around his waist tightly. "I'll change into my swimsuit and T-shirt then."

Kyle was already wearing surfer shorts and a T-shirt.

As the pontoons and variety of boats and yachts came into view, Kyle started to look for somewhere to park up. The water was so blue – vivid and Prussian in spots. It was a direct contrast to the tint of orange and sienna of the surrounding hills.

A group of kids stood on the decking and threw pieces of bread into the water.

"What are they doing?" Tina asked.

"Feeding the carp."

"Excuse me? Feeding the fish?"

"Yeah – these aren't just any fish – these are giant Lake Mead carp!"

Tina jumped out of the car. "This I have to see," she said.

She ran over to where the children were screaming with delight as the fish scrambled over each other with mouths wide open to catch the pieces of bread. Some mallard ducks were getting in on the action and pecking up the crumbs.

"This is so cool!" she said.

Kyle was beside her now and he enjoyed watching her expression. He had seen the phenomenon many times himself but watching Tina made it seem different.

"Do you want to change into your wet stuff?" he asked. "There's a bar over there called the Boat House – we can get a burger there later if you like?"

Tina beamed from head to toe – of course she would like – she liked everything about Kyle and where he brought her and what they did together.

Vicky looked at her phone for the umpteenth time since they'd left the shopping mall.

"I'm sure she's okay," Frank assured her.

"I know – it's just this is a strange place and they have to drive through the desert for over an hour to get to Lake Mead."

"There are plenty of kids her age trekking around the world on their own – you really should just relax – this is our big trip, remember?"

Of course she remembered but sometimes she suspected that Frank didn't understand the responsibility that comes with having a teenager. Coming to Vegas had thrown them out of sync with each other and she didn't know how to read him at all. It was like he was jumpy or fidgety all of the time and it didn't matter who he was with or what he was doing because ultimately he was in a world of his own.

All the emotions that had been welling up inside since her mother died were coming to the surface. The sense of loss and feelings of hopelessness were palpable. There was also the guilt. She was still haunted by the memory of finding her mother cold and stiff and so alone. She couldn't shake the notion that she had let her down in her final days and it was all because of the feud that had been smouldering between them for years – broken intermittently when they unified to wallow in Tina's accomplishments and milestones. Why had it been so difficult? It wasn't as if there were brothers or sisters to compete with for her affections or attention. It was strange that they could never just sit in a room together and be – just *be*. And what terrified her more than anything was the fact that she could see the very same thing happening with her own daughter. The distance between them had widened and was at a dangerous level. The few moments of communication that they did have were nearly always tarnished by some friction and ended with one or the other in tears.

"We'll have to buy new suitcases," Frank said. "We aren't going to have room for all of this stuff."

Vicky looked at him. He was burdened with massive carrier bags. Time to call a halt.

"Frank – do you mind if we go back to the hotel – I'm feeling tired and really want to give Connie a call. Maybe we could take a trip out to Lake Mead?"

Frank stopped in his tracks and put the bags down on the ground. He put the palms of his hands gently on to Vicky's shoulders and looked into her green eyes. "Look, Tina is eighteen years of age. She is with the son of a woman who is doing business with us – you have to give the girl her own space. She's going to be fine!"

Vicky smiled. She needed his reassurance – not just about Tina either – she needed it for herself. She desperately needed to know that her new husband was going to be a support for her and that he wouldn't just up and leave like David had.

"Okay – I'll stop fussing. Just let me ring her, Frank."

Vicky took out her phone and dialled her daughter's number. It rang out and then went to voicemail.

"No answer!"

"She's probably having fun swimming in that lake – it's like a beach. I read about it on the plane on the way over. She's fine."

"Am I really worrying too much?"

Frank gave her a look that told her the answer.

Vicky sighed. "I'm sorry, honey. I should be just enjoying my time with you!"

Frank nodded in agreement. "Yes, you should. Now – let's go buy a couple of extra suitcases and then we can get a taxi and go back to the hotel for a nice leisurely swim. I bet John has been lying by the pool for hours."

"That's if Connie has let him," Vicky said with a giggle.

"She's not his sort – poor Connie – nice lady."

"It's good of her to arrange tickets for tonight though – it will be fun to see a show."

Frank stalled as they came to the Delsey luggage shop. "Everything about this trip is perfect – just relax and enjoy!"

Vicky smiled and followed him into the store. She did trust him and she had faith in him but she couldn't explain the uncomfortable feeling in the pit of her stomach and why it was there.

"Get on!" Kyle called as he settled on the jet ski.

This was the moment Tina had been waiting for – she would wrap her arms around his waist and as soon as he speeded up she would be able to squeeze him really tightly and it would be okay!

Kyle pushed away from the pontoon when he got used to the controls.

"This is so good!" she whispered in his ear but she wasn't sure if he heard over the revving of the engine.

He drove it forward and soon they were out on the water, away from the boats moored to the marina. They were surrounded by lumpy hills formed from red sand and grey and black stone. Eagles and blue herons flew across the lake – their wings flapping in harmony with the sound of the engine's rumbles. The water was perfectly still as the jet ski sliced through it and splashed water on the young couple's legs.

"You okay?" Kyle asked, turning his head to check.

Tina nodded. She could breathe him in from where she rested the side of her face against his shoulder. It was so close and intimate, the way her body fitted so snugly against his. She had total confidence and trust in his every move.

Kyle sensed her buoyancy and took it as a cue to speed up. The vibrations ran between them and they both yelped and screamed with joy as the jet ski pounded over the water. They were like Oisín and Niamh in *Tir na nÓg* – The Land of Youth – Tina made a mental note of the analogy – she would write it in her diary later. She would write every second of this special day down so that she would never ever forget it.

Connie suddenly appeared just as Vicky and Frank were about to step out of the taxi. She beeped loudly and Frank turned around first. He called to Vicky and she followed him over to Connie's car.

"Hi, guys – you've been shopping, I see – did you have a good time?" she beamed.

"Yes, thanks," Vicky said. "Are you coming in?"

"Not yet – I was visiting a client. I've made a reservation for Stack for later – or would you rather try somewhere else?"

"No – that sounds lovely, Connie, thanks." Vicky smiled. "What about the kids?"

"Oh, they won't be home until dark – Kyle sent me a text."

Vicky took a deep breath. Tina should have at least let her own mother know what her intentions were. Still, she had to remain calm and couldn't show her fears in front of Connie.

"See you about eight then? The show starts at ten thirty."

"What time is it over?" Frank asked.

"We'll be finished by twelve thirty! Why don't you guys go for a little rest – recharge your batteries?"

Vicky looked at Frank.

He grinned. "Good idea – see you later, Connie."

The wind blew in Connie's hair as she drove off down the slipway in her cute Chrysler convertible. She was like a breath of fresh air.

"Come on, let's get some sleep," said Frank. "I'm shattered."

They made straight for the lifts. They were in the block with the best view in the hotel, although John had assured them that the view over the Nevada hills was equally as spectacular as The Strip.

"I'll just see if John is in his room," Frank said. He knocked loudly on his door but there was no reply. "He must be down at the pool."

Vicky put the room key into the slot and the lights came on as the door opened.

"I would be much happier if Tina was back – what time is it now?"

"It's only four o'clock," Frank said as he went to the window and pulled over the blackout curtains. He undressed down to his boxers, then slid down under the newly made sheets and let out a sigh as his head hit the pillow. "I could sleep for hours now."

Vicky looked at him. That was what he had every intention of doing by the looks of it. There was certainly no suggestion of anything romantic.

"I might go for a swim myself," she said. "See if John is down at the pool."

Frank had already closed his eyes. "Good idea. Will you wake me an hour before we have to go for dinner?"

Vicky felt like taking her shoe and throwing it at him, but she contained her anger. In as noisy a fashion as possible she put her bikini, towel and lotion in a bag. She slipped her sunglasses on to the top of her head and slammed the door behind her. She was fuming inside. But she wasn't exactly sure who she was cross with any more. Tina for going off with Kyle? Frank for going to sleep? Or herself for the way she expected so much from people and the way she constantly felt let down.

She pressed the button to call the lift and stepped inside. A couple inside were fixing their clothes as she watched the doors close. At least somebody was getting some romance, she thought to herself.

The couple remained silent – holding hands as the lift descended. They were in their fifties but glowed with all the passion of a pair of teenagers.

Vicky envied them. Why was she going down to the pool while her fiancé was snoring in the bedroom?

The doors opened and she followed the signs for the pool. It was quite a trek and along the way she passed enticing tearooms and restaurants. There was so much to see and do it was too much to take in. And her mind was in a haze anyway. The pool area at the Mirage was lush and beautiful. Exotic palms and foliage grew from every plot of soil. The gardens where the white lions and rare animals were housed lay just behind the pool. Wooden decking and cabanas marked out different plots where guests could get as much privacy as they needed. Although it was busy there were some sunbeds free and one of the pool boys was liberally handing out towels. She stood at the poolside, scanning the pool to see if she could find John when the boy approached her with a towel.

"Thank you!" she said.

"Would you like to take a cabana?" he asked.

Vicky looked over at the white tarpaulin tents with beautiful cushions on cane couches. And there, outside the corner cabana reading his book, was John.

"Actually I'll just go over to my friend – I see him over there."

John was wearing a pair of dark-brown surf pants with lemon and green floral motifs. He didn't lift his eyes from his page until she was standing right beside him.

"Vicky – you're back – did you have a good time shopping?"

"Yes, thanks – it took longer than we thought – your brother nearly bought the entire mall."

"Where is he?" he asked looking around.

"He's up in the room. Taking a nap!"

John raised his eyebrows.

It made Vicky feel uncomfortable but vindicated.

"I thought I would take a swim. These huts are cool. Have you been here all day?"

John nodded. He put his book down. "I'll join you if you don't mind? Why don't you change in the cabana – I'll pull over the curtain."

Vicky felt suddenly very shy about taking her clothes off so close to her future brother-in-law. He was looking very fine in his nakedness. His muscles were well developed and he had a classic male proportion that suited his broad shoulders and height. There wasn't an ounce of unwanted flesh on his torso – unlike his brother's.

Vicky berated herself for her thoughts and quickly went into the cabana. She shouldn't entertain such wicked thoughts for John. He was a totally different character to Frank. She needed the steadiness of Frank – he was the businessman – he would mind and protect her and give her the stable life that she craved and needed. John was one of those annoying arty types. He picked up his guitar from day to day and did exactly what he felt like when he wanted.

Up to now, whenever she looked at John all she saw was a man who didn't take his responsibilities seriously. A man who wanted to live his life on his own terms. But there by the pool he looked so attractive and Vicky wondered if the reason he looked so good was because she was aching and craving some physical attention from Frank. She stepped out of the cabana in a chocolate-brown string bikini with a pretty yellow floral motif.

"We match!" John declared. And he was right – the fabric of his shorts was co-ordinating with her bikini. "Come on, let's get in! There's a quiet spot over by the waterfall."

She walked behind him and couldn't take her eyes from his frame. His skin was smooth – pale but sunkissed. She hadn't known that he had a tattoo until now. On his left shoulder-blade was an eagle motif. Its wings spread out and she was fixated on the beauty of the artwork. She never thought that she could ever like a tattoo – she detested with a passion the abominations that Tina had printed on her once flawless skin. But for the first time in her life she had to admit that a tattoo looked beautiful.

She cleared the thought from her head. Her mind was overreacting to the new sights of this crazy town. She continued walking behind John around the curved snakelike contours of the pool until they came to one of the most private corners, just beside the waterfall.

"Okay?" he asked.

She nodded.

Together they walked down the shallow steps. She winced at first as her legs submerged in the cool water but quickly got used to the temperature. John was keen to get in quickly and threw himself into the water head first. Torrents of water raced down the rock face, sprinkling them like a shower.

"Good, isn't it?" he said, shaking the droplets from his dark-brown wavy hair.

"It's lovely," Vicky nodded. She felt brave enough to try a breaststroke and swam close to the waterfall.

John swam over to her and they stood, shoulder deep, in the refreshing spray.

"You see that fencing?" John said, pointing up to the edge of the pool area. "There's a bar for adults only – it's called Bare – they encourage topless sunbathing!"

Vicky laughed. "I don't think I'll be going in there!"

John shrugged. "I don't think Frank will be either."

Vicky thought it the strangest thing to say. What did he mean?

With her hands on Kyle's shoulders, Tina stood up, carefully put her foot upon the pontoon and climbed off the jet ski. She took the rope from Kyle and tied it to the mooring.

"That was really amazing. Thanks a million."

"Good fun!" he said, brushing his long wet fringe from his forehead. "I'm hungry now – what about you?"

Tina nodded. "There's no need to change, is there?"

"Nah – we'll dry off in the sun!"

Kyle led her over to the deck where tables and chairs were placed for guests of the bar.

They took a table at the water's edge with a perfect view of the Marina and all of the moored boats.

"I can't believe I'm here. This place is so cool!" Tina peeled off her top to reveal a skimpy T-shirt covering her bikini.

Kyle looked at the chain around her neck and followed the line of her cleavage. She was like a doll. An exotic doll from far away. He desperately wanted to touch her. He knew last night that he fancied her but now he really wanted to have her. He wondered if she was a virgin. If she went to Las Vegas High School there was no way she would be – but there was something innocent about her. The way she hid behind the black eye make-up and dyed hair said that he hadn't even touched on finding out who the real Tina was. He would make it his business to do so before she went home.

"You kids ready to order?" the waitress asked as she came out with pen and pad at the ready.

"I'll have a burger," Kyle said. "And a Coke."

"Me too!" Tina nodded. When the waitress was gone Tina propped herself up at the table and rested on her elbows. "You know, that was the best fun I have had since . . . I can't remember!"

"It's good – do you live near water?"

"Right beside it. Mum and I moved out to Howth, to Frank's place, six months ago. I didn't want to go but it's not so bad. We have a train called the DART so I can get into Dublin city in twenty-five minutes.

"Do you still go to school?"

"I'm repeating my Leaving Cert – that's my finals. I should be finished but I'm not." She paused. "Last year was bad – my gran died and it hasn't been easy. There's just me and my mum, you see. My dad has a new wife and he lives in Limerick – quite a way from Dublin – with her and his sons."

"So you have half-brothers?"

"I don't see them very much though. My dad's wife doesn't like me."

"That's too bad – but at least you have your mum."

Tina bit her lip. "It's not easy – my mum and I have always had a difficult relationship. I think it's because I'm an only child. She wants to control me. She thinks I'll make a mess of my life. She won't let me be me!"

"Moms do that sometimes – it's because they love us. My mom is really protective of us – she had a real bad time with my dad. He used to beat her a lot. I can remember her screams. Troy and I would hide in the bedroom 'cos if he was in a real bad mood he would come after us with his belt. One day he hit me so hard she packed a suitcase and took us here. I heard a year later that my dad shot himself."

"Oh Kyle, I'm so sorry! That must have been terrible."

Kyle shrugged. "I don't miss him – I'm glad he killed himself – it means he won't hurt her again. Crazy to say you love someone so much and then hurt them."

Tina knew exactly what he meant. She loved her mother. In many ways she was the best mother in the world. But she lived with such fear. She couldn't just let things be – she had to have everything and everyone cornered off into neat little boxes. Maybe Tina was just like her gran – a free spirit who needed to be left to do her own thing.

But where did that leave her mum – how could she get to a point where she had the confidence to be herself?

"You know, I don't think my mum even realises she's unhappy. She thinks marrying Frank is going to make everything okay – give her back that status of a married woman and then she will look good to everyone else. She doesn't realise that most people don't care. My gran told me ages ago that everyone is so caught up in their own world they don't really give a damn what you do."

Kyle nodded. "I know that. But you'd be surprised how many kids I know live their lives worrying about what other people think."

Tina looked admiringly at the boy she found it so easy to confide in. She had never been able to open up to someone about her mother so easily before. He understood her. He didn't judge her. It was how a good relationship should be. She trusted him. The same way as she'd so readily trusted him on the jet ski.

The silence between them was tangible – both were talking about subjects that were incredibly uncomfortable but, when shared like this, they didn't seem so bad.

Kyle leaned his arms over and rested them on the table. He was intimately close to her now and only a few inches from her pink lips – no traces of the lipstick from this morning when he had collected her from the hotel. He looked into her shiny blue eyes that sparkled widely. The black make-up was smudged around them from the water earlier but that only made the whites of her eyes glisten brighter.

"Can I kiss you?"

No one had ever asked her if they could kiss her before. The few times she had been out with a guy, he would just do it. It sounded so romantic to be asked and especially as she wanted him to.

"Yes," she whispered.

He took a moment to look at her. Then put his hand under her chin to gently raise her lips. He leaned forward and placed his lips on hers. They felt so soft. Their mouths remained closed and they kissed again for a little while longer. Each kiss more gentle than the one before.

Suddenly her phone started to ring which broke the moment.

Tina saw her mother's number on the screen. She wondered if she had hired a spy to watch her.

"You okay?" Kyle asked.

Tina nodded. "It's my mum. She can't leave me alone." She threw her phone onto the table. "Sometimes I feel like she's smothering me!"

Kyle put his hand up to her cheek and rubbed it softly. "She loves you – if she didn't she wouldn't care."

"I know – but she has to let me be myself."

Kyle nodded. He was lucky. He had a mom who was happy to let him find himself. He hated to see Tina so unhappy. This was a special moment and it had been interrupted. He didn't know the woman but Tina did have a point and he could see by her expression that she was suffocating in her mother's love.

John dried himself off and lay back down on to the sunbed while Vicky changed in the cabana. He picked up his book and started to read.

When Vicky emerged he was so engrossed he hardly noticed her.

"Eh, I think I'll go and get something to eat – we didn't have much lunch while we were at the shopping mall."

John looked up. He nodded and returned to his book.

Vicky couldn't understand why he was suddenly so quiet. He had been so friendly while they swam in the pool. He most definitely was odd. She had been right all along about him.

"See you later then."

He looked up again and smiled. "See you later."

She couldn't fathom men. Why did they need to be alone like this? She had read *Men are from Mars, Women are from Venus* shortly after she had separated from David. Still, it made no sense. A constant stream of dialogue was normal in her relationships with her female friends. They frequently texted and updated each other on everything from the most trivial purchase in the supermarket and the best tip to get stains off the bath to the most heart-wrenching complexities like dealing with your husband leaving you for another woman. Her female friends all understood her perfectly and she them. They were her body armour and she missed them since she had moved to Howth. However, she still made a special effort to see them at least once or twice a week. But women were so much easier to understand and to relate to – except for Tina, of course.

Looking at John as an object of desire had been delusional – he was far too happy with his own company to connect on a permanent basis with anyone, she concluded. On her way into the hotel she was distracted by a display of beautiful cuddly white lion-cub teddies. One opened up into a bag. She couldn't help studying them and looking inside. How she wished Tina would like a gift like that – but she wasn't a little girl any more – she was a young woman. But Vicky had hope. Frank had made it perfectly clear when he proposed that he wanted a family and that, although he was happy to accept Tina as his daughter, he wanted a child of his own. The words had fallen on Vicky's ears like honey. A new baby would be wonderful for everyone.

Vicky looked at the little bag again. There was no point in buying it – she might have a boy. The thought thrilled her – a son. She could spoil him and look after him just the way she pleased. Maybe she would go up to the room and try and rouse Frank. Get him in baby-making mode before the wedding!

John didn't read much fiction. He liked lots of different types of books but mostly autobiographies. The book he had chosen to bring on this trip was good – he had read it before. *Black Elk Speaks* was a classic document of a medicine man who had led one of the most interesting and prophetic lives of the Oglala Sioux Indians. John was in Indian country now and felt close to the beating heart of Native America. The people that Black Elk wrote about were so much a part of every western that his mother's brother, his Uncle Bob, had recalled with such precision that John often wondered if he had been re-incarnated from a cowboy. There was a strange obsession amongst men of that generation with the Wild West and his Uncle Bob had told him that John's own father was a great fan of westerns too. Crazy Horse, Custer (or Long Hair as Black Elk referred to him) and of course Buffalo Bill and his Wild West show – all legends and part of a past that had left a terrible legacy of injustice and even genocide. John read how the soul of America had been ripped apart by industrialisation. And it wasn't just in America – it was happening all over the world and John worried and cared for every continent and the damage that mining and consumerism had on the environment. These were the issues that really concerned him. He didn't care about bankers and credit crunches – he was in a vibration where the big picture was far more important than finance or ridiculous political power trips. His world was partly in the here and now and partly in a realm of the universal consciousness where he liked to be most of the time.

He had brought his guitar to Vegas. That was his vessel through which he was able to truly connect with his spiritual self. He was lucky to have found this source of joy while still in school and it had helped him to lead an adventurous and fulfilling life. His mother thought that he was one step away from being a vagabond or homeless person. Never for a moment could she imagine how it felt to stand on a stage and transport yourself and thousands of others in the audience to a plane higher than narcotics could take you. And he had dabbled in his fair share of drugs over the years. It was part and parcel of going around the circuit and mixing with the other musicians and roadies. He did have good times and a buzz but this was not how he lived his life now – nor had done for the last decade. He had found his spiritual self and with it the security and balance to be at peace most of the time. That was his way of coping with his mother's disinterest and his brother's erratic stumblings.

This latest one was difficult to watch – especially as John could see from the outside exactly what was going on. Frank wasn't getting any younger – he had to have a child.

John had a different perspective on parenthood. There were enough unwanted children in the world and if he ever felt the compulsion to become a father he would do his best to go out into the world and find that soul that needed him. He realised that adoption as a first choice would be unusual for most men – but not those with a social and global conscience.

In some ways he felt that he could easily have been a monk – only for his love of sex. His need for it was as natural as breathing or eating and he never had any problem finding someone to make love with when the urge took him over. His natural charm and easy-going nature meant that women felt safe around him and more often than not would chat him up.

But the concerns that he had about his brother niggled at him in a way that most other relationships around him didn't. Maybe he was too close. If Vicky was going to be part of his family he did have a responsibility to protect her – but how could he protect her from making the biggest mistake of her life without betraying his brother? The best thing to do was nothing and let them each find their path and travel the journey that they needed, to find themselves. But with his strong gut instinct John knew that the ride was not going to be easy for either of them and for that reason he was sad. He had made a great effort while swimming in the pool with Vicky but she couldn't relax. It was better for now to concentrate on his book and let the drama unfold as he knew it would.

Chapter 10

*What is life? It is the flash of a firefly in the night. It is
the breath of a buffalo in the wintertime. It is the little
shadow which runs across the grass and loses itself in
the sunset.*

~ Blackfoot proverb ~

Ronan stood in Departures at Logan International Airport. The
clouds were tinged with pink against the blue sky and he could feel
winter in the air – it was too early for snow but nothing would
surprise him after the week he'd had.

He was so glad to be going off to sunnier climes. He looked at his
email – still no word from Suzanne but he was hopeful. He smiled as
he thought of her. The air steward took his luggage for check-in.

"Good afternoon, sir," she beamed – thinking that Ronan's
smile was for her. "And how are you today?"

"Good, thank you."

He was good. He had a few days' space to contemplate Laura
and his life. He made his way down to the gate and picked up a
copy of the *Boston Globe*. The flight was short enough – he would
have a couple of drinks and try and snooze on the plane.

The light for his flight was on and he decided to board early. He
really wanted to get comfortable. He handed his boarding card to
the steward and walked down the tunnel to the aircraft.

As he took his seat he heard his phone bleep. Once settled, he
opened it – it was from Suzanne. He had to read it twice. She was

coming to Las Vegas! What had made her do something so impulsive? It was crazy – she would be staying in the MGM Grand – only a short walk through to his hotel. Did she know that he was staying in the Signature? It was mind-boggling. She added that she would be with her friend Eddie – that was odd. Was she in a relationship with this fellow – she did seem to mention him a lot. Maybe he was fooling himself by thinking that Suzanne might have any romantic interest in him. He suddenly felt like he'd been reading the situation entirely wrongly and had been a total fool! He looked to find another email – from Laura this time: Miss you, baby – see you in five days.

He certainly couldn't say that his life wasn't interesting at the moment. Then he had to work in the middle of all of this emotional turmoil.

An air steward came over.

"Can I get you a glass of champagne, sir?"

"Yes, please – actually, can you make that a double gin and tonic?"

He needed to steady his nerves. Suzanne was going to be in Vegas – but she had this Eddie fellow with her. Maybe she would just meet for a drink or a meal and a catch-up on old times but that would be that. To be fair, she had said that she hadn't married but she never said that she wasn't dating anybody! Or even living with somebody. He was confused – why, if she was on a romantic holiday with her boyfriend – or partner – did she want to meet up with him?

Suzanne was showing Leo how to operate the new gas heating-system when she heard Kate coming in through the front door.

Leo was in a state. Suzanne had waited until he had arrived before telling him that she was just leaving! She felt terrible but she just had to grit her teeth and do it. Anyway, it turned out now that Wendy and Grace would be coming to stay also the next day so he'd have some company and support.

Suzanne was doubly glad to be going away. Grace was so

sanctimonious – it would do her no harm to have to care for her elderly mother-in-law!

"I still can't believe you're tearing off to Vegas, Sue!"

"And why is that, Leo – can't I have a life?"

"I didn't mean it like that!" Leo was suddenly very careful with his words, lest she should unleash the wrath of ten years on him.

"Good!"

Suzanne continued to explain the details of the dial for the gas boiler without flinching. She was empowered and had been since making the decision to go to Las Vegas. Since Ronan had contacted her she had been playing the events that led to the end of their relationship over and over and the pain and anger that accompanied those months overflowed and she was glad to be able to let go without taking it out on the one person with whom she was the angriest.

"I keep the vacuum cleaner in here and the bucket in case Mum has an accident there." She pointed at the small closet in the corner of the kitchen.

"An accident?"

"Sometimes she forgets to go to the toilet, Leo."

Discomfort was etched all over Leo's face. "I've got a taxi calling for me in ten minutes – so you can use my car of course. Now is there anything else?"

Leo shook his head. He got the message – loud and clear! And inside he knew that he deserved it.

Eddie answered the door to the taxi driver and dragged his bag out. He hadn't brought much – he had every intention of buying lots of new clothes when he hit the shopping malls of Vegas. He was a seasoned traveller to New York – he loved that town so much – and something inside him said that he was going to love Las Vegas too! His stomach was jumping with anxiety and anticipation at the thought of stepping out on to The Strip and seeing the bright lights and pizzazz.

"Stop off at Kincora Road, please – we're picking up my friend."

The front door of Suzanne's house was open wide. The driver didn't have to beep as she appeared at once with her suitcase behind her.

Suzanne gave Leo a peck on the cheek and strode down the driveway. This was going to be an adventure and one that she truly deserved – she had got to the age of thirty-seven and played by her mother's and everyone else's rules – now she was doing something for herself and she wondered what reception would be waiting for her when she arrived.

Ronan opened the door of his suite in the Signature at the MGM Grand. It didn't feel like twelve months since he had been in Vegas. Strange to think how the events of the last year should have changed his life so utterly. First, Laura having an affair – then becoming pregnant – now wanting to be back in his life in some strange capacity that was unclear. It was confusing. Then connecting with Suzanne again and hearing how her life had turned out. The hope of maybe having something romantic with her suddenly dashed by the revelation that she was probably bringing her boyfriend with her to Vegas.

He went over to the window and drew back the curtains to reveal a perfect view of Planet Hollywood Hotel and the sun shining on the distant hills. At least Vegas was the same. He loved this town. It was the best and worst of mankind all rolled into one and somehow it worked! Even though he would be spending many hours in the Convention Centre on Paradise Road, he had plenty of time to have fun first and for a while he had hoped he would be sharing it with Suzanne. She looked just the same from her photograph on Facebook. He wondered what she would think of him! His hair was speckled with grey now – although it wasn't apparent as it was still a light mousy brown. He felt his chin – it could do with a shave.

The table was laid with a bottle of champagne and beautiful display of exotic chocolate-coated fruit and nuts. He picked up a pecan on his way to the bathroom and munched it hungrily. The suite was sumptuous and had every conceivable mod-con but the bathroom was the pièce-de-résistance. A marble Jacuzzi bath was in the corner which comfortably fitted two as he recalled from the first time he had stayed here with Laura – and there was a double sink and massive shower which could house a small family. It was all there and now that he was on his own he realised how little he needed all of this space. He set to shaving his stubble and took a quick shower. It would be nice to go out for a walk on The Strip.

Chapter 11

May the warm winds of heaven blow softly upon your house. May the Great Spirit bless all who enter there. May your moccasins make happy tracks in many snows, and may the rainbow always touch your shoulder.

~ CHEROKEE PRAYER BLESSING ~

Eddie helped Suzanne out of the taxi – she was exhausted and exhilarated. They looked up and were both in such awe at the size of the mammoth glass structure that was the MGM Hotel neither said a word! The cab driver took out their bags and zoomed off with a new fare. The two new guests went through the glass doors and into the massive reception area. A bronze life-size sculpture of a lion rested in the middle of a bed of flowers. The marble floor had another image of a lion imprinted in black and the logo was echoed in the doors.

"It's amazing – whaddya think, Sue?" Eddie gushed.

"It's like the biggest cinema foyer in the world!"

And she was right. There was something Hollywood and big screen about the place – like they had walked on to a set!

The reception ran along the entire back wall of the foyer and at least a dozen receptionists were checking guests in.

"We'd better get over there!" Eddie urged.

Suzanne didn't know what she had expected from Las Vegas but so far her eyes had been exposed to the most amazing sights and all she had done was travel from the airport.

After the receptionist had checked them in and given them room keys, a bellhop brought their bags over to a trolley and assured them that he would be up with them soon.

As they took the long walk through the casino to the elevators Eddie had to follow a map for directions.

"I think this is the biggest hotel in Vegas!"

"I'm not surprised," Suzanne said, her mouth open.

Suddenly her phone bleeped and she looked down to see a text from T-Mobile welcoming her to the US. She logged on to her email and was delighted to see that it too was working. And not only that but there was a message from Ronan.

Wow – we have to meet up – I'm staying at the Signature – part of MGM Grand. Give me a call when you arrive my number is 671-5556789. Ronan

"Eddie – it's from Ronan – he's given me his number!"

Eddie smiled. "Good – that's the main reason we're in Vegas. Now I'm after booking us a table in Fiamma's – why don't you tell Ronan we will be there after we freshen up?"

Suzanne hesitated. She wasn't sure if she had the nerve – she was exhausted and excited after the flight – she wanted to look her best and be in the right frame of mind before seeing him. Seventeen years was a long time and she wanted him to think of her in the same way as he had before he left for America. But if she didn't call she wouldn't get to see him.

His phone went straight to voicemail.

Hi Ronan – Suzanne here we have a table booked in Fiamma's for 8 if you want to join us? Or I could meet you first for a drink on our own? Give me a call.

Suzanne hung up and went into the bathroom. She would have a shower and do everything she could to make herself as attractive as possible before seeing her old love.

For sure Ronan wanted to see her on her own. He didn't want to play gooseberry on a lover's holiday in Vegas. How could he have been so foolish as to think that Suzanne would still harbour feelings for him after seventeen years? He hadn't even bothered to finish with her. He was so consumed with his new life in Boston and all the fun of college and it was a different world to Dublin. She had been inconsolable as he left from Dublin Airport. Her mother had told her not to go to say goodbye – she was such a strange woman and had done everything in her power to put obstacles between them and their relationship. Ronan had been relieved to be away from all of that tension when he arrived in America and the mothers of the girls that he dated there didn't seem to care what time their daughters came home or where he took them. It was a different world, filled with hurly-burly, and he did love it and although he didn't find it easy to forget about Suzanne all the distractions of the new country did help. There was no future for them and at such a young age he knew it. He did wonder what might have been if he had stayed in Ireland though. He would never know.

But what had he to lose by phoning her now? They could meet – have a drink for old times' sake – and then he would spend any leisure time he had for the rest of the week as he had originally planned with all his computer-geek friends in the strip joints and casinos.

He dialled her number and waited.

"Hello? Ronan, is that you?"

Ronan paused – her voice sounded exactly the same as it had when he last spoke to her over seventeen years ago.

"Yes, Suzanne – hi – how was your flight?"

"Good thanks – we aren't long in – it's amazing – this hotel is so huge!"

"Yeah, the MGM is big – I'm very close to you in the Signature – there's a walkway that connects the two hotels. I'd love to meet for that drink if that's okay with you?"

"Oh great – I didn't know if you would have to go to work or meet some colleagues. How are you fixed now?"

Ronan looked down at the towel around his waist. "I could meet you in twenty minutes."

"Great! You can join us for dinner after."

Ronan stammered. "I, eh, don't want to impose."

"Honestly, Eddie won't mind at all – he's dying to meet you – I told him all about you!"

Ronan was taken aback – this was obviously a very secure and happy relationship if her boyfriend didn't mind her contacting old boyfriends. It made it even worse.

"Look, I do have to meet someone later," he lied. "But I'll see you at the bar in Fiamma's in twenty minutes, okay?"

Suzanne didn't want to show how disappointed she was, so she tried to keep her tone light. "Okay then, Ronan, see you in twenty minutes."

"See you then, Suzanne." He hung up.

He was thrown after hearing her voice – it felt so strange to think that she was so near and in a few minutes he would actually see her. But maybe this wasn't going to be the thrilling trip to Vegas he had hoped for after he discovered that Suzanne was going to be here.

Eddie could read the disappointment in her face as she hung up.

"Ahh – what's wrong?"

"He's a bit standoffish – I was hoping he would want to eat with us – he said that he would have a quick drink but then he had to meet someone."

Eddie rushed over and gave her a hard hug. "Poor Sue – look, we're all going to be here for a few days – this is only the first night!"

Suzanne slumped down onto the bed. She was perfectly groomed after her shower and applying fresh make-up and suddenly felt like she had overdone it!

"What was I thinking of? We only had a couple of emails – his marriage has just broken up – why would he want to see me really? It's one thing flirting in an email but another thing when that person is thrust upon you."

Eddie sat down beside her and gently pushed a strand of hair that had fallen over her face back behind her ear. "Go and see him.

When he sees how beautiful you still are, he will fall in love with you all over again."

Suzanne put her head into her hands. "Eddie – I can't go on deluding myself. My life is so miserable – here I am in Vegas running after a man I dated seventeen years ago who doesn't know me any more and I don't know him. I'm sad – that's what I am!"

"Stop that right now!" Eddie commanded. "You're my beautiful friend and we are going to have the time of our lives in this fabulous town."

He squeezed her tightly and she smiled. He truly was the best friend in the world.

Suzanne got up and went into the bathroom to put on her face. She had planned what she was going to wear before leaving Dublin but somehow had misjudged how warm it would be in Vegas. Although the air steward had warned her on disembarking that Las Vegas got chilly in the evenings this time of year!

It wouldn't do to be too glamorous for a first meeting. She decided to go with a simple red dress and pair of black boots. She would need a cardigan for later so she threw a black cashmere one over her arm. She ran a brush through her hair and applied another layer of lipstick. She was ready.

Eddie took a step back as she stepped out of the bathroom.

"You look stunning!"

Suzanne smiled shyly. "Thanks, Eddie – you always know how to make me feel better! See you down in the restaurant in half an hour."

She picked up her bag and slipped it on to her shoulder. She was ready to meet the man who had made the greatest impact on her life. She had always known deep down that this day would come but never dared to dream of the consequences or outcome. She wasn't certain what she wanted from the meeting but there were hurts that needed addressing and maybe they would get put to rest.

The lift seemed to take forever and stopped at every floor. It was enormous – like everything else in the hotel – including the spacious rooms.

When she stepped out of the lift she had to take a look around to get her bearings.

"Here, you can use this, honey – you're gonna need it!" A tall Texan with a Stetson and southern drawl handed her a map of the hotel.

Suzanne smiled up at him – such a kind gesture from a stranger. "Thank you," she said, taking the sheet.

She scanned the page for Fiamma Trattoria – it was only around the corner and through a parade of slot machines. The theatre for the *CSI Miami* spectacle was across the way and a host of eateries in a massive food hall. She slowed down as she approached the sign for Fiamma. It was very appealing and sophisticated and she went up to the maitre d' who looked like she had stepped out of the pages of *Elle* magazine.

"Hi there – do you have a reservation?" she asked, showing beautiful white teeth.

"Eh yes, but I'm meeting my friend for a drink at the bar first."

"Sure, would you like to see a menu?"

"No, thanks," she said, looking over the girl's shoulder and spotting Ronan in the distance. He was sitting up on a high stool with his right arm leaning on the bar and one eye on people passing by. Suzanne was out of his line of vision and she enjoyed being able to look at him without being seen. She surveyed his jeans and sporty polo shirt. His hair was cut very short and peppered with grey but his face hadn't changed at all. He was exactly as she had left him at Dublin Airport all those years ago.

She braced herself before walking over to him. Her heart pounded loudly and the blood pumped through her veins. It was the moment she had dreamed of and dreaded for so long careering towards her like a freight train. She was almost upon him when he swung around on the stool and caught his first glimpse of her.

"Suzanne!" he exclaimed, jumping to his feet. "Wow – you look fantastic!"

He reached out to give her a hug and wrapped his arms around her.

She responded by squeezing his biceps and kissing his cheek.

"Ronan – it's been a long time."

He was beaming and took a step back to sit on the stool. He called the bartender over.

"Here, let me get you a drink – you haven't changed a bit, Suzanne – I can't believe it – how many years?"

Seventeen years, six months and twenty-three days – she said to herself. She had worked it out – it wasn't difficult to keep a calculation of those terrible days that passed after he went to America.

"Oh, it must be about seventeen years, I guess," she said smilingly.

The bartender came over and asked her what she would like.

"Just a pineapple juice, please."

Ronan nodded to the bartender who was in full body paint as the Incredible Hulk.

"This town goes crazy at Halloween!" Ronan said with a grin.

"I've noticed," Suzanne said. "Fred and Wilma Flintstone passed by over at the slot machines."

"And it will get worse over the next two days – Fremont Street goes crazy! It's a place downtown – anyway, enough of that. Tell me everything – it's been so good getting back in touch."

Suzanne rested her left arm on the bar and ran her fingers through her hair.

"Well, I don't know where to start really – still living at home – it hasn't been easy with Mum sick."

Ronan shook his head. "That is so tough – I'm really sorry to hear about her." He hated the woman but he wouldn't wish Alzheimer's on anyone.

"And I love my job – kids are great to work with. I have good friends and Dublin for all its faults isn't the worst place in the world to live. How have you been – it must be hard for you going through your divorce?"

Ronan winced. He wasn't sure how he was going to describe his situation – it was easier to lie. "Yes, it's been tough, but Laura is gone now and we both need to move on. So tell me about your boyfriend?"

Suzanne looked at him in confusion. "My boyfriend?" Then the penny dropped. "Oh, you think Eddie is my boyfriend?"

"Is he not?" said Ronan, hope dawning.

Suzanne let out a little giggle. "Eddie isn't my boyfriend – he's just a friend. Actually there is more chance of him fancying you than me if you know what I mean!"

Ronan laughed out loud. What a relief! "Oh, I thought as you were on holiday together that you were in some sort of relationship."

"Eddie is a godsend. He is such a support, especially when it comes to Mum."

Ronan looked at her beautiful blue eyes that turned sad when she mentioned her mother. He only realised now what a huge influence and force Mary Quinn had been on her daughter's life – how it might have been if she had a different mother. Probably no different for them, as fate had sent him to America, but he couldn't help sensing that Suzanne's life had been restricted or thwarted in some way.

"What time are you meeting your friend?" she asked, while looking at her watch. She didn't want the time to go so quickly.

"Actually, I was thinking, if that offer of dinner is still on I would love to join you and meet the famous Eddie."

Suzanne beamed. "That would be fantastic."

"I can cancel that meeting – I'll be spending plenty of time with the software people over the next few days!" He looked dolefully at her – searching for the seeds of love in her eyes. Only now that she was in front of him were the warm comfortable feelings of home and Ireland and the past flooding back and put into a real perspective.

Suzanne smiled. She would hopefully have plenty of opportunities to get to know Ronan better. It was long overdue and somehow it felt so right.

Eddie looked down at his phone. He had been anticipating a text message at least by now. His boyfriend was more than surprised that he had packed his bags and decided to hit Vegas. It was very mischievous but that was Eddie's style and put him in a position of power again in a relationship where he had been feeling hopeless. He waded though the crowds of bodies putting money into slots and chucking chips on the green tables. The excitement was palpable in the air. This was a busy time for gambling by all accounts and the majestic lion and two lionesses were almost unnoticed behind that glass panel where they strutted and surveyed the madness.

Eddie went over to take a look. One of the lionesses was chewing on a massive chunk of raw meat. It was bizarre – the whole setting – and yet it was perfectly normal for Vegas. Suddenly his phone went bleep and he looked down to see the message. He smiled. Maybe it wasn't too late!

He quickened his pace as he saw the Trattoria in the distance, hoping Ronan and Suzanne had hit it off. He didn't have to worry. As he approached the maitre d' he spotted Suzanne out of the corner of his eye, engrossed in conversation with a smart-looking guy up at the bar. He wasn't Eddie's type by any means but he did look good at Suzanne's side. Things were obviously going well.

Eddie strode over to Suzanne who didn't see him until he was right at her side.

"Eddie," she beamed. "Eddie, this is Ronan."

Eddie held out his hand. "Pleased to meet you, Ronan."

"Delighted to meet you too – I hope you don't mind if I join you for dinner?"

"Of course not – it will be great to get to know each other."

Eddie had to contain his own excitement. If dinner went well this pair of lovebirds would be only delighted if he skipped off later.

The waiter was wearing a black shirt and trousers and he came over to them with three large menus.

"Would you like to take your table?" he asked.

"Yes, please," Eddie replied, taking the menu from the waiter's hand.

The three walked over to a corner table surrounded by chocolate-brown leather seating. The styling was ultra-trendy and minimal with elegant lines of dark wood swirling over burnt-orange walls. Each table was lit by a tiny candle in glass and a huge modern lampshade made of spiky cane hung from the ceiling. It was categorised as Italian cuisine but you could have any range of European dishes that you liked from the menu.

"Oh, the sea bass looks good," Eddie said as he scanned the menu.

"The speciality of course is the slow-cooked steak. The meat will just melt in your mouth," Ronan informed them.

"Have you been here before?" Suzanne asked.

"I have – a couple of times. I usually stay at the Signature – it's linked to this hotel but it's not on The Strip."

"I had no idea that Las Vegas was such a big city for conferences and shows."

"You better believe it," Ronan said. "It's the best junket for anyone working in the States. The Americans don't travel, you see, so this is the only chance for many of them to get to see the Eiffel Tower!"

Suzanne smiled. Ronan had become so Americanised and he probably didn't even realise it himself. She didn't mind – there was still enough of the old Ronan to make her feel comfortable and relaxed.

"I can't wait to see The Strip," she said. "I've been doing my homework and I spotted the Statue of Liberty across the road as our taxi pulled in."

"Yeah – you're beside everything here – Caesar's Palace and the Bellagio are a short walk over the road. You only have to walk outside the MGM to see Paris Hotel and Planet Hollywood. How many days in total will you be staying?"

"Just five," Suzanne answered. "Will we get to see enough?"

"You will never get to see all of Vegas – there's just so much. That's why people keep coming back. Have you decided what you would like to order?"

"There's too much choice," Suzanne sighed. "You choose – I eat everything."

Already Eddie was beginning to feel left out of the action and that suited him fine.

"Excuse me while I run to the toilet," he said getting up.

"What will we order for you?" Suzanne asked.

"The crab rolls and sea bass – back in a mo!"

He had his phone out of his pocket before he reached the bathroom. There had to be a message. He checked his emails – only two from his friends at home – nothing from the one person that he really wanted to hear from. He was feeling uneasy. He would just have to send him another message and hopefully he would get the reply that he wanted.

Once they were alone again Ronan and Suzanne sank into the past.

"It's so strange to be here with you – yet it feels like only yesterday since I saw you. How can that be?" Suzanne asked.

"Time has a habit of surprising you – or so I've found over the years. I can't believe that I'll be thirty-seven soon."

"The 15th of November." She had blurted it out before she even realised she had said it.

"Wow – I'm impressed. You have some memory, Suzanne."

Suzanne smiled. "I don't remember everyone's birthday – but I always remember dates around you for some reason." There – she had hinted at her secret.

He hadn't reacted – he hadn't a clue of all that she had been through after he left for America. Part of her was aching to tell him but it had to be under the correct circumstances and it was too soon. They had to get to know each other again first.

"Your birthday's in the summer – July, am I right?" he said.

"Very good – the 14th!"

"Bastille Day – of course – sorry, I should have remembered."

Suzanne gave a little laugh. "It's okay – my own brother can never remember my birthday – he can't even remember my mum's. Mind you, she can't either."

Ronan watched Suzanne's expression change the minute that she mentioned her mother. Mary Quinn still had that hold on her daughter – it was obvious. Suzanne didn't need to explain or say a word. She had been trapped in the same way as she had been controlled by the woman. It was obvious.

"How is Leo?"

"Leo is still Leo. You remember how much he liked to do his own thing. He wasn't too happy about minding Mum while I came away with Eddie."

"It sounds like you have shouldered all of the responsibility of your mum since she became ill?"

Suzanne nodded. "It hasn't been easy – it's difficult to explain. In some ways she is easier to live with now than when she was *compos mentis*. But yes – it's the responsibility that is daunting at times. And it does limit lots of decisions that I make."

"What about work – how do you manage that?"

Suzanne took a deep breath and rested her elbows on the table. "Ah, work? I used to work full-time of course – I love my job – kids especially are great to work with. It's so rewarding watching them bounce back to life so easily after an injury. If I hadn't dropped back to job share, I would be a manager now. Everything would be different."

It was the sadness in her eyes as she spoke that really reached out to Ronan. He took her hand and held it for a moment, neither feeling the need to speak. They barely noticed Eddie's return to the table.

As Eddie sat down Ronan took his hand away.

"My God, this place is so big! Even the bathrooms could house a few families!"

"We haven't ordered yet – sorry!" Ronan said.

"That's fine," Eddie grinned. "You know, I was thinking of taking a little wander around The Strip by myself after dinner if you two want to do more catching up. I have Suzanne all the time at home – I don't want to be greedy!" he said with a cheeky wink.

Suzanne felt uncomfortable but Ronan just smiled gratefully at her friend. He was thrilled and entranced by Suzanne and wanted to spend as much time as possible with her.

"Where will you go?" Suzanne asked.

"There is so much to do . . . but, anyway . . ." Eddie looked at his watch, "seeing as it's coming up to 4 a.m. back home I don't think I'll last much longer!"

"Did you guys get to sleep on the plane?"

"Suzanne did. But I just can't sleep sitting up – I have to be horizontal! Now, have we chosen from the wine list?" As he lifted the wine list his phone rang and he picked it up. He could see who was at the other end of the line. "Excuse me!" he said hurriedly to Ronan and Suzanne and slipped out of his seat.

Ronan glanced over at Suzanne with his eyebrows raised as Eddie hurried off.

"I have no idea!" she said with a shake of her head.

"Why don't you pick the wine?" Ronan suggested.

"I usually buy the house wine when I'm in a restaurant."

"You won't go wrong here – the quality is superb. Which do you prefer? Red or white?"

"I don't mind but usually I drink white at home."

"Okay. I see a nice Sancerre here."

Suzanne watched Ronan the man order the wine from the waiter. They were only kids when they had parted. It was a different time and neither of them had done very much in life. Now she could see that Ronan the man was very different to the boy she had dated. He had lived a lifetime since they had been apart and she had to keep reminding herself of this because he wasn't her Ronan any more and she didn't want to be disappointed if he didn't have any notions of romance.

Chapter 12

*When you were born, you cried
and the world rejoiced.
Live your life so that when you die,
the world cries and you rejoice.*

~ White Elk ~

"I'm going to bed, Mum," Tina said and she gave her mother a kiss on the cheek.

Vicky was happy. She had made love to Frank earlier and now there was the comfort of her daughter's return. All was well in her world for the moment and she could go and enjoy her evening in peace.

"But what are you going to do for food, darling – will I ring room service?"

"Honestly, I'm exhausted – I'll be fine. If I get hungry I'll ring them myself."

Her cheeks had a rosy glow and she looked positively healthy and happy. It had been years since Vicky had seen her like this and she had to admit that Kyle was showing her daughter how to enjoy herself!

"Okay but ring me if you get lonely!"

"I will – but, Mum, you'll be in a theatre."

Vicky stalled at the door. "I'll keep checking my texts. Have a good sleep, pet."

She would. All she had to do was get her mum to go!

When Tina was sure that her mother had closed the door behind her she grabbed her phone and texted furiously. She couldn't wait. Kyle was waiting for her to give him the all clear. It was too exciting. Having a hotel room all to themselves! They could do anything they wanted and she already knew exactly what she wanted to do. She had been with guys before but never to go 'all the way'. For some reason she had been saving herself and she realised now exactly why.

She sent the text to Kyle's phone.

Mum gone – come up to room 2734.

She ran into the bathroom to see how she looked. Her face was sun-kissed and her hair was all over the place. Her make-up had worn off and she looked shattered. But inside she was exhilarated and thrilled and it was all because of Kyle.

The theatre in the Bellagio was enormous – easily bigger than the O2 in Dublin – and had all the decoration and opulence of a grand theatre in Paris. Vicky was in awe that this was just one theatre in a series of many others along The Strip. She had organised Garth Brooks tickets as a special treat for Monday night in the Wynn Auditorium – their last night before their big day and on that occasion she wanted to be with Frank on her own.

"These are our seats," Connie clucked with delight. "Right, you go in there, Frank, and Vicky beside you." She handed John his ticket – making sure that he was at the end of the aisle beside her.

John was aware where Connie was going with this but he didn't want to offend and sat down beside her graciously. He had been at other Cirque du Soleil shows but had heard this was something special.

The theatre went dark and the audience mumbled quietly in anticipation. Suddenly the sound of dripping came over the speakers. Frank felt his neck to see if it was actually coming from the ceiling. The show had begun as acrobats started their graceful performance in the rafters. Along the aisles clowns appeared holding umbrellas with huge holes in them.

Connie was buzzing with excitement and watching the faces of her guests with relish. John was absorbed, his eyes fixed on the clowns as they danced between the rows of the seated crowd. Just like everyone else who was enjoying the show for the first time.

The long red drapes lifted to reveal a massive set. A thin layer of water covered the stage as the clowns splashed and danced across it. Suddenly pairs of feet erupted from the centre of the stage and fantastic surreal characters in zebra costumes and long red coats danced along the edge of the pool.

There was so much on view that Vicky found it difficult to take it all in. She looked over at John who was drinking in the music – his foot tapping to the cacophony of unusual sounds and drumbeats. Then she looked at her future husband who was busily trying to send a text message. How could he be so preoccupied?

She nudged him – angry inside at the sly way that he was trying to conceal what he was doing.

Frank nodded and slipped his phone into his pocket. He couldn't focus on the stage. There was too much going on inside his head. He slid into a kind of trance – it was easier like that. The surreal dancers throwing their bodies through the air were not half as difficult to believe as the text that he had just received. His life couldn't get more complicated – he hoped!

Kyle knocked gently on the door.

"Who is it?" Tina whispered – just to be sure that it was him.

"Kyle."

She melted at the mention of his name.

As the door opened he slipped inside the room.

She shut it quickly and stood still – just looking up at him.

She was unable to speak. The anticipation of what she was about to do was too much for her.

Kyle didn't waste any time. He wanted her. From the moment of the special connection they had shared in Red Rock Canyon if he was to be honest. This was the moment he had been waiting for all day. He leaned forward to kiss her and she responded.

She hoped that he knew what to do. Her couple of sexual encounters had been abysmal and ended with her chickening out before going through with the act. But she knew that wouldn't happen this time. Now she was ready.

John was watching Vicky and Frank out of the corner of his eye. Connie had him pinned against the wall as they trudged through the crowded theatre exit. He really wanted to dodge her politely and return to his room for the night.

Frank was tetchy and fidgety but John knew that this mess was one that his older brother would have to sort out himself and the best thing he could do was leave him to it.

"I think I'll hit the sack, Connie – if you don't mind," he said.

Connie was disappointed and tried to hide it graciously. "Of course you guys are still on Irish time."

"The show was great. Thanks for organising it," he said with a smile.

Connie moved forward – hoping for a goodnight kiss. But it was clear that it was not going to happen as John subtly moved back a little.

"Take care, Connie," he said and started to walk out of the Bellagio.

"John!" he heard from behind him.

He turned around as Frank ran up to him.

"John, I need you to say that you're coming gambling with me," he muttered. "I want to go to the high-rollers suite in the MGM."

"You'll have to go alone," John said and continued walking.

The reception area was thronged with people leaving the show and others bustling in to get to the casino and The Bank, which was a hotspot club at the back of the casino.

Frank kept in step with John. "Please say you're coming with me!"

"Gambling money that you don't have," John said curtly. "Come on, don't try and fool me – I know how bad things have been over the last few months – years, to be honest. You're on your own, Frank. I'm off to bed."

Frank was a man in distress. He really needed to go to the casino.

Connie went over to Vicky. She felt suddenly very embarrassed. "I'd better get home too – Kyle will be back. We'll talk tomorrow." She gave Vicky a kiss on the cheek and made for the exit, brushing past John and Frank who were still in conversation. "Talk tomorrow, Frank – I'll let you two love birds get on with enjoying the night."

Connie kept her dignity and strode out the door towards the car attendants.

All Vicky could do was to follow the men, speechless.

Frank turned around. "Do you want me to walk you back to the Mirage?" he asked.

Vicky was beyond words. "I can't believe you're even asking that question!"

"I thought you were keen to check on Tina?"

Vicky couldn't handle much more. She stomped away with her temper just about intact but without saying goodbye.

Tina shivered as she stepped out of the bed.

Kyle pulled at her bare leg playfully.

"Don't go!" he called.

"I have to," she teased. She needed to pee. A part of her was anxious – she had just had unprotected sex and she felt that if she went to the toilet some of the sperm would get washed away. She didn't regret what she had just done but she didn't want to be pregnant. It had all happened exactly the way that she had dreamed it would. She didn't come when he was making love to her but somehow he knew what to do to make her come after by using his hands and that had never happened before. She had released herself as she came and given herself to him truly. She'd only known him a little over twenty-four hours but already he knew her better than any man on the planet and that felt wonderful.

When she returned from the bathroom she carried a towel to cover her bare skin.

"Don't cover up." Kyle said. "I want to see you."

Tina let the towel drop and exposed her nakedness – she couldn't believe she was doing it.

Kyle stared. "I'm the luckiest guy in Vegas."

Tina felt beautiful. She was endowed with a confidence that she didn't know she had before setting off from Ireland. Kyle was the one person who had given her the right to be herself and she wanted to hug him for it.

"Come on, get back into bed quickly!" He was ready to make love to her all over again.

She slid under the covers and let him run his fingertips up and down her stomach.

"Have you had many girls?" She needed to know and was ready to hear the answer.

Kyle stopped moving his hand. "I had a girlfriend in high school for ten months. I did have other girls that I kinda dated but she was my main one. And you?"

Tina desperately wanted him to know that he was the one – the first. He was special. She shook her head. "I have had boyfriends but you're my first real one."

Kyle gasped. His heart pounded. He had wondered but that information blew him away. Then it struck him.

"You're not using the contraceptive pill?" His voice trembled. "I just thought that you would have said . . ."

Tina felt foolish and naïve as she shook her head. What sort of a dumb school kid must he think she is?

"I can get the morning-after pill – can't I?"

Kyle nodded. "Sure, we can go to the drugstore in the morning. Gee, I'm sorry, I would have used something."

"I'm glad you didn't." Tina knew that what she was saying was silly and naïve but she meant it. She had always wanted her first time to be spontaneous and natural and that was how it had been and she didn't regret a thing.

At that moment he leaned forward and pressed his lips hard against hers. He stopped for a moment.

"Why do you have to live in Ireland!" he said, his dark eyes penetrating right into hers and reaching into her soul.

"I wish I didn't – I wish I lived here."

Kyle leaned forward and kissed her deeply. He was pouring his heart and soul into this girl. He didn't want her to go back to Ireland – they had something special.

"You're here now and that is all that matters," he said and kissed her again.

Vicky gulped back the tears. Standing in a lift on her own was not where she wanted to be. She looked down at her watch. It was ten past one in the morning. She was so angry inside and couldn't even manage to show her true emotions to Frank. If she wasn't able to articulate how she felt before she got married, how was she going to be able to do it after the event?

Things like this had never bothered her before. Frank frequently went gambling with his chef friends and clients to the casino on Dawson Street after work and it had never bothered her. But she had just wanted this experience to be special and all she felt was let down and deserted. Why couldn't he be like his brother John and just call it a night?

To avoid a scene she had swallowed her anger with Frank. She did want to see Tina if truth were told but she didn't want Frank telling her that she should learn to let go. She'd had eighteen years practically on her own, bringing her daughter up. David had left all of the disciplining and childrearing to her, until he left when Tina was just twelve. Tina had been her sole responsibility since then and sometimes it was that closeness that suffocated Vicky. Tina's dad was there but he was in essence a child himself. She had been dreaming of the freedom that would come when Tina reached eighteen. Of course that never happened. When Tina turned eighteen she was exactly the same as when she was seventeen and probably would continue to be dependent on her emotionally and financially until she was well into her twenties. Maybe it was because she was an only child – or maybe it was her way of trying to make it up to her daughter for their being on their own.

Either way Vicky wanted to check that Tina was tucked up safely and sound asleep. She opened the door of the suite and the lights came on. She went over to the connecting doors and turned the handle but it was locked from the other side. She tried again, then took the spare room key and walked out into the corridor. She put the key in the lock and opened the door. It was very quiet in the room and the light was still on. She could see a figure curled up in the bed. She stepped forward very slowly and stopped in shock and horror at the end of the bed when she realised that Tina was not on her own. Curled up at her daughter's side, spooned beside her, was Connie's son – sound asleep.

She trembled inside as she spotted their clothes lying on the floor beside the bed. What could she do? This was the most awful abuse of trust. How could Tina be such a little slut? She moved over to her daughter and shook her hard.

"Tina – what the hell do you think you're doing?" Her voice was loud enough to be a scream. *"Get up!"*

Kyle moved first. He looked around and shrieked with shock on seeing Vicky. He pulled the sheet up over his nakedness, then jumped out of the bed and dressed with the speed and alacrity of a cartoon character.

Tina was now awake too. She trembled on seeing her mother's fury – she had never known her to be like this – not even after she got the last tattoo.

"I would move it very quickly if I were you!" Vicky glared at Kyle.

Kyle grabbed his jacket and keys and ran for the door. "I'll call you," he said to Tina on his way out.

Vicky ran after him to make sure that he was going down the corridor towards the lift.

"Don't even think about it!" she shouted after him.

When she came back Tina was lying still and flat on the bed and staring blankly up at the ceiling.

"What the hell did you think you were doing?"

Tina didn't want to answer. She had nothing to say to her mother. She didn't regret what she had done. Anyway she was eighteen and perfectly within her rights as an adult.

"I don't want you to see that boy again for the rest of the holiday – or ever!" Vicky was in tantrum mode now. "I can't believe what you just did and you don't even know him!" Suddenly she thought of another scenario and her mouth dropped. "Oh my god, you could be pregnant – don't you dare tell me that you're pregnant. I will not be looking after any baby that you bring home!"

Tina was sick inside by now. She remained staring at the ceiling, waiting for her mother's rant to be over.

"Just don't leave my sight from now on – is that clear?"

Tina didn't hear the rest of the words as they fell from her mother's lips. She was turned off and on a different vibration.

When Vicky had left through the now unlocked dividing doors, she reached for her phone and texted Kyle. She'd had enough. She couldn't take it any longer. She didn't care if she never finished her Leaving Cert or went to college. She had to get away from her mother. She would leave tonight.

Kyle was downstairs waiting for her call. He knew that he would hear from her. He had seen Vicky in action first hand now and didn't want to leave the girl that he loved anywhere near the psychotic woman. He replied swiftly by text.

Get ur stuff am in car.

It was all she needed to know. As quietly as she could she put essential toiletries and a change of clothes into her beach bag and got dressed. She would be downstairs before Vicky realised that she was missing.

She suddenly remembered her passport and phone charger and grabbed them out of the safe. Her head was all over the place but she had to get out and quickly. Her heart pounded. What she was doing was wrong but to stay would be worse. It was all her mother's fault anyway. She had been desperately unhappy since her mum had started seeing Frank, so this was her just desserts.

Tina pushed past the gamblers who were playing craps and roulette – she knew exactly where he would be. It was so wonderful to feel that she wasn't only escaping from the toxic relationship that she shared with her mother but she was heading off on an adventure and she didn't know where – yet.

Kyle had the engine of his SUV running and he took off the minute she jumped in. They didn't speak but he put his right hand on her left thigh and held it tightly as he careered down The Strip.

"Where are we going?" she asked.

"We can't go to my place – your mom will ring mine as soon as she discovers that you're gone!"

"I have no money!" Tina gasped as she realised what she had done.

"Hey, I have sleeping bags and a tent in the back of the car. The guys often go out to the desert to camp! At least we used to."

Tina's eyes widened – she felt so safe and protected in Kyle's company. He could take her anywhere and she would be fine.

Vicky lay in her nightdress trying to read her novel. She really wanted Frank to be there. He would be some sort of support. She probably shouldn't have brought Tina to Vegas – she really would have been better off with her father. She eventually dozed off but her sleep was restless and erratic.

She woke to find the light from the bedside lamp blaring into her eyes and turned expecting to find Frank at her side. He was nowhere to be seen. She looked down at her watch.

It was 4 a.m.

Where could he be until this time?

She got up to check on Tina and opened the dividing doors. Tina's room was dark and her figure motionless in the bed. Vicky went over to observe her more closely. When she realised that the shape was made by a bundle of clothes she cried out. She looked around the room and saw the safe was open. It was empty. Tina had taken her passport.

Vicky sat on the edge of the bed and put her head into her hands and sobbed. Now she had a runaway daughter and a husband-to-be that had been missing for hours. She desperately needed help. She rang Frank but his phone went straight to voicemail. She didn't want to disturb John – she didn't know him well enough either. But who else could she turn to? She decided to call his room. She regretted it the moment the phone was answered and John's groggy voice said hello.

But she was desperate.

"Please, John, Tina has gone missing and Frank hasn't come back yet."

John rubbed his eyes and yawned. "What time is it?" he mumbled.

"It's four o'clock. I'm so sorry to disturb you."

John didn't sound too concerned. "Say it again – who's missing?"

"Tina – I called into her when I came up from the show and she was in bed with that kid."

John was pleased that Tina was having a good time. She was eighteen after all. But he recognised the panic in Vicky's voice and the sense of despair.

"She has probably gone off in a huff," he said. "She'll be back in the morning."

Vicky wasn't so sure. "I need to find Frank – did he say where he was going to be?"

"Look, I'll help you find him. Give me five minutes while I get dressed."

"Oh thank you, John – I'm going out of my mind."

John paused for a moment before hanging up. "Hey, maybe Connie will be able to say if her kid came home last night – at least then we'll know if she's with him."

Vicky sighed loudly. "John, you're a genius – I'll do that now."

John dressed and thought about the best way to approach this. Frank was going to be in the MGM and he wouldn't be much use to their cause at this stage anyway. He knew what his brother was like in stressful situations – he would undoubtedly make matters worse. Still, he had a duty to support his future sister-in-law.

John rang Frank's mobile but it went straight to voicemail. He wondered if his battery was down or if he had turned it off – his gut told him the latter.

He went out to the corridor and knocked on the door of Vicky's suite.

The fear was etched across her face as he entered the room.

"Oh John!" she cried and felt his arms slip around her comfortingly.

"Are you ready to go?"

She nodded. "Can you get Frank on his mobile?"

He shook his head.

"I can't either," she said. "Did he tell you which casino he would be in?"

"He said the MGM Grand."

"Okay, let's go there." She grabbed her bag and jacket and they left.

"Did you ring Connie?" John asked as they paced down the corridor to the lift.

"Yes, and Kyle hasn't been home all night – poor Connie is concerned now – although something tells me she's not in the same state as I am! She said some crazy stuff about him camping in the desert with his friends and that they'll be fine."

"He knows the city and he has a car," he assured her. "Wait and you'll see they'll be back in the morning."

Vicky couldn't wait until the morning. She needed her daughter and Frank back now.

Frank was listening to the words gushing out of Vicky's mouth but he really didn't know what to say.

"Have you rung the police?" he asked.

John shook his head. "They aren't missing persons yet – they've only been gone three hours – maybe less."

Frank put his arm around Vicky. "We can't do anything at this time – why don't we ring in the morning?"

Vicky had thought she would feel better now that she had Frank by her side but instead she was just more frustrated.

"I don't know why you were sitting here for so long with strangers," she said. "It's our first proper night in the city."

"Sorry, honey – I really should have come back to the room with you. I'll make it up to you tomorrow – I promise." He kissed her forehead.

"Right, I'm off," John said.

He walked away before they could stop him. He had seen the guy that Frank was talking to before – one night in Frank's restaurant – he was sure of it. The guy seemed to recognise him too. John had always suspected but now he knew. This wedding had all the warning signs of a disaster waiting to happen. He considered leaving early and heading off to the Havasupai Lodge. That way he could avoid the fallout. Mind you, if Vicky realised what was going on then she would need someone here for her. She had enough on her plate now that her daughter had gone missing. He owed it to her at least to stay around until Tina was found.

Vicky started to sob as she threw herself down onto the bed.

"It's okay – she'll turn up tomorrow," said Frank as he made his way to the bathroom. "I guarantee it, especially if she doesn't have any money. Kids these days just sponge off their parents so much they wouldn't be able to last."

For once she hoped that Frank's scathing comment was correct. It would mean that she could try and fathom what she had done wrong. Life was so complicated. Why did she feel so alone in the world? Was she overreacting as Frank suggested? Tina was eighteen with no money and not much street sense. Now she had a moody strange guy taking her daughter off to God-knows-where and her future husband was sitting up drinking and gambling with strangers. John was behaving like the only reliable member of their wedding party.

She turned her head on the pillow and closed her eyes. She begged sleep to come and take her away from this nightmare. In her gut she knew that she had brought all of this on herself. If she had a better relationship with her daughter, Tina would not have run away with the first guy to show her serious affection. It was the thought of what might happen that scared her so much. Connie seemed sure that Kyle knew his way around the desert but that wasn't much consolation. She would have to wait until morning to see if there was any word.

And there was something untoward about Frank and the fellow that he was gambling with. They were up to no good – of that she was sure. The way that guy slipped away as soon as she appeared made her uneasy. Frank was a wealthy man but there were some strange dealings going on. A terrible thought crossed her mind – maybe he was dealing in drugs or something else that was illegal. She wondered if she knew her future husband at all!

As Frank slid into the bed beside her she closed her eyes even tighter – she really did not want to be there.

Chapter 13

Those who have one foot in the canoe, and one foot in the boat, are going to fall into the river.

~ Tuscarora proverb ~

Eddie was quite fidgety by the time the text message finally came. It was as he had expected. Suzanne and Ronan were already heading over to the Irish bar in the New York New York hotel. The distance was perfect. He told her that he would see her later in the room. If their night went well hopefully she would go back to the Signature with Ronan. This was the reason he had come and orchestrated the whole plan. He couldn't wait. What was going to happen next?

Ronan and Suzanne giggled like they used to as they walked on the flyover from the MGM Grand to the Hotel New York New York. It was a setting made in heaven with millions of flashing light bulbs and bands of neon sparkling up and down The Strip. From the Pyramid of the Luxor Hotel with its dazzling laser lights all the way past the Statue of Liberty and Eiffel Tower they powered their brilliance as shining homage to man's dazzling creativity.

"It's a bit like being in a crazy virtual computer game – isn't it?"

"Sorry, I lost you there," Suzanne said. "What is?"

"Vegas at night – sometimes I feel like there is so much going on that it cannot be real."

The two paused at the railings and for a moment everything froze in both their worlds. They were in a private cocoon – staring into each other's eyes. Their faces were older, their surroundings unfamiliar, but the connection between them was still there and even more intense than when they were kids.

It was too much for Suzanne to take in. Brain overload and old-boyfriend overload. She might as well be in a show or playing a part in someone else's life because this was not anything like it felt to be Suzanne the Carer as she had lived and breathed since her mother took ill.

She shook herself. "I'm really looking forward to seeing New York – it's my first time!" she giggled.

And although the tension of the moment had been temporarily interrupted, the closeness remained and they set off for Hotel New York New York!

Eddie sat waiting at a roulette table in the MGM Grand. The openers were five dollars so he should get a while out of his one hundred bucks. His lucky number was 18. It was a number that had never let him down.

Eddie swapped his dollars for yellow chips and put five of them down on number 18. The croupier was a tall man with grey hair in his mid-forties. Dressed in a dickie bow and waistcoat he was there to do a job and that was to take Eddie's money. Eddie watched the wheel spin and the tiny silver ball land on 28.

One more try. He put the chips on 18 again. This time his number came up – he had just won over two hundred dollars. Maybe this was his lucky night! He certainly hoped so.

Sitting in the Nine Fine Irishmen Bar in the New York New York, Suzanne and Ronan were catching up on seventeen years of personal history. As each revealed what they had been through, they realised that they had both changed very little.

Suzanne had taken a chance coming to Vegas – she had nothing to lose and she was grateful to Eddie for the way he had set it up so simply for her. Now she was confronting demons that had lurked in her psyche for seventeen years and meeting Ronan had been the right thing to do. The timing was ideal.

While listening to the strains of traditional music, the two were transported back to Dublin. Those were the times when Suzanne had been at her happiest – she'd been so confident that Ronan was the one for her back then. Maybe this was their second chance? If she had found him before this he would have still been married. This was fate – she felt sure of that.

As they at last walked back across the flyover towards the MGM Grand, Ronan was sure of one thing: he didn't want the evening to end. As they came to the foyer of the MGM he paused.

"I don't suppose you fancy playing roulette or blackjack?"

Susan smiled. "Why not – I'm wide awake – can't believe it!"

They strolled through the entrance and made their way past the rows of slots on their way to the green tables.

"I haven't a clue what to do!" Suzanne said as she took a high stool next to Ronan at one of the tables with a low limit.

"Don't worry – it's easy. We just hand over all our money but try and make it last a while before we get cleaned out!" he winked.

Suzanne was enthralled. Ronan the man was strong and safe and even more delicious than Ronan the youth had been. She took a pile of chips from him and he briefed her on the order of the game.

A waitress came over and asked them what they would like.

"Drinks free by the way when you play!" he informed Suzanne.

She was in a spin, giggling and enjoying the night, when out of the corner of her eye she spotted Eddie. He was engrossed in conversation with a dark-haired man at a roulette table about ten metres away. From their body language they seemed to know each other. She took a double take and decided it was best to leave them be. They hadn't seen her and Ronan and maybe it was just as well.

Ronan put his arm around the back of her chair and whispered in her ear. "So we have to get twenty-one . . ."

He spoke on but all Suzanne could digest was the warm and playful affection that he was showing her. She didn't want this night to end. His breath on her ear was so warm. She wanted to feel him closer so she snuggled up next to his chest and he didn't pull away. It was as if they were in a bubble of their own making – holding each other close by an invisible forcefield.

The dealer gave them their cards.

"What does that mean?" she asked Ronan.

"It's good – we have nineteen – a queen and a nine – I think we should stick!"

Suzanne watched as he gambled and played the next three hands, beating the dealer each time. Everything was perfect until Ronan paused and pointed.

"Hey, is that Eddie over there?" he asked.

Eddie was surrounded now by two men and a woman. The woman was waving her arms in the air.

"I wonder what's going on?" Suzanne squinted in disbelief. She watched Eddie stand up and start to walk away. "Maybe I should go and see!"

Ronan gathered up his chips and followed her.

Suzanne couldn't make out what the woman was saying but the tall man at her side was trying to calm her down. The man that Eddie had been talking to was shaking his head and running his fingers through his hair. She hurried past the group, Ronan in her wake, and followed Eddie in the direction of the lifts, leaving the three other people to work out their issues.

"Eddie – what's going on – are you okay?"

Eddie seemed thrown. "Suzanne – I didn't see you. Hi, Ronan. Yeah, they are just some fruitcakes I met playing roulette. I think I'll go up to my room."

Suzanne turned to Ronan. "I think I'll go up too." She was worried about Eddie.

Ronan looked taken aback. "Oh – okay – will I see you tomorrow?"

"Do you have to be at work in the morning?"

"Only for a little while – I can conference call. I'm a couple of days early for the convention. We could meet for breakfast if you like?"

"That would be great – I'll call you. Thanks for a lovely evening."

"I had a great time too," Ronan said. He was sorry to see the night end so abruptly but hoped this was the beginning of an extra-special few days. "Goodnight, Eddie."

Eddie was in some sort of daze. "Yeah – bye."

Suzanne touched Eddie's shoulder to steady him. "Are you drunk?"

Eddie shook his head but she knew that he was.

"Who are those people that you were talking to?" she asked.

Eddie just walked away and Suzanne ran after him. He was behaving totally out of character. "Eddie, have you taken drugs?"

Eddie laughed. "Suzanne – love is the drug!"

"What do you mean?"

"You should have gone up to Ronan's room and had a good time – no need to worry about me – I'm fine."

Suzanne stopped as they came to the lift and put her hands on his shoulders. "Eddie, what is going on?"

Eddie took a deep breath. "You don't really want to know!"

But Suzanne did want to know and she wanted to know now. "Eddie!" she said, only this time more firmly.

"I've just come all the way to Vegas to stop the man I love from making the biggest mistake of his life and he has just told me that he doesn't love me in the same way."

For a moment she thought he was joking but his expression told her he was not.

The lift arrived and they stepped in. They were alone.

"Can you repeat that, please?" Suzanne said. "What did you say?"

"Sue – that was my boyfriend, Frank – and those other people were his brother and his fiancée."

Suzanne could feel her heart thump. It was the most unbelievable way to end the night. She could never have predicted getting on so well with Ronan and she had been so grateful to Eddie, and now she was hearing that the whole trip was planned so that Eddie could meet his boyfriend who had come to Vegas to get married.

Ronan made the trek through the walkway that joined the Signature to the MGM Grand. It was empty and he was in a sort of daze. The night had ended too abruptly for his liking.

He had been excited about meeting Suzanne again but, on a more serious level, had made no presumptions about how he would feel about her. She could have changed so much. It had been such a long time – but she hadn't changed at all. She was as lovely and charming and soft as she had been when they were teenagers. In many ways she had grown into a wonderfully empathetic person but perhaps she had always been and he hadn't appreciated it truly when he was dating her. She and Laura were poles apart. He wondered how his life might have been if he had stayed in Ireland and stayed with Suzanne. Very different – of that he was sure. But the experiences he had enjoyed while spending his young adult years in America were part of what made him who he was today, and he wouldn't change any of that. He had to get it in perspective – they had only spent a few hours together and he couldn't let his emotions take hold of him. Vegas had a habit of transporting people off to a different zone where they believed that anything was possible. That was why it was such a successful venue for him to sell his products. But this development was something totally new for him.

He wasn't sure what he was going to do the next day, but he knew that he wanted Suzanne to be a major part of it. He took the lift up to the stylish suite that awaited him. It was spacious and modern. Exactly the sort of place to bring Suzanne to. He went into the bathroom and brushed his teeth. He looked at his reflection and smiled. What must she really have thought of him? He had changed so much. The crow's feet around his eyes were firmly engraved by Massachusetts sunshine. Suzanne hadn't seemed to mind.

He had to think of something special to do with her tomorrow – he had to think outside the box. Where could he take her to see how she felt about him? He looked into his own eyes and the answer was obvious. He would take her to the Grand Canyon – and he knew the exact place.

Chapter 14

All men were made brothers.
The earth is the mother of all people,
and all people should have equal rights upon it.
You might as well expect the rivers to run backwards
as that any man who was born free should be contented
when penned up and denied liberty to go
where he pleases.

~ Chief Joseph (1840-1904), NEZ PERCE *~*

Tina woke first. She heard a cry and didn't know what it could be. She gasped when she realised that she was in the back of an SUV in the middle of the desert. The noise had probably come from a wild animal. It had been too cold to camp. But snuggled up inside the closed sleeping bag with Kyle curled cosily around her, she had felt safe. It had been one of the best night's sleep in her life.

Kyle was still asleep and she didn't feel the need to wake him. She looked out at the sun rising over the mountains and smiled. It was so beautiful to be able to look forward to blue skies and sunshine almost every day. She wanted to stay here forever. She never wanted to go back to Ireland. She knew now why she had such little interest in the Irish guys that she had kissed before. They were so out of touch with her soul.

Kyle moved a little and then opened his eyes. Immediately he put his arm around her and pulled her into his shoulder.

"You okay?"

She nodded. She was more than okay. She was in heaven. It was a bonding of souls, now that they had run away from her mother.

Kyle knew that his mother would be mad with him too and he decided that it would be best to let her cool down and maybe miss him a little before calling home.

"Hungry?"

She was – starving, and that was something she never felt first thing in the morning.

But she had never felt so exhilarated before either.

"I have some rice cakes and waffles in my duffle," he said as he searched in his bag. He held up a bottle of Sprite like some sort of trophy.

"Oh, I'd love some of that," she sighed.

Kyle opened the bottle and held it to her mouth.

"So what do you want to do today?" he asked.

She didn't care what they did. She just wanted to be with him.

Ronan called the Papillion Tours to organise a helicopter for later that day. Next he had to arrange for a reservation at El Tovar hotel. It was the perfect spot. Maybe a bit ostentatious for a first date – especially when he felt he couldn't even call it a date. But then this felt right. Why couldn't he do something out of character? He had spent his entire married life bending to Laura's rules and doing whatever she had wanted. He hated himself for his lack of drive. He wouldn't let himself be led like that again. From what Suzanne had conveyed to him the night before, she really could do with a special treat.

The operator on the other end of the line was polite and helpful. She organised a pick-up from Las Vegas International at twelve o'clock – they could be in El Tovar by two and have a nice lunch. Then a walk around the National Park and Bright Angel Point. He had been there once before and loved it. Laura wasn't with him that time and he had wished then that she was. But this was going to be a great day – a new adventure with a woman from his past

who only a couple of weeks ago he thought he would never see
again.

As Frank opened his eyes he saw Vicky dialling a number on the
bedside phone. Last night had been a bad dream – he had hoped.
But now in the bright morning light he realised that everything was
caving in on him. He couldn't keep up the charade much longer.
Eddie's arrival in Vegas was surreal. When they were sitting at the
roulette wheel last night, he had lied to Eddie, telling him how
happy he was with Vicky and that this was the right thing for him
to do now. He had made up his mind. He himself would be the
sacrificial lamb. Vicky must never know about the other life he led.
He would give it all up and make things work with her. She needed
him now, especially as she had a daughter who was giving her
nothing but grief. He didn't really worry that anything untoward
had happened to Tina. As far as he was concerned she would be
back before lunchtime. But he had to react appropriately to show
that he cared.

"Are you ringing the police?"

Vicky nodded as the phone was answered.

"Hello," she started. "I want to report my daughter missing."

As Frank watched and listened, she went on and on about the
details of Tina's disappearance. Her face spoke a multitude –
whatever the cop was saying wasn't to her liking. Obviously the
policeman at the other end of the line was thinking the same thing
as everybody else: one spoilt Irish kid who had disappeared with
her boyfriend in tow was no major whodunit. Then Frank gathered
that the cop was promising that he would go over to the boy's
house and interview his parents. When Vicky said that she knew
Kyle's mother, the cop apparently went silent on the other end of
the line. "Hello? Hello?" said Vicky.

Frank hoped that she wouldn't get done for wasting police time.
Vicky's face fell even further when the cop began to speak again.

"Are you okay, honey?" Frank asked supportively as she hung
up.

She nodded but clearly was hugely deflated by the response to her call.

Frank jumped out of the bed. "Come on, we'll get some nice breakfast and do something exciting for the day."

"I can't eat a thing," she said, brushing his comfort aside. "I'm not hungry. Oh God, why did this happen now?"

"Maybe it had to happen at some stage – she's a headstrong girl!"

"What do you mean?" Vicky snapped. "Do you think I have driven her to this?"

Frank was caught unawares. It was exactly what he thought in one way yet he knew, on the other hand, that Tina was very much her own person.

"I'm not saying anything of the sort. Vicky, you have to relax – she's with a guy that knows his way around."

"Some geeky fool who probably shouldn't have a licence. Oh, how I wish we had got married in Dublin!"

Frank let out a little giggle. "Then we would have had my mother to contend with and I don't think you'd have liked that either."

Vicky looked at him in disbelief. "You *do* think this is all me – don't you?"

"I'm just saying you can be a bit paranoid sometimes, Vic. It's what's so sweet about you and why I fell in love with you in the first place."

Vicky had had enough. Frank's attempts to be consoling and supportive were backfiring drastically.

"I'm getting out of here!" she said, grabbing her bag and room key.

"Where are you going?" Frank asked in dismay.

"Just out." She stomped out of the suite, slamming the door behind.

She had no idea where she was going. She just couldn't look at her fiancé. She ran straight for the lift and got in beside a group of guys who looked like they were on a stag. The lift seemed to take an age and when she reached the foyer she stormed past the lush Polynesian reception and walked out onto The Strip. She took a left in the direction of the TI hotel and walked. She didn't care where she was going. She hoped that maybe, just maybe, she would spot her daughter somewhere.

Eddie woke up feeling worse than he had ever felt in his life. It had been a big mistake coming to Vegas. He had made a total fool of himself with Frank. He had arranged the meeting in the MGM so that they could discuss their feelings for each other but it hadn't worked. Frank had been distracted and, Eddie suspected, itching to try his luck on the games tables. He couldn't understand Frank's compulsion to gamble when he had a lover and fiancée in states of high anxiety. Now he wasn't so sure that Frank had ever really liked him. It was a disaster.

Suzanne was already up and walked out of the bathroom with a mock frown on her face. She could never stay mad at Eddie for long and, in this scenario, she felt that she was definitely having the better time. Her feelings had moved quickly from anger and resentment at being used, to pity and affection for her poor misguided friend.

"How do you feel this morning?" she asked.

Eddie was ready to face the music. It really was all his own doing.

"I'm sorry for not coming clean with you, Sue!"

Suzanne smiled. "I guess you should have before we left Dublin. I thought you were trying to get me and Ronan back together!"

"I was!" Eddie protested. "I mean I did – I *do* want that. But, apart from Ronan altogether, I really think it was important for you to come – not just to have a break which you desperately needed but to break out of the trap your life in Dublin has become! But I also came because I thought my boyfriend really loved me! How stupid, huh?"

"Let time settle things down. It was probably a shock for him. Let's try and distract you. What do you want to do today?"

Eddie scratched his head. "Well, I wouldn't mind breakfast for a start. Then I have a good mind to go shopping."

"That sounds like a good idea," Suzanne agreed.

Suddenly her phone rang. She looked at her watch – it was ten o'clock. Her heart pounded with excitement – it was *him*.

"Morning, Suzanne – did you sleep well?"

A brilliant smile erupted across her face, shining brighter than the Nevada sunshine.

"Good morning, Ronan – yes, I did actually. And I'm feeling remarkably awake this morning."

"Okay – that's good!"

"Why?" she asked playfully.

"Because I had something in mind for today if you're free."

"Yes, we are," she said.

Ronan paused. He hadn't planned on including Eddie on the trip to the Canyon.

"Actually, I hoped that you and I could take a trip alone . . ."

Suzanne knew exactly what he meant. She looked guiltily at Eddie. She felt sorry for him. She accepted the fact that he had orchestrated the entire trip for her as well as for his own sake. Things had not worked out for him and now she was going to desert him too.

"I'll just check and see what Eddie wants to do."

Eddie looked up at her and with a flick of his hand gave her his blessing to disappear for the day. "Go – I want to be on my own anyway to shop in peace!"

"Actually, Eddie has plans, so yes – what had you in mind?"

"It's a surprise! Do you think you could be ready by eleven to meet in the foyer of the MGM?"

Suzanne was very sure that she would be ready. "Of course I could. We'll be getting some breakfast first. Do you want to join us?"

"I got some room service – I have a couple of calls to make before we go – see you then?"

"That sounds great – see you then."

"You've gone pink!" Eddie teased as she ended the call.

"Please – give me a break!" She felt her cheeks nonetheless and they were hot.

"One of us may as well be happy!" Eddie said with a shrug.

"Come on, let's go downstairs and get some breakfast. You can ring your boyfriend – what's his name?"

"Frank."

"Is he really getting married?"

Eddie nodded. "He says that he is. I really thought if I came here I could bring him to his senses and get him to be true to himself but he just doesn't want to hear. I've seen so many gay guys get married and have families and then make a mess of other people's lives. He is in complete denial – and now he's told me to leave him alone for the rest of my stay here. I guess I was the one in denial, come to think of it!"

"Does his fiancée realise he has been having an affair?"

"Not a clue," Eddie said, folding his arms. "She doesn't even realise that he's into men. This is the drastic attempt of a man in his forties to play straight and have kids. I would like to have kids – we could adopt!"

Suzanne looked at her friend sadly. It was so unfair – he would make a great dad too. But then she would have made a great mother and that wasn't to be either. It was no wonder that they were bound together as friends. They saw so much in each other that nobody outside their friendship could see.

"Come on, let's go!" she said again.

There really was no simple answer to any of it. She just hoped that, now she had embarked on this rollercoaster ride with Ronan, they would be strong enough to face up to the secrets and hidden hurts that would have to be dealt with at some stage.

Eddie's phone rang and he stopped just as they were about to leave the room. It was an international number – and he knew whose it was. He could feel his stomach churn. But he had to answer.

"Yes."

Suzanne watched his face rise and drop. He was so vulnerable for all his brave talk.

"Okay, I'll see you then." Eddie finished his call.

"Are you okay?" Suzanne was truly worried.

Eddie nodded. "I don't know what he's playing at now but we're meeting after breakfast."

Suzanne hoped that it was okay leaving him alone with his vulnerable heart. But she had no option – this was her chance to deal with the past. It wasn't going to last long and she might never see Ronan again after this trip. But she couldn't help worrying about Eddie – it was in her nature to be a carer now and part of who she was.

"Where are we going to?" Tina asked as Kyle started the car.

"My friend Len – I mentioned him before – he's a Hualapai Indian and we can go stay at his reservation, have a clean-up and decide what we're going to do next. Is that okay?"

Tina nodded her head. "Sounds great! I always wanted to see a reservation."

"It's really good – and Len has a really cool granddad. He says crazy stuff – he really is fun."

Tina was ready for the adventure.

"I texted my mom," said Kyle, "and told her that we were okay – that we were just giving your mom time to cool down."

Tina's mouth dropped. "Did you tell her everything?"

Kyle shook his head. "I didn't need to – she could read between the lines okay! She's mad as heck with me but knows that telling me to come home will only make me stay away longer!"

"Sounds like you've done this before."

He laughed. "Yeah – this isn't the first time I've taken off into the desert. I find it hard to fit into the ordinary. That's why Len is so lucky. He can come out here and be an Indian whenever he wants – or go to school and be like the other kids."

"Don't you want to go to college?"

Kyle shook his head. "I want to play my guitar."

"I haven't heard you play – I really would like to."

Kyle smiled. "Later – Len's granddad always makes me play when I stay with them. They light an open fire at night and sit around it. Even in the winter like it is now!"

"Sounds cool."

"Okay then, let's go!" He leaned over and kissed her on the lips. She was the happiest girl in the world.

"A helicopter!" Suzanne exclaimed. Petrified at the prospect of flying over a fissure taller than the Empire State Building, she was also exhilarated and excited.

"Are you okay with that?" Ronan could sense her anticipation.

"Fine." She smiled nervously.

Ronan laughed. "Would you like me to fly it?"

"Wow – you learned to fly – that's amazing! You will have to tell me about that later!"

A lot had happened in seventeen years and Suzanne was just realising that she had no idea what his life had been like and vice versa.

"Today we are going to be flown by a pilot. I can fly but my licence isn't current and they do like to make a song and dance about red tape over here!"

The propellers whirred in the air and were getting louder as they took each step.

Ronan was ready. He wanted to make Suzanne's time as special as he possibly could. The pilot came over to them and shook their hands.

"Pleased to meet you – I'm Ted and I'll be looking after you today with Gerry."

Gerry waved at them from the cockpit.

Suzanne felt like she'd been transported into a movie set. Ronan took her hand and helped her into the tiny cockpit where Gerry showed her how to fasten her seatbelt.

So much attention and fuss and she hadn't time to think of how her mother was or what her mother would have said about what she was about to do. She had managed to blot her out of her head and she realised that this was probably the first time in her entire life where she had decided to do something that her mother would not approve of and it felt great. Mary had opinions on helicopters – she tolerated airplanes but would never get into a helicopter. That was why this flight was so important for Suzanne.

"Ready, crew?" Ted said with a wink. He was dressed in a white shirt with four gold bars across his shoulders. His tie was black but hung loosely under his open top button.

Ronan reached out and took her hand before take-off. He didn't look at her as both were staring out the window at their own side – but his touch was enough. She was transported up into the air as the chopper flew high above the Las Vegas Strip and the towering skyline that now appeared like tiny models below.

"Refreshments are in the boxes beside you and we estimate our journey time to be one hour and thirty minutes," Captain Ted said.

They followed the straight line of concrete road below that led them out to the desert. They were flying for only a few minutes when Ronan pointed out the Hoover Dam. It was like a tiny piece of Lego stuck in the middle of a rock – holding back a massive pool of deep blue water. Spectacular and awe-inspiring, Suzanne had never seen such an arid and dramatic landscape. It resembled a crumpled brown-paper bag which was used so many times it was torn in places. The tufts of flora sprouted up in spots and then covered large areas like carpet but what amazed her most was the vastness of the wide-open space. It seemed to just go on and on forever. A massive crater in the ground signalled the start of the canyon followed by a tapestry of sculpted rock that danced rhythmically across the landscape.

Captain Ted started to tell them about the pioneering John Wesley Powell who mapped out the canyon back in the nineteenth century but it all went over Suzanne's head. She didn't want or need to know the history. It was so beautiful and desolate, the perfect setting to enjoy having Ronan at her side – holding her hand.

The landscape changed, becoming greener, as they flew into the airport at Grand Canyon National Park.

A car was waiting to pick them up and after they said their goodbyes to Ted and Gerry they drove through the lush pines and sequoias to Bright Angel Point.

Suzanne squeezed Ronan's hand as they came to the village and the car slowed down.

"We are here!" he said with a smile.

Suzanne let the driver open her door and they entered Bright

Angel Lodge – a log cabin with a stone fireplace on one side of the entrance and a coffee and gift shop on the other.

"Come on!" Ronan tugged her hand to go through to the back door. "This is what we came to see."

The lodge was dark and sparsely furnished – more a greeting area that led to the gift shop and coffee dock. Suzanne had no idea what was on the other side of the door and no words could have prepared her.

Ronan proudly presented the view as he opened the door. A narrow pathway with picnic table and a low stone wall stood between them and the Grand Canyon. It was so vast it took Suzanne's breath away.

Ronan enjoyed watching her reaction.

"What do you think?"

"Ronan, it's spectacular."

Ronan put his arm around her shoulder and she rested hers about his waist – both looking straight ahead at the pleated layered rock that resembled a slice of exotic terrine. The vastness of the scenery conveyed endless possibilities and Suzanne felt that anything could happen.

Vicky had lost her bearings. It was hopeless really but at least by walking and searching she felt like she was actually doing something. Then she saw the Encore Hotel and found herself back on The Strip. She went past the Wynn, and walked on in the direction of Venezia Tower and the Venetian which were almost back where she had started. With each step she took she thought of Tina and a niggling little voice inside her head, that sounded remarkably like her mother's, kept saying: *You drove the girl to this. You have made her feel stifled by your fear and turned her into a rebel that you despise. She needs your support now and you have managed to push her away all by yourself. You can't blame David for this.*

And with each step in the warm sunshine she felt more and more ill. Nevertheless she passed her own hotel and walked on as far as the Paris Hotel where she went inside to find a place to buy a bottle of water. It was really picturesque and reminded her of happier times with David when they had stayed for a weekend in Paris. Her mother had minded Tina. It was on her insistence that they had gone. She warned them to put time and effort into their relationship and not focus all of their attention on Tina. Of course Vicky had ignored her advice. Instead Tina became the very centre of her world, at the expense of her relationship with her husband and her career. She drove Tina to every Billy Barry dance class and gymnastic class that she wanted to attend. Tina learned to play the piano up to grade five and rode ponies in a stable that took up every penny of the Children's Allowance. Tina never wanted for a bike, a Baby Born or whatever doll was the flavour of the moment. All the things that she, Vicky, had desired so much as a child instead of a crazy artist mother who would let her sit up past midnight while her painter friends sketched her. All the adult events that she had attended while her friends were doing kiddie things with their families were so painful for Vicky. She had been brought up like an adult and fitted into that world to suit her mother but she made sure that the same thing didn't have to be endured by her daughter. And so Vicky's world always revolved around whatever Tina wanted or needed to do.

She was exhausted with the amount of horrible situations she was imagining for her daughter and went over to the café to buy the water that she so badly needed. The smell of the croissants and delicious pastries made her sick. She couldn't eat – she wouldn't eat until she found Tina.

She drank some water and then walked out onto The Strip and crossed over to the Bellagio. There was no sign of the kids there either. She was frustrated and felt that her walk had served no purpose at all – if anything it had only set her imagination into overdrive. She decided to call John and Frank but hadn't realised that she had left her phone in the hotel room until she searched for it. She was furious with herself for being so stupid.

Back at the Mirage, she rushed up to the room. She flung open the door and called out for Frank and Tina, but there was no reply.

Grabbing her phone from the table beside the bed, she searched for a message or a missed call but there was nothing. She went into the bathroom to see if Frank's swimsuit was still there but it was gone.

She rang him just to check and he told her to come down to the pool where he was swimming with John.

Vicky grabbed her bag and raced down to the pool.

Frank and John were lying there taking the sun.

Frank jumped up immediately and gave her a hug. "Where did you go? We don't want to be looking for two of you! I saw your phone on the locker and thought it best to leave it there. Connie is on her way here."

Vicky nodded. "I just walked around looking for Tina. I feel so helpless – there's absolutely nothing I can do!"

Just then Connie appeared. She was hiding her concern behind a rather strained smile.

Vicky rushed over to her, anxious to hear if she had been in touch with her son.

But the look on Connie's face didn't reassure Vicky.

"Vicky, honey! I have just come from the police station and they say they are not concerned about two kids who are over eighteen. The kids have turned off their phones but their car was seen on the highway. We know that they are out in the desert and possibly heading in the direction of the Indian reservation – I bet they're going to Len, Kyle's friend who lives there."

"Is that far away?"

"About a two-and-a-half-hour drive. Kyle sent me a text message last night and he said that he would call today. I'm so sorry, Vicky – I won't tell you what I'll do when I get my hands on him."

It wasn't much consolation for Vicky. She wanted to see her daughter and quickly. It wasn't Connie's fault but the poor woman was beginning to irritate Vicky immensely.

"If you like I'll ring the station and talk with the police," Frank said, pulling on his trousers. "Put a bit of pressure on them!"

Vicky was in despair. "It's hopeless. You heard what Connie said – the police aren't interested." She realised after she spoke how desperate she sounded. She was beginning to lose confidence in herself and faith in her fiancé. "Can we go out to the Indian reservation?" she asked Connie.

"We could go out there, honey, but we can't drag them home."

"Just watch me!" said Vicky.

John had been pretending to be intent on his book up to this point. He didn't want to contribute to the mayhem that was unfolding but he had a plan to get Vicky to relax.

"I have something to do, girls – I'll only be half an hour!" Frank announced.

They all looked at him in disbelief.

"What could you possibly have to do that's of any importance at this point?" Vicky demanded.

"Just a bit of business – you're okay now that Connie is here – right?"

Vicky didn't want to cause a scene so she didn't respond. In any case, the way she was feeling it was maybe better if her fiancé wasn't around.

As Frank started to walk away, John jumped up. He told the women that he would be back and ran after him.

Frank was almost at the door to the hotel when John caught up.

"What's going on, Frank?"

Frank looked up at his brother. "I need to see someone."

John stared deep into Frank's eyes. "It's time for the truth, Frank. I can keep Vicky busy and help her while we look for Tina but what are you really doing? Are you gambling or is it something else – maybe something to do with the guy you were with last night?"

Frank's heart pounded. He found it so difficult to admit the truth even to himself.

"I'll only be half an hour!"

John shook his head in disappointment. His brother was so self-centred. "Go and do whatever it is that you have to but when you get back – I want the truth!"

John spoke with such conviction that Frank felt even more uneasy.

When John returned, Vicky and Connie were putting together a plan.

"I'm meeting a couple at three but you can take my car," Connie was saying. "I can get a cab home. Do you think you can find your way to the Hualapai Indian Reservation?"

"Actually I know it," said John. "I've spent some time there."

"But what about Frank?" said Vicky. "We have to take him too."

"Actually I have a suggestion, Vicky," said John. "I get on better with Tina than Frank does – do you think she might be more likely to respond to me – being the crazy step-uncle and all?"

Vicky had to agree. Frank would not help the situation and John was the least threatening adult in the party.

"Okay," she said. "Only now I need to speak to Frank and tell him that we'll be gone for hours."

"I'll text him," John said reassuringly. "Now go up to the room and get some warmer clothes – the desert gets chilly when the sun goes down."

Connie nodded her head. "I think it's best."

Vicky did as she was told and a short while later they were dropping Connie off at the Chapel of the Flowers.

"Call me when you find them – I'll let you know if I hear anything."

"Thanks, Connie, we will," Vicky said.

They drove off down the highway. Considering the tension around the trip they were about to take, Vicky was amazed at how calm John remained. She was almost pleased that she was with him instead of Frank. Under these circumstances anyway . . .

Eddie was confused. Frank had made it quite clear to him last night that he didn't want to see him for the rest of the stay and now they were to meet at the Paris Hotel. Frank was waiting at the foot of the Eiffel Tower.

Eddie took a deep breath and walked over.

"Are you trying to tease me, asking to meet here?"

Frank shook his head. They had spent a weekend together two months before in the French capital. Frank had been like a different person – true and relaxed with himself and his nature. But Eddie was dismayed at the way that he reverted to his clandestine self on returning to Dublin. He had expected such a reaction but hoped for something else.

"I remember Paris!" said Frank. "But I really picked it because it's between our hotels. I'm sorry about last night. I got such a shock when you turned up here. I mean, you should have said you were coming before I left Dublin."

"I was afraid of your reaction."

Frank shook his head. "Well, you got it! But why have you done this? What were you thinking of?"

"I was trying to prevent a disaster – people are going to get hurt if you go ahead."

"And you imagine no one will get hurt if I jilt Vicky at the altar?"

Eddie bit his lip. It was true. People were going to get hurt no matter what Frank did.

Frank sighed. "I don't know what I'm doing here . . . and now, to make it all worse, Vicky's daughter has gone missing."

"She's what?"

"She's run off with the wedding planner's son into the Mojave Desert – only known him two days – why do I attract these disasters?"

Eddie gasped. "You couldn't make that up, Frank." Then he started to giggle. "It does provide us with a useful distraction though!"

Frank couldn't suppress a smile. "I know, it's all so unbelievable – but the fact that we're in Vegas makes it seem normal or something – it's a town where anything can happen!"

Eddie sat down at the foot of the tower and rested his hand on Frank's thigh. "Well, I'm totally responsible – mea culpa, Frank. I'm sorry that I came but I'm glad that I did."

Frank was more confused than he had ever been in his life. He should be supporting his fiancée and looking for his future stepdaughter but instead he was here at the foot of a mock Eiffel Tower fretting over someone who was only ever meant to be a fling. It was a fling that had gone on too long and was really now a relationship. He had managed to live a double life in Dublin which was not easy – with two people of different sexes. And now he was marrying one of them so that he would have a child some day when really he was too much of a child himself and too irresponsible to look after anyone.

"Eddie, you're better off without me – I just wanted to apologise for last night and explain what's going on. Vicky's in a state because Tina went missing in the middle of the night and I don't really know what to do now . . . it's all a mess."

Eddie pursed his lips. He was glad that he didn't have Frank's troubles. "Do you have any idea where this missing teenager might be?" he asked.

"As I said, she's gone off into the desert but she could be anywhere now – Vicky is in a panic dreaming up all sorts of unlikely scenarios."

"I'm sorry – I don't know what to say to you. I'm glad I came to Vegas though. Suzanne has found the old love of her life and is heading off for a romantic trip around the Canyon so at least someone is happy!"

"It's probably best if we don't see each other though – you know, I just wanted to explain about last night."

"Hey – it's okay."

But Frank noticed Eddie's face fall in disappointment. "I have to rush now – Vicky is back in the hotel with the wedding planner – I have to see what they're doing."

"I understand," Eddie said. He couldn't resist giving Frank a peck on the cheek – it was something they would never have done on the streets of Dublin but somehow Eddie felt he had nothing to lose. He watched Frank walk away, even though he was dying inside. He would do the only thing he could think of to distract himself for the rest of the day – shop!

Frank's phone beeped just as he reached the hotel. He couldn't believe the message. John and Vicky were gone and would be gone for the rest of the day at this rate. He was angry with Tina for going missing – with John for rushing off, playing knight in shining armour – with Vicky for letting him – and worst of all he was raging with himself.

Still, he could always make the most of a bad situation. He went to the safe and took out two bundles of cash – he had all the time he needed now to do what he really came to Vegas for.

Ronan took Suzanne's hand and led her along the pathway around Bright Angel Point. With each step the view changed, each as stunning as the one they had seen a few seconds before, and each with the most spectacular array of colours that could not be reproduced through the lens of a camera.

They passed an indigenous-style building with small windows.

"That's the Hopi House – it's a museum and craft centre – Einstein visited it – I'll show you the photo of him later wearing a feathered Indian headdress!"

Ronan brought her along the snakelike path until they came to a large wooden building with an extensive veranda. It was furnished with colonial-style rocking-chairs all facing outwards to survey the best views of the canyon. Ronan told her it had been constructed over a period of years with extension after extension, giving the exterior different levels and heights, and a wooden turret crowned it beautifully. It was chillier on the edge of the south rim than it had been in Vegas and they soon went inside.

Carved into the lintel over the porch were Higgins' words – *Dreams of mountains, as in their sleep they brood on things eternal.*

"That's just beautiful," Suzanne said, her eyes pinned to the ornate script.

Ronan gently tugged her hand and led her into the hotel foyer. The crackling sound and smell of burning logs were their first experience and the cosy intimate surroundings swept the two back to a time of cowboys and Indians and saloons. They were pioneers looking for shelter. Logs lined the walls and a sweeping stairway led up to an impressive hexagonal balcony. In the corner was a reception desk with a shiny brass bell and large registration book. Above the main entrance and adorning the walls in several spots, moose and caribou heads looked down at the patrons. Beside the fireplace were two large armchairs carved in the same wood as the staircase and the mouldings. A glass display case showed historical artefacts of a bygone era. Although it was very dark, the mood was intimate and inviting, and Ronan was delighting in Suzanne's surprise at every step.

"You're going to love the dining room."

He had made a reservation for a table by the window with, he said, the best view in the entire mid-west of America and arguably the western world.

The back wall was covered in Native American craft and artwork and each dining table was simply decorated with wheat and flowers of the Halloween harvest. Pumpkins adorned the table where the best wines and desserts were on display.

They both ordered French onion soup for starters and soon were sipping on it with relish.

"This is so lovely, Ronan – I can't thank you enough for bringing me here. Eddie and I hadn't time to discuss what we would do when we got to Vegas and I wouldn't have thought of coming out to the Canyon – it would be such a pity to come all this way and miss this experience."

Ronan smiled. "Today was the perfect day to bring you here – I'll be busy during Monday and Tuesday – and I'm so glad you've seen the Canyon at its best."

"I feel so small when I look out there. It truly puts my place on earth into perspective. The stories this land could tell must be amazing."

"America is fantastic but there are very few places like Ireland. I miss it." Ronan scooped up another spoon of soup and sipped.

"Would you ever consider moving back?" she quizzed. "I don't mean to pry but I'm sure you've been all over the place since your separation from your wife."

Ronan looked at her. If only she knew how complicated his divorce was becoming. "Maybe I'll go back to Dublin but it really would depend on the economic climate. It might not be so easy to get a job and I'm doing well in Boston. I'm not only a director but a shareholder and, although the shares are not worth what they used to be, I have a lot of say in what goes on in the company and

I like being in that position of power. I wouldn't fancy starting off again with an entirely new company at my age."

"You're only young!"

Ronan laughed and took another spoon of soup. "I guess so, in relative terms. But it's comfortable and what I know."

Suzanne took a sip from her glass of red wine – they had ordered a half bottle and in hindsight that wasn't going to last them to the end of their starter. Maybe she should slow down, stay in control. She didn't want to dream that something could happen between them – he hadn't even kissed her. She had to be realistic about their meeting again. She was feeling too emotional and getting lost in the romance of the setting.

Ronan had ordered the beef stroganoff served with egg noodles and Suzanne the pistachio-dusted pork loin roast. It all looked wonderful when it was served up.

No, she didn't want to dream but, as she looked up from her food and caught him gazing at her, she was sure that he was having the same feelings as she was right at this moment.

Outside the sun cast shadows which seemed to ripple along the north rim, changing the light and mood every few minutes.

Ronan held up his glass and Suzanne clinked hers off it – their eyes met and fixed as the glasses touched.

"To us!" he said.

"To the Grand Canyon – and thank you for a lovely day that I'll remember forever."

Ronan grinned. "Do you know what this reminds me of?"

"What?"

"You know that song by Lou Reed – 'Perfect Day'?"

"Oh, I love that," Suzanne sighed.

"I know you do. I put it on my iPod for when I go to the gym and when it comes on I always think of you."

Suzanne blushed. "I always think of you when the leaves turn in the autumn."

"I guess we both knew in our hearts that we would meet again some day."

174

"Hoped . . ." Suzanne said, "but I could never have imagined it to be in a place like this."

"No, I suppose this is where serendipity took over." Ronan still hadn't lifted his knife and fork. He wanted to grab the moment. He reached out and rested his hand on the back of hers. He wanted to kiss her but stopped and picked up his knife and fork instead. This wasn't the moment – yet!

Tina and Kyle drove into the reservation. The area around the lodge and guest quarters was relatively deserted, with only a pickup truck and old wagon outside.

Len was waiting for them there.

"Hey man, how you doing?" Kyle stepped down from the Jeep and slapped his friend's palm with a high-five.

"Kyle man, I've been trying to call you – your mother was on the phone to my folks. You guys have to get out of here."

Tina rolled her eyes and inhaled. It was her worst nightmare.

"When did she call?" Kyle asked.

"About an hour ago. My grandfather promised he would call her if you came and you know what he's like . . ."

Kyle nodded. "He's a man of his word. That's what's so good about him. I thought we could lie low here."

"I have an idea – my cousin Alberta is working in the Luxor Hotel – she says, if you make your way back now, she'll get a room for you free of charge."

Kyle looked at Tina. "It sounds good to me!"

Tina nodded. She would love a shower and some food.

"Alberta remembers you from the last pow-wow – she'll give you a voucher for food too."

"I don't know what to say – thanks, Len."

Len was tall – about six foot three. His hair was the colour of jet with a brilliant shine and rested on his shoulders. He had a piercing in his left ear and was wearing regular American clothes. He smiled at Tina. "Take care of this guy – he's a good one."

It was as if he knew something that Tina and Kyle didn't.

"Come on," Kyle urged.

Tina jumped back into the car. She didn't fancy the long journey back but she hoped that at least they would get some more time together before her mother found her.

They drove sometimes in silence, sometimes commenting on the music. Then Kyle asked her why her mother was the way that she was.

"I think it goes back to my grandmother – she never got on with her, you see. My mother is an only child and felt that she was responsible for her mother." She giggled. "You'd want to have seen my gran – she was always painting or gardening. She wore a crazy turban – you know, like the ones cancer patients wear. She lived in a big old house, five stories high – with cats crawling around it and cobwebs on the cobwebs in all the corners and crevices."

"I'd love to see an old place like that – everything is so new in Vegas."

"Yeah, her house was great – she always had the fridge filled with chocolate cake and smelly cheeses. And then there were her bookcases – she sorted books by colour – all hard-backed and some of them centuries old. She had a real old record player and used to play hippy music from Woodstock days on it. This was up until a couple of years ago – and Phil Lynott and Thin Lizzy were her favourite! Do you know that music?"

"I've heard of them. She sounds fantastic."

Tina nodded. "She was something else. She hated fools and liked everything done her way or no way!"

"I wish I'd met her."

"She would have loved you! And she would have loved you taking me off like this – driving my mum crazy!"

Kyle looked at her with penetrating eyes. "That's not why we're running away – it's because I've never met anyone like you, Tina – I don't want you to go home. I can't explain it but for the first time in my life I feel like I've met someone who really gets me!"

"I know, I feel it too." Tina did.

The road went on ahead of them and they listened to Jim Morrison and thought of where they were really going.

After dessert Ronan suggested they move into the lounge. A cosy fire burned in the dark oak-panelled room. Paintings of the canyon by local artists covered the walls. They sat on a couch reminiscent of the kind found in a saloon during the pioneering days of the Wild West.

"Would you like another drink – or perhaps some coffee?" Ronan asked.

"Coffee would be lovely. And thank you, Ronan – you're spoiling me – this really is too much."

Ronan ordered a pot of coffee and sat back comfortably on the couch.

"I never could have imagined this start to my business trip!" he smiled. "Especially after the last few months."

"Was it acrimonious with Laura or civil?"

Ronan rubbed his chin. How to answer it without shooting himself in the foot? "We are on civil terms but it's complicated now that she's pregnant – naturally I don't want to upset her in her condition."

Suzanne couldn't imagine the emotional complexities involved in a divorce – she could barely imagine what it must be like to be married in the first place.

"So there's no chance of reconciliation?" This she really needed to know.

Ronan shook his head. "No way – not for me. It's really over."

Suzanne tried not to smile. It was difficult. She had felt his energy all over her during lunch and the tension between them was tangible. She shuffled up closer to him while the logs on the fire crackled, wanting him to make some sort of romantic move.

He responded like Pavlov's dog. He slipped his arm around her shoulder and she slid easily into the shape created by his side.

Both looked at the fire because they knew the next time that their eyes turned to each other this would be it.

A waiter appeared with the coffee and put it down on the table in front of them. He turned away hastily and left them alone again.

Ronan leaned forward but stopped and instead turned to stare at Suzanne.

She looked up and the moment was perfect. With ease he tilted his head and their gazes met. Both paused before the inevitable kiss.

Suzanne gasped as his lips landed on hers. It was like being torn out of the new millennium and transported back to 1993. She had forgotten how soft his lips were. How salty and delicious he tasted. How long their kisses used to go on and on.

Ronan was so keen to have more of her he knew he could very easily lose himself and this was much too public a place. He had never felt so raw with Laura for the duration of their relationship – how could he have forgotten what it was like to feel this way? Any more thoughts of Laura were gone after another kiss and another.

Suzanne pulled away first. "Are we going to drink this coffee?" she giggled.

"I really don't mind!" Ronan said with a wicked wink. "What I'd really like to do is get a room!"

Suzanne didn't know where her voice came from but the words were out before she had a chance to consider. "Well then, why don't we?"

Chapter 15

Tell me and I'll forget. Show me and I may not remember.
Involve me and I'll understand.

~ NATIVE AMERICAN PROVERB ~

It was almost dark when John and Vicky reached the reservation. There was something about the desert that made Vicky nervous. She had tried to call Frank en-route, to no avail. She was furious that he had turned off his phone.

John seemed totally at ease as he stepped out of the car. A group of young people sat on a wall and one of the guys walked over on seeing the new arrivals.

He introduced himself as Len, Kyle's friend, and said that he had spoken with Connie about Kyle but the young people had not shown up yet.

John wasn't surprised – it was a long shot coming out to the reservation but he realised that Vicky needed to feel like she was doing something to find her daughter.

Len brought the two Irish people over to meet his grandfather who was the head of the tribe and the person they had spoken to earlier.

Vicky smiled politely at the old man with long grey hair tied back in a loose ponytail. He was wearing a suede jacket over a check shirt and had a necklace with beads and feathers around his

179

neck. His eyes were framed by years of sadness and knowledge – a deep understanding that she didn't see in many old people. It did however remind her of her own mother and she felt a pang of emotion that shook her.

"Good evening, Chief – thank you for coming to greet us. I believe Kyle has not called out this way?"

"You have my word, Mr John," the old man said. "The young people have not been here. They are very welcome but must honour their parents. Running from your life will only cause pain – these children are young but they will learn."

Len watched on anxiously – he didn't like to lie to his grandfather and he felt bad on seeing the distress that the ordeal was causing the Irish girl's mom but he had to be loyal to his friend first and foremost.

Vicky put her head into her hands as John comforted her by putting his arm around her shoulders.

"Please come into my home – take a drink," the chief said. "You must be tired after the long drive from Vegas."

John and Vicky followed the chief into a log cabin and sat down on a wooden couch covered with woven blankets.

Len appeared and offered to fix them coffee which they thanked him for.

"These young people must be sorry for what they have done to their mothers – it is not good to behave like jack rabbits. The desert is no place for young people to hide."

All sorts of terrible notions started creeping inside Vicky's head. She let out a loud sad sigh. The strain of the day was catching up on her fast.

"Vicky – are you okay?" John watched the colour drain from her face. "You've gone white."

She shook her head and the tears started to flow. John tried to comfort her but soon she was shivering and sobbing in his arms.

The old man nodded gently. "I'll get her some medicine."

Vicky slumped like a rag-doll in John's arms, her breath coming short and shallow.

When the chief returned he had a basket with a rattle and

feathers in it, a clay bowl and a bunch of sage. He took a bottle with stones out of his pocket and placed it at Vicky's side. He then put some sage in the clay bowl and lit it. Taking an eagle feather, he began to waft the smoke around her and, as she breathed in the scent of the sage, she became calm.

Time passed as the chief alternately spoke, chanted and used his rattle and feathers. John quietly let her know what he was doing at each stage, explaining that he was cleansing her aura and extracting negative energies that were blocked by years of fear and tension.

John knew that this ceremony would have a profound effect on Vicky but the ultimate outcome was uncertain. John had faith that the chief was the man who was meant to do it and hopefully their trek into the desert would have been worthwhile.

"Her energy is sad," the chief said. "You must stay here tonight. When the young people show up we will get them together and form some peace."

John had spent time with the Havasupai tribe in the basin of the Canyon before and was aware of the Indian's innate ability to see beyond people and identify their truth.

Vicky was a woman on the edge and John had sensed this when he first met her – his brother was the same but he had almost given up hope of his recovery. This healing that the chief was offering would hopefully help her to find her soul. John realised that there were millions of people all over the world going around without their souls. They had sold them for the love of money, materialism and greed for power and things that would never make their souls sing. John wanted Vicky to find peace – he wanted her to find her soul again. She might not realise it yet but maybe losing her daughter was the best thing that could ever have happened to her.

Kyle parked outside the Luxor and a doorman took his car keys.

Then he and Tina walked into the tomblike reception. A giant sphinx and decorated columns surrounded the desk and hieroglyphics covered the wall behind. A barrage of signs and directions on a post pointed across to the escalators which crisscrossed in a labyrinthine fashion as they climbed the interior of the pyramid.

Kyle searched for an Indian girl with the blue-black hair that was typical of Len's people. Just then a girl approached him, smiling. Alberta had recognised him from an MMS she had received a few minutes earlier. Len's description of Kyle's girlfriend had been perfect.

"Can I help you, sir?" she asked in a professional manner, then added quietly, "Kyle?"

Tina was relieved that finally they were going to get refuge for the night.

"You guys are lucky – we are very full as it's Halloween and all, but I have a room on the seventeenth floor of the pyramid – you'll like it!"

Tina was going to love it.

Kyle thanked her profusely. No exchange of money took place and he was grateful to Len yet again for being such a good friend.

They expected it to still be noisy when they got into the room but it was serenity at its best, though the casino and restaurants below were visible from outside their room. Tina opened the door to the ensuite and gasped when she saw the beautiful tiles and reproduced hieroglyphics in the shower.

"Why don't I order room service?" said Kyle.

Tina nodded. "Good idea – we don't want to be spotted, I guess."

Kyle hadn't texted his mother as promised. He didn't want to. He wanted just one more night with Tina in peace – because when her crazy mother found them he knew that they would not be free to do whatever they wanted for the rest of her time in Vegas.

"I'm going to jump in the shower!" Tina exclaimed, desperate to ease the tensions of the day.

Kyle raised an eyebrow. "Want some company?"

Frank was down to his last five thousand dollars in a matter of hours. He had been relatively lucky the night before but he couldn't get any good hands now. He had lost track of time and couldn't remember how long he had been there. The waitress had brought him drinks every fifteen minutes and he had been careful to have a drink of water in between the odd beer. He was getting hungry now too but was determined not to leave the table until his luck turned.

There was another reason why he had chosen the MGM to gamble – he hoped that at some stage Eddie would walk by. He had kept an eye on the lifts while he was playing cards. But there was no sign so far and he needed to pee. He gathered up his chips and set out in the direction of the bathroom. He was almost at the door when it was opened suddenly and Eddie stood on the other side.

"Hello!"

Frank gasped. "Eddie – hi, I wondered if I would bump into you!"

"Are you not looking for your stepdaughter?"

Frank shook his head. "It's got complicated."

"Are you on your own?"

"For now I'm waiting to hear how Vicky and John get on in the desert."

"The desert?"

Frank nodded. "The kids may have gone out to an Indian reservation in the Grand Canyon – John knows the place and volunteered to take Vicky out there."

"Well, as you're on your own and so am I – I don't suppose there's any harm in two friends going for something to eat?"

Frank looked around but only anonymous faceless crowds swept by. "I'm starving – maybe if I give it a while my luck will turn." Frank looked at his phone. It had no battery power left in it. "Damn!"

"What's wrong?"

"I was so engrossed in the game I didn't realise that my phone was dead – Vicky could have been ringing me."

"Look, put your SIM card into my phone – you can check it out."

"Thanks – I'll take you up on that."

"Come on, let's go over to the Studio Café – get a burger?"

Frank used the bathroom and then met again with Eddie. He fiddled with his phone while they walked through the rows of slots and tables to the food hall. He hoped that Vicky would find Tina soon but he also needed some time to make back all the money that he had lost!

"Oh . . . some missed calls . . . and a text from John – they're staying in the Indian reservation for the night!"

Eddie grinned. "Well, that's a liberal start to the marriage – the bride and the best man – and the groom and his boyfriend!"

Frank didn't respond. He took his SIM card out and handed the phone back to Eddie.

"Thanks. At least they won't be back till morning – unless they find the brat and decide to drive home in the middle of the night!"

"You don't fancy being the father figure then?"

Eddie loved to tease – he wasn't the one living a lie. Besides, sarcasm was a good way to hide his own hurt.

Frank shook his head and dragged his fingers through his black hair. "I need to charge the phone – I need to ring her."

"You can use the charger in my room if you like?"

It was all falling into place conveniently for Eddie and he hoped that Frank wouldn't run scared. But no matter how fussed he seemed last night and earlier when they spoke in the Paris Hotel, he did seem happy to be in Eddie's company now and that was just the way that Eddie wanted it.

"Let's run up and charge it," Eddie said.

Frank grinned at him – he was glad to be with Eddie but he was in a rush to get back to the hotel now that Vicky was gone for the night. "Eh, I'll wait for you in the Studio Café if that's okay – what do you want me to order for you?"

"A burger, thanks!" Eddie was disappointed that Frank wasn't taking the bait but happy to be in his company for a while.

It was getting late and Ronan had to make a call. The sun had gone down and the helicopter was on its last run back to the city.

The room had been an idyllic place to make love for the first time in seventeen years.

"We have to decide now if we are going back to Vegas . . . or . . ."

"Or if we want to stay the night?" Suzanne finished.

He nodded.

"I really want to stay but I'm feeling bad for poor Eddie."

"Of course – whatever you feel you must do," he said but disappointment was what he really felt.

Then something stirred inside her – she was tired of always having to do what was right for someone else. She loved Eddie but he'd had his own agenda all along for coming to Vegas. This happiness she was experiencing with Ronan might not be so easy to arrange again when they were both back living in their homes an ocean apart.

"Okay, then, let's stay."

Ronan beamed. "Oh good – I'll ring the guys and try and get us back on a flight tomorrow – worst-case scenario we can join some group on a bus!"

Suzanne nodded, her eyes wide and bright.

"Now we can see the canyon at night – which is the very best time to be here!"

Suzanne was naked in every sense – all her emotions exposed. The clocks had turned back to a time when she had been at her happiest and in love with Ronan. Although Ronan the man was older, he smelt the same, he tasted the same. Her feelings were stronger and deeper now and she wanted to stay in his arms forever.

Connie was using her best contacts in the hotels along The Strip to find out if her son was staying anywhere there. She was getting more concerned the longer she went without hearing from him. The countdown to Halloween had begun and the town was buzzing but she felt flat and sad. That gorgeous Irish guy was off in her car in the desert now and she wished that she was with him. Why did she have to watch so many couples come and go and always she was on her own? She really wanted some fun. She would call her friend Georgia and go to one of the clubs – sure, she was the wrong side of thirty for the really trendy clubs like JET, but Studio 54 was always good fun at Halloween. And Georgia loved Studio 54.

Georgia was already out partying when Connie got through to her.

"Get a cab – I'm in the MGM – I'll see you in the bar!" Georgia screeched down the phone. "I got a crazy soldier whispering wicked stuff in my ear, babe!"

Connie didn't need to be told twice. She fixed her make-up and called a cab. She dialled Kyle's phone one more time to no avail. In the back of the cab she continued dialling but each time her call went straight to voicemail.

She would drive herself crazy at this rate. She hoped that he had the good sense to look after himself. Still, a few texts around to the people in her phone would do no harm. She made it brief and not too panicky but she wanted to get the message across.

Vicky sat on a bed in a little cabin with a woollen blanket wrapped around her shoulders. She was no longer shivering but she was numb and unable to use more than monosyllabic words.

"Is that okay?" John asked.

"Yes," she replied. She didn't want to leave without her daughter and this was her best hope of finding her.

"We are having a sing session in a few minutes – do you want to join us?" Len asked.

"Sure," John replied. "That okay, Vicky? It might help take your mind off things?"

Vicky just nodded. She wasn't going to last very long. She wasn't able to do much after the healing the chief had sent her. She'd been in a daze as he shook his eagle feather and rattle in the air around her. Under normal circumstances she would have run out of the room but she was so far out of her comfort zone and so afraid for her daughter that she hadn't the strength or energy to tell the chief to stop.

The chief directed them out to the campfire which had stools placed around it. A group of ten guests were sitting and a man from the tribe was strumming softly on a guitar.

The night air was clean and cool and in the distance the wild native animals could be heard howling and hooting.

Sitting beside John, Vicky listened as the man began to sing. It was a ballad she had never heard before and, as she lost herself in it, everyone and everything before her appeared to be a dream.

She looked at John who had been transformed since their arrival in the canyon. He was so graceful and relaxed in this environment. It was no wonder that he disliked the world of shallow one-upmanship and finance where his brother thrived.

But indeed she didn't last long, soon asking if she could go and lie down. Len brought her over to the cabin she was in before. Inside it was basic but clean. The walls were made from logs and the décor could easily have been a set in an old western movie.

She waved goodbye to Len and slipped off her shoes. She didn't undress. She tunnelled under the covers and pulled them up under her chin – leaving a light on in the middle of the room.

She was desperately trying to figure out what sort of ceremony the chief had performed. Whatever it was it had caused a shift inside of her.

It had been a groundbreaking moment – one of great realisation. Like the one she'd had two years ago when she realised that she could no longer be on her own – the years of minding Tina had mounted and she hated the fact that soon her daughter would be grown up and would leave and, more than that, she realised that she needed a man in her life. She didn't want the man to be a casual boyfriend who came and went for weekends. She didn't want a man who had commitments to another family, carrying tons of baggage. Once she'd opened herself to the truth of her emotional needs, her way was clear. She needed a man for herself and Frank fitted the bill perfectly. He was charming and charismatic in work – an excellent boss and a good listener. He was a man of means and status in Dublin and the perfect person to give her a fresh start and the chance of another child. A chance to break the duck of "only children" that ran through her family. If she had another child, Tina would be part of a new family unit and everything would fall into place so much more easily – or so she had thought. But since she had been engaged to Frank she had found him to be more absent than present at the key times when she needed him there. That was why she had decided to sell her house and live with him. She hadn't expected to be on her own as much then, but she soon realised that being the wife of a chef or restaurateur meant that he had to be out at least five nights a week. There were only so many novels she could read and night courses in Pilates she could do, before she realised that maybe her life with Frank would not be how she had anticipated.

But marrying him meant that she would now be back in the world of outwardly contented couples, wrapped carefully in their co-dependence with an invisible layer of clingfilm. Yes, that was what she was buying into, marrying Frank, and that was what she had thought that she wanted. But the proposed nuptials hadn't brought the security and stability that she had hoped. Instead she had driven her daughter away and was now more alone than she had ever felt in her life.

While the chief chanted over her she realised that truth. It was like a veil had been lifted – one that had been hanging over her eyes since David had left. Now her current life seemed like a lie. Her emotions had been swung like a pendulum back and forth across the great canyon beside where she now lay. She didn't know how long she had been lying there transfixed when the door opened suddenly.

John came into the cabin and bent over the bed where Vicky was curled up like a wild animal.

"Just checking to see if you are okay?"

Vicky nodded, her head the only part visible above the tucked blanket and sheet.

"I'll sleep on the sofa over there," he said.

She nodded again. "Thanks for looking after me, John."

"I did nothing – it was the chief who did it all – feel any better?"

"I do feel calmer – a bit numb to be honest."

John knew what she was going through but there was no way that he could explain it to her – not in normal language anyway.

"I'm going to go back to the camp – is that okay? They asked me to sing!"

"I'm fine here, John. Thanks for everything."

John smiled. "I called Frank earlier and told him that we were staying here – waiting for Tina to show. He's fine." It was a lie – he

had tried but had no reply so he texted and hoped that Frank would
have the sense to ring soon.

Vicky just nodded. She hadn't the strength to do much else. She
didn't care where he was. She had too much of her own internal
emotions to digest.

When Eddie returned to the Studio Café he was horrified to see
Frank sitting at a table and chatting with a fit young guy. Eddie
could feel the blood pulse through his veins but he composed
himself and walked over to them. Frank's arm rested around the
young guy's shoulder and he was punching him playfully. The
stranger had brown curly hair and a smooth even tan. There was a
twinkle of bright intelligence in his hazel eyes.

Eddie stood quietly near the table and waited until Frank
spotted him.

Frank jumped to his feet. "Hey, Eddie – you'll never believe who
I bumped into – this is my neighbours' son Charlie from Howth –
he's a professional poker player."

Frank was so open and animated about the guy that Eddie felt
silly for the jealousy he had felt. Probably this guy was straight and
saw Frank just as one of his parents' friends.

"Charlie's father is in the restaurant business too – he's so proud
of you, Charlie, and your track record on the global poker circuit –
always talking about you in the casino in Dublin."

"Hey," Charlie said, putting his right hand out to Eddie.

Frank was on a roll. "Charlie's going to a show me how to play
Texas Hold 'Em – he advised me to forget blackjack – especially
after last night."

"Oh great!" Eddie said reluctantly. That was not what he had in
mind for the evening after finding Frank at last. He hadn't let on
that he had traipsed the Mirage casino floor for three hours in the
hope of seeing him and now that he had found him he didn't want
to share him – even if it was with a straight guy.

A waitress delivered burgers and a pitcher of beer and Charlie
produced a pack of cards.

"Will you play a hand too?" Frank said, looking at Eddie excitedly.

Eddie agreed. He liked the young man's style and he explained the terms and rules so simply that even Eddie felt as though he could tackle a turn at the tables after it.

The three were laughing before long and by the time it came to pay the bill Charlie was looking at his watch. "Hey, you know, you're good at this!" he said to Frank. "Do you fancy coming in on the game with me in the Bellagio?"

"How much do you need to enter?" Frank was very keen but embarrassed that he had left himself with so little capital. He still had to get through two weeks and the wedding with only five grand left!

"Thirty," Charlie replied.

"Thirty hundred?" Eddie asked.

"No, 30K!" Charlie said in all seriousness.

Eddie nearly spit out his beer with shock.

"Eh, I don't have that on me!" Frank said as he tried to think of excuses. "Not cash-rich at the moment."

"Hey, I can stake you if you like – you can put it in my bank account when you get home if we lose – but that's unlikely!"

Eddie thought the young man's confidence was verging on arrogance and besides he didn't want to be watching a card game all night.

Frank on the other hand was hooked. He couldn't believe his luck – this was his chance to make back the ninety-five grand he had lost and maybe some more. "Count me in – maybe we should have a practice at the tables inside first – what time is the game?"

"At eleven – we have an hour to play here if you want to practise – we won't be playing the house like we are here – you'll be playing each player at the table but these guys have more money than card savvy!"

Charlie seemed to have the whole thing sewn up already.

"Who are these people we'll be playing?" Frank asked anxiously.

"One is a Chinese tycoon who comes to Vegas a couple of times a year. Young guys like me get the call if we're free to come in to a game like this – it's like taking candy from a baby!"

"Well, if you're sure," Eddie said protectively – he didn't want Frank to wind up in even more trouble than he was in already.

Lying in each other's arms, they had watched the sun disappear over the canyon and the stars light up like lanterns against the dark blue velvet sky.

"Should we get up and have something to eat?" Ronan asked.

Suzanne nodded. "I don't mind whether we do or not. It's so wonderful to be looking out at that beautiful night sky."

"It'll be cold outside now but we can go for a walk later if you like."

"Yes, let's do that," she smiled.

They had certainly made up for the lost years. Their lovemaking was wonderfully mature – so different from when they were teens. It was the difference between sipping a brand-new Beaujolais or a very fine vintage St Emilion that had been kept for a special occasion only.

Reluctantly they dressed and Ronan took the key off the beautiful mahogany dressing table.

They shut the door and walked down the carpeted hallway where old colonial pictures hung and tasselled lampshades covered the light bulbs.

"Actually I'd like to go outside now before eating – the bar will serve food for a while longer, don't you think?" Suzanne suggested.

"Sure they will," Ronan said.

There were very few people outside and only the odd light on the pathway around the hotel. They walked along a dirt track to a sylvan setting with the smell of night and pine.

"It's so bright – I had no idea that the stars could create such light," Suzanne exclaimed.

"Look behind you – it's the moon."

Suzanne gasped. The moon was magnificent. It hung like a huge disc, its craters clearly visible. "It's so beautiful." She shivered. It was all like a dream.

Suddenly his phone rang.

"Aren't you going to answer?" she asked.

Ronan was reluctant to check it – he had a hunch that it was Laura. He turned his phone off.

"It's not important," he said, putting it into his pocket. He didn't want to be disturbed – he was falling in love with Suzanne all over again and wasn't letting anyone interfere with this moment. He would deal with Laura when he returned to Boston. This evening was incredible and he wasn't letting anyone or anything ruin what was unfolding between him and this wonderful woman.

At the other side of the Canyon in Hualapai country John was taking a walk behind the lodgings and out to the Eagle Point – a stunning cliff face that strikingly resembled the lines of an eagle with wings outstretched. Len's granddad accompanied him.

"It is the Moon of Changing Leaves," the old chief said. "A time to rest and consider what is best for the winter ahead."

"The Moon of Changing Season was last month – right?"

The old man smiled. "You know something of my culture – I saw it in your eyes. That is why I did the healing for your friend."

"Thank you for looking after her."

"It is good that she came to me when she did. I would fear for her soul. She has so many years' sorrow in her heart, she could have lost her soul forever."

"I have learnt some shamanic ways and trust in Spirit. I think it's good for Vicky that she has found you and if her daughter hadn't disappeared she wouldn't be here."

The old man paused. They stood on the edge of the cliff. Down below was a drop of hundreds of metres.

"I think it is lucky for her that she met you. You have an important part to play in this woman's life. She does not realise it – she may never realise it but it is good that she is here now."

"Do lost souls often come to you?"

"My son, he runs this ranch and the tour for the visitors – my ways do not interfere with his work. But the matters of the spirit of the tribe must come through me. I don't usually stay with the visitors but I knew today when I heard of the lost girl that I had work to do. It is the mother that needed to heal. The daughter needed to disappear to let the mother heal."

To some people the old man would sound crazy but to John he spoke perfect sense. John lived in a world without blinkers – one where the spiritual and real world blended and now he hoped that the gauze had been lifted from Vicky's eyes and she would find some peace that would ultimately help her relationship with her daughter. He felt an incredible sense of relief, as if he had completed his task in accompanying his brother to Vegas – whatever happened now, he had done something proactive. He would have to wait and see in the morning how things developed for them all and if it was time for Tina to return.

The practice session in the Bellagio was brief but Frank had the order of the game and even though they were at a low-limit table they were up ten thousand dollars. Frank was buoyant with confidence and Charlie was at the stage where he was giving him inside tips on how to capitalise on a good or bad hand!

Eddie wasn't sure how the organisers of the game would react to a new player at the table but Charlie appeared to have a huge amount of influence because everywhere he went the casino managers seemed to know him and nod with great respect. Now that he knew the full story about Charlie and how he had earned eight hundred thousand dollars last year alone, he considered that maybe this was a golden opportunity for Frank and he had better take it with both hands.

The place they were heading to was Bobby's Room – named after the winner of the 1978 World Poker Series who at that time was the youngest in history – the legendary Bobby Baldwin. It was right at the back of the casino and the glass doors could be seen through from the inside only. They took table ten which was the first one on the left as they entered. Eddie was not allowed to sit at the table because he wasn't playing so he sat slightly behind under the portraits of famous poker players who had graced the tables at one stage. A live boxing match was being televised in the corner on a plasma screen and the waitresses were carrying bottles of whiskey and champagne on large silver platters. They were in the big time now and Frank couldn't believe his luck. Charlie was dressed in a casual polo top with sunglasses resting on the top of his head but the other players were all in smart shirts from Saville Row or Fifth Avenue. The Chinese billionaire was introduced to them as Mr Lee but he could have had any name and Charlie knew that they often liked to use false names and it didn't matter anyway – he was happy to take his money whoever he was. The manager had rung him because he knew that he played fast and hard and the rich tycoons who travelled to Vegas wanted to see action with people who knew what they were doing.

Frank had been prompted that if he had a good hand he was to rub his index finger along his left eyebrow and Charlie would run his fingers through his hair if he had a good hand. That way the two would not bet against each other if they had a good hand. It lessened the odds and they agreed to split the pot, whoever won the most.

Eddie wished that he had Charlie's confidence and Frank's naïve sense of certainty. He was on the edge of his seat watching the hands being dealt. They opened with a five grand bet before the flop had been dealt. Eddie's mouth dropped but he was impressed by Frank's ability to carry it off with confidence and when Charlie won ten thousand with the first pot he settled into some sort of trust of the young man's ability.

The hands were played and played until overall Charlie was up eighty thousand and Frank was up seventy. Charlie had to nod at him to calm down at one stage but he needn't have worried because things were about to get very interesting.

Mr Lee was up fifty thousand and the other players – an African moghul and Arabian sheikh were losing hand over fist. Then they were asked would they mind if another player joined. He was of Chinese and English descent but had an American accent. Charlie recognised him from playing the circuit in the other high-rolling rooms in the hotels and when he appeared the pots usually multiplied rapidly.

"Hi, there – Chester Forde's the name," the player said as he took a seat beside Frank.

Kyle and Tina collapsed onto the bed. They were more in love than any other two people could ever be. Tina felt confident of her body as Kyle stroked it gently – massaging her face and the length of her arms before cradling her small breasts in his hands.

"Kiss me," she teased.

He leaned down and started to suck on her nipple. She shuddered.

She was transported to a new place in her head where she was confident and happy and fulfilled. "I wish I could stay like this forever!" she exclaimed.

Kyle slid up alongside her, resting his head on his palm. He looked intensely into her blue eyes and knew at that moment that this was the woman he wanted more than anything in the world.

"You can't go back to Ireland," he said.

Tina giggled. "I have twelve more days!"

"You have to stay – I've decided I'm not letting you go!"

"And how can I stay – I don't even have a student visa!"

"There is one way!" he said with his eyebrow raised.

Tina could feel her heart pound. There was only one way. He couldn't mean it – she knew that it was common in Ireland for non-EU nationals to have marriages of convenience to stay in the country but could Kyle mean them to marry?

"How?" she bleated.

"We could get married!"

As he stared deep inside her, she knew that he wasn't messing. Her head spun and her pulse increased. She knew exactly what she wanted – the answer was easy. It was a crazy mad thing to do – but she didn't need to use words to reply. She wrapped her naked limbs around his and they were lost in their own world.

Mr Lee was jigging up and down and Charlie had an angle on reading his body language over the last two hours – he knew to fold. Frank on the other hand was raising the stakes and Charlie was beginning to wonder if he had set the bar too high by bringing Frank into the game with so little experience. But Frank reassured him by rubbing his eyebrow and Charlie watched as Mr Lee and the new player raised their stakes by fifty thousand each.

Eddie was shaking – he felt helpless but he was also inspired by Frank's guts – he had a greater nerve than Eddie had ever realised and then it hit him that his lover had to be super-confident to carry off his relationships with Vicky and him simultaneously for the last six months. Frank wasn't flinching as the stakes were raised again and again. He held fast and the flop was not a very interesting set of cards at all – two threes, a seven and an eight. There was a lot of money on the table for such a weak set of cards. Even Eddie realised the relevance of the picture and high cards over the smaller ones.

It was Chester Forde who caved in first. He checked and watched as the others continued to re-raise. Frank who had been up by eighty was now back to his original five thousand. But Mr Lee decided to raise it by another fifty. Frank needed an IOU and he called over to Eddie who had to pretend that he had the rest of the money. The next card was drawn and Mr Lee checked at last. Frank was confident but Mr Lee seemed more so as he revealed a pair of sevens – giving him a full house.

But Frank didn't flinch. He set down the other two threes in the pack. It was a poker and the pot was his.

Even Charlie breathed a sigh of relief.

But the loss didn't put Mr Lee off – he seemed even hungrier to play more and harder and they continued for another hour as the hands continued to flow for Frank. Eddie counted the chips at Frank's side and he stood at one hundred thousand dollars. Enough to make any normal man delirious. But Frank wasn't a normal man – he was a man full of complexities and emotions and Eddie wondered if he really knew him at all.

When they finally left the table and bid Charlie goodnight, Eddie got the old Frank back – the one he knew in Dublin when they were together and alone and Frank was adamant where he wanted to spend the night after cashing in the chips at the Bellagio – they both walked over to the MGM Grand and went straight to Eddie's room.

Chapter 16

As a child I understood how to give. I have forgotten
this grace since I have become civilised.

~ *Luther Standing Bear*, Oglala Sioux ~

Connie woke with her head thumping and no idea where she was.
She looked over at the bed and saw her friend Georgia wrapped
around a male torso. Her flame-red hair poured over the side of the
bed and most of her bronzed smooth skin was visible.

An army uniform lay on the floor.

Suddenly a man sauntered out of the en-suite, wearing nothing
but a big smile.

"Mornin', sweetie-pie," he drawled.

He looked vaguely familiar to Connie as the pieces of last night
slowly started to come together. She shrieked when she thought of
Kyle and Tina – how could she have been so negligent? She
searched for her phone but had to find her bag first.

"You looking for this, honey?" the soldier asked, lifting her tiny
handbag.

"Yes, please – I need my phone."

"Sure thing, honey, but after you give me a kiss."

Connie didn't know if she was going to barf or hit him. "I need
my bag, please – I don't have time."

"You had all the time in the world last night, honey – why did you sleep on the couch and leave me in this big ol' bed on my own?"

Connie was shaking. She couldn't remember getting to the room and it worried her. She knew by the décor that she was in the MGM Grand – she had stayed here before but under very different circumstances.

"Hey, Connie – what time is it?" Georgia asked on realising where she was and that her friend was there too.

Connie looked at her watch – it was ten to eleven and she had a lot of work to do today. It was one of the biggest days in the year – it was Halloween.

Frank and Eddie walked together out of the hotel room, both high after the excitement of the night they had spent. They'd been in a state of euphoria and neither wanted the buzz to end.

"I think we should have called room service," Frank said.

"Don't be silly – it's going to take Vicky and Frank hours to get back to the Mirage."

The two trekked down the corridor.

"Okay then, I'm starving!" Frank agreed and hit the button to call the lift.

Connie checked her phone and couldn't believe it. There was a message from her friend Paula in the Court House. It had been a long shot leaving a message there but it had come up trumps. Connie had asked her to look out for a girl with an Irish passport. A couple by the name Kyle Haycock and Tina Hughes had called by to get the necessary licence which would permit them to get married.

Couples coming to Vegas to get married usually had all their paperwork well ordered and organised. Getting a licence at this late time on a Sunday morning meant that Kyle and Tina would be lucky to find any chapel to marry them – especially on Halloween of all days.

Her dumb and crazy son was getting married. She had very little time to get around every chapel in Vegas – hopefully she wouldn't be too late. She had to get a car somewhere and was furious with herself for letting John and Vicky go off in hers.

She waved goodbye to Georgia and stomped past the randy soldier who had pursued her all night.

She brushed past people along the corridor as the doors of the lift opened. Inside a couple were kissing. They were startled when the doors opened – it was Vicky's Frank and he was kissing another man!

Kyle drove up to the MGM and parked. He had a voucher for food there and this would be their wedding breakfast. The town was buzzing with locals and tourists dressed for Halloween.

"What are we going to wear?" Tina giggled. She was in a trance since Kyle had proposed in the Hotel Luxor the night before.

"I think we should dress in something seasonal – maybe a vampire costume. I never want to forget this day!"

Tina was so caught up in the romance of what they were about to do, she agreed. "I would love to be a vampire – something really dramatic. It will be wild."

Kyle nodded. *She* was wild. They were wild together. This way Tina could stay in America forever if she wanted. It was so simple – he couldn't believe he had thought of it. He had to rescue her from that screwed-up mother. This was the best way around it.

"We'll get something to wear after we eat – okay?"

Suddenly his phone rang – he checked the number, then answered eagerly. He had no cash and had been ringing around his friends and contacts looking for help.

"Hi?" He smiled as he listened to the voice at the other end of the line.

It was a girl he used to go to school with – who was now working in the Viva Las Vegas Chapel.

Kyle smiled widely as he turned off his cellphone. "I have good news. I have a friend who works at the Viva Las Vegas chapel and if we agree to let Fox News film us they will do the ceremony FOC and throw in the costumes!"

Tina beamed. It was really going to happen then – getting the necessary papers from the state registry had been exciting but now they had a venue. She put her hand on his thigh as the car came to a stop. Adrenalin pulsed through her veins – she was with the wildest guy in Vegas and soon she would be his wife.

Suzanne rolled over and opened her eyes. She had forgotten in slumber where she was. Ronan was breathing quietly and calmly and he opened his eyes slowly and looked at her. She felt as though she could melt again – the same way as she had yesterday afternoon and again last night after they had come back to the room after watching the moon and stars. Ronan was right – there was something special about the Canyon at night. She had experienced a kind of peace there that she had never known before – ever. Whether it was because she was with Ronan or not she wasn't quite sure.

"Sleep well?" he asked.

"Mmmm," she replied with a smile.

"It has been so wonderful – thank you."

Suzanne felt like she was going to burst. He had made her feel like the most wonderful warm sexy woman in the world and he was thanking her.

"Are you ready to return to the madness?" he asked.

"Oh, I love Vegas – I haven't seen much of it yet!"

Ronan raised his torso – leaning on his elbow he was now able to observe Suzanne more closely. He propped his head on his hand and smiled.

"I have a treat for tonight," he said. "Mix is the best restaurant in Vegas – you're going to love it!"

Suzanne didn't think she could like anywhere better than El Tovar – it was already the nicest place she had ever been and the perfect spot for rekindling her love with Ronan.

"Okay but I have to ring Eddie and see how he's getting on – I really feel sorry for him!"

"Don't feel bad because you're having a good time for once! From what you've told me it sounds as if things haven't been easy for you, Suzanne."

Suzanne nodded. "It's great that I can tell you what it's really like – you understand – and you knew what my mum was like before!"

Ronan didn't want to elaborate. He remembered the wrath of Mary Quinn with clarity. It wasn't an issue any more and for the duration of their stay in Vegas he certainly didn't want to be reminded of her. He was enjoying himself in a way he wouldn't have under Mary's watchful eyes and now her daughter was able to relax as well.

The language from Frank's mouth was obscene – though he had waited until he was sure that Connie was out of earshot.

"Look, she didn't see anything! I could have been checking for an eyelash in your eye!" Eddie tried to assure his friend. "But in any case what does it –"

Frank threw his head back and roared. "I think she's a woman of the world and knew exactly what we were doing, don't you? What the hell is she thinking! Her son's missing with Tina and now she's caught us!"

An old dear with a blue rinse on her way to the slots stopped and stared at him.

Eddie grabbed him by the elbow and dragged him off to the nearest hotel exit.

"Frank! What does it matter now if she's seen us? Surely you're not going through with this wedding after last night?"

Frank was perplexed. Now that he had won back his money and made a little profit he was certainly going to marry Vicky. He saw his last night with Eddie as a sort of swansong. But this was not the way that it was meant to go. How could he face Vicky in front of Connie? There was no way he could go through with it, and the additional news that Tina was going off to elope was the greatest head-wreck of all.

"Eddie, I honestly don't know what I'm doing now!" he said

with a shake of his head. "I have to go and help look for Tina – I'll call you later."

"Will you stay for breakfast at least?" Eddie begged.

"To be honest, I'm not hungry." He couldn't stomach anything after the encounter with Connie. "I'll call you later." He walked off and disappeared behind the slots.

Eddie felt terrible but nevertheless was very hungry. He decided to go to the café where they had eaten the night before. He took a seat at the bar and read through the menu card.

A couple sat up beside him, giggling with all the anticipation of youth. Eddie envied them.

"What will you have?" the young guy asked.

"Do they have the pancakes here like in the Mirage?" The girl's accent was unmistakably Irish.

Eddie couldn't resist – he had to say something. "Hi, are you from Ireland?"

"Yes," the girl giggled. "I'm from Dublin – Howth."

"I thought so!" Eddie smiled. "I live in Clontarf myself."

"Wow! Small world!"

"Are you staying here?" the young man asked.

"Yes – I'm with my friend but she's all loved up and left me."

"Oh, that's terrible," said the girl. "How could she do that?"

"Oh, it's okay – she's not *that* kind of friend. She has my blessing. So how do you like Vegas?"

"Well, Kyle is *from* Vegas. And we're getting married today! Though I actually came to Vegas because my mum is getting married here! Isn't that something?"

Eddie couldn't believe his ears. He put two and two together and was clearly getting four. He was with the missing elopers and Frank and all the rest of their family were off looking for these two crazy kids. He decided to play along with them.

"Incredible! Eh, where are you getting married?"

Tina turned to Kyle. "What's the name of the place?"

"The Viva Las Vegas Chapel. They are going to televise our wedding on Fox News this evening if you want to look out for us – we are going to be dressed as vampires."

"Well, you won't be out of place today – everyone else is dressed up – in fact, I think I'll be the only person tonight that looks a bit odd!"

Kyle laughed.

Eddie didn't want to be obvious now that he had found out the important information, but he really needed to call Frank at once.

He stood up. "Gotta go – I've just remembered something I have to do. I hope you guys have a great day."

Tina waved goodbye. They did seem happy, he thought. He had to text Frank and quickly. As he walked away he couldn't get the digits to flash up quickly enough – he pressed send and waited.

John answered Vicky's phone and he was glad that he had. Vicky was in a heavy sleep. Connie was breathless and flustered at the other end of the line. She relayed as much as she knew but she needed her car and she needed John and Vicky to help her search the wedding chapels before it was too late.

John listened carefully to Connie's directions but dreaded the task ahead. He thought that last night had been difficult for Vicky but didn't know how she was going to react to the latest news.

"Okay, Connie. I'll touch base when we get to the Fast Lane Wedding Chapel."

That was their first port of call. Connie would have as much of the town covered as she could by that time. It would take two hours to get back to Vegas at the very least.

He gently shook Vicky and she stirred very slowly.

She looked around as she opened her eyes – checking her strange surroundings.

"Vicky – you okay?"

She sat up in the bed. "Have they found her – did they arrive?"

John hated to be harbinger of bad news but hopefully it would all be over soon – one way or another.

"We have to get back to Vegas. Vicky, Connie has a tip-off that they've got a marriage licence."

Vicky couldn't believe her ears. She jumped out of the bed. "Oh

God – what are they doing?" Vicky seldom cursed but a cacophony of colourful abuses flowed from her mouth as she frantically got ready to leave.

Connie took a loan of Georgia's red Cadillac. Georgia was going to be occupied for the day with her soldier.

Connie was a woman on a mission. She was not having a good day. She was seldom wrong about a couple and she'd had a hunch that Vicky and Frank were not the perfect couple but nothing had prepared her for what she'd seen in the lift! When Frank tried to explain, it just made things worse. She resented the fact that he tried to make out that she hadn't seen what she clearly had! She was so disgusted with his behaviour that she hadn't even told him the news about the kids.

Her head was racing since she'd heard. Her dumb son! Getting married! She would never have believed it – how did the fool think he was going to be able to support a wife when his mother still looked after him like a baby?

She had sent out an email to all of the directors of the hundreds of wedding chapels across the city. Even at that, it was a long shot as there were so many places they could have chosen to marry in. She did know that they would be relying on a cancellation as this was one of the most popular days of the year to get married. What she needed was John and Vicky to get back as quickly as possible. It was all hands on deck if they were to rescue this situation from disaster.

Vicky looked out the window of the car as they drove on and on through the desert. John felt so sorry for her. The fact that she had slept so heavily and soundly meant that the illumination enacted by the chief had left her exhausted. Poor Vicky had been through so much since she came to Vegas – quite apart from the shocking news from Connie.

The signpost read *Vegas 10 miles* and he sighed with relief. He hoped that they would get there before it was too late. The radio was playing the sleepy sound of "Take It to the Limit" by The Eagles and John listened as Vicky sat silently with her anxiety.

As the high-rise towers of the Vegas hotels started to come into view he noticed her fidget in her seat. She was like a lioness waiting to pounce as the car rolled down the highway. Just a few more miles and they would be on The Strip.

Eddie's phone rang out and Frank was on the other end of the line.

"Hi, are you okay?" Eddie asked.

Frank presumed he was talking about the shock of seeing the wedding planner at the lift and grunted.

"Frank, I've just been speaking to a couple of kids in the MGM and they are going off to get married in the Viva Las Vegas Chapel and Fox News is going to televise their wedding! The girl is Irish and said she lived in Howth and had come here for her mum's wedding. And the guy's name was Kyle."

Frank gasped. He had to call Connie and quickly. "Thanks, Eddie – you might have saved the day!" With that he hung up.

Eddie looked at the phone and wished that he had saved his own day!

Connie had already visited the Chapel of the Flowers, Cupid's Chapel, the Little White Chapel and half a dozen others. She was going to the Vegas Weddings and Fast Lane Drive-Thru now. All the times she had driven couples to these places and shown them the settings for their nuptials, she had never suspected that she would end up searching for her own son in this way. Suddenly her phone rang. It was John. He was coming down The Strip and she gave him directions to where she was going. From there she would give him a list of places to check so they could cover as many chapels as possible. She knew in her heart as she pulled up at the Fast Lane Chapel sign that her son wasn't there but she went through the motions nonetheless. She heard the familiar sound of her car engine roll up beside her and she got out of the Cadillac.

Vicky was visibly shaken and there were rings around her eyes but in a strange way she did look better than she had before she set off for the Canyon.

"Where are you going next?" John asked.

Connie looked at Vicky first and then back at John. Her heart broke for the woman who had no idea that her husband-to-be was busily occupied with another man while she searched for her daughter.

"I'm going into the Wedding Chapel – you guys go around the side to the Fast Lane Drive-Thru." She handed the keys of Georgia's car over to John. "Here, you take the Cadillac and give me my car back – I can talk on my hands-free then as we go around the chapels."

"Who owns the car?" John asked, admiring the vintage red Cadillac.

"It's my friend Georgia's – she's not going to need it today."

"Have you any more leads?" Vicky spoke for the first time.

Connie shook her head. She rested her hand on Vicky's arm. "We will find them today!"

Vicky nodded.

Connie thought she had got away with it until Vicky grabbed her.

"Have you spoken to Frank?" she asked.

Connie hesitated. She saw John's eyes narrow and knew he had guessed that something was wrong. "I saw him, yes, but . . . I didn't know about the wedding at that point . . . Well, we'd better get going!"

Vicky let John lead the way as Connie rushed off into the large reception where beautiful gowns and flowers were on display.

Suzanne and Ronan were in mid-air flying over the Hoover Dam when Eddie's call came.

Ronan could tell by the look on Suzanne's face that she had a story to tell.

"Okay, I'll see you in about an hour, I guess," she said before hanging up.

"Everything okay?" Ronan asked.

"He had a good night by all accounts but now his boyfriend is up to high doh – oh, I don't even want to go there!"

Ronan put his arm around Suzanne.

"Just focus on us – this is your time away – Eddie has had you around him for years. I want to be selfish and keep you all to myself while we're here."

Suzanne loved the words he used. She felt blissfully happy but part of her was concerned that when the trip was over she would be left with nothing but memories. He was clear on his desire to stay in the States – he hadn't made any shallow promises either. On the contrary, he kept dwelling on the fact that this was a special short time that they had together. Maybe she should just accept that wonderful memories might be all she would have to take home.

The responsibility of minding Mary Quinn was hers. She hoped and prayed that this weekend would lead to something much more but she didn't want to get her hopes dashed either. So instead she focused on the spectacular high-rise scenery of the towers of Vegas in the distance and she smiled at Ronan and let him kiss her the way that she wanted to be kissed.

John asked the girl at the window of the drive-thru if she had a Kyle and Tina on her list for today or if she had seen them since opening.

He quickly took Vicky's arm on getting a negative response and they waved at Connie as they got into the Cadillac and she climbed into her own car. It was a nice car and John liked the feel of it under his feet. The top was down. It was the sort of car that he would enjoy driving through the desert. But he realised the seriousness of the job in hand and with one eye on Vicky and the other on the road he drove to Cupid's Chapel. Suddenly Vicky's phone rang – it was Connie.

John watched Vicky's expression as Connie spoke.

"Yes?" he asked as the call finished.

She looked at him, her eyes wide and distraught. "She's been reliably informed by Frank of all people that the kids are in the Viva Las Vegas Chapel. She's on her way there now."

"Are you okay?" John asked, even though it was perfectly apparent that the onslaught of the last few days was now taking its toll.

They were nearly there.

Chapter 17

The Earth does not belong to man,
Man belongs to the earth.
All things are connected,
Like the blood which unites us all.

~ Chief Seattle ~

The coffin lid opened and a man dressed in Edwardian costume complete with top hat stepped out. Red face-paint dripped from his lips, resembling blood.

Tina's heart beat heavily in her chest as Kyle reached out and took her hands.

It was the most intense moment either had ever experienced. They repeated their vows solemnly and lovingly to each other as the music started in the background.

Suddenly a loud clatter came from the back of the chapel as the entrance doors were flung open.

Vicky pushed past the man standing inside the door – knocking over his television camera. Dry ice rose from the floor, tinted lilac by the flashing spotlights. Candlelight illuminated the dark walls and the strains of a church organ playing a macabre melody filled the air. Large cobwebs draped down from the rafters and hung over the aisles and Vicky pushed them out of her way to get to the bizarre altar.

Kyle stood on the left with a pallid face and blood dripping down his chin. To his right Tina was standing, wearing a long green satin dress and black shawl.

Vicky tripped over a tombstone in her anxiety to reach her daughter. Hysterically she waved her arms in the air and screamed. "Where have you been? Tina, what do you think you're doing?"

The organ started up with the Dead March as two trapeze vampires glided through the air over their heads.

"I'm getting married," Tina replied. Her voice trembled – this wasn't the way she had planned it.

Vicky shook her head in disbelief.

"Tell me this is some kind of joke – you can't honestly be getting married!"

Tina moved in by her groom's side and he put his arm protectively around her.

"This is my wife," the boy said brazenly. "And we *are* married!"

"Tina Hughes, come with me now!" Vicky roared.

"Her name is Tina Haycock now," the young man said coolly. "And she's going with me!"

Connie came out from the shop and reception desk of the Viva Las Vegas chapel. She had missed the spectacle but met her son and now daughter-in-law as they signed the register. She looked around for Vicky and John and saw them at the entrance, standing in the brilliant sunshine. John was comforting Vicky as she sobbed against his chest.

"Guys – I'm going to take the kids back to my house if that's okay – they don't seem to have realised what they have done."

"They know exactly what they have done and it's all your fault! You and that blasted son of yours!" Vicky was hysterical. "He told me that I couldn't speak to my own daughter. I wish I'd never come to Vegas!"

Connie realised that she was completely in shock after what she had seen in the chapel. It must have been traumatic – she had only missed the ceremony by seconds herself and could see that Tina was visibly shaken after her encounter on the altar with her mother. For now she would let Vicky calm down and take care of the kids – because that was all that they were and it was all she could do.

John helped Vicky into the Cadillac, all the time trying to stop her sobbing.

"I'll text Frank and tell him to meet us at the Mirage."

Vicky nodded and blew her nose into a tissue. Her tears were relentless but she didn't know who she was crying for any more.

"At least we know that she's safe. Connie will keep them at her house."

"I shouldn't have shouted at Connie – it wasn't her fault!"

John agreed but didn't say anything. He started the engine after sending the text and drove as quickly as he could. He wanted to get some head space for himself.

Suzanne flopped down on the bed of her hotel room. Eddie was nowhere to be seen. She sent him a text to see where he was, closed her eyes tight and tried to imagine that she was back lying on the bed that she had left earlier that morning. Ronan was so amazing. She couldn't have dreamed how she was going to feel after spending only one day and night with him. There was a familiarity and safety about him that she hadn't experienced with any of the other men that she had dated since him. The fact that she felt eighteen when he kissed her helped too. They were free spirits. It was so strange that all of the years had passed and neither of them had had children. It wasn't as if they were young either and most of the people they had known back in those days were now parents. She wondered if she should share her secret with him yet. She didn't want to ruin what they had found and it was very early days – but she did want to clear the air and get the truth off her chest. She had carried the knowledge around on her own for too long and it broke her heart every time she thought about what she had done. At least now she could share the grief and pain and they could start afresh. It was too much to dream of at such an early stage but she knew how she felt and, from what Ronan had said and the way they had been for the last forty-eight hours, they were both on the same wavelength.

Suddenly the door opened.

Eddie came through it with gaunt cheeks, rushed over to Suzanne and gave her a massive hug.

Suzanne could see in his eyes that he was an emotional mess.

"Eddie – what happened?"

Eddie sat down on the bed beside her, his head hung low.

"It's all gone pear-shaped – you won't believe the craziness of the last twenty-four hours – don't leave me again!"

"What's happened?"

"I spent last night with Frank –"

"You told me – but what about his fiancée?"

"She was searching for her daughter who has eloped and I met the crazy kids on their way to get married – it's all gone bonkers – anyway Frank won a fortune last night when he met an old friend and we spent the night together – it was amazing fun – and this morning the wedding planner caught us kissing in the lift –"

"Slow down," Suzanne giggled. "I can't take all this in!"

Eddie gasped. "Enough of my troubles – what did you get up to?"

"Oh Eddie, I had the best night ever. Ronan brought me to the Grand Canyon and we spent the night in this really old romantic hotel – it was so gorgeous."

"And . . .?"

Suzanne didn't want to kiss and tell – it was too special. "And it was wonderful and he is taking me out to dinner this evening if that's okay."

"Sue, at least one of us is living the dream – I thought after last night things had changed but Frank is not the man I thought he was – I really thought we were back on track. He's going through with this wedding on Tuesday."

Suzanne rested her hand on his thigh. "Poor Eddie. Maybe you have to forget this guy – try a night club – there's bound to be other nice guys in Vegas and it is Halloween – Ronan says the town goes crazy tonight."

Eddie thought for a minute. That was what he would do – try and forget Frank and have some fun of his own. Although it wasn't what he really wanted. He knew what he wanted and that was Frank.

Kyle sat at the kitchen table. His face still smudged with traces of red make-up and his hair dishevelled.

Tina was relieved because she didn't have to go and talk to her mother who had totally overreacted as far as she was concerned.

Poor Connie didn't know what to do! Vicky had behaved totally out of character by cursing at her outside the chapel. But Tina didn't seem to want to talk to her mother and Connie felt that at least, if she had her confidence, she could keep the young couple in one place overnight and try to reason with them the next morning.

"Do you want some coffee?" Connie asked, trying to bring some sort of normality to an abnormal situation.

Kyle nodded.

"Can I have a drink of water, please?" Tina asked. She had a still and numbed expression on her face since the wedding. She certainly didn't look like a blushing bride.

Connie poured the water and turned to Kyle. "So the guys at Viva let you marry free of charge if you let the Fox TV guys film you?"

Kyle nodded. "And they gave us the costumes."

Connie put the coffee into the pot and poured in the boiling water. "You got a good deal," she said with a little laugh. "But that doesn't mean I'm not mad as hell with you kids."

The reality of what they had done was hitting them. The last forty-eight hours hadn't been real somehow but now as they stood in Connie's kitchen everything seemed different. Kyle did love Tina – of that he was certain – but that was all that he was certain of now. Tina was worried about her mother. She had felt like going over to her when she followed them outside but Kyle and Connie had taken her with them and she hadn't said anything. She should have spoken to her at the very least. She wondered where Frank was and why her mother was with John. It was all surreal.

"Do you mind if I lie down for a few minutes?" she asked.

"Sure, honey – go into the guest room – it's the last on the right."

As she took her glass of water and walked away, Kyle began to follow her

"Kyle!" Connie said firmly. "Stay here. She needs some space."

Kyle did as he was told and let his bride walk away.

When Vicky got back to the room Frank was waiting for her. He put his arms around her and John watched as she sobbed into his brother's shoulder. John wondered how much of her reaction had to do with the shamanic ceremony. One thing he knew was that Vicky Hughes would never be the same again. The chief had whispered in his ear before he left that Vicky would feel strange for a number of days and that finding her daughter would help her to find herself. She had found her daughter but lost her again unless they sorted out the mess that they were in.

"I'll leave you guys," John said. "I have to get the car back to Connie's friend. I'm going to give her a ring now."

"Thanks for everything, John," Frank said. He really had a lot to thank his younger brother for. He needed to speak to him – come clean about what had happened.

He needed to tell him the truth. "Hold on for a minute."

When they got out to the corridor and he was sure that Vicky was out of earshot, he faced his brother and forced himself to speak.

"John, I have something to t-t-tell you," he stumbled. "I spent last night with someone."

John didn't flinch – nor did he help. He just waited. Frank had to finish all by himself.

"Well, you see, this someone – it was someone from home – someone that I've been seeing and, well . . . it's . . . not a woman." He paused and took a deep breath. "This someone is a man."

"I don't know why you haven't told me before – I always knew," John said.

Frank was genuinely shocked. "How? I mean I didn't realise it myself. I have had such mixed feelings. You've no idea."

"Well, I know that woman in there has been through enough – she needs looking after – you can't go through with the wedding now."

Frank gasped. "Of course I have to – especially now after everything that has happened."

John shook his head. "Look, don't leave her in there – she's had a ceremony on the reservation that will be leaving her a bit shaken, quite apart from everything else that's happened."

"What sort of ceremony?"

"It was a shamanic illumination – the chief of the tribe did it."

Frank laughed. "Hocus pocus, you mean!"

John stared at him in dismay. "How can you be so scathing about something that you know nothing about – especially when you don't even know yourself?"

That remark certainly put Frank in his place. He had lied to himself and to everyone else. But he was going to put everything right now.

"Where will you be?" he said.

"I have my phone on – ring me when you've told her the truth!"

Frank watched his brother walk down the corridor. He had no idea how he was going to handle the mess that he had got himself into now.

But he definitely was not going to tell his future bride the truth.

Chapter 18

May the stars carry your sadness away,
May the flowers fill your heart with beauty,
May hope forever wipe away your tears,
And, above all, may silence make you strong.

~ Chief Dan George ~

Suzanne didn't know what to expect as they stood in the lift of THEhotel at the Mandalay Bay. It was like any other high-class hotel in a big city and very different to the Mandalay Bay itself. No slot machines or roulette tables in the foyer. They were greeted by a doorman who led them through reception.

It took less than a minute to get to the sixty-third floor where the restaurant was situated. Ronan told Suzanne that the hotel was actually forty-three stories high but they skipped some to make it seem taller – either that or they didn't want floors that mentioned the "unlucky" number four to put the Chinese guests off their luck. When the doors opened they were met by a wall of glass and the most amazing panoramic night-time spectacle that Suzanne had ever seen. The airport runway was to the right and the beacon at the top of the pyramid of the Hotel Luxor shone high into the sky. All the lights and towering hotels of The Strip were visible in a fantastic display of neon and colour, from the Excalibur beside them up to the Stratosphere at the very top of The Strip.

Ronan watched Suzanne's reaction with great pleasure. He wanted this to be special. Since their return from the Canyon he had been able to think of no one and nothing else but her. The two hours they had spent apart while she was with Eddie were unbearable. He had decided that he didn't want his time with Suzanne to finish with this trip. She meant too much to him and he wanted to make her a permanent fixture in his life again. He hadn't returned Laura's call either. But he would. He would tell her gently but firmly that he had met someone he felt he had a future with, and she would just have to accept it and go along with the divorce proceedings that *she* had started!

The restaurant was laid out beautifully with starched white linen tablecloths and fine elaborate chandeliers that hung like thousands of bubbles over the tables and staircase. The maitre d' introduced himself as Pascal to Suzanne and shook Ronan's hand as if he were an old friend.

He led them to the decking outside and seated them beside a heated lamp at what was unquestionably the best table in the restaurant – they certainly had the best view. Their waiter handed them the most exquisite menu that Suzanne had ever seen. It was quality beyond anything she had ever experienced and so far not a morsel of food had been laid on her table.

"The French chef, Alain Ducasse, runs this restaurant," Ronan informed her. "It's going to be very good."

Suzanne smiled as the waiter lifted her napkin, shook it and rested it on her lap. It was going to be wonderful.

Connie left the two kids in front of a DVD with a bowl of popcorn. The evening resembled so many that Kyle had spent when he was having a friend over on a sleepover – it certainly was nothing like a groom and his bride on their wedding night. They promised they'd stay put. The poor kids were so confused. They'd had too much adventure over the past two days and she believed they wouldn't wander again.

But she wanted to see John and make her peace with Vicky. They also needed to sit down and sort out the mess that their children had created.

217

"Are you guys okay if I leave you now?" she asked.

"Where are you going?" Kyle asked.

"I've got to meet Georgia – John is giving her car back."

"Will my mum be there?" Tina asked anxiously.

"No, honey. Your mum is having a rest at her hotel – she's happy to leave you here for the night but you're gonna have to talk to her tomorrow."

Tina realised that. She had got over the shock of the day and was glad to be sitting quietly in the safety of Connie's house. She had no doubts that she loved Kyle and wanted to be married to him but she hadn't thought through the seriousness of her actions. She wasn't sure any more if she wanted to live in the Nevada desert for the rest of her life but living in Las Vegas was the only life that Kyle knew. In the same way that living in Dublin was all that she knew.

"Be good and see you later," Connie said as she took her bag and left the room.

Tina and Kyle looked at each other. They had seemed so much older and more mature when they were on Lake Mead and driving through the desert. But sitting now in front of the plasma TV – him in his T-shirt and boxers and her wearing one of Connie's nightdresses – they felt like two little kids although neither would say it.

"How do you feel?" she asked, scared of his reply but needing to know. He had been very quiet since they left the chapel and his mother had been around.

"Fine – I don't regret it – do you?"

"No!" Tina replied, a bit too quickly. "It's good that we are here now, though. I do want to see my mum. She's not such a witch really. I feel sorry for her."

Kyle thought that she seemed like a witch earlier in the chapel but either way he knew that Tina would have to speak to her soon – the hiding was over. They'd been so caught up in the passion they had felt for each other that they hadn't thought it all through.

He looked at Tina and could read the fear in her eyes. He put his arm around her and snuggled up closer.

"It's gonna be okay!"

Tina nodded. Whatever happened it would be okay.

Suzanne ordered the Filet Mignon Rossini for her main course and Ronan ordered the Atlantic Sea Bass. The starters had been exquisite and the quality living up to its Michelin stars – the wine was an aromatic French Chablis and the company had been perfect.

Ronan and Suzanne looked out at the sparkling lights of The Strip and he moved his hand and placed it on top of hers. The moment couldn't be more ideal.

"You know, Suzanne, I hope I'm not jumping the gun here but it's been really amazing seeing you again. You have made me remember what it feels like to be really in the here and now – living in the moment."

Suzanne smiled softly. "I know – I feel the same!"

"I just want you to know that I want to see you – if you do – after we both go home." He seemed apprehensive and nervous as the words came out. "I don't know how we can do it – but maybe you can take a trip to Boston or I can visit you in Dublin. We are only a few hours away from each other really!"

Suzanne nodded her head. "It's not easy for me to leave Mum – I've explained why already – but, yes, I would like to see you soon too."

Ronan beamed. "Good. I wanted to say it – I didn't want you to think this was just a fling for me. I really would like to continue our relationship."

Suzanne was flushed with the joy of the moment. She wondered how she would be able to make it happen – Ronan had no idea how restricted she was by her mother. She had contemplated telling him about her secret but now she was certain she had to tell him. She wanted the slate wiped clean and the truth out so that they could move on.

"Ronan – I want that too – it won't be easy with Mum but I'll do whatever I have to, to see you again."

Ronan's smile was wide. He truly felt on top of the world – the setting was ideal for what he had revealed and even the thought of Mary Quinn couldn't dampen his spirits. This was the start of something new and exciting for them both.

"But, Ronan, if we are going to have a relationship there's something I have to tell you that's been cutting me up for years – since we were last together."

Ronan was puzzled. He couldn't imagine what sort of teenage dilemma would need laundering all of these years later.

"If this is about the way I didn't write – I'm truly sorry. It's typical of guys – especially young guys like I was."

Suzanne shook her head. "No, Ronan – this is about me. This is about after I left you at the airport. Do you remember the night before?"

Ronan smiled – of course he did. Their last goodbye was extra special. They had gone to his friend Keith's and used his bedroom for two hours. They had made love like it was the last time they would ever see each other and until a few weeks ago that is exactly what it was.

"Well, I have a confession – I should have told you then but my mother was adamant. You weren't around and you didn't reply to my letters. I did try to phone and your mum said she would tell you but you didn't call me back."

Ronan was aghast. "I didn't get any message that you had phoned."

"I did phone – not that it mattered. My mum was furious and she took total control. She saw to it. I tried to put it into a letter but . . . you hadn't answered the ones that I had sent before."

Ronan was confused. "Your mum saw to what?"

Suzanne looked into his eyes. He had no idea what she was about to say.

"The abortion, Ronan – I was pregnant."

The silence between them was deathly.

"I was pregnant and had to have an abortion – I had no choice – my mum was furious and she made me get a plane to London and I spent the night at a clinic . . ." She had to gulp back the tears. "I had to have it – my mum gave me no choice."

Ronan's eyes widened. His pulse pounded in his ears. "I can't believe it – why didn't you tell me?" His voice was cracked and hard.

"I told you, I did call but I couldn't reach you . . . then it all happened so quickly. When I tried to explain with letters it was hopeless – you hadn't replied to the ones I had written to you anyway."

"I didn't know that you had tried to call me! How could you go ahead without telling me?"

Suzanne frowned – the hurt and upset of the ordeal was still too fresh in her memory. "What was I supposed to do? My mother threatened to turn me out on the street. You didn't call and I was all alone!"

Ronan put his head back. This was information overload. All he could picture was Laura at the medical centre as they were told that he had a low sperm count – he wished he had known then what he knew now – his ego needn't have taken such a hammering. And now he had to face the news that there was a child that he fathered but it had been taken away from him without his ever knowing. He was shaking with the information. He looked at Suzanne with pain in his eyes.

"How could you do that?"

Suzanne was trembling now. She could feel her stomach muscles clenched at the shock of his reaction. "What do you mean – how could I do that? You were the one that left Dublin. I was on my own with my mother – you remember what she was like – you remember how bossy she was and how she tried to control my every move. How dare you? You have no idea what I went through – what it was like for me and what I have had to live with every day of my life since the abortion!"

Ronan watched her become more animated and angry as she spoke each word. She was on a roll and the words tumbled from her lips.

"You have no idea how it feels for me when I watch my friends come home from hospital with babies – how I watch mothers in Temple Street with their kids and long to hold them and look after them. And now I'm left with a seventy-year-old baby that nobody wants to mind – not even her own son. You have no idea what life has been like for me!"

She didn't know where she had found the strength to say what she had said. She stood up and threw her napkin down on the linen-covered table.

"I'm sorry for upsetting you, Ronan – but *I* have been upset for a very long time!"

She grabbed her handbag and rushed off past the poor confused waiter. She looked behind but Ronan was sitting very still at the table – looking straight ahead.

Suzanne pushed the button for the lift and threw herself into it. She wanted to be home – not in her hotel room – she wanted to be back in Dublin. This was a big mistake – how could she have got it so wrong? She thought that he would be sympathetic – empathetic at the very least! She had known it would be a shock for him but she had not expected condemnation from him. She had been young, alone and penniless, with a domineering mother!

On the street a cab passed by and she hailed it. She jumped in – the MGM was only a short walk away but she didn't want anyone to see her sob. She would rush through the foyer, go to her room and hide away until she caught a flight back to Dublin. She never wanted to see Ronan again as long as she lived.

John arranged to meet Connie and Georgia on Fremont Street. He would return the Cadillac and then might as well check out the action downtown. He wanted to give Vicky and Frank a chance to sort themselves out properly. Besides, he was curious to see what Halloween was like at the Fremont Street Experience.

He liked driving the Cadillac. Connie had told him to drive up Carson Avenue and park it up in the Golden Nugget car park and meet her there in the casino for a drink.

Rush Lounge was at the centre of the action – a spacious lounge with high stools set around the curved bar and smaller tables in a modern streamlined design. John spotted Connie straight away but it was the dazzling woman with striking red hair and piercing green eyes that caught his attention.

He strolled over to them and sat on the stool beside Connie's beautiful friend.

Georgia's eyes twinkled as she was introduced to John. She held out her hand and he shook it politely – their eyes met and in an instant she was hooked.

Connie was quick to spot the attraction and quickly intervened by asking John what he would like to drink.

"A beer, please – unless you would like me to drive the car home for you, Georgia?"

Georgia laughed. "I'm not driving tonight, honey – it's Halloween. They know me here and let me park my car here all the time."

John took out the keys and car-park ticket and handed them to her. "Before I forget!" he said. "And thank you for lending it to us."

Georgia smiled a bright wide smile – her lipstick was cherry-red like her hair and she was beaming now at John. "Honey, if I'd known such a cute Irish guy was in town I'd have collected you from the airport myself and driven you around."

Connie was used to Georgia's hypnotic effect on men but wasn't too pleased that she was flirting so overtly with this one in particular. Georgia was meant to be with her soldier tonight but had dropped him for no apparent reason other than it was Halloween and a chance for some interesting people-spotting in town.

"Are you playing cards tonight?" Connie asked.

"I don't gamble," John said with a shake of his head.

Georgia laughed. "Have you seen Fremont Street yet – it's *awwwesome*!"

"I've never seen it at night-time."

"Well, you picked a *gooood* night," Georgia beamed. She could feel the glares from Connie burn onto the side of her face. "Excuse me, guys, while I go to the bathroom." She batted her long eyelashes as she slid off her seat and walked away with a sway of her hips that she knew would be in John's full view.

When Connie was sure that her friend was out of earshot she cleared her throat and moved over to the stool beside John.

John didn't know what was coming next but he knew that Connie was a sharp woman and figured that she was already concerned about the upcoming nuptials.

"Hey, John, do you know if this wedding is going ahead? I mean, this is crazy but I'm kinda related to Vicky now." She shook her head and brushed her long dark hair back. "I don't know if Frank told you that I saw him in the lift yesterday kissing someone?"

John didn't know but that would explain Frank's confession earlier. "I can't speak for my brother, Connie, but I've known for a long time that Frank would find it hard to settle with a woman. He sees all women in the same way as he sees our mother. She has a strong influence on him and always had." John stopped and scratched his head. "I have to admit that I tried to talk to him about guys that were his friends but he never opened up to me. Now he has and there is someone who has come over to Vegas and wants to be with him. He's got to decide whether he wants to spend the rest of his life with a woman or a man."

Connie felt for John. He was trying to keep the wedding party together since he had arrived. "I feel bad for Vicky – I mean I feel bad for me too – I can't believe what my stupid son has gone and done. Vicky has to sort her relationship out with Frank and soon, or it's going to be impossible to try and reason with the kids. I mean, how are the kids going to listen to the adults if they aren't honest with each other?"

John knew that Connie had a point. He had wondered the same thing himself. This Eddie character was lurking around Vegas too and who knew where he would pop up next.

"Maybe you would come back to my place and talk to the kids?" Connie asked. "I mean, I don't know how Tina will take it but Vicky said that she can talk to you? Not now, of course – I mean in the morning?"

John nodded his head. "Sure – if you think I can help I'd be happy to. But what are you going to do with the kids? I mean, they are legally married."

Connie picked up her drink and took a sip. She had thought about that. She needed to talk to Vicky before they could reason with the kids. She knew it was rougher on Vicky than it was on her. She was on her home territory and she didn't have a fiancé with an identity crisis to contend with as well.

"I hope that he's going to come clean with her," John said.

Connie shook her head. "Poor Vicky – this is some nightmare for her."

"It is."

Georgia came back to her stool and brushed her revealing cleavage against John's elbow.

"Oops, sorry," she said with a dazzling smile.

Connie scowled and John winced. Georgia was wildly attractive – he would definitely like to fill his night with her company. But matters had become so complicated he didn't need to make them worse.

The waiter came over to Ronan and placed the beautifully presented sea bass on the table.

"Would you rather I waited until the lady returned?" the waiter asked.

Ronan's head was in a spin. He didn't know how he really felt. He was so hurt, so shocked – such a plethora of emotions swimming around inside him that he could barely speak.

"Eh, she won't be back," he said.

The waiter was utterly professional and disappeared discreetly.

Ronan put his head into his hands. He really had messed up this time. After only two days Suzanne hated him. He was so numbed and raw with the information he couldn't get a grip on his emotions. He hadn't realised until this moment that having a child was such a big deal for him. Nor did he understand the pain he had felt when Laura had left him and announced that she was having another man's child.

It was like a jigsaw being made before his eyes. This new knowledge helped him to see himself. But now he had upset

Suzanne and he didn't want to make her feel any worse – he had no idea what had happened. He looked down at the splendidly dressed fish and the aroma wafted up and filled his nostrils. He couldn't eat – he was sick inside.

He had never been in a situation like this – his own hurt and thought of the termination of his unborn child was all he could focus on. He needed to speak to Suzanne and comfort her too. How could he have let her just slip away like that? He called the waiter over and handed him his credit card. This had to be sorted out before she disappeared out of his life again. He hoped that he wasn't too late.

"It's a shame to be calling room service when there are so many nice places to eat," Frank said as he leafed through the room menu.

Vicky was prostrate on the bed as she had been for most of the day.

"I'm sorry – I just can't seem to pick myself up at all." She was pale and shaken and nothing Frank said or did could shift her from her daze.

"Well, at least we know Tina is safe in Connie's house."

Vicky turned her head and closed her eyes. She had to choke back the tears. She had found her daughter and lost her again. She didn't know how she was going to get her back. Frank hadn't a clue. He was so out of touch with everything that had been going on since they arrived in Vegas. If truth were told, he was out of touch with her life back in Dublin too – but no more than she was with his.

"What's going on, Frank?" she finally said, opening her eyes and looking sadly at the man she was about to marry.

"Well, I've been putting off telling you this but something big has happened."

Vicky's heart pounded. She was anxious but ready to hear what he was about to say.

"I had a run of luck at the casino last night. I didn't want to say anything because you were looking for Tina but it's a good chunk and should help us out over the next few months."

Vicky looked at him in disbelief. She couldn't even think of money – not after the last two days. So while she was out looking for her daughter Frank was gambling heavily all night. Was this the sort of man that she wanted to marry?

Georgia led the way with John and Connie at her side. She swaggered with each step she took and Connie watched how her hips had caught John's attention.

"Hey, let's dress up?" she suggested as they passed a shop called Western Village, displaying a huge range of wigs, masks, paint and zombie-style clothing.

John liked the sound of it and he liked Georgia – she was a lot of fun. She wore her heart on her sleeve.

They went into the shop and Georgia picked up a squaw wig. She adorned her neck with tassels and feathers and put on a suede waistcoat. John stuck on a hippy moustache and put on a massive peace symbol chain. He finished the look off with a long wig and headband. Connie was not in the mood to join in – it irritated her that Georgia could just push herself on people and get away with it. She tried to smile and explained that she had a hell of a day and wasn't in the mood – but all the time the other two were getting more and more familiar and she didn't like it.

Eddie left the hotel room and made his way to Planet Hollywood – he knew that if he got there he would only be a stone's throw from Krave Nightclub. He had taken Suzanne's advice and was going to go out and enjoy himself. The previous night had been magical – from winning the money and then sleeping together in his suite. It was like a dream but one from which he had been rudely awoken in the lift. Secretly he was pleased that the wedding planner knew about Frank and him. Maybe she would feel the compulsion to tell his bride. It was a long shot but Eddie would try anything to get Frank back. The street was alight with buzz and fun and he guessed that he was almost there.

But his phone rang and it was Suzanne in a flood of tears.

"Where are you?" he asked.

"I'm up in the room – I really need you!"

She was sobbing so hard he turned on his heel and started to walk back towards the MGM.

"Relax and I'll be there in five minutes," he said as he picked up speed.

Suzanne was choking back the tears. Her insides were burning with the pain and loss that sat in her stomach – something that she had managed to control for the last decade with such skill. It was too raw. She went over to the mini-bar and poured herself a brandy and ginger ale. It was strong and sharp on her tongue but she needed the consolation that alcohol brings. This was too awful – she had rehearsed the words for so long but never expected to get the reaction that she had. He made her feel like a murderer – because that was how she had felt herself when she arrived home from the London clinic. Her mother never let her speak of the experience once they returned. It was as if it had never happened. And as the months and years passed Suzanne's confidence waned until she was left the sad and shy spinster in the department that nobody asked about her love life any more. She could cope with all that because she had held fast to the dream that one day she would tell Ronan and his reaction would be one of consolation and understanding. But she got the very opposite and she couldn't face dealing with the emotions that he was going through. She had to go home. There was no other way around it.

Eddie arrived through the door and rushed over to where she sat on the bed. He put his arms around her and let her sob wholeheartedly into his shoulder.

"There, there, Sue, tell Eddie what happened!"

Suzanne started to tell the story as if she was under a stopwatch – she couldn't get the words out quickly enough.

Eddie listened with care and understanding even though the entire situation couldn't have been more alien to his ears.

"So, my love, what are you going to do now?" he asked, wiping a lock of her blonde hair away from her tear-stained cheek.

"I don't know!" she sobbed. "I didn't expect his reaction to be like this – I don't think I can face him again – not while we're in Vegas anyway."

"At least he doesn't know your room number," he said as he lifted the phone to call reception.

"What are you doing?" Suzanne asked.

"Telling reception not to put calls through for you from Ronan in case he rings."

Suzanne shook her head. "I don't think he will – he hates me, Eddie."

Eddie spoke to the receptionist and then hung up.

"Now, my love – I'm getting you a drink – what's it going to be? Vodka? Brandy?"

Suzanne nodded. "I've just had a brandy and ginger ale but I'll have another."

Eddie fixed her the drink and handed it to her. Then he sat down beside her and watched her take a gulp.

"Do you want to lie down?" he asked, turning and fluffing up the pillows on the bed.

Suzanne shook her head.

"Maybe you'd like to go out? Escape from your thoughts? What about taking a trip downtown?"

"I really don't think I can face that."

Eddie tilted his head and looked at her dolefully. "Sue, it might be just what you need. Hey, we're in Las Vegas! All too soon we'll be back in rainy Dublin – and you'll be *so* sorry you didn't hit the town with me!"

Suzanne smiled despite her heavy heart. Poor Eddie! He had his heartache too but here he was, trying to comfort her. He was right – better to go out into the bright lights than stay here in her misery.

"Okay then," she said, "if you insist."

"I do. Go and fix your make-up, girl!"

"But, Eddie, I don't want to bump into Ronan again."

Eddie grimaced. "Vegas is a big place – and he'll be working tomorrow – let's just get on with enjoying tonight – okay?"

Suzanne went into the bathroom and got ready – Eddie was

right and if he could stay in Vegas, with all that he had to deal with, then so could she.

Frank watched as Vicky slept – she had taken a sleeping pill and was not likely to wake until morning. He was tempted to call Eddie but resisted. He had won so much money but was tempted to try for some more. He decided to call Charlie instead. Charlie was on his way to a game in Binion's in Fremont Street. It was a real change of scene – he seldom played downtown but because Fremont Street was the best spot to enjoy Halloween he had agreed to go there.

Frank went into the bathroom and splashed on his Boss aftershave. He was going to hit the town. He put on a new shirt and brought out his favourite linen jacket. He smoothed back his long black locks – Eddie loved it when he wore the linen jacket. Eddie knew him better than Vicky. That was the irony of his situation – he really wanted to spend his life with a man – and if not Eddie some other man. He looked at Vicky and sighed. After all she had been through, he couldn't turn around and explain to her now. Even though he knew by now that it was the right thing to do.

Fremont Street was heaving and Eddie and Suzanne were enjoying watching all the different costume-clad people strolling by. It was the first evening they had spent together and, after the turmoil earlier for each of them, they were happy to lose themselves in the madness of Halloween. Overhead the strains of "Thriller" rang out loud and the epic video flashed on the mile-long screen. It was something out of this world and surpassed any illuminated display either had ever seen.

Vegas Vic sparkled brightly amongst the countless light-bulbs glaring from the casino façades. The crowds moved in waves – angels, pirates, devils and bunny girls, Flintstones, gladiators, hippies and men in drag.

Suzanne even managed to forget about her emotional outburst with Ronan earlier and followed the flow of characters past a big white stagecoach – transport for a zombie bride being pulled by the skeletons of two horses. A whip cracked loudly from the coach and a shotgun blasted as the crowd cheered in a frenzy.

"Let's go and do some gambling," Eddie said. "Binion's is meant to be one of the oldest and most famous casinos downtown!"

Suzanne nodded and walked beside him, saying nothing but smiling and watching everything going on around her.

When they entered the casino it had a crazy vibe – full of ordinary Americans who had come here to play very serious card games. Every table was packed – the carnival atmosphere was electric.

"Fancy playing some cards?" Suzanne asked.

"What games do you know?"

"I watched that movie about the college kids who played Blackjack – *21* I think it was called. And I had a couple of goes with Ronan in the MGM the other night."

"Okay – let's try it." Eddie said enthusiastically and rushed over to a table. He didn't want to speak about Ronan again – they had come to Fremont Street to try and forget their unfortunate love lives.

Vicky was in the deepest sleep of her life and, although she knew that she was in slumber, her dreams were so lucid she didn't remember what it was like to be her waking self. The images were all symbols of different stages in her childhood. Her mother was there with her, feeding and caring for her. At her side was a man, tall and handsome, and he paced up and down in what used to be the kitchen in her mother's house. He was bellowing loudly, words so strange and long and harsh he could have been speaking another language – but now as an adult watching it all like an old film she could see that he was berating her mother. Putting her down and bullying her with each syllable. As a child all she understood and could focus on was his blond hair and strong features. But in this clip that rolled before her eyes she saw her mother tremble and sensed the urgency with which she was trying to put the food into Vicky's mouth because she was anxious to pick her up and carry her out of the room. The man was smoking a pipe and the air was heavy with the pungent aroma from the tobacco.

Suddenly she was another age – about seven and standing at a graveside clutching on to her mother's coat. There were people all around the hole in the ground but she couldn't see their faces – all she could focus on was a sea of black and her mother's silence. It was the same silence she had encountered in the kitchen when her father spoke. The next scene that flashed before her was her mother again with tears in her eyes. Vicky had never remembered seeing her mother cry but now that she was thrown back to her early teenage years she could understand the frustration that her mother was feeling as she tried to help Vicky to find herself and the path in life that would make her the happiest. She was always trying to get her to do something artistic or musical – she had to go to drama school for three years until eventually at the age of fourteen Vicky said no – she did not want to be a painter or an actor or a poet but to learn to type and get a good job as a secretary and meet a man and get married.

Her mother hadn't explained then why she was so unhappy with her choice of career direction and even all of these years later she couldn't come to terms with her mother's views on most of the important choices in life.

All Vicky ever wanted was stability. She loved David – he was all that she wished for and she hated the way her mother used to pass remarks when she came to visit them. She thought that he was boring and dull and would never understand how to make her heart sing.

On one occasion Vicky asked her mother if maybe she wasn't such an expert as she had led her to believe and maybe she just couldn't find anyone to match up to her husband. Of course Vicky couldn't recall much about her father and she had no one to tell her about him. Her mother never spoke of him – she only showed photos and said that was enough. Even up to the day she died she would never give her any more information. But as Vicky sat again in the high chair and listened to the intense, coarse and humiliating language that he was using to her mother she suddenly understood why her mother had remained silent and maybe why she never wanted to be in a position where she would have another man speak to her this way. She was a feisty woman who loved life and it seemed so odd to see her scared and meek in her husband's company. It explained why she loved to express herself so much through her painting once she had regained her independence. And why she had never remarried!

Then Vicky was back in the Canyon but this time Tina was with her – the chief was there too and he was blessing them both using the eagle feather and stones. Sage burned in the background and her mother joined them and they formed a circle with their hands and all the energy of the women amalgamated and became strong. A wind blew around them but left the three untouched. It was magical and mystical and Vicky felt the peace of all the loving feminine energy around her. She didn't need a father to mind her – her father was not the person whose memory she carried around in her head like an idol since he had died when she was seven. Her husband David was not the strong supportive rock that she had clung to for the duration of her first marriage and, now with the imprint of Frank on her mind, she realised that he was not and could never be who she wanted him to be either. He was dressed in a clown costume and dancing on the sideline, being spun around by the powerful wind. It was too much to bear and as the wind sped faster and faster around her . . .

She woke up. She sat up in the bed and looked around.

She was on her own. Then she put her head into her hands and cried and cried and cried bitter and sweet tears – for her mother and father. And still she had more – many more – they were for Tina and for herself.

She couldn't go back to sleep. She wondered where Frank had got to. She picked up her phone and dialled his number but it went straight to voicemail which was no surprise. Her head was light and she wanted to get up and do something. It was almost twelve o'clock. She went over to the safe and punched in the numbers to get some money – she got a shock when she saw only five hundred dollars in cash inside. Frank had brought a few thousand at least – or so he had told her.

She needed to speak to someone that she trusted about Frank – after the distressing dream she needed help. So she called the one person that she knew she could rely on.

John picked up his phone when he felt it vibrate – he couldn't hear it with the music blasting from the Oktoberfest side-shows and overhead speakers. He saw Vicky's name flash up and answered it promptly.

"John – sorry to annoy you again – you've been so good."

"No problem, Vicky – is everything okay?"

"I fell asleep but Frank's not here – where is he?"

"Sorry, Vicky, I don't know – hey, I'm down on Fremont Street with Connie and her friend – why don't you join us?"

Vicky flinched. "Eh – thanks but I don't think I should see Connie – I feel like such a fool for the way I lashed out at her earlier – it might be better if I see her in the morning with the kids as we arranged."

"Well, I think you shouldn't be on your own – I have no idea where Frank is. He said that he was staying with you." John hesitated. He had a good idea that Frank had run off with his male friend. "Look, will you please jump in a cab and meet me? I'm going to Binion's now – I can meet you in, say, half an hour by the tables on your right as you go in. How does that sound?"

Daunting – but she didn't want to say that. The slightest thing had her nervous and anxious and that was the way she was about everything in her life at the moment.

"I don't feel very safe getting a taxi on my own, to be honest!"

John understood. "But if you get it at the lobby they use good cab services that will take you straight to the Golden Nugget – then just walk on to Fremont Street and Binion's is in front of you."

It still sounded fairly daunting but she really needed to talk to him. Her dream had been so clear and she knew that she couldn't trust Frank but she didn't know what was best to do.

"And Vicky – it *is* Halloween – you might not recognise me at first." John laughed.

"Have you dressed up?"

"Yes – I'm the creepy hippy with long black hair and a purple headband – mind you, there are a few of us in the street."

Vicky managed her first laugh of the day. "Okay – I'll see you in about half an hour."

"Great," John replied. "Take care – it's mad down here but great fun!"

Then he was gone. Vicky looked at the phone. Fun – that was what she needed. She changed quickly and ran down to the foyer where the queue was short and she only had to wait behind five people before jumping into a cab!

Eddie couldn't believe his eyes. It definitely was him.

He turned around quickly, looking so shocked that Suzanne grabbed him by the shoulders.

"What – are you okay?" she asked.

"It's *him* over there at the Texas Hold 'Em table."

"Who?"

"Frank and he's with the guy from last night – Charlie! I can't believe it – oh God, I've been such a fool! And he's more concerned about gambling and making money than anyone or anything!"

Suzanne wanted to go over and throttle Frank for hurting her friend in this way. But she also wanted to know the truth – was Frank here to get married or was he just trying to recoup some cash? It wasn't adding up and now Frank had his arm around this Charlie and was getting too close for comfort, whispering in his ear. She dragged Eddie to a spot where she was sure Frank and Charlie were well out of sight. She didn't want him to see how Frank was laughing and joking with his friend.

"Eddie, you're going to have to confront Frank. His behaviour is way out of line!"

"It's cutting me up, Suzanne – I've been played with so much – can you imagine what his fiancée has been going through?"

Suzanne grimaced. "I don't think he's a nice person, Eddie – he has been playing around with so many people he doesn't deserve anyone. Maybe it's time you told him what you thought – stood up for yourself?"

Eddie had to agree – he definitely needed to do something, and soon, or else he would go insane.

John stood by the door and waited for Vicky. He watched while Connie and Georgia played some blackjack with cards being dealt by a woman wearing a bunny-girl outfit.

He had become more than protective of Vicky – he saw a vulnerability and innocence in her at the Grand Canyon that he hadn't seen before. His concern and desire to look out for her was growing as his tolerance of Frank was waning with incredible alacrity.

Vicky sat nervously in the back of the car as the driver assured her that the Holocaust during the Second World War was an idea entirely concocted by American Jews. He added that there were aliens and UFOs in Area 51, a short ride into the Nevada Desert and that 9/11 was definitely an inside job caused by operators of the Dow Jones stock exchange.

She desperately wanted the car to speed up but was nervous about the way that the driver weaved in and out of the lanes along the freeway. When she saw the horseshoe lights of the Golden Nugget come into view she breathed a massive sigh of relief.

She paid the driver and was happy to mingle with the masses swarming like bees in the direction of Fremont Street. She had to push her way through the crowds and eventually arrived under the twinkling lights of Binion's Casino.

She texted John and hoped that he was near. Her phone bleeped with a text from John. He was waiting at the entrance to the casino, he said. She turned and walked past the throngs until a tall man with a long black moustache and headband grabbed her. She got a fright and then realised it was John.

"Oh hi – you look good!" she said, managing a smile.

"Come on over to the girls."

Connie and Georgia were playing at a five-dollar limit table.

When Connie saw Vicky she jumped off her seat and gave her a big hug. "Good! You came! Now I can show you Vegas – the kids are safe and tucked up watching a movie."

Vicky gave a little smile. They could tackle the issue of their offspring in the morning – this was definitely not the time or place for serious discussions. It was a display of people behaving like kids in a giant Disneyland for adults. Vicky could feel herself getting caught up in the buzz of the festival.

Connie picked up a margarita from the tray of a passing waitress. She handed it to Vicky. "Here you go, honey – get in the holiday mood!"

John stood behind Connie as she took her seat again and continued to play. They laughed and joked with the dealer and Connie was the only one who seemed to be making her pile of chips bigger rather than smaller.

Suddenly Vicky let out a yelp. She had been looking around the room and had been intrigued to spot a man who looked like Frank – until she realised that it actually *was* him. She tugged on John's sleeve.

"Over there – look – it's Frank – who's he with? That guy looks familiar!"

John looked over to where she pointed and sure enough it was his brother. He wondered who the young man was at his side. A terrible thought struck him – could this be a boyfriend? This was not the place for Vicky to find out about Frank's alter ego!

"Eh – I'll go over and get him to come and join us," he said hastily, getting off his high stool and indicating that Vicky take his place. "You play on for me – I'll only be a minute."

Connie saw what was going on – but that guy at Frank's side was not the one that she had caught him kissing earlier in the morning. He really did know how to get around.

"Hey, Vicky, how are you doing? Got a good hand?" she said, leaning in closer to the Irishwoman and using her enthusiasm for the cards as a distraction.

"Sorry – Frank's over there – I want to go over to him – will you take over Georgia, please?" Vicky said, getting up to go.

237

Georgia sat down and watched Vicky walk away.

"What's up with these crazy Irish people?" she asked Connie.

Connie shook her head. "You don't really want to know. That woman's fiancé is gay and I hate to say it but I don't think there's going to be a wedding!"

The boss had been called from the pit – it was a lot of money for one player to gamble. Frank was on a buzz – so far he was up 250K. He felt invincible and with Charlie at his side he could take the casino.

A lot of high cards had been played and Frank had a pair of kings – another one had been dealt in the flop and he didn't think he could be beaten – a pair of fives were there giving him a poker – it was the house he was playing and he had a good chance of making a killing. If he hadn't been with Charlie there was no way that his bet would have been accepted but the pit bosses liked to see the young pro players in the downtown casinos.

He got the thumbs-up from the man in the suit who told him that it was okay to raise the stakes to one hundred thousand. Frank could see his money troubles dissipate before his eyes if this hand was his. Now that he had a cash flow it would make a big difference to his life and the stresses that he had been living with. He was about to call when he felt a tap on his shoulder.

Suzanne had tried to keep Eddie occupied with the cards as they were dealt but every few minutes she spotted his head turn in the direction of Frank's table. Eddie was a bag of nerves. Suzanne had never seen him so cut up about anyone or anything. She understood exactly how he felt – only a few hours ago she was the one in a heap. What was it with this town for bringing everyone's emotions to the surface?

"Why don't you just go over?" she'd said at last. "I can see that it's killing you. At least you'll know what he's up to."

"Okay!" Eddie had declared as he stood up. "I'm going over to him."

Suzanne had gathered up the chips and smiled at the dealer.

It was like a scene from a movie as Eddie strode over to Frank's table.

Frank didn't recognise John at first.

"What's going on?" John asked. "Who's your friend?"

Frank was about to play the biggest hand of his life – he didn't like his brother's accusatory tone. "What do you mean? For God's sake, John, I'm playing a massive hand!"

The dealer was glaring at John. He didn't want to lose such an amount on his table but it was looking that way, and already Frank had aroused a huge amount of interest from passers-by who wanted to see some of the action.

"Vicky is over there – you just left her alone in the room!"

Frank ignored him. He had no intention of dealing with anything except the game right now.

"Frank – answer me!"

But Frank just pushed out the chips.

"Thank you, sir," the dealer said and he pulled out a card from the shoe.

It was another king – unbelievable! Frank was trembling and Charlie congratulated him with a pat on the back. He turned around but his brother wasn't there and in his place was Vicky with pain and hurt in her eyes.

All Frank could feel was the ecstasy of the moment and the thrill of the win until Eddie appeared in his line of vision, right behind Vicky. Eddie was clearly furious – all he could do was point at Charlie with his finger wagging in the air. He stepped forward, not noticing Vicky by his side. Then he let out a roar and turned his pointing finger towards Frank's face.

"You lying cheat! It's bad enough having to share you with a woman but I won't share you with another man!"

Frank thought that he was going to implode on the spot. Had Eddie not noticed the woman who was standing at his side?

"Eddie!" he said, shock and horror drawn all over his face. "This is my fiancée, Vicky!"

239

The dealer started counting out the chips as the crowd around the table gasped.

"What's going on, Frank – who are these people?" Vicky was in total shock – like a little lost child. What was the man with the shaking finger implying? She had seen him before in the MGM the night that Tina went missing. Who was he and what was he saying about sharing Frank with a woman but not with a man? The penny slowly started to drop. Her mouth fell open – it was too much to take in – on top of Tina's elopement – her crazy dreams – this was the last straw. Was her Frank really having an affair with this man – both these men? Was this some bizarre nightmare? Her head started to spin and everything in front of her seemed to blur together. She was in darkness as she hit the floor.

"Oh my God!" a woman screamed.

Connie and Georgia came rushing over as John held the crowd back and Frank got down on his knees beside Vicky. Eddie was appalled on realising the scene that he had caused.

Suzanne knelt beside Frank. "I'm a physio – I can help – excuse me, please." She checked Vicky's respiratory tract and, holding her wrist, took her pulse.

Vicky opened her eyes and moved her head. She had fallen on the carpeted floor in a manner that didn't seem to have broken any bones or caused any serious injury.

"Are you okay – can you see? How many fingers do you see?" Suzanne asked, holding up two fingers.

"Two," Vicky said. She was groggy and still in shock.

Frank turned around to see Charlie was gathering up the chips.

"I'll take care of this!" said Charlie.

Frank watched his money being chucked into a bag and wanted to go to the cashier with Charlie but he couldn't leave Vicky.

The dealer had closed the table and the crowd was dispersing. John and Frank propped Vicky up on a stool and Connie gave her some water. Suzanne was trying to get Eddie to move away but couldn't – he was staring with such utter contempt at Frank that she was afraid there was going to be another scene.

John whispered in Eddie's ear. Suzanne couldn't make out if he was being threatening or just concerned but she knew that they had to get out of the casino and quickly.

Poor Vicky was speechless. She put her elbows on the table and her head into her hands. Then she looked up at John.

"Please, can you take me back to the hotel?"

Frank touched her arm but she shook him away and nestled into John for protection.

"I'll take her back to the Mirage, Frank," said John.

The night was over and this was one wedding party that had got more than it had bargained for from Vegas.

Frank stood in shock as he watched John lead Vicky away. Eddie was trying to apologise but Frank was numb and not listening. He had brought all this on himself. He had lied to everyone and hurt those who meant most to him in the process.

Connie followed John and Vicky as they approached the entrance. Catching up with them, she put her arm around Vicky.

"How you doing, honey?"

Vicky was now in tears. "Connie, Frank has been having an affair!" she sobbed.

"There, there – you've had a lucky escape, honey!"

"B-b-but why didn't I figure it out? I've been an idiot."

"You won't be the first bride to find out that her husband is gay before her wedding and you won't be the last!"

Vicky looked at Connie. She hadn't mentioned anything about Frank having an affair with a man! She realised in that instant that Connie already knew. Did she know all along? Why was she the last to know? She felt such a fool!

Georgia was bewildered by what was going on and traipsed behind with an air of disappointment. She'd been getting on so well with John, she had thought! But it was obvious by the way that this Irishman was so protective of Vicky that she was the real object of his affections.

When they stepped out on to the street Georgia decided that she wasn't going to miss out on the fun – she was dressed like a squaw and getting lots of attention from cowboys and vampires.

"I'm splitting, Connie," she whispered in her ear. "You coming?"

Connie felt that she should go with Vicky but it was becoming apparent that her services were not needed – she was feeling more like a gooseberry and maybe Frank wasn't the only one who liked someone that they shouldn't.

"Maybe I'll come with you," she answered Georgia. "Are you going back to the hotel, John?"

"Yeah – I'm taking her back to the Mirage. I'll see you tomorrow morning – with the kids if that's still on – okay?"

"Sure thing!" she replied. "Get a good night's sleep, Vicky!"

She watched them get into a cab outside the Golden Nugget. She looked on forlornly and Georgia gave her a big hug.

"Come on, this town is full of men just waiting for us to meet them! That big Irish guy only has eyes for Vicky."

And Connie knew that she spoke the truth. But she was so disappointed. When was she ever going to have someone for herself!

"Georgia, do you mind if I go home too? I don't feel up to painting the town tonight."

Georgia was visibly disappointed but in a way she understood. She could see why Connie had been so smitten by John – it was a pity that he was into somebody else.

"All right, hon – talk tomorrow," Georgia said.

Then she kissed her friend and let her walk to the cab rank. She would have to paint the town red on her own!

Vicky didn't speak in the back of the cab as they drove to The Strip and the Mirage. John stroked her hair gently away from her face and held her tightly to console her.

"John, I can't thank you enough for everything you have done for me – first with Tina and now with Frank. I had no idea – I feel such a fool!"

"Don't – I doubt he even realised himself until a couple of years ago."

Vicky shook her head. "How could he not have known his own sexual identity?"

"Believe me – we were brought up rather strangely. You know what our mother is like – she wouldn't believe it possible for someone in her family to be gay."

Vicky felt her stomach lurch. She took a deep breath and the moment passed.

"Almost there – you can stay in my room if you like – there are two beds."

Vicky nodded. She couldn't face Frank – and she didn't care about her make-up or clothes or anything – all she wanted to do was sleep.

John kept his arm protectively around her shoulders as they walked through the Polynesian foyer and the casino.

"Nearly there," he said comfortingly as they approached the lift.

In the room Vicky let out a loud sigh and flopped on to the bed.

"Would you like something to drink – a brandy maybe?" John asked.

He had read her mind. "Yes, please." She took the glass gratefully from him. "John, I don't know how to thank you – I don't know how I could have got through the last couple of days without your support and patience. You've been so kind!"

John shrugged bashfully. "I would have done it for anybody – but I could see that you needed minding. I had a bad feeling coming out here, to be honest, but I was hoping for the best."

Vicky took a gulp from her brandy glass, then put it down on the bedside table. She swung her legs up on the bed and settled into a more relaxed pose on propped pillows.

"How long have you known Frank was gay?" she asked, picking up her brandy again.

"I knew before he did – as a kid he was different – things he said and did. The funny thing is that he didn't know himself. I mean, he knew deep down but never addressed it."

Vicky shook her head. "I don't understand. How was he able to be with me?"

"He likes women too – he's had other girlfriends in the past – but he would never have been looking for a relationship in the same way as other guys."

"But he's over forty years of age – how could he have kept it inside?"

"Lots of gay men get married and never tell their wives. Why does anyone do anything that isn't true to their nature?"

Vicky could figure that one out on her own. "Fear?"

John nodded. "Fear is the cause of all our problems in this world. If only people were more themselves and less afraid of what others thought of them, the world would be a happier and better place."

Vicky looked in awe at the tall and handsome man sitting beside her on the big king-size bed. How could she have thought him selfish and lazy and misjudged him so badly? John was a real man who was comfortable in his own skin and never tried to be anyone or anything that he wasn't. He had nothing to prove – he'd lived the celebrity life and yet settled back into living an ordinary life with ease.

"Do you think I live in fear?"

John could feel an eggshell moment coming on – he was never going to answer this question correctly. But then maybe Vicky needed to hear his opinion. And after the illumination maybe she would be ready to hear it. He had to be gentle.

"I think you haven't always had it easy, Vicky, and like so many people you do care about what other people think – maybe to your own detriment?"

Vicky felt ashamed but he was so right. She had always cared what other people thought of her and to such an extent that it had prevented her from finding her true self. She didn't feel that way now. Her daughter had left her and got married and her fiancé had had another lover all along. All she wanted was someone for her and the way John was looking at her right this moment she wanted him to be that person.

She let out a little cry. "Please, John – will you hold me?"

Their bodies were perfectly placed on the big bed to fall into a lovers' embrace and that's exactly what they did.

It was so warm and loving and real in John's arms that Vicky felt free for the first time in many years. It was different to the way Frank had held her – she realised that now. And John smelt different – he was raw and clean and strong. Her mind cleared of all the things that had happened in Vegas and all she could focus on was John and the touch of his cheek so close to hers. She moved carefully and gently to search for his lips.

The first kiss was so soft and gentle it made her tremble. His tongue slipped so softly between her lips she felt as if she was being kissed by an angel. He was so delicious she craved more of him. She thrilled as he slid his leg over hers, engulfing her figure like a cocoon.

John knew how to arouse a woman – he was an expert. The same skilful sensitive fingers that drew music from his guitar now moved her towards a climax. She hardly noticed her clothes being peeled off like the skin of a ripe fruit. She was bursting inside. As he started to fondle her breasts she tingled from his touch. He told her how beautiful she was – how much he desired her and what he was going to do to her. She didn't blush because she wanted it as much as he did. Nobody had ever caressed her this way before. His hand slid between her legs. He whispered to her, making her move in rhythm with each stroke. She was able to come to orgasm from his tender fingers – something she had never been relaxed enough to do with any other man. As he stripped she watched his smooth figure and fine muscles revealed. He slipped inside her with such ease and pleasure that she gasped. This is how sex is meant to be, she thought to herself. Because in all of her years of marriage to David and all the nights she had spent with Frank – she had never experienced anything like making love to John Proctor!

Tina was asleep in the spare room when Connie arrived home.

Connie expected Kyle to be with her in the big double bed but instead he was up and still looking at the TV. It was an ideal opportunity for her to talk to her son before meeting with Tina's mother the next morning. Poor Vicky – she had been through so much these last couple of days. And she was meant to be preparing for her big day which now wasn't going to happen. Connie couldn't help feeling sorry for herself also. Her own son's wedding hadn't been what she had hoped for him. She walked into the lounge and sat down on the couch beside him. He seemed relieved that she was home.

"How you doing, son?"

He smiled and let his head fall on her shoulder like he used to when he was a little boy. Connie lifted her arm and cradled him with it. She understood he was feeling shell-shocked. The romance and passion of young love had moved very swiftly into the realm of reality and he would have to take responsibility for his actions.

"Mom, what have I done?"

"Fallen in love, son – it's not easy."

Kyle wished he had some answer to sort out the mess but he couldn't come up with one. "Mom – I'm very confused about the future."

"You have both had a crazy few days, honey – you let it all happen too fast."

"I knew what I was doing marrying Tina – I don't want to change that."

Connie sighed. The reality was a very different thing to what he wanted but his young mind hadn't properly thought through the consequences of his actions.

"Nobody is saying you can't stay married but how are you going to support yourselves – where will you live? Which country for openers?"

Kyle had thought that marrying Tina would guarantee her right to stay in the US but now he was getting the impression she didn't really want to stay in the States. He had never considered living in Ireland – he had never been out of the States – he had no idea what it would be like on a little island on the edge of Europe.

"I just wanted to give her the chance to stay here – not go back to Ireland with her crazy mom."

Connie fondled her son's long fringe, running her fingers through it. "Oh, sweetie – it's not that simple. Vicky is a good mother and deep down Tina loves her. She's young and confused – and you guys did something very romantic but also very stupid. You might not be able to stand each other in a couple of months' time."

4am in LAS VEGAS

Kyle started to get defensive. "We have a special bond – we knew what we were doing."

"And did you use a condom?"

Kyle felt his cheeks burn – he hadn't the first time they did it – he hoped they would be okay. "Of course I did. Jeez, what's that got to do with anything?"

Connie sighed – she wasn't going to win with a one-to-one like this. "Try and get a good sleep tonight and see how you feel in the morning. You have a few days to see how it all pans out. If she really doesn't want to stay here, she could go back and you guys can Skype each other and visit during the school holidays – don't forget Tina is doing her SATs or whatever they are called in Ireland. Her mom has high hopes for her to go to college and I would like you to go to college too."

Kyle's face showed a multitude of emotions. "I could go to school in Ireland, couldn't I?"

Connie wasn't sure. "It would be very expensive. Sleep on it and we'll find an answer in the morning – okay?"

Kyle nodded. He was exhausted. He kissed his mother goodnight and walked down the hallway to the spare bedroom. Tina was sound asleep so he closed the door and turned around and went into his own bedroom – it was where he felt safest and happiest. He would deal with everything in the morning.

Eddie and Suzanne got back to the room in the MGM and threw themselves on their beds.

"I don't think I can take much more of the excitement in this town, Eddie!" Suzanne declared. "And I couldn't bear to run into Ronan either!"

"Has he tried to call you?"

Suzanne looked at her phone – there were no messages. "I doubt I'll hear from him again!"

Eddie said nothing but deep down knew that it was only a matter of time before there would be some sort of communication.

"What are you going to do?" she asked.

"About Frank?"

She nodded.

"I don't have an option – watching him fawning over that Charlie was bad enough but watching him gambling and fawning over all that money, I have to say I saw him in a completely different light. I'm not sure that I would like to have a relationship with him any more!"

Suzanne was shocked. But it was an epiphany of sorts and she was delighted to hear her friend speak such sense. "Well, good on you! You deserve better and I'm lucky to have you as my friend, Eddie – that I know," Suzanne sighed.

Eddie pushed himself up on his elbow. There was something he wanted to know. "Why did you never tell me about the abortion before, Sue?"

Suzanne hung her head. "Oh, Eddie – I've been so ashamed. It felt like the wrong thing to do at the time – I would have loved a baby – even back then."

"Could you not have run away from your mother and had it?"

Suzanne had asked herself the same question over and over after the deed was done.

"Run where? Pregnant? If I looked for help the social services would have just sent me back home! Besides – I can't explain – my mother had such a hold over me – I always needed her approval and opinion before I did anything. And now she doesn't even know me half the time!"

Frank was all alone and fumbling in his pockets for some cash. He had let Charlie slip off with all of the winnings and he hadn't enough to get a cab home. It should have been the best night of his gambling life but it looked like he had gambled on too much and too far. He stepped out on to Fremont Street and took out his iPhone to see his position on the map. The Mirage was a good long walk away.

How could he have been so foolish as to let Charlie walk away with his chips? He decided to phone him and see where he was.

But Charlie's phone just rang and rang.

4am in LAS VEGAS

He checked the Google Map again on his iPhone and started to walk – at least this way he knew that he was going in the right direction. Then he saw the Stratosphere ahead in the distance and once he reached that he was on The Strip.

His head pounded as the scene in Binion's played back in his head. He really should not have gone out and left Vicky. It was all over. Vicky would probably never talk to him again and he couldn't blame her. He had used her and the idea of a wife to forge a respectability that he thought would help him out of the mess that he had created of his life. All the years of decadence and indulgence left him with nothing but debts. He wondered why he found it so difficult to be true to himself and who he really was. Even the way he spoke was a lie – why couldn't he speak with his natural northside accent like his brother? Maybe because he wasn't grounded like John was or happy in his own skin. But it was easy for John – he had always liked women and understood his sexuality. John didn't have to live up to their mother's expectations either. Their mother was a pivotal reason why he himself had never explored his sexuality until he was well into his thirties. Somehow the fact that he concentrated on his career and not women and relationships like his other friends was a source of pride and pleasure for his mother – little did she know that the real reason was because he preferred, and always had preferred, to look at men's bodies and fantasise about them.

The power and control that Bernadette held over Frank had been a source of intrigue for Eddie. He couldn't understand why Frank had to visit his mother so many times during the week. It was easy for Eddie to judge – he was only one of a huge family that lived miles away.

Frank wondered how he had fit it all in over the past year – Vicky, Eddie and his mother. On top of all his financial and business worries. But as he walked through streets with packs of zombies and ghouls he also felt a kind of relief. It was all out in the open now – he would have to return to Dublin and deal with the consequences. The huge win would certainly help. He would sort Charlie out in the morning. He would sort everything out in the morning. For now he put his head down and concentrated on getting back to the Mirage and the start of his new life – whatever that was going to be!

Georgia went back to the Golden Nugget and scanned the casino floor. She didn't want to sit up at the bar of Rush Lounge on her own – someone could take her for a hooker. Then she spied the handsome young guy that had been sitting at the table in Binion's in the middle of all the commotion. He was fit and handsome and had won a major pile of chips. Georgia wasn't a gold-digger but her regular job as florist in the littlest chapel didn't exactly pay big time. She was in her early thirties but, although this guy was younger than her, she felt sure that he would be interested.

She slipped on to a stool next to him and flashed him a wide smile.

He smiled back with a smug satisfaction that said he was a man in his element. He was playing for fun now – Connie could read his body language. At his side was the bag of chips from Binion's and she wondered how much was in it.

Connie was in her sixth year in Vegas and it hadn't turned out to be the money pot that she had hoped it would be – she had a nice lifestyle but her job was boring and she really didn't think that she could spend much longer in the city. She always said that she would return to Florida one day but not until she had made enough to buy a little house by the beach and have some put aside. She had contemplated becoming a hooker when she arrived first but quickly realised that twenty-eight was old by Vegas standards. At thirty-four she was ready to leave but hadn't even got her own house – she was still renting and she had never met her millionaire and got swept off in a coach like Cinderella and now she realised that it was never going to happen.

But something possessed her on this devilish night of ghouls and vampires – she could always do it another way!

Vicky lay on the covers with her nakedness on display and she didn't mind. It was another first. Neither spoke nor felt the need to.

It was a perfect moment and Vicky felt peace on a level she had never experienced after making love. She didn't have a huge list of lovers to compare John with but she realised that she had experienced something special and true that would change her life forever.

The Volcano erupted outside and the pounding of the Polynesian drums started.

John let out a little laugh and Vicky joined him.

"I feel really happy – I know it's wrong but it feels right!" she whispered.

John turned his head so that he could see her face. "Why is it wrong? We are two consenting adults – we are not married to anyone else. I think Frank would have to admit that he can't talk!"

"I know he's a strange character. All I want is a simple life – I guess I got more than I bargained for when I got involved with Frank. And I'm not just talking about his secret boyfriend!"

John nodded. "You have to understand where he's coming from. He always had aspirations way back – even when he was a little kid. The Celtic Tiger was the worst possible time for someone with an addictive character like he has."

"I knew that he gambled – back in Dublin – but not to such an extent. I'm beginning to realise that I had no idea what he was doing with his time when we were not together – I thought that he was working hard in the restaurants."

It was time to explain a few home truths to Vicky. John had to be gentle in the way that he did it.

"Frank made a lot of money on paper with his investments in property – with each apartment he bought he could accumulate collateral to buy another and another but when the bubble burst on the property market he found himself left with a whole load of negative equity."

"So he doesn't have money from the restaurants?" Vicky was aghast. She always presumed that he was a wealthy clever businessman – he certainly always gave her the impression that he was anyway.

"His love of gambling doesn't help – but at the end of the day as each apartment block and tower went up along the skyline of

Dublin a little piece of who we are as a nation was lost. Frank and all his friends would think I'm cynical saying that but it's true."

He continued as Vicky listened intently. She loved to hear him speak with such truth and wisdom – before, she had thought he was a dropout not living in the real world, but maybe he was the one with vision and solid grounded beliefs and all those running around accumulating their euros and properties were the delusional ones.

"I like a quote I heard a few years back from one of the Chippewa Indians," he said. "*I do not think the measure of civilisation is how tall its buildings of concrete are, but rather how well its people have learned to relate to their environment and fellow man.*"

"Oh that's beautiful, John," Vicky sighed. If Frank had listened to his brother maybe he wouldn't be in such a state now – if he had been true to himself. But it was easy to judge someone else. As she rested her head on John's chest a litany of truths occurred to her. If she had been less concerned by what other people thought she would have been a better daughter and a better mother. Her relationships with those that she loved would be true also. She had been living behind a veil in the lovely house on the Hill of Howth while her fiancé had been gambling and cavorting with another man. It was no wonder that Tina had eloped – it was a desperate cry for help. Tomorrow was another day and a chance to find out who she really was. No time to be afraid. Things had changed in Vicky's world – radically.

Chapter 19

*Do not judge your neighbour until you walk
two moons in his moccasins.*

~ CHEYENNE PROVERB ~

The next day was bright and gloriously sunny – just like the one before. Tina had slept well, considering, but was nervous and anxious about meeting her mother. Kyle wasn't in the bed beside her. She slipped out from under the sheets and made her way to the hall. There wasn't a sound from anywhere. She made a quick visit to the bathroom and then started her search for her husband. She didn't know what was behind every door in the house and wondered how to get to Kyle's bedroom before she accidentally opened the door to Connie's. There was nobody in the kitchen or lounge. It was early – twenty to eight. She crept quietly around until she heard Kyle's snoring. She opened the door of his bedroom, slipped in and watched him sleep. He had chosen to sleep here rather than in the guestroom with her – he had returned to what he knew – to the place where he felt the most comfortable. He was only a kid – not some great superhero that was going to whisk her away to safety and a new life. Besides, she didn't want to stay in Vegas – she knew that now. And even though she had so much to complain about, living at home and going to the Institute, now she wanted to be home in her own house in Ireland. And most of all she wanted her mummy.

Vicky stirred in the bed and almost forgot where she was. John turned on hearing her movements.

"Did you sleep okay?" he asked.

"Mmm, thanks – and I didn't have any crazy dreams for a change."

John laughed.

"Why are you laughing?" she asked.

"That will be the illumination that the chief did when we were at the Canyon – you will be fine in a couple of days. I'm so glad you had it done – you will probably need all the strength you can get for the next few days."

"Do you really believe in all that shaman stuff?"

John seemed offended. "Of course I do. It has been around a lot longer than conventional medicine."

Vicky smiled. "My mother would have loved you!"

"Why?"

"She was such a hippy – so alternative. I guess that's why I disregarded her beliefs and was so conservative with my own views – she scared me."

John stroked her hair gently. "The truth is scary. It's easier to believe everything you're told in the media – on the news and in the papers. The reality is that we all make our own worlds and each person is the centre of a different universe."

Vicky frowned. He had lost her now.

John looked deeply into her emerald eyes – she really was a lost soul. Maybe that was her attraction. She brought out a need in him to protect and nurture and nobody had ever made him feel that way before. The fact that her mother was high-spirited and her daughter definitely was too, made him wonder if subconsciously he saw something deep inside Vicky's psyche that needed to be drawn out – maybe that was his role in her life and why she had met Frank and why they were all here now in Vegas.

This belief made sense to John and as they looked at each other with their hearts open they kissed. There was no rush to go to Connie's place – the urgency was here and now and they were together for a reason.

Georgia had checked into a room in the Sahara with Charlie. She wasn't known there and it was the perfect spot to enact her plan. She had laced Charlie's drinks – getting him doubles and triples until he was well and truly intoxicated. Then she brought him to the bedroom. He wasn't able to perform and she was happy to sacrifice the sex for the job at hand. When she was sure that he was asleep she opened his bag and was startled by the weight of the chips. She had no idea that they were playing for so much. She had figured that maybe he had twenty or thirty hundred but she had no idea that he'd had such a huge win. There was 350,000 dollars' worth of chips in his bag – enough to change her life forever. And to think this young kid had made all that in one night! She had learnt nothing in her six years here. But this was her chance to escape. No more wedding bouquets or late nights in the chapel watching others in love. She could pack up and start her journey back to Florida today. He was so drunk he could have left the chips anywhere and, besides, as far as he was concerned she was some crazy squaw. All the CCTV cameras would show her as such if he did figure out how he lost the chips. It was the perfect crime.

Charlie stirred in the bed so she had to be extra quiet. She put back on her squaw wig and put the chips in a laundry bag. She checked his wallet, leaving him just enough to pay for the room. Then she tiptoed out of the bedroom and into the hallway. She would get her car in the Golden Nugget and collect her belongings from her rented apartment. She could be out of Vegas in an hour.

Frank wasn't sure how long he had slept but it hadn't been that long. He looked at his watch. He did wonder where Vicky had spent the night and suspected that it was with John – platonically of course!

255

He needed to apologise and talk to her but his head was buzzing over the whereabouts of his chips and he decided that even though it was early he just had to speak to Charlie. Frank dialled his number but couldn't get through – it went straight to voicemail. He wondered if Charlie had made it home safely with the chips or if he had cashed them. He did trust Charlie but was concerned nonetheless. He wouldn't be happy until he had the cash in his hand.

He tried John's number and this time it rang out. John was usually prompt in answering his phone – things were getting strange. He thought about calling Eddie but he felt he had well and truly blown it with him. Eddie's outburst in Binion's was clearly the last straw for him. Frank didn't blame him either for his frustration. Nobody deserved to play second fiddle in the way that he had for so long. All this time he had hoped that Eddie would go off him like the couple of other men that he'd had brief flings with, but Eddie was different – he was sincere and much more sensitive. It was a shame that he couldn't be with him publicly but that was never going to be an option – not while his mother was alive anyway.

Tina thanked Connie for the cup of coffee and plate of toast. She had to act like a grown up now that she was a married woman – but what she really wanted was a bowl of cornflakes.

Kyle sat quietly at the other side of the table sipping on his mug of coffee. He was numb after the night and looked sadly at Tina who seemed very different to the spirited teen who had driven with him through the desert.

"So, your mom is going to be here in a few minutes, Tina, and it would be good if you had figured out what you're going to do," said Connie.

Tina took a sip of her coffee and hid behind the mug. She had no idea what she wanted to do. All she did know was that she wanted to go home to Ireland. She looked over the rim of her mug at the handsome young man at the other side of the table – her husband. It was totally bizarre – she'd had no idea what she was doing the day before – she realised that now.

Kyle was quiet too.

"Well – do you want me to leave you two alone to figure out what's going to happen? Because you don't have much time!" Connie was getting impatient. The teens had put them through enough and now it was time to talk the talk.

"It's okay, Mom – stay. We just haven't figured out where we want to live," Kyle said.

Tina nodded. "Yeah – that's it – we just haven't thought it out."

Connie shook her head. "Well, you guys are all married and grown up now so you really should be in your own place – shouldn't you?"

Tina gasped. She wasn't ready to fend for herself. She was still at school. "I want to go to art college – I always have."

"Well, Kyle – are you going to put your wife through art college?"

Kyle blinked. "I, ah, want to play music – you know that – write songs and . . . I thought we'd live here, Mom!"

Connie smiled softly. "I love you, son, but you're a married man now – I was only nineteen when I married your father and we were living on our own. Jeez, I had you and your brother when I was only twenty-two!"

"I really need to go to art college in Ireland but my mum won't let me even try!" Tina blurted out.

"Then go to art college here!" Kyle exclaimed.

"And are you going to pay for your wife?" Connie asked. "College is expensive. You have any idea how much your brother's expenses are and he has a scholarship?"

The truth was that Kyle didn't – he had no idea how much it cost to survive in much the same way as Tina didn't either.

Kyle and Tina looked at each other silently.

Connie's no-nonsense practical approach resonated with Tina – she wished her own mother was more like her.

"Well, kids, Vicky is gonna be here in twenty minutes – she just called and you guys had better know then what it is that you really want to do. But, much as I love you, you can't stay here – I can't afford to support the two of you and put you through college."

Connie lifted her coffee cup and left the kitchen. The silence she left behind her assured her that she had done the right thing. It was a much better way to make them realise the consequences of their actions. She sat out on the porch and watched the sprinklers start up and spray her lawn. She had worked hard and come a long way from the woman who had left California on that fateful night. Her son would have to realise what it meant to fend for himself now – she had to be firm. It broke her heart to be this way but it was for the best.

Ronan felt terrible when he woke. He couldn't get the thought of his unborn child out of his head and the tear-stained face of Suzanne haunted him even more. His phone rang and it was one of the reps from work. Yes, he was up and ready to meet at the Convention Center. Yes, he had done his prep and brought all of the paperwork. Yes, he would be there in thirty minutes. It was awful to have such a pain before facing a new project but somehow he knew that this pain wasn't one that would easily fade away.

John held Vicky's hand in the back of the taxi. Connie's house was just a ten-minute ride away.

"Are you sure you don't want to see Frank after this?" he asked.

Vicky shook her head. "I can't stand the thought of speaking to him. I don't know what I would say for a start. Right now I just want to see Tina and get this mess sorted." She had been through enough.

John stroked the palm of her hand with his thumb. He had awoken something inside her that touched his soul and he was happy. He wanted to be there for her every step of the way – with the teenagers and when she decided that she would be ready to speak to Frank.

The car drove into a salubrious estate with perfectly placed trees and flowers in the gardens. Vicky spotted Connie's car in one of the drives and the taxi pulled up outside.

"Thanks," John said as he paid the driver.

Vicky waited at the kerb for John to get out of the car. They were at the porch before Vicky saw Connie sitting on a chair in the corner.

"Hi there," Connie said. "Do you want a quick word before we go in to the kids?"

"Hi, Connie – good idea," John said.

Vicky took a seat beside Connie. "Thanks for last night and everything. I have been a bit of a drama queen, Connie – sorry."

"Hey, honey, it's okay – you've had a lot to deal with." Connie was careful not to mention Frank. It was an unspoken weight that hung between the three of them – unmentionable until the present situation was sorted out.

"What have the kids said this morning?" John asked anxiously.

"Those dumb kids don't know what they want!" Connie said, shaking her head in dismay. "Tina wants to go to art college and Kyle thinks they can stay here and live with me – they don't know what they want!"

Vicky tensed up. "I could shake her – she knows how I feel about art college – that has nothing to do with this mess she has got into. Have they said anything about an annulment? You would know the situation, Connie – surely they can just get one?"

Connie shook her head. "They both want to stay married and be with each other, Vicky, that's the message at the moment but maybe when they realise that life isn't a bowl of cherries in the real world they will consider something on those lines."

"That's ridiculous," Vicky couldn't hide the emotions she was feeling. Her face was now red. "They have to get an annulment or divorce or whatever before we talk about college or anything else."

"If we bully the kids into doing that they will gang up and just run away!" Connie said. "I know my Kyle!"

John took Vicky's hand to placate her. "Connie is right. It's much better for them to see the reality of what they have done and have to deal with it – more chance of them coming to that realisation themselves – if we make them split they will get tighter."

Vicky gasped. She hadn't considered any option other than her own initial conclusion. John and Connie had a point and maybe she could try and be more flexible. She didn't really have a choice – she was way out of her depth.

"I think we should ask them what they are going to do – put the ball in their court?" Connie suggested.

The other two nodded.

"Are we ready to go in then?" John asked.

"Okay," Vicky said.

The kitchen was big and bright and the two young people sat at the white table in the middle of the room. Kyle had moved over to be beside Tina – he knew that she would be uneasy about seeing her mother.

Vicky burst into tears on setting eyes on her daughter. The relief and emotion of the past two days rolled down her cheeks in huge drops. Tina didn't stir but felt troubled on seeing her mother this way. She had caused all this upset and she felt bad.

Connie pulled up a chair and urged John and Vicky to do the same.

"Okay, guys," John said with deadpan seriousness. "I've spoken with your mom, Tina, and we want to know what your plans are?"

"Oh!" Tina gasped. "We haven't really decided."

Kyle knew their mothers were playing a game of chess. He realised that they had to be careful or they would end up looking like two idiot kids – which in many ways was how he really felt. How had he thought they could live happily ever after in his mom's house?

"Well, you had better make up your minds because this trip is going to be cut short!" Vicky announced.

It was news to Connie and John but they were happy that Vicky was feeling strong enough to join the debate.

"We're going home early? Why? Is it because of us?" Tina asked.

Vicky shook her head. "No. I'm not going to marry Frank. I think it's best if we go home."

Tina gasped in surprise, her eyes wide.

"No way – we need more time to figure out what we're going to do!" Kyle protested, wrapping his arm protectively around her.

"Well, I'm going home. Tina, if you're coming with me you had better let me know." Vicky's tone was very matter of fact and in complete contrast to the tears earlier.

Tina was panicked by the news but at the same time bursting inside with joy that her mother wasn't going to marry Frank. "But why aren't you going to marry Frank?"

Vicky did not want to answer that question. "It's been a long few days. We can discuss it another time but for now I just need to know what you're doing."

"Can't I spend the next few days with Kyle like we had planned?"

Vicky shook her head. "I'm going home on Wednesday and whoever wants to can come with me! If you stay with Kyle, I'll take it that you don't want to live with me!"

It was putting a gun to the newlyweds' heads but this was obviously the approach that was needed.

"I want to go back to Dublin, Mum, but I want to be with Kyle – we love each other. You never listen to me and what I want."

"You don't know what you want – you're too young!" Vicky exclaimed.

John could see how the last remark was setting Tina up to pounce on her mother's words. Why couldn't Vicky have stopped when she was in control of the situation and was winning her daughter over?

"Look, Tina – emotions are still running high," he said. "Do you want us to come back later?"

A stubborn look took over Tina's face. She was not going to take this from her mother – had she been so foolish as to think that she would really listen to what she had to say?

"I'm glad you saw through Frank at last, Mum, but I need to be with Kyle – we need time to sort out what we're going to do."

"Well, you didn't need time to decide to get married, did you?" Vicky snapped.

It was the remark that turned the conversation around and backfired on Vicky.

Tina burst into tears.

"This is not helping anyone," John said. "Your mum and I'll go outside, Tina, and let you two talk with Connie okay?" With that, he stood up and ushered Vicky out to the porch. She was a bag of emotions and needed to take stock.

Vicky sat on the wooden chair and put her head into her hands. "I've gone and done it again – made things worse."

John sat beside her. "Don't beat yourself up. Things are not easy and you've had more to deal with over the last couple of days than most people would in a couple of years. What are you willing to do with the kids?"

"What do you mean?"

"Well, what do you want?"

"I want my daughter home and back with me and not married."

John held her hand to calm her down. "Well, you might not be able to get all of those things but maybe you could meet in the middle."

"What do you suggest?"

John shrugged. "Kyle could come with her back to Dublin. They will probably be bored with each other after a few weeks anyway when reality kicks in and she has to go back to school. If he has to get a job it will all be very different!"

"I don't even know where I'm going to live – I mean Frank and I co-own that house in Howth!"

"Don't worry about that – I'll sort Frank out. I won't let him move you from your home."

"I shouldn't have moved from my old house – oh God, what a mess I've made of my life! And here am I, attacking my daughter for making a mess of hers!" Her head fell against his shoulder.

John let her cry her heart out. He was happy to be her support. Something big had brought them together and when he awoke all those passions and possibilities in her the night before, he knew that she was the woman he had been waiting for all his life.

Suzanne and Eddie were enjoying a day by the pool, surrounded by lush tropical vegetation and palm trees. Waterfalls gushed into the clear blue water and the prospect of some pampering in the world-famous spa awaited them later.

It was Eddie who'd insisted they spoil themselves and make the most of the short time they had left in Vegas.

"Are you feeling any better?" he asked.

Suzanne took a sip from her cocktail glass. She looked stunning in her little blue bikini with her dark shades resting on her blonde hair. "Thanks, Eddie – you know, I really am. I can't remember the last time I spent a day doing nothing like this and it's wonderful!"

"Well, you deserve it," Eddie said. "Ronan and Frank don't realise how good they had it with us!"

Suzanne smiled. Eddie was better than any girlfriend – he really knew how to make her feel better. She stuck her head into her book and tried not to think about Ronan. She had to make the most of the next twenty-four hours – before she knew it she would be back on the British Airways 777 bound for Heathrow airport. She had rung Leo earlier while it was late at night in Dublin and he was finding the going tough with their mother. It was definitely a good thing that he got to see what life was like for her. She would be interested to see how he was on her return. She sighed. It would be so lovely to have the same freedom back in Dublin to date and feel love as she had with Ronan in the Grand Canyon. At least now that she knew what it was like, she could search for it again. Part of her resistance to dating had been a lack of confidence and the past twenty-four hours had shown her that she had the ability to be in a relationship. She would treat life with new gusto when she returned to Dublin.

Ronan stood at the stand in the massive Convention Center. The hall was filling up and already two big firms had placed substantial orders. By now he would normally be buzzing but all he could think about was Suzanne and the way she had left him in Mix. He hadn't the nerve to call. There was still so much he wanted to ask her. Had she been holding a candle for him all of this time? He had been so self-absorbed, with his new life in America, that he'd just put all thoughts of her to the very back of his subconscious but spending those two days with her in the Grand Canyon had awoken emotions in him that were carried in the depths of his soul.

"Do you carry voice-recognition software?" a very pert woman in a light grey business suit asked.

"Eh yes – we have several to choose from," he answered robotically.

As he leafed through his company's brochure flashes of Suzanne came up on every page. The humming of voices from all angles around him agitated his mind. He really was tormented by what could have been and how different his life would have been if he'd had a child with Suzanne.

The woman continued to speak and although Ronan could see her lips move he couldn't take in what she was saying – she was like a pneumatic drill and her constant drone reminded him of Mary Quinn. He thought he was going to be sick.

"Can I get one of the experts in this area to talk to you?" he said, calling over one of the reps who had just arrived in Vegas. The woman didn't seem pleased to be fobbed off in such a manner but Ronan didn't care. He took out his handkerchief and wiped his brow as he strode to the bathrooms which were a good walk away on the other side of the hall. Suzanne's face was following him with every step that he took. When he finally reached the toilet he took a cubicle and shut the door with a bang. His stomach heaved and he vomited violently into the bowl.

He went outside and rinsed his mouth out at the sink. He stared at himself in the mirror, seeing the sweat on his brow, the hurt in his eyes. All his youthful dreams and aspirations came flooding back, the hopes and desires that had floated into the stratosphere and he'd thought were gone forever. Why had he been so hard on Suzanne? It clearly wasn't her fault that she had the abortion. She'd been in a hopeless and powerless position. And he remembered exactly what Mary Quinn was like and how she gave her daughter such a hard time. He had to call her to apologise for the way that he had behaved in the restaurant. He cleaned himself off and went out to the corridor where he found a quiet corner. He dialled her number and it went straight to voicemail. He paused and opened his mouth but no words came out. What had he intended to say? I'm sorry that you had to go through all that trauma on your own but I wish you hadn't killed our baby? It sounded selfish and accusatory! Maybe it would be better if they spoke face to face? Maybe she would see him before she left? He would have to be quick – this was her last full day – she would be on the plane home by lunchtime tomorrow.

Frank was uptight. So far he had made ten calls to Charlie and each time they went to voicemail. He checked the safe in his room and found the last five hundred dollars still safely there. The 350K that he had won was going to be the difference between bankruptcy and a hopeful future.

His head pounded every time he thought of Vicky. He hadn't wanted her to find out about Eddie and least of all in the way that it had happened. He tried John's number and got through this time.

"Where are you?" he asked.

"I'm with Vicky in Connie's. We are trying to sort something out with Tina."

Frank huffed. He'd forgotten about that mess on top of everything that had happened the night before.

"Oh – can I speak to Vicky?"

"She doesn't want to speak with you, Frank. She's very upset."

"Look, I'm going to go back to Dublin as soon as I find this guy with my money."

John wasn't surprised by his brother's reaction. Everything was immediate and everything reflected his needs.

"What about Vicky? She needs time but you shouldn't leave without speaking to her."

"I just *asked* to speak to her and you said she wouldn't speak with me!"

John was disappointed at his brother's lack of sensitivity. After creating this mess he was going to jump ship. "She needs a couple of days."

"I don't have a couple of days. I see a call coming through from Charlie – I'll call you back!"

Frank waited attentively to hear the voice on the other end of the line.

"Hello?"

"Hey, Frank – I've got some bad news."

Frank didn't think that things could possibly get any worse. "What news?"

"Your money, Frank – I was cleaned out last night by a woman – she stole it from me in the Sahara."

Frank looked at the phone with complete disbelief. "You lost my money?"

"Yeah – this chick came back to my room and she was dressed like a squaw – when I woke up this morning she was gone and so was the bag of chips."

"You're joking, aren't you?"

"No!" Charlie sighed. "I really didn't think this girl was a hooker!"

Frank thought he was going to choke. "Charlie, I need that money – I mean it – I'm bankrupt if you don't get it for me!"

"Sorry, Frank – there's nothing I can do – anyway the tournament starts tonight so I won't be able to see you again – it lasts all week and then I'm off to Brazil. But tell my folks I said hi when you get back – sorry about the cash. It's a pain!"

"*Sorry? Sorry!* That's not good enough, Charlie – that was *my* money!"

"I feel bad – got to go, Frank – enjoy the rest of your stay in Vegas!"

With a click he was gone. Frank was aghast. His whole world was caving in on him. He had lost his boyfriend, then his fiancée and now his money – when he returned to Dublin there was a good chance that he would lose his businesses also. He sat at the edge of the bed, put his hands over his face and cried and cried. He wanted to speak with his mother but she was the last person that he could tell his story to. He felt so ashamed. He had made a complete and utter mess of his life.

Connie got a text from Georgia – it intrigued her.

Thanks for being a doll. I'll miss ya!

Chapter 20

*The soul would have no rainbow if the eyes
had no tears.*

~ CHEROKEE PROVERB ~

Leo was counting the hours before Suzanne returned. It had been the most stressful few days he could remember – even the days after bringing Wendy home from hospital when she was a baby couldn't compare. He saw his sister in a new light too. She had carried the responsibility of their mother single-handedly and it really was unfair to expect her to do it any longer.

"Paddy, is that you?" a voice hollered. "Don't let my father find you here – we will both be in terrible trouble if he sees you again!"

Leo didn't know who Paddy was but he certainly must have been a feature in his mother's life at some stage! She did recognise Kate and never got her name wrong. It was difficult to take. Kate told him to introduce himself when he entered the room and that way it would be less confusing. Of course Leo forgot more often than not and that left him being called Paddy for the rest of the time.

Kate said that she had tried to discuss with Suzanne the prospect of Mary moving into a nursing home that specialised in Alzheimer's care but Suzanne had dismissed it immediately.

He would broach the subject when she returned and maybe they could work out the costs by selling the house. He didn't know how he was going to manage that but he would suggest something.

Vicky had been able to forget the last few days as she revelled in the electric atmosphere of the Wynn Auditorium. She had been expecting to go with Frank – this was meant to be the night before their wedding – the wedding that never happened. John had gone to Frank's room earlier and it was cleared out – no trace of clothes and the safe was open and empty.

He had left Vegas.

Vicky had had enough on her plate trying to figure out what to do with Tina and she didn't want to see Frank for a very long time. Tonight, however, she was getting some well-deserved respite. Garth Brooks had been sensational and John had been most attentive.

"Fancy going for a drink in the Revolution Lounge Bar?" John asked as they entered the casino at the Mirage.

Vicky was enjoying the evening so much she had no difficulty deciding what to do.

"Is that the place on the way to the lifts?"

"Mmm – it's kinda cool!" he said, slipping his arm around her shoulders.

The casual way he draped himself protectively around her made her feel sensual and desired. It was bizarre – too much to carry in her head. Her spine tingled with the excitement of spending more time with John. The night before had started out as a strange sort of consolatory smooch but turned into the most intense and enjoyable night of lovemaking that she had ever experienced. And now she was going to a trendy ultra-modern Beatles-inspired lounge. How could she have misjudged him so badly? It was on Frank's scornful comments that she had formed her opinion of him and she couldn't have been more wrong. The way he viewed the world fascinated her – he always had an alternative, more interesting way of looking at situations.

Go-go dancers were grinding provocatively in the massive letters spelling out the word *REVOLUTION* that formed the boundary of the bar. The queue was long outside but John took out a card and flashed it at the bouncer who ushered them in with a big smile and welcoming gesture.

Inside, it was rocking with more go-go dancers – complete with knee-high white boots and micro-minis. They paraded along the counter at the back of the bar – in between the glasses and bottles of spirits. Portholes dotted along the wall showing visual images from under the sea – as if they were in a psychedelic submarine – and huge columns showed illustrated scenes from "Lucy in the Sky with Diamonds".

John grabbed a tall white stool that looked like it had been taken off the set of *Barbarella*, moulded with smooth lines out of plastic and aluminium.

"What do you fancy?" he asked.

"Why don't you choose?" she suggested. She had a feeling that whatever John ordered she would like!

He ordered two cocktails but wouldn't tell Vicky what was in them. They were delicious. In the corner the dance floor was heaving with pretty young things and ultra-trendy guys – it was like being back in an early Bond movie.

"Look, there's a booth free over there – want to take it?"

Vicky followed him over to the big white comfortable sofa and put her cocktail on to the white square table. Immediately the surface of the table lit up and lines of love hearts cascaded from the top to the bottom of the glass.

Vicky's eyes widened.

"Look!" John said as he brushed his hand across the top of the table and the lights went out. Using his fingertip as a pen he started to write the word '*Love*' across it. As his finger passed it left a stream of light, leaving the word in perfect view. Then it disappeared beneath a layer of more love hearts until the table-top turned white again.

"You could play with that all night!" Vicky giggled. "I've never seen anything like it before!"

"You can even create pictures like that and they project it onto those big pillars." John shrugged. "That's Vegas for you!"

"Magic!" said Vicky.

He sat back in his seat and she moved to fit in snugly beside him.

"It's a really remarkable place. I'm glad to have been here – even if it hasn't worked out the way it was meant to."

John took a sip from his glass and put the drink back on the table. "But it *has* worked out the way that it was meant to – don't you see that? Things happen for a reason!"

Vicky was starting to understand what he was saying. Before now he seemed to be speaking gibberish but that was before she *got* him. And there was a lot more to John than she ever could have imagined and something told her that she hadn't even scratched the surface yet.

"Vicky, do you mind if I suggest something?"

Vicky shook her head. "Go on!"

"A lot has happened over the last couple of days. Do Tina and Kyle really have to give you a final answer tomorrow? I mean, if they had some more time together they might come to a better decision on what is best for everyone. And we could have a good time – maybe go back to the Canyon for a couple of days?"

Vicky paused. What was she rushing back to Dublin for? Frank was back there but really she couldn't face him for a while. John did have a point. And she could enjoy this time with John – he was opening her eyes to the world. It made perfect sense the way he suggested it too. How had she never heeded his advice and wisdom before? And then she thought, maybe she wasn't ready to hear it before.

"Okay!" she nodded. "Let's stay like we are meant to for the full two weeks. As you say – who knows how Tina will feel when she gets to know Kyle better!"

John squeezed her and kissed her cheek.

She fluttered inside like a teenager. She was letting herself go and loving it!

"We *are* going to Krave!" Suzanne insisted. "I really don't mind and you might get to meet some hot guy!"

"You're too selfless, Sue – I can't have you in a gay bar on your last night!"

"It's one place I'm sure that Ronan won't be so it suits me fine!"

Eddie gave a small grin. Suzanne was trying to make him feel better and he knew it – it was just her style. What a wonderful friend and partner she would make – Ronan was very stupid to upset her and let her go.

"Well, if it's no good you have to promise you'll go to one of the other night-clubs on The Strip!"

Suzanne nodded. She was going to enjoy the fun and atmosphere in the hottest gay night-club in Vegas. The theatrics and entertainment would be a good distraction from what was going on in her head.

"Okay, hurry up!" she said as she hurtled into the bathroom and ran a brush through her hair. She already had full make-up on. She was wearing a pair of dressy jeans and a glittery red top that would have been a little too loud for Dublin but here seemed almost subdued!

Eddie was still wearing his bathrobe and fingering through the numerous shirts and trousers that he had bought in the retail park. He decided on a salmon shirt and cream jeans.

Suzanne sipped on a glass of sparkling wine and watched him check his look in the mirror. "You're gorgeous!" she exclaimed. "If I were a gay guy I would definitely chat you up!"

He did look smart – his hair was cut to only a few millimetres in length and he had let a small beard grow since they had arrived in Vegas. It complemented his big brown eyes.

He blushed when she said it. "Okay, I'm ready to hit the night!"

Suzanne turned off the TV and took the room key and slipped it into her bag.

"What about your phone?" Eddie asked, pointing to where she had left it on the table.

Susanne picked it up and checked it. "One missed call – him." Her heart beat as she went to voicemail but there was silence. "No message."

Eddie watched her disappointment. He wanted to punch Ronan

– but at least he had rung. "Are you okay, Sue? Do you want to ring him back?"

She shook her head and said nothing. He should have had the manners to leave her a message.

"I'm fine, honestly," she said brightly – hiding her feelings as she had learned to do living with Mary.

The buzz in the foyer of the MGM was palpable.

"Come on, let's go out this way!" Suzanne beckoned. They walked out to The Strip and she slipped her hand into the crook of his arm. It was so exciting and wonderful to be here. She had managed to keep all thoughts of her mother at bay – in less than twenty-four hours she would be back to her old routine and she wanted to remember all the marvellous memories that she had made in Vegas and the Grand Canyon. She would need them to cling to as the nights got longer and the caring for her mother became more difficult.

Ronan increased his bribe but the receptionist wasn't having any of it – she had got a reprimand from her boss for giving the room number of a client before. That client had been chased around the casino floor by a hooker.

With the knowledge that Suzanne would be on a flight back to Dublin at lunchtime the next day he decided to call it a night. He was unsure what his best move would be now.

Krave was throbbing with life. A divine specimen of manhood resembling a Greek god danced on a podium wearing a white leather thong and a smile. His skin was bronzed and glistening under the flashing lights. He caught Eddie's eye the minute he entered the room.

"Now that is what you need to get your mind off Frank," Suzanne teased.

"That fella would help you forget about Ronan too!" Eddie grinned.

Suzanne gave a little smile – she wasn't going to be able to forget about Ronan in a hurry.

On a podium nearby a girl wearing a pink bikini and thigh-high boots was dancing provocatively on her own.

"Your one over there is enough to make a man turn straight!" he giggled.

The room was easily eighty-per-cent male but Suzanne felt safe and relaxed. The majority didn't even see her as she passed.

Eddie's eyes were about to pop out of his head. "It's nothing like the Front Lounge, I tell you!"

Suzanne had been to the Dublin venue with Eddie and his friends and she had to agree. There was so much physical beauty all around her it was difficult to digest.

"I'll get us a drink – do you want to take one of those stools over there?" Eddie pointed to a table beside a pillar.

"Okay!" Suzanne went and sat up on the high stool and waited. And waited. She was glad that she had something nice to look at and keep her mind from thinking of Ronan. She kept wondering what he had rung to say and why he couldn't leave a message on the phone. Eddie was gone for half an hour and when he returned he wasn't alone.

At his side was a tall man whose freckled complexion and reddish hair gave his Irish identity away.

"Suzanne, this is Harry – you'll never believe it – he drinks in the Front Lounge!"

Suzanne recognised him. Eddie had had a crush on him two years before. After the Temple Street Christmas Party Eddie had made her follow him to the Front Lounge to see this gorgeous guy who had brushed past him the week before. But back then Harry was heavily involved with an older man and Eddie was left disappointed when he reached the Front Lounge that night and saw Harry wrapped around him. How ironic and coincidental that Harry should turn up in Vegas – and now hopefully unattached!

"Hi!" Harry said with a smile and he held out his hand. "Pleased to meet you."

He spoke very well – probably a southsider, Suzanne deduced.

"Would you like to dance?" he asked Suzanne.

It was kind of strange – men were dancing with men and women with women and men with women – anything went in this place.

Eddie seemed happy for her to dance with Harry and, even though Harry was only trying to be inclusive, she didn't want to offend him and joined him on the floor. The music was current with a heavy beat and easy to dance to.

Harry leaned forward and shouted in her ear.

"How long have you known Eddie?"

Suzanne shouted back. "About seven years. He's my best friend. A really good guy!"

"I can't believe he's here – I saw him getting the drinks – I noticed him a couple of times in the Front Lounge. I couldn't believe my eyes when I saw him here!"

Suzanne laughed. "Eddie used to go there in case he'd see you! Funny that?"

Harry gasped – he was in luck. "I have to know – is he seeing somebody or is he available?"

"He's very available – he's just come out of a relationship that wasn't very good for him. I'll let him tell you himself!"

"Oh good!" Harry said and started to dance more vigorously than those around him. He was in his element and as Eddie watched from the side of the dance-floor something inside told him that very soon he would be too.

Kyle and Tina sat in front of the big screen in Connie's lounge for a second night. Only this time Connie joined them. Tina felt awkward and wanted to go out and do something but Kyle seemed happy to just chill.

"Would you like some coffee?" Connie asked as she got up to brew a pot.

"No, thanks," Tina replied. "Would you have some Coke?"

"Sure – I'll get you some now – what about you, Kyle?"

Kyle grunted. "I'll help you!" He jumped up and followed his mother into the kitchen.

Connie was pleased by the gesture but somehow guessed that it wasn't just to help her out – he needed to talk.

"What is it, honey?" she asked as she put the coffee granules into the pot.

Kyle paced up and down the kitchen floor. "I want to go out and see Greg – I've been with Tina non-stop for four days!"

"Well, honey, you're gonna be with that girl a lot longer than that – you married her!"

Kyle ran his fingers through his long fringe. He was so out of his depth.

Connie went over and put her hands on her son's shoulders. "Why don't you see if Tina wants to go to Greg's with you – include her in your life – give her a chance to see what American life is like?"

"Okay!" he agreed and went in to speak to Tina.

Connie sighed as she put the water on the coffee. She worried for those hapless kids. She also wondered why she couldn't get through to Georgia when she had rung her earlier – she would call around and see her tomorrow. For now she would take a break and watch a movie – this had been the craziest Halloween in Vegas since she had moved here.

Chapter 21

When all the trees have been cut down,
when all the animals have been hunted,
when all the waters are polluted,
when all the air is unsafe to breathe,
only then will you discover you cannot eat money.

~ CREE INDIAN PROPHECY ~

Ronan couldn't sleep a wink and when Laura's call came through he really didn't want to take it. But he felt that he had no choice.

"Hello?"

"Why haven't you been returning my calls?" Laura demanded.

"It's been crazy busy here!" he lied.

"Well, I guess I'll have to forgive you! When will you be home?"

Ronan looked at the phone. Home? What did she mean? He hoped sincerely that she wasn't in his apartment still. What were her expectations?

"I'll be back in a couple of days."

"I can't wait! You know, I was thinking about our apartment in Arlington Street – why don't you move back there with me? It's much more central than Fulton Street."

"I thought we had it on the market to sell?" Ronan was amazed. The woman must be on some sort of speed the way she chopped and changed things around. He realised in that moment that he had been too passive during their marriage and let her get away with too much.

"I've taken it off the market – I won't be buying the house with *him* now – we are so over! I can't wait for you to come home!"

There was that *home* word again! Ronan didn't know how to answer. He was torn from the glorious two days with Suzanne in Vegas and dreaded returning to Boston.

"I have to go here – I've got a meeting!"

"At twelve midnight?" Laura was perplexed.

"I know, it's very busy – meetings all day and night – gotta go!"

Ronan switched off his phone and stretched out on the bed. He hit the button on the remote and turned on the movie channel but he soon turned it off again. He was too upset. He closed his eyes and all he could see was Suzanne's bright and beautiful face. It was a wonderful second chance with a sweet and caring woman and he had let her slip through his fingers for the second time!

Frank looked out of the small oval window at the green landscape down below. He could make out the church in Howth village, the boats in the marina and the lighthouse at the end of the pier. He was sure that he could find which house was his and Vicky's but he hadn't the heart to search. He had a right to be there because it was his home too but he didn't want to. He might go to one of his apartments that hadn't been let for a while. At least there he could have privacy and anonymity. The other weight on his mind was meeting his mother. She really would have so many questions. How he wished he could just turn up on her doorstep and tell her the truth about everything that had happened! But he could not honestly say that he could ever see the day where he would be able to do that.

"Five minutes to landing," the air steward announced over the intercom.

Perhaps he should try his mother's place first. There was something about home comforts at a time like this.

Frank collected his case from the carousel and hailed a taxi.

"Where to?" the driver asked.

"Could you take me to Cabra Road, please?"

He was glad the words had fallen from his lips before he had a chance to consider. This way he could get the worst bit over before Vicky and John got home. At the back of his mind he was thinking about what he would say to Charlie's parents if he saw them but then he figured there wasn't really any point. They mightn't even realise how heavily their son was involved in such a hugely high-stake scene.

Dublin seemed much darker and drearier than it had when Eddie dropped him to the airport only a few days before – how strange the whole scenario in Vegas had been. He wished he was with Eddie now and he wished that he could have changed things before they had got so out of control.

It was eleven o'clock in the morning. Bernadette Proctor would be on her way home from Mass – or she would be at home already.

It didn't take long to get to Cabra. Frank paid the taxi driver and went up to the red-painted door on his mother's council house. It was a purchased house now and she was so proud when she paid the council for it back in 1987. Frank had tried to get her to move but she would hear none of it. Why would she want to live in one of his swanky apartments that resembled a glorified hospital as far as she was concerned? This was where she had spent all her life and she loved her neighbours and the local shops.

So Frank had to come to Cabra when he wanted to see his mother and that was the way it would stay. He took out his key and turned it in the latch. The alarm started to sound and he quickly hit the code into the box at the side of the door beside the light switch. She must still be at Mass, he thought. He went into the kitchen and put the kettle on. It was an old habit. No sooner had it boiled than he heard his mother's familiar voice call out in the hall.

"Who is there? Is there somebody there?"

Bernadette let out a little yelp when she saw Frank standing there – she realised instantly that something was terribly wrong.

"Ffff-rrrank," she stuttered. "You're meant to be in the States getting married – why are you here?"

Frank rushed over and gave his mother a hug. He wasn't able to say anything. His tongue was tied and his heart was aching. He had let her down and didn't know how to tell her the awful truth!

"Sit down, Mammy – I have the kettle on – let's have a cup of tea."

Bernadette had a bag of groceries that she put on the kitchen table. She untied the knot in her headscarf that rested under her chin, and pulled the scarf off.

Frank sat down beside her and held her hand as he stared into her eyes.

"Frank, what's happened – why are you home so soon?"

"Mammy – it's all been a bit difficult. Vicky is not the girl I want to marry after all – she . . ." He had to think and quick! "She's having terrible trouble with her daughter who has got married to a young lad in Vegas – and I had to come home – it's crazy out there!"

"That's just awful," Bernadette gasped. "The selfish little wagon trying to upset your big day! But Vicky is a sweet girl – I mean, you can't let her daughter get in the way of your happiness – you were so happy before you left for America. Maybe you'll get married in Dublin now?"

Bernadette got up, kissed her son on the forehead and walked over to make a big pot of tea.

Frank was dismayed. His mother was the last person on earth that he could ever hurt. He wanted to tell her the truth about everything – his business – his money situation – his sexual persuasion – but he couldn't bear the thought of shattering her perception of him.

He took the mug of tea that Bernadette put down in front of him and sipped it. He would wait until later. Yes, he would tell her later.

Eddie was fidgety and jittery as he put his bags on the belt for weighing.

"You're so giddy!" Suzanne said with a laugh.

"I can't remember a night like it – and Harry will be home on Saturday!"

The steward handed him the boarding passes and passports and they walked down to the boarding gate.

"Whose wedding did you say he was in Vegas for?"

"His sister's. The whole family were over and making a holiday of it!"

"I think it's amazing that you had to come to Vegas to meet him!"

"I'm sorry things didn't work out for you, Sue – I have a feeling that Ronan will contact you again though."

Suzanne hoped so and yet another part of her was still angry with him for the way he had taken her news. "Come on, tell me all about last night again – how lovely are the rooms in the Bellagio? I'm very jealous!"

Eddie recounted the romance of his night with Harry and the many people they knew in common and all the places they had been. It was fate, Eddie declared, and Harry was happy to go along with that.

This was the right time and place for Eddie and Harry to meet and Suzanne couldn't be more pleased. She needed to feel that there was love and happy endings.

Vicky stepped out from the ensuite in her bathrobe, shaking the heavy drops of water from her hair with a towel.

"Do you fancy going down to the pool before breakfast?"

John laughed. "I'm glad we stayed now – aren't you?"

Vicky nodded and went over to him as he lay sprawled out on the bed.

"Push over!" she said and snuggled up with her head on his chest.

"Hey – I'm getting all wet!" he said playfully.

"Mmm!" she said with a cheeky grin. "And?"

"And what?" He knew what she meant but liked to tease. The little smile and longing in her eyes said only one thing.

She had transformed into a different person. She wasn't thinking about Tina or worrying about what was happening with Frank or anything – she was just enjoying life and this was the best place in the world to do it.

Chapter 22

It does not require many words to speak the truth.

~ Chief Joseph (1840-1904), NEZ PERCE *~*

Frank was still in Bernadette's house after more than a week and she was becoming suspicious that maybe her darling son hadn't told her the complete story. Why would John still be in Las Vegas with Frank's fiancée? And Frank hadn't spent so long with her in her house since he had become a commis chef. It was time she heard the truth but she couldn't ask him straight out – that was not her style. She always spoke gently and carefully with her son.

Frank galloped down the stairs and grabbed his coat.

"I'm going in to the restaurant, Mammy!"

"Will you be back for your tea, love?"

"I'll be back for a while but don't make anything – I'll eat in the restaurant."

Bernadette heard the front door bang and she hugged her cup of tea to her cheek. He was so mixed up – always was – even when he was a toddler. No matter how much she had tried to guide him he was always attracted to the wrong things – money and glitter and the shallow people that were now all scampering like rats from a drowning ship as they watched their millions in assets just disappear. It was sad to see a whole generation flapping about without direction. Frank was one of those – even when he was flying high at the height of his success he wasn't happy and Bernadette realised this – it was why she had encouraged him to find a nice girl and think about settling down. But from the moment she saw Vicky she realised that they were not suited and Frank didn't have the empathy or wherewithal to be someone's stepfather. But at the time Bernadette was just relieved that he had found someone and was settling down. She had had such dreams of happiness for both her sons – John was going to be fine, he was always fine – but Frank was the son that she worried about. He was always more misdirected than other kids. She took a sip from her china cup. She had wanted so much but now all she wanted from Frank was the truth.

Ronan shut the door on his apartment in Fulton Street – glad to be in the privacy of his own place at the end of the day. There was so much work to be done following up contacts and orders after the fair. They had been good distractions and helped him to keep Laura at bay. She hadn't taken the news well. But then again it was the first time in her life that he hadn't caved in to her wants and desires – she had never seen him that way. He hoped that she would respect his wishes and give him space.

He took a beer out of the fridge and turned on the TV. Boston was so cold compared to Vegas. He wished he was back in the Canyon with Suzanne.

Suddenly the buzzer went off and he went to see who was at the door.

Laura was standing there looking larger than usual with her rotund stomach.

"Laura – come in."

Ronan could do without this – he wondered what she wanted now. He went over to the door of his apartment and held it open.

"Ronan," she said with a nod of her head in a matter-of-fact tone.

"Laura," he replied. He felt absolutely nothing for the woman – emotionally or otherwise. But he did feel a little contempt for himself – for the way he had let her control him and their marriage.

"I hoped we could talk and I didn't think you would want to speak on the phone after our last call."

It had been a heated debate and Ronan wouldn't have been the one to contact Laura so quickly. Whatever she wanted he figured that she must want it really badly.

"Would you like a drink?" he asked.

"No, thank you Ronan, I'll be brief," she said with a sigh. "I want to stay in the apartment in Arlington Street – buy you out."

Ronan was shocked but pleased. This would cut ties between them completely.

"So you want to stay there?"

She nodded. "I'm having this baby on my own and I'll need to be close to work – I can get a live-in nanny and it will be the best solution."

Ronan was perplexed but relieved that this was all that she wanted. No doubt there would be a sting in the tail – either over the price or some other matter, but for now he was pleased that it meant he could be released from all attachments to Laura. Matters like money meant nothing to him. All he wanted was his freedom.

"Oh, and I left some cosmetics in the bathroom – is it okay if I take them?"

"Of course," he nodded.

"I'm sorry things didn't work out for us, Ronan. I messed up – I know that."

Ronan felt sad for her. It wouldn't be easy but he needed to sort his own life out.

It was a painless solution and meant that she would be happy to go through with the divorce now instead of just venting anger as she had done when he returned from Vegas.

"I'll go then – my solicitor will make you an offer – it will be at market value and then hopefully we can both move on with our lives."

Ronan gave a small smile. "That would be good, Laura. I wish you well – hope it goes well with the baby!"

Laura kissed him on the cheek on her way out.

It was a sad parting but Ronan felt better. He would move on with his life now – whatever that might be. He looked at his watch – it was a good time to catch his sister on the west coast. He went over to his computer and Skyped Martina in San Diego. She was on line and appeared by video call a few seconds later.

"Hey, bro – how are you? Good time in Vegas?"

She was bronzed and the picture of health. All that sunshine and good food, Ronan figured.

"Hi, Martina – yes, good and bad and strange – you'll never guess who I met."

Martina was eating from a pot of yogurt. "Who?"

"Do you remember Suzanne Quinn?"

Martina thought for a moment. "The blonde girl from Clontarf?"

"Yeah – she was in Vegas – I found her on Facebook a while back and she was going there on holiday."

Martina nodded. "She was a nice girl – really pretty – she had that awful mother I remember!"

Ronan felt a pang of guilt. "Yeah, well, her mother has Alzheimer's now."

"Wow – is that Karma or what?" Martina gasped as she licked her spoon clean.

"I think that's a bit cruel to say, Martina."

"Yep – sorry, but I mean what a witch! I remember calling around to Suzanne's house – she was a year ahead of me in school. She was always so nice to me – probably because I was your little sister!"

"She's still the same – but she dropped a bombshell – you're the only person I can tell this to."

"Go on!"

"Apparently she was pregnant just after I came to the States and she had an abortion and I never knew."

"Wow!"

"What do you think of that?"

Martina shook her head. "That's amazing. I presume you were the father?"

"Yep!"

"How did the poor girl get over it – I mean, I'm sure she probably hasn't – has she any other kids?"

285

"No."

"Oh, wow – that is sooo sad!"

Ronan felt bad for only thinking of his own feelings, for the way he had treated Suzanne. "I'm afraid I reacted badly. I tried to call her in Vegas before I left but didn't get through to her. I didn't leave a message – I didn't know what to say."

"What did you do, bro?" Martina looked crossly at the computer screen.

"I wasn't very sympathetic – I was so hurt that she had the abortion – I mean it's crazy and I might have felt differently back then but I can only say how I feel now – I wish we'd had the child."

Martina tut-tutted. "You had better make a big gesture of apology – you were way out of line being angry with her!"

Ronan felt ashamed. "I know that – but it was a shock. And now I just don't know how to handle the situation. I can't handle all the emotions at the moment. Laura is finally settling for a divorce – she's buying me out of Arlington Street."

"Glad to hear that you're finally getting closure there – I knew she was no good for you!"

"Well, it's over now. How are things in San Diego?"

"Things are great out here," she nodded. "I've a big group coming for a weekend of meditation. Sounds like you could do with some time here."

"When I finish with the work I've brought back from Vegas I'll come down for a weekend."

"Do that and tell Suzanne I said hi!"

Ronan smiled. That was his sister's way of telling him to contact Suzanne. She was a clever and tuned-in lady. She always trusted her gut. That was why she led such a holistic life. "I will – talk soon!"

With a tap to the keyboard she was gone.

Ronan respected his sister's opinions on matters of the heart. He knew in his own heart that he had messed up with Suzanne and that had given him the strength to finally tell Laura that he no longer wanted to be a part of her life. Suzanne helped him to see that he had been blind while in his marriage to Laura. He really had to do something and soon. He went straight on to Facebook and composed a message.

The return to Dublin had been traumatic for Suzanne. Her mother was the same and it was like she had never been away. But she was so angry with Leo. He wanted a quick fix to his mother's problem and had the audacity to think that he was helping. To top it all, he wanted to kick Suzanne out of her own home. Even if they did sell the house in Clontarf, with the capital raised they couldn't afford to keep Mary in a nursing home for long. But it was the heartless way that Leo approached the issue of their mother's care that really hurt Suzanne. She had sacrificed so much of her life already and she wasn't going to compromise her mother now.

She looked at her watch. She had an hour before she had to be in work. Eddie was besotted with Harry and she had seen little of him since Harry had returned from Vegas. They were in that glorious honeymoon period and Suzanne was happy for him. She tried not to think about Ronan too much – although he cropped up several times a day. Each time she thought of him she was in the Canyon and surrounded by love. If only she could freeze those moments and relive them over and over again like a kind of Groundhog Day!

She hadn't been on Facebook for a long time – not since before she went to Vegas. But something urged her to turn it on – her mother was asleep in bed and Kate hadn't arrived yet.

She wasn't surprised to see lots of photos of Eddie and Harry posted all over her news page. He was the picture of happiness. There was a message from her friend in London and a couple of make-up and hair company invitations.

Then she checked her email, which she had avoided doing since her return from Las Vegas. She didn't know whether she was fearing she would see a message from Ronan, or fearing she wouldn't. But there it was. She was trembling as she opened it.

Dear Suzanne

I hope you got home safely and enjoyed the rest of your stay in Vegas. I'm sorry about my behaviour in the restaurant. I did try to contact you but the hotel wouldn't give me your room number and your phone turned straight on to voicemail. I won't try to make excuses because my behaviour was awful – I was just thinking of myself. I hadn't thought about all the pain that you must have gone through. I still find it difficult to get the image I have of our baby out of my head. I think it would have been so beautiful – providing he or she looked like you of course. You see, I would love nothing more than a child – I guess you get to a stage in your life when you realise that having a child is going to be the biggest and most important thing that can happen or else you decide that you're not going to go down the parenting route. I went through so much with Laura and carried the blame when she couldn't conceive – that was part of the reason why she went off with another man. Recently she tried to convince me that was the only reason and wanted a reconciliation – but that's Laura! I realised when I was with you in Vegas that I never really loved her properly. I was caught up in a whirlwind of emotions with her and never true to myself. Being with you was incredible. I was truly happy. And, although I'm making excuses again, it was the shock that made me react the way I did.

I don't know if you want to get back in touch but I feel it is an opportunity that we can't let pass. If there is any chance you might feel the same, maybe you could come to see me or I could come over to you in Dublin – please think carefully about this – I need to see you again.

With love
Ronan

PS Are you on Skype? It would be nice to video call?

Suzanne cried as she read and re-read the email. It was all so simple for him – all so simple for Leo – none of them understood her sense of responsibility to her mother. She would love to just go off at the drop of a hat to Boston – she was only young and had a desire to travel and see more of the world. She didn't answer immediately – she would think about it before she replied.

Vicky, John, Kyle and Tina boarded the plane together. To Vicky, it felt surreal. It certainly was not the end to the wedding adventure that she had planned but she couldn't help smiling when she remembered the fortune-teller's predictions.

Connie had shed more than a few tears as she watched Kyle walk to the boarding gate. His decision to move to Ireland had been against her advice but John assured her that he would take him under his wing and help him get set up in a new rock school that a friend of his had opened. It was the best-case scenario and Tina was beside herself with joy at the prospect that she could work on a portfolio and apply to art college. The happy party buckled their seatbelts and sat back and waited for the plane to take off – each of them a little unsure about what their new lives were going to be like when they returned to Dublin.

John looked over at the two young people who were happily engrossed in the programme of entertainment for the 12-hour flight. He had helped them all to reach a compromise that suited everyone's needs. The young people were able to be honest with him in a way that they could not be with their mothers and it roused a sense of responsibility in him that he enjoyed and hoped to nurture.

Vicky took the in-flight magazine from the pocket in the seat in front of her and placed it on her knee. She threw her head back against the headrest and turned to John.

"Thank you."

He smiled cheekily. "For what?"

"For being there and for getting Tina to come home – for everything really."

John was enveloped in the positive vibes from the woman sitting beside him. "I'm not finished yet!" he grinned. "Among other things, we have to talk to Frank about the house and see him at some stage – but there's no rush. Is the house in your name?"

Vicky nodded. "It's in both our names."

"It will make things simpler if he just signs the house over to you and, after what he has put you through, I can't see him denying you that. The sooner he does it the better." He paused and looked seriously at her. "Vicky, I've been remiss in not telling you – Frank's money troubles are more serious than you might think. The day before we left for Vegas he was in with his bank manager – he may have to declare bankruptcy in the near future."

Vicky frowned. She was sorry for Frank. She didn't have the same feelings of betrayal that she would have if Frank had had an affair with another woman – this was different. She couldn't compete with sharing his affections for another man. In a strange way she understood what had brought them together as a couple. For her it was the security and stability and being part of a couple that she longed for – she could only presume that for Frank it was the prospect of a child and outward respectability that mattered. Either way they were both fortunate that this had happened. At least they had a chance of finding happiness and maybe even love. She studied John's profile as the thoughts passed through her head. He was strong and beautiful – the type of man that she wouldn't dream of approaching in a million years. Yet he wanted to be with her and help her and heal her. She was a very lucky woman.

Eddie called around on his own to Suzanne's when her mother was asleep.

"So – tell me more about Ronan," he said, holding the cup of hot coffee in his hands. "I knew he'd contact you!"

"Yeah, well, it's not that straightforward. I can't just go off to Boston at the drop of a hat!"

Eddie huffed. "Can I help – maybe move in and let you go over for the weekend?"

"Eddie – I'm not made of money – and, besides, I'm only just back – my mother likes it that I'm back."

"Lily – where are you?" a roar echoed from the hallway.

Eddie raised his eyebrows, his silence saying more than words.

"Coming, Mum," Suzanne said, getting up and going out to her mother's assistance.

When Suzanne returned with her mother on her arm, she put her sitting in the armchair in the corner and went to make tea for them all.

Eddie took up where he had left off. "Well, I would be happy to stay here and help – Harry would too!"

Suzanne poured the boiling water into the teapot and slammed the lid on top.

"I don't know if I want to see him again – I don't think I could deal with rejection again!"

"Oh for God's sake, Suzanne, would you ever live a little?" Mary trumped up from the corner of the room.

Suzanne nearly dropped the teapot. It was the first time in three years that her mother had addressed her by her name.

"There's the sign!" Eddie said with a beaming smile. "Good on you, Mary – you tell her!"

Mary looked over at Eddie from under her scowl. "Who are you?"

Eddie laughed. "I'm Paddy – your boyfriend – remember?"

A glazed look passed over Mary's face. "Oh, Paddy – how I have missed you!"

Suzanne was beginning to think that maybe she should reconsider Ronan's request. But after Ronan's initial reaction in Vegas she wanted to be sure that his feelings were genuine. If Ronan wanted to see her he could come to Dublin.

"Eddie!"

"Mmm?" he asked, delighted that his point had been backed up by Mary so unexpectedly.

"How do I set up Skype?"

Frank woke in his mother's house for the tenth night in a row. Bernadette was more than suspicious about the events that had happened in Vegas and she wanted answers. He, on the other hand, was surprised that the overwhelming desire he had above all others was to see Eddie. He missed him like a limb. And the fact that he was at rock bottom in every other aspect of his life made him miss him even more. He would call him later – after he went to see the bank manager. He was through with lying – he had to get sorted out once and for all.

Connie's house felt big and lonely. She had watched her boy walk through the boarding gate with pangs of loss that only a mother can feel. This meant that she was on her own. She had been so busy working and providing for her sons she hadn't expected them to leave her so soon. Her life was flashing before her and she had no idea what she wanted for herself. Maybe she should have gone to Dublin with Kyle – but then he would have felt that she was fussing. She needed to focus on herself – maybe go skiing this year in Lake Tahoe – she had put that off for so many reasons but now she had no excuses. Except she had nobody to go with! Georgia had disappeared off the face of the earth and her flat had been cleared out since Halloween. People were strange, she decided. She found herself in her early forties alone in a lovely bungalow waiting on other people who were happily getting married. Maybe that was meant to be her lot.

She looked at her watch. Another appointment awaited her and with smiles and all the joviality that was required she would meet this couple and make their day really special – because she was a professional and everyone deserved to be happy.

Suzanne went to work next day with a spring in her step as she thought about her reply to Ronan's email. It was open and honest and it felt right. She would know very soon what his genuine intentions were towards her. It was all very well bathing in the glory of the Grand Canyon in El Tovar but how would he feel when he came home and saw her life in full colour in Clontarf?

She was optimistic that maybe they could start afresh and take it one step at a time. But she didn't want to get her hopes up either. She breezed into the staffroom and put on her uniform.

Her first patient of the day was the little boy who'd had a dislocated thumb. She remembered him. It was around that time that she had first found Ronan on Facebook – had it really only been four weeks? Either way she couldn't have imagined what a difference going on line would make to her life.

The little boy smiled when he saw her.

"I haven't missed any matches – the pitches have been too hard with the cold weather."

"I'm glad to hear that," Suzanne said with a gentle smile.

She loved her job and she loved working with young people. They were full of hope and innocence. She had to put the past behind her. Even if things worked out with Ronan a family might not be on the cards. She would do her best to do what felt right and wouldn't compromise herself or anyone else.

Suddenly Eddie walked into the treatment room.

"Now, I think you'll make that football team this week!" Suzanne said, patting the boy on his back.

The little boy looked pleased. "Thanks – but my mum says it's going to snow so there'll be no match anyway!"

"Make sure you have gloves on if you throw any snowballs," she said with a smile.

When the little boy was gone Eddie launched into what he had to say. "You'll never guess who called me?"

"Frank?" Suzanne said as she tidied away the dressings and equipment.

"How did you guess?" Eddie was aghast.

"He was bound to, wasn't he? So what did he say?"

Eddie was jittery with the news. "Would you believe he said he wants to see me and he misses me? He came home the next day – hasn't married his fiancée either."

"Good!" Suzanne said in the matter-of-fact way that she liked to deal with most aspects of her life – except for Ronan! "And how do you feel?"

Eddie took a sharp breath. "I think I'm over him – not just

293

because I'm crazy about Harry but I see that Frank was not for me. Harry is so full of life and he's just so cool. Hey, I can't believe that I'm actually over Frank!"

Suzanne smiled. "And I have some news!" she said gleefully. "I invited Ronan to stay with me in Dublin!"

Chapter 23

*Even the seasons form a great circle in their changing,
and always come back again to where they were. The
life of a man is a circle from childhood to childhood,
and so it is in everything where power moves.*

~ *Black Elk*, OGLALA SIOUX ~

Enormous cumulus clouds tinged with pink and bursting like
marshmallows hung against a powder-blue sky. It was the perfect day
for Tina to take Kyle for his first walk along the cliffs. The wind was
sharp but they were well wrapped up and Kyle's arm securely hugged
Tina's shoulders. Seagulls hovered in the air and screeched as they
glided along the invisible jets of air, soaring and diving.

"It's a pretty awesome place, this!" Kyle said as he stopped still
for a moment.

"I'm glad you like it – I never really appreciated it before – I
always associated Howth with Frank." She kicked a stone off the
path. "So you've no regrets about coming to Dublin?"

Kyle didn't answer quickly enough to reassure Tina. "The rock
school is cool – but not really what I thought it would be."

"What's missing?"

Kyle shrugged. "I guess I thought it might have more equipment
and stuff and the classes are freezing!"

"Ireland is cold!"

Kyle realised he was hurting Tina's feelings and responded
quickly. "It's good to be beside the sea though – really cool!"

Tina had found the return to school difficult but she didn't want to complain. She was spending time on her portfolio now for art college and hopefully would be able to start a course next year. She was aware that it was more difficult for Kyle, fitting in to a new country and she had to consider his feelings above hers. It was a tough lesson but John's presence had been helpful. Her mum was like a new person in some ways – then at other times she was the same. John was so good for her – she hoped that he would stay around.

John called around to his mother. It was time that she heard the truth about her eldest son.

Bernadette was in the kitchen cleaning the sink when she heard the key in the door – she had expected that John would call sooner.

John leaned down and kissed his mother on the cheek as she continued to scrub. She put the sponge on the draining board and picked up a tea towel to wipe her hands dry.

"Will you have a cup of my Maxwell House? I know you usually only drink that fancy stuff in the pot."

"Maxwell House is fine, Mam."

John took a seat and waited for the third-degree questions. But they weren't coming and that was when John realised how seriously concerned Bernadette was. He had an inkling she suspected and didn't want to be told the truth.

"So Frank is staying with you?" he started.

"Yes – he's not himself – I'm so worried about him, John. Can you tell me what happened in Las Vegas? They should never have gone – I should have kept an eye on the two of them more. I thought she was a nice girl."

"Vicky is a nice girl, Mam. She's also a very simple and naïve girl in many ways and Frank was never right for her. Frank isn't in any position to marry anyone."

Bernadette shook her head and held her cup of coffee up to her cheek as she had a habit of doing. "Where did I go wrong – I did my best?"

"None of this has anything to do with you, Mam – we all agree that you worked hard and did everything for us – this is about Frank."

John took a sharp intake of breath. There was no easy way to say this.

"Mam do you remember when Frank was younger how he was more sensitive about things than me – even when he was playing football he couldn't cope with certain situations. He was always trying to be two people – the person inside the house and the person out on the street who wasn't really himself at all."

Bernadette took a gulp of coffee and looked straight ahead at the wall. She knew what John was implying – God knows she had thought about Frank so many times and worried about him.

"Frank would never be happy with Vicky," John went on, "and not because she is Vicky but because she is a woman."

Bernadette almost tipped her cup over as she placed it down on the table. Her heart sank – it was true. But it was also better that she knew the truth. She put her head into her hands. It was all too much to take in. She had always known this but hearing it from John made it real. She couldn't ask the details – it was too painful.

"And what about his business – what's going on?"

"Frank got in over his head with investments and developments, Mam – he's broke."

Bernadette threw her head back to contain the tears. "I don't know why he didn't tell me – I have savings and could have helped him."

John smiled at his mother's naïvety. "Mam, Frank owes millions of euros."

Bernadette seemed startled by his revelation. "But how – I mean his restaurants surely are doing so well?"

"Mam, there's a recession – every business has been hit in some way. But the bigger issue I think is the need for Frank to be true to himself and who he really is."

Bernadette had hoped by discussing her son's business dealings she could avoid talking about his sexuality. "So what can he do now?"

John shook his head. "He has to sort himself out – be true to himself. You should be glad that he didn't marry Vicky and mess up her life too."

"And why did you stay on in Las Vegas?"

John wasn't proud of the way that he had stepped into his brother's shoes but he wasn't afraid of telling the truth to his mother. "I was helping Vicky out and we have become close over the last couple of weeks in Las Vegas – she's a lost soul too who needs help – especially with her daughter."

Bernadette stood up and started to clean away the cups from the table. She huffed and puffed but couldn't find the words to answer John.

"And would you not think about how your poor brother must be feeling instead of worrying about some stranger?" she finally said.

"Mam – Frank is a grown man – and anyway I have feelings for Vicky."

Bernadette shook her head. "Feelings! You should be worried about your brother!"

John stood up now – it was time to leave. "Mam, Frank has always had you worrying about him – he doesn't need the two of us – you've never been concerned about me."

Bernadette gasped. "That's not true – I always treated you both the same."

John smiled. "Whatever you want to think is fine by me, Mam – I don't have any issues any more – I've found out who I am and I'm happy. Maybe if Frank wasn't so caught up in pleasing you all the time he would have found himself before."

Bernadette's cheeks turned pink. "Are you saying it's my fault that he's in all this mess?"

"No, Mam – I'm not blaming you or anyone. He just needs to stand on his own two feet and find himself."

Bernadette couldn't stop the tears – they cascaded down her cheeks.

John went over and wrapped his arms consolingly around his small bird-like mother.

He kissed her on the top of her head.

"It's okay, Mam – it will all be okay – it always is!"

Bernadette held John and thanked God that she had one son who had grown up and could stand on his own two feet.

Living in a house with two teenagers who were married was not easy. Vicky had listened to John's advice and let it ride but her routine was upset and she had too much to cope with. Kyle and Tina weren't pulling their weight with housework as they had promised they would do before leaving Las Vegas. It was all getting too much for her and she found herself falling into the old mindset of her past, fussing over the things that used to matter to her before she went to the Canyon with John. Traces of the old uptight Vicky that had boarded the plane to marry Frank were creeping back into her consciousness.

So this morning she found herself in the new routine of tidying up the breakfast dishes for four adults and cleaning down the worktops and scrubbing around the hob. Nothing much had changed and yet everything had changed. What had she achieved for herself? As she sprayed the sterilising liquid across the chrome surface she tried to focus on what she was doing with her life. Who was she any more?

John wasn't the same either. He would disappear and come back at irregular times – doing recordings or just meeting people that she didn't know. It freaked her out in a way that Frank's absence hadn't – at least when she was ignorant of Frank's affair she presumed that he was working but that was not the case with John. He made it impossible to quiz without her sounding like some sort of paranoid maniac.

And in a way that was what she felt like. Always imagining him with other women and wondering why he liked her at all.

Frank had called and been very decent about the new arrangements – his relationship with John hadn't been damaged and this amazed her. Had Frank thought so little of her that he didn't mind the fact that she was now sleeping with his brother? He had even come out to the house and gathered up most of his belongings and all of his clothes. He seemed so much lighter.

Everyone else was in control except her. And then there were the neighbours. She couldn't stand the way the curtains twitched every time John or Kyle walked up the drive. They were giving her funny looks and this tormented her. She found herself too embarrassed to explain who the new houseguests were and where Frank had gone.

She needed to have words with the men in the house later – she needed to get order and structure in her life. And to top it all it had started to snow!

Suzanne was so excited. She stood at arrivals with baited breath waiting for a glimpse of Ronan. Communicating by Skype and text for the last few days had helped them move things forward but she had butterflies in her tummy and wasn't sure how they would be when he came through arrivals. The traffic had been horrendous on the way to the airport. It was touch and go whether or not the flight from Logan International would be diverted but she had just been informed that Ronan's was the only flight landing in Dublin airport today from the US. Destiny was lending them a helping hand.

Her mother was oblivious to the news of a visitor to the house and it was probably just as well. It had taken them seventeen years to get to this stage but they had got here and that was all that mattered.

When Frank returned from work Bernadette was waiting for him in the kitchen. He hoped he could just go up the stairs but she called him down when he was only halfway up.

"Frank, I need to talk to you."

He trod sheepishly into where she sat at the kitchen table.

"Mammy?"

"Did you have any trouble in the snow?"

Frank shook his head and stood at the door, unwilling to engage in conversation.

"Come and sit down, Frank."

Reluctantly Frank pulled the chair back and sat down.

"Your brother called by earlier."

Frank kicked his feet out in front of him, his left arm resting on the table – fingers strumming on the wooden surface. He remained silent.

Bernadette was composed. She'd had some hours to think about what she had to say. "Frank, I'm very worried about you – what has happened?"

Frank didn't shrug although that was what he wanted to do. This moment reminded him of the time that he got a horrific report for his mock-Leaving Certificate.

"You're in trouble – I know that – with the business. But you're in trouble in your heart too!"

Frank shook his head. He wasn't ready for this conversation. He would kill John the next time he saw him.

"I'm fine, Mammy – I'm sorting the business out – it's the property market that's the cause of this mess."

"Tell me the truth, Frank. I need to hear it from your lips."

Frank wasn't keen to divulge. He wasn't sure how he felt any more. At the moment he didn't love anybody. Eddie had made his feelings clear during their conversation. He never wanted to see him or have anything to do with him again.

Frank swallowed hard. "What did he tell you?"

She said no words but tilted her head in a gesture that spoke a multitude.

"Did he tell you that I was gay?"

Bernadette smiled at her son. "I suppose I always knew. Son, never underestimate what it takes to be a mother – it's the most wonderful and terrible job in the world. We carry you in our wombs and bring you into the world and have to watch as you grow and get battered and develop and blossom and all the time we have to stand on the sidelines and watch while sometimes our hearts break. All any mother wants is what is best for her little one – and you're still my little one. I love you – no matter who you love or what you do."

301

Frank felt a lump develop in his throat. He had never expected such a speech from his mother's lips – it was like she had used someone else's voice for the sermon.

But a great relief came with the knowledge that he didn't have to pretend any more.

"Thanks, Mammy." He sighed. "It means a lot to hear you say that – I'm in a right mess."

Bernadette slapped the palm of her hand down on the table. "And you can get out of this mess – sell off those bloody apartments or give the keys back – concentrate on the restaurants. I'll help you – you can always stay here as long as you want. Whatever it takes – I'm here for you."

Frank leaned forward and gave his mother a hug. "Thank you for being so understanding. I'm sorry if I've been a disappointment."

Bernadette stroked his head as he nestled against her shoulder. She thought of what John had said earlier. "Don't worry, love, it will all be okay."

And for the first time in a long time Frank actually believed that it would.

The roaring was loud from the kitchen and Vicky pulled on her dressing gown to go and see what was going on. Kyle was standing at the sink waving his arms frantically in the air and Tina was sitting at the table with her artwork covering the surface.

Vicky could see by the look in his eyes that Kyle was not keen to continue his argument with her present. She began to back out of the room.

"No, Mum, stay!" said Tina.

Kyle threw his arms in the air and stormed out past Vicky in the direction of the bedroom.

"What's going on, Tina?" Vicky asked.

"He says I'm spending too much time on my art – I should spend my evenings with him because he doesn't know anybody and he hasn't got any money and he can't find any work . . . and that this country sucks!"

John came into the kitchen.

"Everything okay?"

Vicky glared at him. She was cross with him for not coming home as early as he had said he would. When she had quizzed him on where he'd been he wouldn't tell her.

"I can handle my daughter, thank you!"

"Vicky, I'm not getting into an argument with you – I shouldn't have to tell you where I am twenty-four hours a day – I don't even live here!"

Vicky put her palms on her hips. "Well, why don't you go home then? You're the one making the big deal by not telling me."

John shook his head. "It's just your own paranoia!" After all the mediation he had done and coaxing and caring for her hurts and fears, she couldn't trust him. And without trust there was nothing for John. He wasn't entering into a marriage – he had never suggested any such arrangement. He was a free spirit and maybe he would be better off just remaining that way.

Suzanne and Ronan snuggled under the duvet.

"You know I might not be able to give you children," Ronan said sadly.

"There's no need to say that – you never know – I mean it did happen once!"

But no matter how much Suzanne protested, Ronan's sense of realism prevailed.

"Don't try to spare my feelings – it's okay – I've come to terms with it," he insisted. "But I have to be sure that you're okay with it."

Suzanne looked up at his face and smiled. "I'm happy just to be with you – it took us long enough to get here – we can overcome anything. My mother for a start!"

Ronan grinned. "It's kinda fun to be in the same house as Mary Quinn, sleeping with her daughter, and she's not going to do anything about it!"

"Ironic!" Suzanne said. "Why do mothers and daughters harass each other so? At the end of the day all that matters is that we are happy."

"Absolutely," Ronan said as he kissed her playfully on the nose. "Now I don't want to have to go in and tell Mary Quinn exactly what I'm going to do to her daughter!"

The thunder roared. It was the first time that Vicky had ever known snow in November in Dublin. The sky was a strange pink and with each flash of lightning she cried into her pillow. How could she have sent him away like that? Now she was left alone with two angry teenagers in her house.

Outside the flakes teemed down and covered every branch and wall and pot in the garden. It was so cold and even though she had the heating on at full blast she couldn't heat herself. The electric blanket was on and she moved her feet around the warm area to circulate the blood. She thought of him out in the cold air – it was quite a walk to the DART and the footpaths were treacherous. He had better not slip or hurt himself – then she would carry the guilt forever. Why had she driven him away? He had been so supportive while she was in Las Vegas and set things up so that she had her daughter back. As he stood in the kitchen earlier and told her that she was paranoid she had yelled at him. She'd really wanted to throw something at him. She had to admit that it was more emotion than she had ever shown with any man in her life. He was the only person who could draw her out of herself – for better or for worse. She felt like she was her true self in his company and it scared her.

When she told him to leave and never come back – he just grabbed his bag with the couple of things that he had been using and disappeared. He had been followed by Kyle but Kyle came back a short time later. No doubt John had spoken to him in the calm collected way that he had a habit of doing and soothed the teenager's anxiety. But Kyle wasn't the same since he returned. Everything had changed very suddenly with the fall of the snow and the abrupt standstill in the streets – so too was her life reaching some sort of climax. She couldn't explain it and didn't know what it was yet but something big was happening around her that she had no control over.

The next morning Ronan and Suzanne woke slowly – bodies curled into each other.

"Sleep okay?" Ronan whispered in her ear.

"Mmm . . . best night's sleep ever."

"I'm moving back – I have to be with you, Suzanne."

Suzanne turned her head. The way he spoke, so matter-of-fact and certain, scared her.

"To Dublin – for good?"

He nodded. "I don't know how I'm going to manage it with my work but I can't let you slip away . . ."

Suzanne stopped him. "Wait, what's that smell?"

"What smell?" he asked putting his nose up to the air.

Suddenly the smoke alarm went off on the landing.

Suzanne jumped out of the bed and pulled on her dressing gown. Smoke was billowing up the stairs. She shouted out, "Mum – where are you?" She looked in her mother's bedroom but she wasn't there. Ronan followed behind as she stumbled down the stairs calling for her mother.

She ran into the front room and found her asleep in the armchair wearing her dressing gown and slippers.

Ronan went into the kitchen – as he opened the door he was hit by a wall of smoke and flames danced along the worktops and cabinets.

Suddenly the electrics in the house tripped.

"Phone 999!" Suzanne called frantically.

"Just get your mum out of the house, Suzanne – leave it to me."

Suzanne tried to arouse Mary but she wasn't budging.

"I need help!" Suzanne called.

Ronan shut the kitchen door – it was too dangerous to try and tackle on his own. He ran into the front room and took Mary Quinn in his arms. Suzanne had left her mobile conveniently in the hall beside her car keys so she was able to call the emergency services as Ronan carried her mother out into the freezing snow.

"I must go next door!" Suzanne said, shoving her car keys into his hand. "I have to warn them." The house was semi-detached.

Ronan put her mother into the ice-covered car which was on the road because the driveway was covered in sludge and snow. He turned on the engine to heat her up and so that it would be ready to move.

In what felt like an hour later but was probably ten minutes the fire-brigade arrived. With hoses they pushed in through the kitchen door and attacked the flames. It took ten minutes before they were sure that every flame was out but by then the entire downstairs was destroyed and upstairs deemed unsafe.

"You must be freezing!" Suzanne said, realising that Ronan was only wearing a T-shirt. "Just as well that you pulled your jeans on!"

"We are all safe – that's all that matters!"

Mary was dazed and distraught. She couldn't understand why she wasn't allowed into her home. "Who is that man, Lily? Did he set the house on fire?"

"I can't understand why the smoke alarm didn't go off in the kitchen – I checked it regularly," Suzanne sighed.

Ronan put her head on his shoulder. "Relax – it's only bricks and mortar. I think we might go and stay in a hotel – what do you think?"

"I think we need to get some clothes and find somewhere safe for mum."

Ronan brushed her hair with his fingertips. "We'll do all that," he said reassuringly and Suzanne felt so relieved that he was there.

Vicky needed help – real help – and she had to be strong. She called John who was in his city-centre apartment. It had taken him four hours to get to the city the night before and even if he wanted to call out to Howth the DART wasn't working and the bus wasn't getting up Howth Hill with the snow.

"Sorry about yesterday," she started.

"I think we need some space."

Vicky gulped. She felt her heart drop. "I'm sorry I was like that . . . but I didn't know where you were . . ."

4am in LAS VEGAS

"I was with my mother," John said flatly. It was her lack of trust that had hurt him.

Vicky closed her eyes drew a deep breath. "I didn't realise that – I thought you were with someone else."

"Vicky, you should know that I don't lie – why would I need to? If I was going to be with someone else you would know because I would have told you."

And Vicky realised that he was being honest – it was his style. He wasn't like other men – he was so confident that he could say those things.

"Hold on," he said. "My mam's trying to call me – I'll call you back."

Frank had the worst meeting of his life. In such a short time the banks had decided to close on him. His business was unsustainable. He was going to have to close the restaurants. It was his life's work gone. He was distracted and trying to avoid the slush and ice on the pavement. If he closed his restaurants it was all over. He had messed up with Eddie and messed up with Vicky and now he had messed up in a way that he didn't think he could recover from. The traffic was moving slowly and he was keen to get to the restaurant before it got too busy. He had bad news for the staff. So this was what he had to show for his life's work – all the glitz and glamour of the life he had once known dissolved. He would be penniless and forced to stay with his mother in Cabra Road. It was ironic. In his rush to improve himself and become "The Big I Am" he was back where he had started. He realised that now – his whole life had been a lie.

He took a step onto the road. His Italian leather loafers couldn't have been more inappropriate as he crossed the road and put his foot into a puddle.

Suddenly a truck laden with kegs of beer swung around the corner. It wasn't going fast but had to swerve to avoid a cyclist who was out of control.

The snow was falling heavily now and Frank pulled the collar of his coat up over his ears. He didn't see the truck coming. It only nudged him slightly but the puddles of sludge and snow made it impossible for him to correct his balance. He hit the road as the truck ran over his leg. The crunch was loud as it cracked under the tyres but it was the fall on his temple that killed him.

Kyle came through the back door and slammed it shut.

"This bloody country," he mumbled. He was covered from head to toe in snow. "I was in the village buying some Coke and look at me!"

Tina was working at the table – her collages and drawings covered it completely.

"I didn't know where you went."

"I could have frozen on the side of the hill for all you care – goddamn it, I wish I was back in Vegas!"

Tina wished he was back in Vegas too. He was around the house far too much.

Vicky came into the kitchen with her mouth gaping and the phone to her ear. She was in a kind of daze.

"What's wrong, Mum?"

Vicky was shaken to her core. "It's F-f-frank – he's dead!"

"What?" Tina rushed to her mother.

"I-I-I can't believe it – it's not right!"

"Sit down, Mum." Tina ushered her mother to a chair.

The veins in Kyle's neck were throbbing so hard they could be seen. "Hold it!" he demanded. "I'm talking to you, Tina! We have to sort things out once and for all."

Tina watched as her husband selfishly demanded all of the attention. It was in that moment that Tina grew up.

Suzanne and Ronan checked into Clontarf Castle with a bundle of shopping bags filled with essentials and some basic clothes they had bought in a local shopping centre. It was a welcome break from the trauma of the events of the last twenty-four hours. They had spent the night in Eddie's while Mary stayed in Beaumont Accident and

Emergency but Suzanne was relieved now that her mother was admitted into Highfield Nursing Home in Santry that specialised in care for Alzheimer's sufferers. A series of unexpected circumstances meant that a bed was available for this week. Leo had investigated the place while he was over and insisted that he put the number in her phone – she was pleased that he had badgered her into it before he left. However, she was furious when he confessed that he hadn't replaced the batteries in the smoke alarm in the kitchen when it bleeped while she was away.

So now at four thirty in the afternoon of the day after the fire, she and Ronan collapsed onto the king-size bed – both looking above them in silence and disbelief, thinking of what the last twenty-four hours had brought.

"Why did you suffer it all – why did you look after her for so long?" Ronan asked.

Suzanne turned her head to face Ronan and stared up into his eyes. "Because she is my mother and you only have one mother!"

Vicky drove the car to the airport with Kyle in the front and Tina in the back. They parked up and saw Kyle through Departures. The goodbyes were awkward and sullen, as to be expected from two teenagers who had fallen out of love as quickly as they had fallen into it.

"At least he'll be home with his mother for Christmas!" Vicky said comfortingly.

Tina just stared into space silently.

"Do you fancy getting a coffee or hot chocolate?" Vicky asked when the last of Kyle had disappeared on his way to the boarding gate.

Tina nodded. She was slightly in shock.

They sat at a table and Vicky brought over a cappuccino for herself and a hot chocolate for Tina.

"Are you okay?" Vicky asked, seeing the strain of the last few weeks on her daughter's face.

But there were other more positive changes Vicky had noticed –

the make-up wasn't so heavy and Tina had taken the piercing out of her nose. It took only one call to get her up in the mornings and her dedication and industrious attitude towards her artwork had astonished Vicky. She should have had more faith in her daughter and listened to her before this – perhaps then they would never have had to endure so much upheaval on such a huge scale. John would say that they both needed to experience all the upset in order to get to where they needed to go.

Tina nodded. "I don't need a guy in my life – I know where I want to go and I want to spend some time just being me for a while."

"It's been a very difficult time for us all."

"Are you okay about Frank and John?"

"It's so sad. I feel terrible for Frank's mum – nobody should have to bury their child."

Tina tried to empathise but, though she knew what had happened was hugely tragic, she could only think of her mother's feelings.

"Are you going to date John?"

Vicky shrugged. "You like him, don't you?"

Tina nodded vehemently. "He's so cool, Mum."

"Probably too cool for me – he's a good friend but you know what I would like?"

"What?"

"I'd like a bit of girl power in our house – the sisters doing it for themselves – what do you think?"

Tina grinned widely. "I think that's exactly what we need to do, Mum. You know, if we had never been to Vegas we wouldn't be here!"

"I think you're right Tina – but we are here now and it's a new start for both of us!"

Tina giggled. "Gran would have loved that – I can see it now!"

Vicky took another sip from her cup and smiled. "You know, I think she would."

Connie was happy to have her son back. She wouldn't scorn him again when he complained about having nothing to do. Then, of course, she had a book full of weddings to organise. Another couple had just called from Ireland – Suzanne and Ronan – who planned to marry at the Canyon. It was so romantic.

She flicked through her diary and added their names. Suddenly the door opened and there in the doorway was the most handsome man she had ever seen. He was wearing a Stetson and tipped it politely as he entered the office.

Connie had to stop herself from involuntary drooling at the sight of his broad shoulders and square jaw. His skin was tanned and his eyes a dark grey-green.

"Howdy ma'am, the name's Lucas Mc Shane."

Connie opened her mouth but words failed her. She held out her hand and he shook it vigorously.

"I called you on the phone two months back to organise a wedding for my fee-on-say – Meg Draymore. We had a date for Thursday next and I'm sorry to say that the wedding has been called off!"

Connie sat upright. "Oh, I see, Lucas – yes, I recall talking to you on the phone. Let me take a look." Her mind was calculating what sort of a woman would let this hunk slip through her fingertips.

"You see, my fee-on-say has had a change of heart and she wants to live in Nu York but I'm here on my bachelor party with some guys. Say, would you know of a good place to go this evening?"

Connie thought quickly. "Bank at the Bellagio is an excellent night club."

Lucas was staring at Connie and she could feel her pulse race. "You know, it would be so great to have someone show us around – would you be free to maybe come out with us?"

Connie didn't need to be asked twice. She picked up her bag and keys and turned the sign on the door from *open* to *closed*.

"Hey, of course I would – always pleased to show a nice guy around town!"

With that she locked the door and walked with the stranger out to her car. As he sat beside her and strapped on his seat belt, she felt a warm glow of satisfaction inside. At last she had found him and she wasn't letting him go!

Epilogue

Four months later

Tina rushed to the door as the postman delivered the envelopes. Today she would know if she had been accepted for art college. In only eight weeks she had managed to do four months' work and she had pulled it all together to create a portfolio of work that astounded her mother.

Vicky watched her daughter's expression to get the first glimmer of success or failure. Her heart pounded in her chest as she heard her daughter whisper the words in disbelief.

"I got in!"

Vicky burst with emotion and hugged her tightly. She never thought that she could feel this closeness with her daughter and the joy of succeeding was eclipsed by the bliss of sharing a special moment together.

Vicky was so proud – she was meeting John for a coffee later and looking forward to telling him. He was bringing her to the shamanic centre to celebrate the spring equinox. They were on a voyage of discovery as friends. And for now friends was good. Vicky had had enough to deal with after the shock of Frank's death – the upheaval for his mother and the huge change in herself.

But this was a special moment to relish her daughter's glory. They were becoming friends too. In a different kind of way – a way that only a mother-daughter relationship can be. But in the short time since they had taken the flight to Las Vegas everything had changed in their lives. Vicky was applying to do a course in psychology to try to find out how the brain really works. She was doing this hand in hand with some healing work that John had suggested for her. Reiki for starters and after a while she was going to try some more types of therapy. She was a sponge waiting to soak up the knowledge that she needed to get to know herself properly and her daughter most especially. John had assured her that the last thing she needed now was a man in her life and she had to agree with him. How could she be ready to share herself with someone until she knew herself truly?

John had started the ball rolling and now she was able to share cups of coffee and chats with him as he mourned the loss of his brother. John was philosophical about Frank's passing. It was a tragedy, yet a blessing that he had come clean with Bernadette before the accident and he felt that was Frank's redemption and what he had to do in this life. Bernadette was inconsolable but that was understandable. She would never recover. But that was the nature of the circle of life, John had said last time they met and she had to agree with him.

For now the future was bright – she didn't know where it would lead or what would happen but, instead of fearing, Vicky had made a new promise to herself that she was going to embrace each challenge head on as she met it. That was what she wanted to do.

On the other side of the Atlantic Ocean, high in the Grand Canyon National Park, Ronan and Suzanne stood to take their vows. The sky was blue. The Canyon, a rich tapestry of oranges, ochres and sepias below made it a picture-perfect setting as Suzanne in a white silk dress stood with yellow flowers in her hands. Ronan was bursting with pride in the woman by his side. The transition to Dublin hadn't been easy at first but it was early days – he would make it work and so would she. They had already looked into adoption and were going to do everything in their powers to get their baby – he or she was out there waiting for them. Of that they were sure and they would know when they met the one for them. They had been warned that the process could take up to three years but they didn't mind. In the meantime they could take their chances and maybe make a baby themselves – they were due a happy ending. It all felt right.

Eddie and Harry were groomsmen and relishing the loving couple's happiness. They were on sacred land and this was a sacred scene. As the couple exchanged their vows Eddie couldn't help grinning – he'd told Connie to play a certain piece of music as they kissed.

Connie obliged. The strains of "Viva Las Vegas" filled the Canyon and everyone laughed – even Lucas who had come along for the ride! He came to Vegas most weekends now . . .

If you enjoyed

4am in Las Vegas by Michelle Jackson

why not try

One Kiss in Havana also published by Poolbeg?

Here's a sneak preview of Chapter One

Michelle Jackson

One Kiss in
Havana

Prologue

The sun also riseth and the sun goeth down
Ecclesiastes 1

September 3rd

Emma woke as the first beam of daylight slipped through the break in the bedroom curtains. She rubbed her eyelids and lifted her head with its raven-black hair off the pillow – careful not to wake her husband. She was trying to relieve writer's block and getting up extra early was her latest attempt at establishing a new routine. Emma was by nature a night-owl and found six o'clock a difficult start. She went down to her study, turned on her laptop and waited as the icons appeared one by one. She had waited her whole life to write her first novel – now she was beginning to wonder if that was all she had to contribute to the world of words. Her husband Paul was so patient, giving her all the support and space that she needed to get the second one finished. She continued working as a journalist on a part-time basis, taking only jobs in magazines and periodicals that interested her, and had plenty of time to work on her novel as she pleased. She realised that she was in a position of freedom that most writers only dream of.

She organized her documents folder and went online to check for emails. Then she put down a few words and, before she realised it, it was seven thirty and time to wake the men of the house.

319

Finn was snoring gently but she crept into his bedroom to check that he was sound asleep. She watched his chest rise and fall and smiled with the satisfaction that only a mother can feel when watching her child sleep. He wouldn't be a child for much longer – he was already in fourth class.

Confident that her son would lie on for another few minutes at least, she set about waking her husband. This morning she was feeling alert and sexy after tapping at the keyboard for nearly two hours. It would be a nice midweek treat!

She laid a hand on to his forehead which was surprisingly cold to the touch. Very gently she put her lips down to his cheek – it was then she noticed that something was terribly wrong.

Louise was cutting the crusts off the sandwiches and putting the neat little squares of bread and ham into plastic bags, wondering how she ever managed when she used to rush out every morning to her job as a music teacher as well as get her children up for school and crèche.

She was still wearing her pyjamas but had been the second member of the Scott household to get up. Donal was already on his way to work – he liked to get to work early so he could finish in the evening and be out of town before the rush-hour traffic. During the summer and early autumn he used that extra time to go out to the yacht club for a sail before the light disappeared.

Suddenly her house phone rang out, startling her – it seldom rang in the mornings. The usual callers at this hour were the mums she knew through the local school calling to arrange lifts and play dates and they would always ring her mobile. She lifted it to hear her sister's voice on the other end of the line.

"Louise!" Emma sobbed. "Help – it's Paul – he's not breathing!"

Sophie breezed past the receptionist with a friendly nod, a cup of Starbucks coffee in her hand. It was going to be a great day –

most days were great for Sophie. As she sat at the desk in her small but smart design office she opened the drawer and removed her mirror to check how she looked after her brief walk to work. Her strawberry-blonde curls held their shape perfectly and her lips were glossy and shiny. She hit the mouse on her state-of-the-art Apple Mac and waited for her emails to appear on the screen. She quickly scanned through them, looking for something from *him*, then double-checked the list – not quite believing her eyes – he always sent her an email before he started work. Suddenly her mobile phone rang and she searched her bag frantically – eager to hear his voice.

But it wasn't him.

"Sophie, it's Louise."

Sophie knew by her older sister's tone that something was not as it should be and she took a deep breath.

"Yes?"

"It's Paul – I'm on my way to hospital now – he's had a heart attack."

Sophie felt the blood drain from her face and rush all the way down to her toes.

"Oh my God! How bad is it?"

"It's bad, Sophie."

"What? He's going to be all right – isn't he?"

"He's in an ambulance – they're trying to resuscitate him."

"What do you mean?"

"I think he's dead – I'll call you back when I know more."

Sophie wasn't able to reply. Her stomach clenched in spasm with the shock and she felt as if she was about to vomit. She closed her eyes to keep from fainting. It couldn't be – not her beloved Paul. He was her favourite brother-in-law. He was her rock. He was her lover.

Chapter 1

Easter was falling early this year and Louise wanted to be prepared for it – in the same way that she had come to be for all festivals and holidays. When she was working she used to imagine how relaxed her life would be if she didn't have to go into school every day and jump to attention every time the bell rang to signal the end of a class. But staying at home hadn't proved to be the bed of roses she had expected. For one thing, since she gave up work Donal quizzed her regularly about how she spent her day and she wasn't always able to give a satisfactory answer. The truth was, she often found herself fussing over the trivial things that before she used to do on her way to and from work without thinking. She also seemed to create work for herself by choosing the more time-consuming option of doing a task. For instance, this morning she needn't have gone all the way into Dublin city to buy the Easter eggs.

The doors to the DART slid open and Louise took a seat immediately to her right. She settled the bags of chocolate eggs at her feet – not focusing on the man wearing the leather jacket sitting opposite.

He spoke first.

"Louise?"

She looked up, startled.

"It's Jack!" the young man said.

Louise's mouth dropped. It was him. His blond hair was now the colour of sand but his eyes were still that unmistakable translucent blue. She stared at his perfectly sculpted nose and the smooth line of his cheek – unable to reply.

Emma turned the key in the mailbox. Most of the letters seemed to be addressed to Paul – she never realised how much of the household mail came to him until he was gone and she was left to open them. The majority were bills or business-related – they weren't too hard to deal with but, when someone wrote a personal note who hadn't heard of his sudden death, she found it hard.

Nothing she had opened so far was to leave her so traumatised as the smooth white envelope in her hand.

She walked back into the hall and then the kitchen. Something told her that she would need a cuppa nearby before she opened the envelope. It was embossed on the front with the logo of Evans, the graphics house where Paul had worked.

Six months had passed so quickly. After his death she used to have six bad nights a week. Slowly as the months passed the bad nights were turning to good. But last night she woke at seven minutes past one and jumped out of bed to soothe the trembling. Wrapped in her dressing-gown, she went into Finn's room to check that he was breathing. It was something she had given up doing when he turned two but since finding his father dead on that bright September morning she didn't take anything for granted any more. If she lay in bed her mind would start to wander and she would torture herself for hours wondering why Paul had decided to leave her and her son when he had so much to live for.

So she did what she usually did and rang her friend David in

Sydney – he was the only other person apart from her brother-in-law that knew Paul had died under such dark circumstances. It was safe to tell someone who was so far away that they would never tell anyone else in her family.

When the call finished she turned to surfing the internet – YouTube managed to have enough on its site to keep her occupied until the next wave of distress hit at around a quarter to four. Then it was time to return between the sheets, with a toilet roll to hand for mopping up tears, until Finn had to get up for school.

So far today was going okay – until she received the post. She hit the switch on the small stainless-steel kettle and it whimpered for a moment before bursting with steam and shutting itself off again. She wondered how many times a day she did that – the kettle was the best workhorse in the house without a doubt. And it was always tea that Emma liked to drink. Hot and strong with a drop of milk. Paul knew just how to make it. It was one of the many things about him that she missed.

Finn was at school and never saw his mum in a state when she read the mail. He was at the age where he preferred to be with his friends. Although she realised that he adored her and was fiercely protective of her, she knew that she couldn't halt his progress in the normal rites of passage of a nine-year-old. Soon she would know all about the difficulties of being a single parent to a teenager and she hoped that she would be able to cope when the time came.

Emma picked up the kettle and added hot water to the teabag in the china mug. She pulled back a chair, grating it on the terracotta tiles, and sat down. Without any fuss she ripped open the envelope and took out another that had the setting-sun emblem of a travel company printed in the top left-hand corner. Folded up inside it were three sheets of paper with neatly typed documentation. A leaflet fell out and rested on the table-top. It was brightly coloured with decorative edging and the word *CUBA* emblazoned across the top. More junk mail – Emma thought – almost dropping it in the bin. But instead she unfolded the other pages and let her eyes scan over the documents. Key words bounced off the page – *thank you – reservation – tickets – enclosed – travel – restrictions – visa*. She was reading a travel itinerary for two. These pages were all that were required for a ten-day holiday in sunny Cuba and the date of departure was only six days away.

Emma blinked and read the documents again – more carefully this time. The names printed across the top of the page were Mr P Condell and Ms S Owens. They had printed her initial incorrectly. She wished that they said Mr and Mrs Condell – she should have changed the name on her passport when renewing it after Finn was born – it was a tiny detail but now that she had lost Paul she wished she had his name on all of her documents. It hadn't mattered before. The date of booking was seven months ago – only a few days before Paul was taken so suddenly away from her. She picked up the outer envelope – it was addressed to Evans Graphics House. If Paul told them to send it to his work, then he must have wanted to keep it a secret to be a surprise – that was just the sort of attention to detail that Paul gave to everything that he did. In his work as a graphic designer he was more fastidious and precise than any of his colleagues and it was one of the things about his character that used to drive Emma mad. How happy she would be now to take all those times he was fussy and neat and hug him and his sweet ways, just to share some more time with him.

In recent years Emma had been longing to go to Cuba to see La Finca Vigía – Ernest Hemingway's home outside Havana where he reputedly spent some of the happiest years of his life. How wonderful of Paul to do this for her! But now he would never know how she felt about this lovely gift. She was engulfed by emotions that she hadn't felt since discovering him lying cold in the bed, that morning in September.

Suddenly the phone rang and she couldn't bring herself to

answer it. All she could do was take her mug and ascend the stairs, seeking the comfort of bed before Finn got home from school.

Louise listened to the phone on the other end of the line ring out once, twice, three times before switching to the answering machine.

Hello, you've reached the Condells – we can't take your call but if you leave your name and number we'll get right back to you.

Louise was familiar with the deep West of Ireland tone of the man's voice. She hadn't suggested to Emma that she change Paul's voice from the answering machine but did wonder if leaving it was part of her sister's grieving process or just an oversight. Maybe her sister was not the best person to call – she was too caught up in her own pain to understand how shocked Louise was feeling after the short trip on the DART earlier.

She hung up the phone and tried to think about the next job on her list for the day. It was all becoming so tedious. She had given up work after the birth of her youngest child.

She and Donal had been happy with two children and doubly thrilled that Molly was a girl so Tom's arrival two years later was unplanned. It was difficult for Louise to work full time and co-ordinate a baby and a five-year-old starting school. She had tried job-sharing for a while but eventually took a career break to be a full-time mother. But with her new role she found it hard to fill her head with things that fed her brain. Shopping and cooking and cleaning had never been high on Louise's agenda – they didn't suit the lifestyle of a bohemian musician. But then again it was a very long time ago since she was either of those. The bohemian part of her personality was gradually smothered by the classroom in her role as a teacher. Now she didn't even play her piano any more.

Jack Duggan. Over the years she had forgotten about him as the children came along and she relished the role of mother, but seeing him a few hours earlier on the DART brought her right back to the first time that she realised she was in love with him. She hadn't felt this distressed since her wedding day.

She recalled her reflection in front of the long oak-framed mirror in her parents' house.

"You look beautiful," Emma had said with such sincerity that Louise almost believed her. But she didn't feel beautiful and a single tear had trickled down the side of her cheek.

Emma took a paper handkerchief and wiped it away. "We can't have you spoiling your make-up on your big day," she said sympathetically.

Louise had sighed with relief – knowing that there was somebody who understood what she was going through. She wondered if she would have been so empathetic towards Emma had the shoe been on the other foot.

She hadn't meant to fall into an affair with Jack Duggan six months before her wedding day – it had started out as a mild flirtation that was common enough in any workplace. But it subtly changed one evening in May when she knew that very soon Jack would be gone and she might never see him again. They both knew that what they were doing was wrong but neither could help it.

She had done the right thing by letting Jack go. She had done the right thing by Donal and held true to her vows for the last fourteen years and bore him three beautiful children who were the centre of both their worlds. So why did she feel so guilty for talking to Jack Duggan on the DART?

Damn, Louise thought. She was trembling inside. Her head was so full of thoughts of herself and Jack making love that she found it difficult to focus. Her stomach flipped as she recalled his eyes – the way that when he looked at her she felt as though he was reaching into her soul. If she stayed on her own until it was time to get the kids she could go out of her mind.

There was nobody else that she could speak to. Maybe Emma was at home but just hadn't answered the phone. She grabbed her handbag and car keys and slammed the door behind her.

Luckily her sister was only a short ten-minute car ride away and she could tell her the incredible news before picking up Tom from school. She opened the doors of her Zafira MPV and slid onto the seat. Her heart pounded as she thought of Jack and the way he smiled at her. She felt in her pocket for the business card that he had handed her hours earlier. He was alive and well and living in Dublin – only a few miles away from her. Thoughts flooded her head and she had to be careful to focus on the road. She was so curious to know more about him and where he had spent the years that they had been apart. Did he have a wife? Kids? Did it matter? Of course not – hadn't she a husband and three children of her own? She had to speak to Emma and quickly or she would suffocate with her thoughts.

The roadworks on the Howth Road put an extra five minutes onto the journey and she cursed every second that it took her to get to Sutton.

Emma left the curtains open in the hope that the rays of spring sunshine might warm the room. She loved the fact that her bedroom looked out over Dublin Bay, with the familiar ESB chimneys in the distance marking the entrance to the Port of Dublin. The backdrop of the Dublin Mountains changed colour several times a day and had helped Paul and her to make up their minds to buy the house all those years ago.

"But isn't it too dear?" Emma had said at the time of the first viewing – two hundred thousand pounds was an enormous sum of money.

"Not as dear as it will be in two or three years!" Paul had assured her and of course he was right – as he had been about most things. Even with the collapse of prices in the housing market the house was still a bargain.

She missed his certainty and nose for predicting what was going to happen and his handling of the household finances.

That wasn't all that she missed. The scent of him on his

pillow had gone even though she had put off washing the bed linen for as long as she could.

Suddenly the doorbell rang out – one loud and long ring that meant it could only be one person. At least Louise was used to seeing her in this state and wouldn't mind. But her impatient younger sister rang again even when she must have been able to see Emma's reflection through the glass door.

"Louise!" Emma said with a sigh. "Come in."

Louise barged past her and went straight into the kitchen where she hit the switch on the kettle. She looked as if she were about to burst. She propped herself up against the island in the middle of the room.

"Emma," she gasped, running her fingers through her long brown hair. "I had to tell someone – I saw him – today on the DART!"

Emma sighed because in typical Louise fashion she expected her older sister to know instinctively who she was talking about.

"Who?"

"Jack Duggan, of course!"

Louise's sureness brought a smile to Emma's face. "We haven't had a conversation about him in at least ten years so how in God's name did you expect me to know who you meant?"

"Who else would have me in such a state?" Louise raised her arms in the air and shook her wrists, the bangles on them jingling.

"Hey, I've seen you this worked up when talking about the state of your hair when it was cut shorter than you wanted!"

Louise closed her eyes and took a deep breath. "That's different – we are talking about Jack."

Emma didn't have much patience for her sister today. Anyway, Jack Duggan was someone from her very distant past. What was her problem?

"Were you talking to him?" Emma knew that it was always best to just listen to Louise when she was like this.

"Yeeesss!"

Emma shrugged. "Go on."

"You won't believe it but he's been living in Howth for two years and I never knew!"

"And what did he look like?" Emma proceeded to make tea while her sister elaborated.

"Just the same – God, he is so gorgeous – my heart was thumping as I spoke to him. His hair is much shorter and sandier than when I last saw him and he was wearing a really cool leather jacket and denim jeans."

"Is he married?"

"I didn't get a chance to ask – he got on at Connolly Station and I had to get off at Killester."

"Did he ask for your number?"

Louise shook her head. "He gave me his business card though. We were both in such shock we didn't say much – it was awkward. He did say that he'd been in the States for six years and was now a journalist for *The Times*."

Louise started to pace the tiles from the kitchen island to the table and back.

"So he didn't go on and become a rock star after all?"

"I guess not. I never thought he'd end up writing like you!"

"Come and sit down. I have something to tell you too." Placing the two mugs of tea on the table, Emma took a seat.

Louise joined her, looking a little impatient at Emma's announcement. She could think of nothing but Jack.

"I got a bit of a shock this morning in the post," said Emma.

Louise took the folded documents from Emma. "*Cuba*" was the first word that she read and then she scanned the travel documents one by one.

"God, Emma – that was so nice of him."

Emma nodded her head sadly.

Louise read on silently. "Hey, it says here that you'll be finishing the holiday with three days in Havana!"

Emma nodded. "I saw that – it would have been perfect."

"What do you mean 'would have'?" Louise said lifting her head. "What's stopping you from going?"

Emma shook her head. "I wouldn't want to go all that way on my own."

"Take Finn."

"You know how he complains about travel – he got cabin fever last summer in an airplane and we only flew to Bordeaux."

Louise thought for a moment. "What about me? I'd love to go."

"You have three kids and they'll be on school holidays for most of it."

Louise pondered for a moment. She could see Emma's mind race. She was always quiet when she was considering something and Louise felt that she knew instinctively what her older sister was thinking.

"I suppose you would want Finn to stay with me then?" Louise wondered why she was asking the question – the answer was obvious and Finn would rather stay with her than anyone.

A smile of relief washed over Emma's face. Louise's eldest son, being two years older than Finn, was his idol.

"Oh Louise, would you? He adores Matt. That would be brilliant – now all I need is someone to come with me. I bet Sophie would be on for it."

Louise felt the words like a blow. She wasn't surprised at the suggestion – life had a tendency to follow certain patterns and it was usually Sophie who landed on her feet. She never had to work hard to get approval or achieve anything and now she was going on a dream holiday with Emma – life was so unfair. But would she have the nerve to go? If she did, Louise didn't know if she could keep from telling Emma the truth. Surely Sophie's conscience would get the better of her?

"Why don't you call her?" she said, biting her lower lip.

"Okay. She's not away today?" Emma got up and went over to the phone.

"No. Not this week as far as I know!" Louise said, trying to hold back the angst in her voice.

She watched as Emma launched into conversation.

"It's me . . . how are you? . . . Sophie, I got a bit of a shock today – I got a letter in the post about a holiday to Cuba that Paul booked before he died . . . I know! . . . I'm still shaking . . . it was a surprise."

Louise watched silently as the one-sided conversation continued.

"Louise is here and she thinks I should go . . . it's in six days' time for ten days . . . Listen, Sophie, would you be interested in coming? . . . I wasn't going to use them but Louise has convinced me to go . . . come on, Sophie, you're the only person who can go off at the drop of a hat that I know . . . call around after work and we'll talk about it . . . bye."

"So I take it that's a yes from our little sister?" Louise said, unable to hide the disappointment in her voice.

"I had to twist her arm but I'd say she'll come. Are you sure you don't mind taking Finn?"

Louise smiled. However jealous she felt about Sophie going off on a holiday, she wanted Emma to enjoy her trip – after all that she had been through she deserved it and she would keep her reservations to herself. It was a strange twist that Paul would not be going now but his wife and lover would be going together.

"Sorry I haven't had a chance to talk to you about Jack – maybe another day," said Emma. "I have to do some bits now before I pick Finn up from school."

"That's fine – no problem." Louise took the cue even though she was sorely disappointed that she hadn't got a chance to discuss what action she should take with her new information about Jack.

The thought of Sophie with Emma's husband brought her back to reality. She kissed Emma goodbye and got into her MPV, feeling her stomach churn as she recalled the awful moment of revelation of her younger sister's affair with her brother-in-law.

It was a few weeks before Paul's death that Louise had found them together. She had called around to collect a dress that she had lent Emma and needed to wear that night while Emma was away on a long-overdue spa weekend with a friend. Louise had let herself in with the key that Emma had given her. It was to be used only in case of emergency but Louise thought that the house was empty as Paul's car was not outside. Nothing could have prepared her for what she was about to see.

At first she thought the noises coming from upstairs was a burglar but she noticed a set of keys on the hall table and Paul's jacket resting on the end of the banisters. Then she realised someone was groaning and, thinking her brother-in-law must be in pain, she ran up the stairs. The bedroom door was open and she could see Paul's body rise and fall under the bedclothes. She felt awkward and embarrassed when she realised that he was not alone and presumed that Emma had come home early. But then the mass of strawberry curls on the pillow gave the woman's identity away.

Suddenly the couple stopped moving as Sophie realised that someone was present. She let out a yelp and pulled the sheet over her naked torso.

Paul jerked and turned around to see what had startled his lover.

"Louise!" Paul cried.

Louise was so shocked she turned and ran down the stairs as quickly as she could. She was out the front door before either Paul or Sophie had emerged from the bedroom. She still shivered to the bone every time she remembered that moment.

Sophie pressed *Save* on her computer screen and rolled her chair away from the desk. She didn't feel like doing any more designing today – she'd have to tell Rod that she needed the time off. It was just as well that the spring/summer ranges were all complete – it would be difficult for him to deny her the leave. She had brought in as many orders as last year and in such recessive times it was a major achievement. An early lunch was called for and she needed to clear her head.

She had wondered when her eldest sister would find out about the trip to Cuba. Paul had consulted her on every detail when they were planning it and now that she was getting to go on the holiday she felt a certain sense of satisfaction – a kind of compensation for losing him and the life with him she had been looking forward to.

It was all right for her eldest sister – she could mourn him openly – while she herself had to hide every trace of her anguish and there was much that she had to carry around silently and sadly since his death.

She decided to take the bull by the horns and go straight in and ask Rod for the leave. He wouldn't want to risk losing her now that she had made such good contacts with the UK buyers – they trusted her and for the last collection she was the only one that the larger stores wanted to deal with – a designer was much less threatening than a sales rep. If only they knew, she thought with smug satisfaction. Subtle manipulation was a game that Sophie was expert in – she had been doing her apprenticeship from before the time she could walk. The key to her success was her charm – nobody ever minded giving in to her – especially her father and her sisters.

Sophie flicked her long strawberry-blonde curls back off her face and strode into the corridor and past her colleagues – she was the first designer in the company to get her own office. But of course Sophie was worth it because she had assured Rod that she was special and he was so lucky to have her working for his company – and of course he believed her. Now he would be convinced that he simply had to let his golden employee take ten days off work. Even in this time of recession when designers were clamouring for work Sophie wasn't concerned. She would get the leave because she was Sophie Owens and she always got what she wanted.

"Hello?"

"Louise – it's Donal."

"Hi – will you be home for dinner?"

"Kevin wants me to take a look at a boat – he thinks it might suit us."

Louise sighed. The sailing season hadn't started yet but the preparation and excuses were well and truly back. "I thought you weren't going to change this year."

"We're just looking."

He was killing time before coming home and they both knew it.

"All right then – you can heat your dinner up in the microwave."

"I might get something in the club."

Louise wanted to scream. What was the purpose of her day? She had been to Superquinn – cooked the beef stroganoff from scratch – and now he wouldn't even be eating it. At least when she was at school she had papers to correct and classes to prepare which left her so busy she didn't have time to fret if Donal came home late from work. She found herself lately checking the time for *Desperate Housewives* or similar programmes once the kids were in bed.

"I'll see you later then," said Donal.

"Bye," she said abruptly and hung up.

If only she could find a balance: appreciation for the charmed life she had rearing her beautiful children and an interest that kept her fulfilled during her free time.

Her head was filled with thoughts of her encounter with Jack. She reached into her pocket and took out the small but slick business card that he had given her earlier that day. She wished that she was strong enough to chuck it in the bin – maybe rip it up beforehand. But she knew that she couldn't do that. After all, Jack had been nothing but gentleness itself towards her during all the time they had spent together. Hadn't she been the cruel one that had broken his heart and left him angry and hurt on that sad October afternoon fourteen years ago?

The trees were turning to all shades of orange, purple and brown as the chill in the air heralded the end of their affair. He had blamed her – told her that she was cold – he said she had planned this outcome all along. Her tears couldn't convince him otherwise, couldn't convince him that she held his future as a priority over her own feelings. But deep down she hoped that he hadn't meant it because they both knew that their love was the purest and most wondrous that either had experienced.

What was she going to do with his card now? Her head warned of the can of worms that she would be opening if she were to ring the number but her heart was egged on by the sureness in the pit of her stomach that she had to see him again – and soon!

She waited until the children were in bed – or in their rooms at least. Matt, the eldest at eleven, could often be heard pottering around his room until the small hours. Molly loved her sleep and often had to be shaken awake in the mornings. Tom was six and protested the most before going to bed but he could be bribed easily with a packet of *Match Attack* cards.

With the house to herself, she shut the kitchen door and, using her mobile phone, she pressed the same numbers as those on the card that Jack had given her. She waited with bated breath as the phone rang out – each ring leaving her feeling more and more apprehensive. Finally the ringing stopped as the voicemail clicked in.

Jack here – leave a message and I'll get back to you.

Louise lost her nerve and turned off her phone quickly. Her heart pounded in her chest.

What would she have said if he had answered? There was so much she wanted to say to him, so much she needed to say, yet she couldn't put it all into words – she could barely put it into ordered thought – but she needed to speak to him like a junkie needed a fix.

·◆·

If you enjoyed this chapter from
One Kiss in Havana by Michelle Jackson,
why not order the full book online
@ www.poolbeg.com

POOLBEG WISHES TO
THANK YOU

for buying a Poolbeg book.

If you enjoyed this why not
visit our website:

www.poolbeg.com

and get another book delivered straight
to your home or to a friend's home!

All books despatched within 24 hours.

POOLBEG

WHY NOT JOIN OUR MAILING LIST
@ www.poolbeg.com and get some
fantastic offers on Poolbeg books